Jadwiga's Crossing

Jadwiga's Crossing

a story of the Great Migration

Aloysius A. Lutz and Richard J. Lutz

iUniverse, Inc.
New York Lincoln Shanghai

Jadwiga's Crossing
a story of the Great Migration

iUniverse books may be ordered through booksellers or by contacting:

iUniverse
2021 Pine Lake Road, Suite 100
Lincoln, NE 68512
www.iuniverse.com
1-800-Authors (1-800-288-4677)

Website: JadwigasCrossing.com

Cover:
Charles Frederic Ulrich, (1858–1908)
In the Land of Promise, Castle Garden, 1884
oil on wood panel, 28 3/8 x 35 3/4 in.
Corcoran Gallery of Art, Washington DC
Museum Purchase, Gallery Fund 00.2
© The Corcoran Gallery of Art/CORBIS

ISBN-13: 978-0-595-38127-2 (pbk)
ISBN-13: 978-0-595-82495-3 (ebk)
ISBN-10: 0-595-38127-8 (pbk)
ISBN-10: 0-595-82495-1 (ebk)

Printed in the United States of America

For Lena

Acknowledgments

The authors are grateful to the following for assistance with research:

Krystyna Baron, The Polish Institute of Arts and Sciences in America
William M. Borodacz
Stanley Cuba
Won Kim
Abbas Labbauf
Dr. Donald Mushalko
Fr. Marek Sotek
Jan Weiss
The staff of the Dunkirk Free Library, circa 1953-1961

...and to the following for comments, criticisms, and corrections:

Peggy Brooks
John Cosgrove
Susan Cosgrove
Kasia Edelman
Clarence Hartlieb
Jeanette Hartlieb
Linda Heimer
Jackie Judd
Matthew Katz
Clemens Lutz
Bill Parks
Sally Stevenson
Ronald L. Stuart
Kay Thompson
Charlie Valentine
Judith Webb
Winifred Webb

Foreword

A story of the coming of Paul and Jadwiga is told among the old fishermen of the Lake Erie shore, at Dunkirk. Their tellings carry the haunting
tone and phrases of legend. It is the kind of story people repeat when
they don't recall the exact truth, or never knew it, or think it tells better
their way.

As wondrous as the legend may be, there is a truth, and I tell it here. I
know the truth, for my father told it to me. And he told it to me as he
heard it from Paul, and when he asked her, from Jadwiga herself.

It is a story of young dreams and young love.

It is a story of those dreams, and that love, and what they can achieve.

It is Paul's story, Jadwiga's story, and the story of their coming to
America.

BOOK ONE

Chapter 1

Across centuries of seasons, there have been willows greening for the Polish Spring on the Baltic shore at Gdynia. Invaders and occupiers have come and in time they have gone. The glowing beach has sometimes ebbed with a shift of wave or current, or swelled with a new deposit of sand. Even the dunes have grown or waned in their time.

But there have always been the willows, clinging to life through summer storm and winter freeze. It is as though they have studied the ways of the fishing people, who have learned how to pass through storms and how to judge the bending required when invader or occupier appears.

There have always been the willows, and always the fishing people.

And always the young ones—the children of those who fish—innocent, wide-eyed sprites who are unpretentiously delighted by the simple things.

It is today as it was then, on a sunny Spring day in 1869, when in the greengrowth separating the Baltic beach from the shore road, the children impatiently awaited the new Head Father of St. Teresa's church. They could ignore the thither and yon of fishing schooners in mere daily routine, but not the first appearance of a new priest. Boys climbed into trees to peer into the distance, then swung on the branches. Little girls picked flowers, assembling bouquets of veneration for the newcomer.

Among them was Jadwiga, third child of Edmund Wdowiak. She was out of place—too old for this group. This past winter, almost unseen, she had encountered a magic: The directionless energy of childhood had become a special something deep in her eyes. Seeing it in Jadwiga by the fresh light of Spring, the fishermen called it *żywotność*—a special vitality.

She was all the more out of place because she wore her second-best dress, which was all the more blue for being near her eyes.

She was pretty. Some said her face was a striking recollection of her mother's smile. Others countered that all the Wdowiaks were born with a half-smile already on their faces, anyway, and it was nothing for them to come aglow for the slightest cause. But all agreed that Jadwiga, daughter of Edmund Wdowiak, was an incitement to the eye.

When the holy one appeared, the gray mass of his long garment cresting a gentle slope, the younger children called out and ran to meet him.

Jadwiga's features were quickly alive with anticipation, as well, but she didn't run. Nor did she follow her impulse to bolt to the beach, for he had already noticed her. He had noticed, and later this day he would see her again, and he would remember.

Alerted by the cries of the children, older people now joined them to surround the new priest in greeting and to guide him to the ceremonial matters awaiting him at the pier. He slowed his determined walk in accommodation of their pace.

"I hear much of sinning and irregularities here," the priest said. He glanced at Jadwiga and she could feel a scolding in his eyes. In her *żywotność*, she had outgrown the blue dress, and it was too snug. Gradually, she moved to the edge of the group and to its rear.

"What's this I smell?" The salt breeze was profane with the odor of roasting pork.

An old man explained: "On Fridays no fish are left so we eat a pig we have taken in trade for fish. It is as though the pig is a fish, is it not? We eat fish all the rest of the days, anyway."

Seeing that this did not satisfy the new Head Father, an old woman added, "We know we must do better, Father."

It always happened this way. The old men taunted a new priest with their pretense of innocent trespass upon the Lord's rules. Later, in the fish-house, someone would give an exaggerated performance in an imitation of his reactions, and make the others laugh. The old women, who knew it was best not to explain too much of the ways of fishing people on a new priest's first visit, always said the things necessary to pacify. Today, they would make an even greater effort, at least until the holy one put in the good word to God for Old Lady Slomiany, may she rest in peace.

"Only when there is a wedding, when you are all drunk, do you come to church."

"But we come at Easter and put enough in the basket for all the Sundays," a man said. Other men nodded in affirmation of this claim.

An old woman added quickly, "But we know we must strive to do better, Father."

While the priest sowed disapproval and reaped his harvest of contrition, Jadwiga slowed her pace, dropping behind. When it would no longer be noticed, she dashed between willows down to the beach. Pausing only to remove her sandals, she sprinted on the firm sand at the waterline, her hair and blue dress billowing.

From the pier, Skipper Edmund Wdowiak watched his daughter as she outdistanced breaking waves and a swooping seagull. And in his daughter, he could see his wife. So like her mother at eighteen, he thought. So quick, innocently graceful, so vivacious. How very much like his Helena on the day they ran together on this same beach, and he caught her and asked her to become his wife. How ready his Jadwiga now, in her own fullness of *zywotność,* for marriage.

And yet, how impetuous, running through wet sand in her second-best dress. Half-way down the pier, she even sang out: "He's coming. The priest is coming!"

The Skipper planted a foot aboard his fishing schooner, grabbed one of the taut stays running from mast to gunwale, and swung his big frame aboard. When Jadwiga was close enough to hear, he spoke to her.

"Jadwiga, wear your dress in your mind, too, not just upon your body. Remember, this is a day of funeral."

"Yes, papa. The priest is coming, papa."

Stirred by her shout, a party of mourners emerged from the fishhouse. They carried the body of an old woman on a wide plank, a large stone tied at her feet. She wore the traditional clothes of her wedding day. In her hands, a crucifix was wrapped tightly with a rosary. A daughter followed, now old herself, then a grandson and his wife, who carried a great grandchild in her arms.

Jadwiga stepped into her sandals. In deliberate solemnity, she walked across a makeshift gangplank provided for the priest and mourners. Despite the dress, she could easily have stepped directly from pier to boat. Her two brothers smiled at this excessive solemnity in response to their father's reprimand, and they glanced at him to urge his indulgence. But the Skipper would say nothing more. Like his sons, he understood that for Jadwiga, this day was more than a day of funeral.

The bearers followed Jadwiga aboard, carefully positioning the deceased on the deckhouse. Other mourners placed flowers around the body, then made way for close relatives, who drew close to shield their matriarch in her last journey.

Now the priest arrived, helped by the old people in his first uneasy steps onto the gangplank, then by the Skipper, who took care to make his extended hand appear more greeting than assistance. Jadwiga took her place at the schooner's helm, while her two brothers stood ready to raise sails. Two helpers on the pier, eyes fastened on Jadwiga but alert to the Skipper's signaling nod, loosed the lines mooring the schooner fore and aft, boarded quickly, then pulled the gangplank after them. As her brothers raised the schooner's sails to receive the breeze, Jadwiga wheeled the boat away into a reach for open Baltic.

"Oh God have mercy upon us and deliver us from evil."

Even with her head bowed, Jadwiga cut the breeze cleanly to take the best tack to the burial waters. But after a while listening to the priest's prayer, tears came to her eyes, and Edmund Wdowiak knew his daughter's thoughts had gone to another such trip, six years past, when the body on the hardwood plank had been her mother, finally taken into the Lord's Special Peace after a hard and grasping illness.

In taking Helena Wdowiak, treasured wife of Skipper Edmund Wdowiak, death had also claimed their plans, so carefully made, to leave partitioned Poland—to leave the Germans—even to forsake the valued contract for the Baron's schooner. They had wanted to take their family to America, the new land where men were free to fish or farm for themselves.

But in the Year of Our Lord 1863, just as word came of the insurrection in the Russian partition, the sickness had struck, lingering to claim life a small bit at a time. At her mother's bedside in the last months, Jadwiga heard the stories of America again and again. But she gradually came to understand that her own dreams of a mother recovered, and of a family strong once more for such travel, were lost in a patient wait for death.

For Edmund Wdowiak, his wife gone, it had not been difficult to make the decision to stay in familiar surroundings. The crushing of the dream of America was the smallest of hurts, seen beside the loss of his wife. And in his fishing community on the beach at Gdynia, his twelve-year-old daughter could grow to womanhood among people of the right priorities.

Watching Jadwiga at the helm, he knew it had been right to stay. She had become a fine young woman. She was radiant with a glow from within; personable, even more than her mother. As her mother had foreseen, she could have her pick of the young men.

She was smart, too. At the school, against the Prussian rules, she had even learned to read while teachers pretended instruction in sewing. She made him proud. It had been right, staying and making the best of it. His sons, Konrad and Konstanty, had become fine men. They were not so full as Jadwiga of the dream of America, but they were strong young men who could fish with the best.

This year, the fishing was the best in Gdynia memory. And this year, Edmund Wdowiak intended that his neighbors should come together in a wedding celebration.

Beyond the invisible line separating the bay from the greater expanse of Baltic, the burial waters were known to the fishermen by the overlapping of two peaks in the distant Oksywie Hills. At her father's glance Jadwiga eased into a closer angle upon the wind, and all aboard adjusted their footing as sails luffed and the schooner gave up its challenge of the waves. When the priest paused and nodded, Skipper Wdowiak quietly snapped the count of three and the young fishermen slid Old Lady Slomiany to her grave with hardly a ripple.

"God have mercy upon her soul."

Then came the silence for the priest to mumble and communicate with God in altogether a different language. It was an uneasy silence. On a boat it was a good time to change the tack and lean to the other foot.

"I want you to come to my house for wine and fish so that we can talk about a wedding," the Skipper said softly into the ear of the priest.

The Father snapped back. "I intend coming to your house and every house on the beach today. And before we talk about weddings we will talk about funerals and you will tell me how many bodies are sent to the bottom of the sea without permission of God and Church."

"Father, I have never had a funeral on my boat without a priest," the Skipper said, raising his hand in testimony to God.

Then the priest turned to the elders who had come to pray for Old Lady Slomiany. "Already this year you people have had three weddings and five christenings." He raised his hands to point at his fingers to show that God and Church had been counting. "Eight drunken celebrations, yet only one funeral."

Even the young fishermen opened their eyes a bit wider with these numbers held up in evidence of sin against the ways of the Church.

"You spend for vodka for the weddings and you spend for wine for the christenings. But you will not spend for wood for coffins. Why can't you bring your dead to the church and bury them in God's ground like other people?"

"It is not so much the spending," an old man said. "It is because we know the fires of hell cannot get us with all that water down there."

But the priest was neither satisfied nor amused and among those who stood together on the boat, there was an awkwardness of eyes cast downward.

Jadwiga's brothers chose this moment to draw sails still tighter. The breeze was steady and strong and it was a good day for sailing the Bay of Gdansk. But for them this was now a holiday and the trip back was a bit faster.

The Wdowiak family shack was on the beach, back among the willows that marked the beginning of good soil where the things of dry land might grow. From years unremembered, it had been passed along from one strong-bodied fishing man to another to be home for the blended generations of old and young. It was made of things yielded to the beach by a generous sea—materials too good for a thrifty man to cast away. It had been rebuilt after storms, expanded in good times, patched in bad.

But Edmund Wdowiak knew that a good home was more than jetsam fit together as shelter for bone and flesh. A good home was shelter for the soul. Thus he felt no shame in making the priest comfortable under a low willow branch in a sling chair of sturdy fishnet.

Jadwiga served the fish and wine. It was understood: she would serve, listen, and keep the helpers away so her father would have no interruptions in his talk with the man of the Church.

"I will pay in money to a woman of your choosing to come here and arrange a wedding for my daughter," Skipper Wdowiak said. "It has not been the same since the mother died and I want a dependable woman to see to it that everything will be as it should be. I want to meet this woman and arrange for pay and whatever time she will be needed. I will give generously to the church for this wedding and I will pay this woman well if she will do well by my daughter."

But with this new priest it was not to be so easy. His mind was troubled with other matters. As though the Skipper's words had gone unheard, he spoke softly to no one in particular. "If only the church had a team of horses, a wagon and sled so that I could come here often, summer and winter." Then he spoke more directly, his eyes finding those of Edmund Wdowiak. "I was told—you people are getting away from God, farther and farther."

But the Skipper's deep-set blue eyes met the challenge of the priest's. "Holy Father, we don't come to church every Sunday because most of them we are out on the Baltic. We fish from March to November. Then comes the snow. And then we have only enough time to mend our nets so we can start fishing again."

"It is not only the coming to church. There are these other matters. Every Sunday morning there is a bashed mouth or a broken rib, a torn ear, a cracked head. All this happens on this side of the road to the young men from the other side of the road. Why? Can you tell me why?"

"I have heard of no such things, Father." He looked at Jadwiga, who shook her head. Neither had she heard of such things. "Władek and Zdenek—my helpers—they fight, Father, between themselves. But it leaves them no time for fighting with others. We are a peaceful people."

"It is said this is likely to happen to the young men from town, or from the farms, after the dances at Gostomski's Hall."

"Sometimes they walk Jadwiga home from the dances, but always she is also accompanied by the helpers, and there is never talk of trouble. My daughter is a virtuous young woman, Father."

"Yes, yes. Perhaps now that she will be married there will be less of this mayhem on Saturday nights."

"It is not possible that she is the cause, Father. But the wedding is the important thing. I'm glad you have brought us back to this matter. Soon the other fishermen will come to take you for a celebration to welcome you as the new Head Father, and there is only a little time for us to talk."

The Skipper put a shiny new coin in the priest's pocket. "This is for the church, but it is also to remind you tomorrow or perhaps on Monday to send a woman here, to the shack of Wdowiak the fisherman—a smart woman who knows about weddings."

The priest sighed and nodded, resigned that he would get nowhere in this discussion of the injuries brought to church on Sunday mornings. He even smiled. And now, for the first time, he spoke to Edmund Wdowiak's daughter.

"Jadwiga, may God bless you with a good man, a happy marriage, and many children."

Now happiness crested like a wave across Jadwiga's features. She bowed her head toward the priest in acceptance of his good wishes. In her smile and in his mind, he could see the cause of the fighting among young men at the dances. Were he a younger man, and not a priest, he too might fight for the favor of such a smile.

Among the fishermen of Gdynia, it was well-known that Edmund Wdowiak and sons had struck good fishing grounds this early Spring season of 1869. The numbers marked on the calendar in the fish house showed the Skipper well out in front of his contract with the Baron. And hadn't his nets yielded at least one fist-sized clump of amber? Some even whispered in speculation that he was getting it into his head to marry again. There was evidence—the private talk with the priest. Certainly there had been no talk of a husband chosen for his daughter.

And now there was more evidence—the fastidious couple from the church, asking for him at the fish house. The woman with her hair in a bun, and with embroidery around her wrists and neck like a pouter pigeon. She held a kerchief to her nose to fend off the thick odor. And the man who played the organ—a long, fine mustache, a sparkling white shirt, a necktie, even, and matching pants and coat.

The man's eyes darted nervously among the fishing people, who stared from everywhere. At first he was reluctant to speak. He even took the woman's elbow and looked up the road away from the pier.

But the woman edged closer to the Wdowiaks—smiling at father, two sons, and daughter. And the Wdowiaks smiled back.

"I am Alfons Posienko and this is my wife, Lilianna," the man was heard to say. "The priest sent us."

There was this evidence. The fishermen of Gdynia knew Edmund Wdowiak was up to something.

Outside the Wdowiak shack, Jadwiga sat on a hammock, looking with big eyes at the distinguished *gospodarz* and *gospodyni* who were to supervise her wedding. The Skipper offered the Posienkos those chairs he judged would best fit their posteriors. His sons, Konstanty and Konrad, took seats, ears tuned to their father's words.

"God called my wife six years ago and now I find I need someone to arrange my daughter's wedding," he said.

The helpers, Władek and Zdenek, peeked from among the willows, then inched closer. When they were close enough to hear, Jadwiga turned to them. "Get my sandals from the boat," she commanded, and both ran to please her.

"One man we know made a good profit for himself on weddings," Alfons Posienko said. "Of course, he had four daughters." He sat in a barrel chair with his arms spread as if having his portrait painted, looking even more distinguished than when standing.

"A wedding is only as big as the people make it," the woman said. "The more people, the bigger the wedding. And the bigger the wedding the better it will pay for itself."

When the helpers returned, each with one sandal, there was an awkward pause in the talking. Konstanty whispered to her, "Take them for a walk. Go with them. Come back when they're occupied." For only a moment, she set her jaw in defiance. Then she obeyed her brother. Władek and Zdenek followed her down the beach.

"I am not looking for profit from my Jadwiga's wedding," Skipper Wdowiak said to Alfons Posienko. "I want only to see her in the beautiful costume of her wedding day, as I remember my wife, surrounded by the little girls. And I want the children to sing for her like angels and after that I want everybody to go to Gostomski's Hall where there will be food and music and dancing."

"But what kind of a wedding will it be if the bride does not sit in the middle of the hall while the girls attending her dance around her with every man they can catch to put money in the apron?" Alfons Posienko asked.

"I don't want my Jadwiga sitting in the middle of Gostomski's Hall on her wedding day. I want her to dance in the middle with her husband. And I want the bridesmaids dancing around her with the groom's men. It will be like in heaven."

Lilianna Posienko leaned slightly in her chair to watch Jadwiga and the helpers. Down the beach, they were joined by two brothers and a sister from one shack, and two sisters from another. They walked together, but Jadwiga was the center of attention from the young men. The helpers maneuvered and played tricks to keep the others from walking beside her.

"Will there be money to pay for the dressmaking, counting for the little girls with the flowers?" Lilianna asked.

"There will be money to pay for the finest dresses you can make. There will be money for everything."

"Counting the food on the table, the pay of musicians, our pay, the rent of the hall?" asked Alfons.

"Counting even that we will hire the Sadowski brothers," Skipper Wdowiak said. "They are the strongest and the meanest two on the beach. And for some money they will stay sober and they will bash the head of anyone who starts a fight or the smallest commotion on my Jadwiga's wedding day."

Alfons looked at Lilianna, but she seemed not to have heard this suggestion. She knew how to write and she was making marks in a small book. "And when is this wedding to be?" she asked.

"That part, the part about when, I don't yet know. And you must keep the secret," Skipper Wdowiak said. "The wedding may be the month after next. Or it may be the next or still the next. And it may not be until next year. But I will come to you and let you know ahead of time."

He spread his hands in reassurance. "I speak to you now so that you will have ample time. But from now until I let you know, you must forget. This is a matter for us alone, and you must not speak of it."

And with a nod of the head and another toast of wine, Alfons Posienko assured the Skipper Wdowiak that he would certainly forget. Especially now, he thought, that he could go home with one more coin in his pocket than he had come with.

"It is as I have always said about these fishermen," Alfons said to Lilianna on their way home. "They bounce on the waves. Their heads become loose on their shoulders. It is fortunate that as long as we had to have a day with them, at least we were paid. For drinking wine yet, and eating fish, and for forgetting." He glanced backward disdainfully. "Not even a young man yet!"

"Oh, there will be a wedding," Lilianna Posienko said. "I can't wait to dress that girl. She is the prettiest thing. It is only that she has not yet made up her mind."

Alfons nodded at this confirmation of his conclusion. "And that brings us right back to what I said about fishing people. Heads loose on their shoulders."

As time went on, Jadwiga's brothers teased her more and more. They plagued her about this one and that one—that one and this one. About Augustin Nowicki from downtown Gdynia and Rysiu Racek from near the church. Both were good dancers who really twirled her Saturday nights at Gostomski's Hall.

"To dance with, yes, but not for husbands. Neither one is tall enough," Jadwiga said back to her brothers.

"Jan is tall," Konrad would say.

"But Feliks is taller," Konstanty would follow.

"Katarzyna can have Jan. He's not in my dream," Jadwiga said. "And Feliks is too fearful. He's afraid of Władek and Zdenek, even one at a time."

"Then perhaps you should marry Władek?"

"Or Zdenek."

"Teresa can have Władek and Klara can have Zdenek. They are in love with them but those stupid ones don't know it. Anyway, none of them has the money to go to America. None of them are in my dream."

With Jadwiga, it was always the one in her dream. A tall one, she said, handsome, with broad shoulders and small ears and eyes the color of the sea. A man of patience and good humor. A man like her father. He would be brave, kind to her, and good.

He would take her to America.

"From the time you leave home until you come back, do not trust anyone you don't already know," Edmund Wdowiak said to his daughter over and over as Easter approached. "Poznań is a big city with all kinds of people, good and bad. Make certain that you have enough money to bring you back, wherever you go. And don't carry it all in one place. You must have some in your purse, some in your stocking, and most of it sewn in your underwear. You must always have a place to reach if someone steals your purse.

"When you get to Poznań, go to Stawicki's farm," father said to daughter. "It is far from where the Germans will let the soldiers out of their army. It's two hours, walking—a good place for girls to stay. For men with bad thinking, too far to walk."

"Yes, Papa."

"And daughter, do not be saddened if you don't find the one in your dream."

"No, Papa."

"Jadwiga, I mean this. Listen. Dreams are good, but God dreams better for us than we do for ourselves. He may have a surprise for you."

"For a woman it is to follow her man," Jadwiga's father always told her when they talked out on the water.

"But sometimes a woman has to point for her man, so he will see the way to go," he would add with a wink. Jadwiga knew these winks. She knew her father didn't mean she should point with her finger.

Chapter 2

Easter Monday was a day of joyous celebration.

And a day of marching.

Among Poles exultant that Christ had risen, it was a day of frivolity. Boys cut switches from the redbush and chased girls, even into their homes, to whip them about legs and buttocks. It was Śmingus-Dyngus Day, and it was the custom. It was a day of dancing the polka and the mazurka, the better to mix the young ones. It was a time for mating.

Among Germans uneasy that the spirit of resistance remained strong among the people, it was a time for showing strength. In all the big cities, the occupying forces of Otto Eduard Leopold von Bismarck-Schonhausen, Premier of Prussia, would parade precisely at noon.

The drums spoke softly, deliberately.

Squadrons stood at sharp attention, ready in their flashing boots of ceremonial march.

Polish soldiers, at last to be mustered out, would march, too. Unlike the Germans, they would carry no rifles. But on this last day of their forced service to the plague of Prussian militarism, neither would they have to carry their picks and shovels.

In all the cities, the drums spoke loudly now. All was ready.

But in Poznań, where the parade would twice circle the flowered hub of the city, there was a disruption. In the fourth row of the first squadron, a German who suddenly became ill had to be taken from the ranks. His place was quickly filled with a replacement from the second squadron, and that from the third, and so on down.

But it left an unsightly gap in the last row of the fourth squadron and this did not satisfy the critical eye of the commanding officer.

"Fill that hole!" he barked.

And here it was only seconds to the first beat of march.

Otto Niebel, First Lieutenant and quick thinker, suddenly ordered the stricken German taken out of his uniform. "Put that Polack into it," he commanded, pointing at the one in the front row—Paul Adamik, the sergeant whose kick-stepping he had once seen. "Out of those greys," he yelled at the Polack in the German tongue. "Into these blues."

Surrounded by his comrades, the Polack scrambled to change and take up the rifle. The drums became a rumble.

"And march as you have never marched before!"

With a click of his heels, the Polack saluted and turned about-face. He stood with Bismarck's finest, rigid and straight.

And proud. From all the Polacks, he, Paul Adamik, was the one chosen.

Now the drums were thunderclouds resounding.

Shots rang out, setting the cadence of march. The Polack stiffened, his chest thrown out. He was marching, stomping precisely to the beat just like the Germans. They were one big, powerful locomotive—a hundred iron horses, a thousand—a huge wheel dominated by the blue of the German uniforms. Not a boot was out of place. Walnut-stock rifles sprang out precisely in arcs of the manual of arms. Spectators stood in awe as the marching machine made its turns about the circle.

Then the lines straightened, spinning into sharply defined columns of march, followed at last by the Polish soldiers in their gray uniforms.

Young, pretty girls in fancy dress now flung themselves at the Polish soldiers, sending rank and file askew. There was screaming, hugging, and kissing. Caps were stolen, buttons torn from uniforms. But it didn't matter—the Poles were being discharged and the uniforms were theirs to keep. There were more girls than soldiers, so there was even some fighting and hair-pulling. Soon, all that remained of the disciplined precision of parade march was the front part where the Germans—and Paul Adamik—stepped out with zest.

As in all the big parades, he could see, there were the few tramps—the girls who ignored the men of their own country and followed the Germans to consort with them when the parading was done. Paul Adamik noticed that one even had her eyes on him—on the counterfeit German—on him, the misplaced Polack in the wrong uniform in the middle of the last row.

But most of the time he looked only straight ahead. This was no time for girls. This was a time for marching proudly with the best.

"She is for me," a goosestepper next to him said in his German tongue.

"She will be mine," said the one on the other side.

Now commotion and disorder was even infiltrating the ranks of Germans—professional soldiers whose future depended upon order and precision. They were turning their heads and rolling their eyes, all because of this young flirt in the pink dress and white lace. She was relentless. She ran up front and then back again to look from all angles and she always came back to march along with the very last row. And each time her eyes were fastened on him.

But his eyes were fastened forward where they belonged. He would not fail Lieutenant Niebel.

But now she ran to the other side, then back, dancing graceful half-circles from one side to the other, always looking straight at him. She made goosestepping uneasy for him.

"Come with me, sweetheart," a German whispered hoarsely.

But still she looked only at him. When close again, she even touched his shoulder, patting him from behind as though to claim him.

But he would concentrate. How honored he was to be chosen in this emergency. How well he had marched in the intricate circular maneuver he had never even practiced, making not one mistake in the manual of arms. Even this German-chaser was mistaking him for a genuine soldier of Bismarck. How clear that she singled him out. How her blue eyes glistened at him; how vivacious she was in her running this way and that.

But suddenly, as the parade turned into a cleared field, the girl was gone. And so was his hat.

"*Achtung!*" Lieutenant Niebel snapped.

Now everything was spoiled for him. Everything would have been perfect if not for the one in the pink dress.

"What explanation have you for losing a hat tied with rawhide under your chin?" Lieutenant Niebel quizzed. "How could any girl get in front of you? Even then, how could she untie it?"

He didn't understand every single German word. But he knew what the lieutenant was talking about. And he was mortified.

"From behind," he said with German words.

"Be at ease. Show how this could happen."

"She was like a butterfly. She untied it," he explained with his best German words.

"I can't see how a girl could untie it from in front, let alone from behind. Find that girl so she can show us."

He saluted. "I will find her," he said.

"It won't be hard. She's the one with a parade hat of Bismarck's finest," Lieutenant Niebel said, and the other Germans laughed.

Paul Adamik looked and looked. He searched the field from one end to the other, looking for a pink dress and blue eyes. He searched the clusters of young women, and it seemed to him that not one of the others was so bright or spirited as the one who had taken his hat.

When finally he saw her it was only because another girl pulled her hair, trying to steal the hat from behind, then yelling when an elbow struck her forcefully in the stomach.

He yanked her out of the crowd. "You are coming with me and you will show how you can take a German army hat from a soldier's head."

She giggled, almost laughing at him. Then she marched with him, step for long step, when he had thought he would be dragging her along. He was embarrassed, then, and angry. He knew he looked like just a boy swinging hands with a girl.

Then she stopped him abruptly, in mid-stride, snapping her hand free of his grip, and spoke as though just remembering something. "Let me look at you," she said.

Now, he looked closely at her for the first time. Her face was framed in the light blue of the hat. He looked at the sparkle in her eyes, and saw they were sharp, yet soft—innocent, yet playful. Then her dimples danced with a new smile. As if for good measure of mischief, she touched the tip of his nose and said, "You are the one."

So befuddled he became that now she was leading him by the hand. "Let's go where we can sit and talk," she said. "I am Jadwiga Wdowiak and I am from Gdynia."

"I am Paul Adamik and I am from near Kalisz," he said.

She steered him sharply away from the German encampment to the high ground where she could sit high on a knoll and fan out her pleated pink dress. She placed herself in the center of all the color, then gathered her skirt to one side.

"Sit here and talk," she said. "I want to hear you talk."

"And I want to hear you talk. How did you know I'm Polish when I'm in a German's uniform?"

"I knew because you are tall and straight and handsome with smooth skin and you have eyes the color of the sea, and a small nose and small ears." He captured her hand and held it as she reached to touch his nose again. "I have seen you many times in my dreams and in the clouds and waves."

"Perhaps it's because I marched with the shortest of the Germans that I appeared tall," he said.

"Then it's good you marched with the short ones so that I could see you."

He didn't know what to say. Her eyes drew him to her.

"Did you ever see me in your dreams?" she asked.

It didn't occur to him to lie. "No, I never have."

She became sad and the sparkle left her eyes. She took back her hand to raise herself away from him.

Quickly, he drew her back. "It's only that I could never dream anything so pretty," he said, immediately pleased with himself that he could save the moment so cleverly.

The sparkle came back to her eyes and her dimples danced all the more. She touched his lips with hers and they held tightly together for a long time. "You're the one," she whispered, almost to herself.

"And you are something," he said into her ear.

He leaned back on his hands and brought his knees up so she would be comfortable leaning against them. She settled there, her arms around his waist.

They hugged and looked into each other's eyes, and lost touch with time. Around them Polish soldiers and their girls gathered, sitting on the knolls where they could get away from the Germans and the crowd. They were hugging and kissing and drinking beer and sharing plates of ribs and sauerkraut. And only then did it occur to Paul Adamik and Jadwiga Wdowiak that they, too, were hungry.

Because he was wearing the blue, they waved him to the head of the line and made certain to fill his drinking pail to the brim with beer. They even gave him two platters. Thus the two of them were conspicuous among the Poles, Paul in the blue uniform, Jadwiga with her own platter and fork. She held her head high with this importance.

Together, they took a drink from the pail of beer, leaning cheek to cheek so none would spill. "Like two pigs," Paul said, and they laughed together.

Then, mischief in her eyes, Jadwiga suggested another drink, but as they stooped she quickly took her head away from the pail and doused his face with beer. Then she sprang to her feet to run and he had to chase her. He caught her eventually and held her in a tight squeeze.

"How can you be such a devil when you look like such an angel?" he asked.

"You are the one," she whispered in his ear again.

Then she wriggled out of his arms and they went back to eating and talking.

"Where did you learn to fight?" he asked. "I saw what you did to the girl who yelled—with your elbow, striking backward."

"I watch Władek and Zdenek."

"You learn from watching two men fight?"

"They're always fighting. They even fight over me sometimes." This made him jealous, so she added, "But they're like clowns in the circus. I wouldn't have a clown to father my children. And anyway, neither of them has money to go to America. But they are good workers—they're fishermen who work for my father."

"Your father is a fisherman?"

And so are my brothers. You'll like them all. And my father will like you."

"Perhaps not so much. Perhaps he hopes that you will find a man of means. I come from poor people."

The poor people are the best ones, she told him.

"My father and mother and brothers are farmers," he told her.

"My mother died when I was twelve years old." Saddened, Jadwiga bowed her head and signed the cross.

"I'm sorry," Paul said, and he lowered his head, too.

Now their talk became a guessing of ages. First Jadwiga tried, then Paul, and both were wrong. Then they tried again and this time Paul guessed right. "You are eighteen."

"And you are twenty-two," she said, her eyes growing wider. "You are already a man." She snuggled close as though for the protection of his strong arms.

And now it was his turn to hold his head high with importance.

Otto Niebel and his subordinate lieutenants had stayed together to eat and drink, argue and speculate. The notion was advanced that the Polack must have helped the girl take the hat, but the First Lieutenant argued otherwise. "This Polack is upright. He marched with integrity. He was telling the truth. The girl untied it herself."

There was even a wager. If Niebel was correct and the girl could once again untie the hat while the Polack marched, as senior officer he would be first to have his fling with her. But if she failed, it would be every man for himself. They would take turns pouring beer into the wench, and from there on they would see who could teach her things about German knots and other manipulations.

Jadwiga was first to see them coming, marching two by two as if coming to make an arrest. "They cannot have you back," she said.

"Let go," he snapped. Because she would not, he had to salute from a sitting position.

"Be at ease," Lieutenant Niebel ordered.

"I forgot," Paul said, piecing German words together.

"With such a *piękna panienka* I would forget, too," Lieutenant Niebel said. He mixed Polish with German, stressing the Polish words *pretty girl* while trying to capture her eyes with his. But she seemed not to hear.

"Tell the *piękna panienka* what we want her to show us," the Lieutenant said, stressing the Polish words again and gesturing to the hat tied around Jadwiga's neck.

She quickly took the hat from her shoulders and gave it to the German. "Take it and go away," she said sharply.

Paul gave a start at this insolence, but was immediately relieved. They hadn't understood her. They squatted to examine the unusual four-petal flower she had tied in the streamers.

"They only want to know how you untied it from behind."

Now Jadwiga's smile returned. She released his arm so he could tie his hat on.

"Now take it just as you did when I was marching into the field."

"I can do it even with my eyes closed." She put her hands around his neck, untied the knot and took the hat from his head with such ease and quickness that the Germans hardly had time to open their mouths in amazement. She had distracted them by pointing to her closed eyes, then opening them to show their blue depth.

"It's a simple knot," she said, putting the hat back on Paul's head. "It can be tied for left-handed people, too."

Then she showed another slip knot with enough rawhide left to make small fists on the ends. "This one is better," she said. "The fists will bounce when the soldiers march. It will be pretty."

A small crowd was gathering—mostly Polish soldiers curious about what was so interesting to German officers. Soon they were joined by another officer under whom Paul had served. Lieutenant Herman Shubert's precise military German had become ragged with too much beer, but he carried papers in his pocket for Paul, and he drew him aside.

"You have until the first of the year to come back," he said. "If you do, you'll begin as a master sergeant. You are a good soldier." Formally, they saluted each other and shook hands. Then Lieutenant Shubert yielded to his own curiosity about the show in the circle of uniforms.

Jadwiga was tying the four-petal knot for Lieutenant Niebel. "Too fast, too fast," he said.

"And I thought I would be dancing today," Jadwiga said.

"Is this the girl who has been waiting for you?" Lieutenant Shubert asked.

Paul blushed. "Perhaps."

Otto Niebel and his sub-lieutenants suddenly knew they had lost their chances with the pretty Polack as she walked away with Paul Adamik and Lieutenant Herman Shubert.

"This is good," the Lieutenant said, and he put his arm around Paul. "If you decide not to stay in the army, I have land here in Poland to be managed. You come from farming people. It would be good work for you. You would have a comfortable house."

And then he presented a gift to Paul—his own knife and sheath, which he took from his belt.

Paul was moved.

But Jadwiga tugged at him. "Come now," she said. "Before long, you will be drunk, too."

He tried to silence her but she was faster with words.

"I didn't come this far to be bamboozled by a German soldier. I came to find a Polish one," she said. "Come. I must be back on Stawicki's farm at midnight and counting that it is two hours walk from here and counting that we have yet to dance in Poznań we have no more time for Germans."

No more time for Germans. As though it was for her to determine this for him. Chasing her after she made her mischief, he had thought her so young, such a child, because of the quickness of her feet in taking the long stride of men and because of her tireless running even after the parade. He had to move his fastest to catch her. But even in mischief he was happy with her, not only because she was so sweet and pretty but because she came from fishing people, and she was so clever with knot-tying. She even caught the interest and admiration of the Germans—even a First Lieutenant.

She wasn't so childlike after all.

So much was happening. Already he had forgotten everything right up to the time he first looked into this Jadwiga's eyes and saw that they sparkled when she looked at him. And now it was becoming an effort to remember the things that had happened just since that first look.

He was forgetting his knapsack, which he was entitled to keep. And he was forgetting the other Polish sergeants—the ones he had agreed to go to town with, to the dance.

Already she had him fully confused, awash in mystification.

And hadn't she mentioned America, even? What was it she said about America?

Chapter 3

There had been other girls, to be sure. Other times when the storm within was both joyful and ripping. Other moments of blended ecstasy and uncertainty. Other occasions when sense was absent and senses unreliable. But there was something more about this Jadwiga.

It was as though she alone knew all the words and all the melody of the song now playing inside him—as though she were the leader of an orchestra within him which, until now, had only been rehearsing. About her, there was something special.

When she let him kiss her, he felt a deep anticipation that gave way immediately to a longing when she grew cautious of his advancing passion.

At the dance in Poznań, it seemed they were born to dance together. In the polka, they swung wide and leaping, and though he could not remove his eyes from her face, somehow there was never anyone in the way. Her eyes would lock to his, and he would drown in their blueness, penetrating to the depth of her soul and finding a flirtatious love of which he wanted more.

When she laughed at his military ways of discipline and straightness, it was a child-woman's laugh telling him that in a grander scheme of things, it was a mere amusement to her. He could not help himself, and he laughed, too.

Later, when she trusted him and allowed herself to fall asleep leaning against him after a long trek through the moonwashed night to the distant farm, he felt charged with a strength and responsibility such as he had not experienced before, even under Prussian discipline. He was her protector, even though he could not imagine from what she might need protecting.

She was so innocent, yet so delicately in command.

Paul Adamik wasn't sure what he must do to know this Jadwiga Wdowiak better, but he sensed there was more to know, and he longed to get on with this course fate had somehow set before him. That feeling drew him along when she awoke with a start near light of dawn and spoke of the train to Gdansk. In her mind, there was no question: He would be coming along.

At the train station it surprised him when she suddenly had the price of her fare in hand. He had been about to spend from his mustering-out pay for second-class tickets, but she bought third-class. "You must save it," she said. "We will need it for travel to America." Then she was off, not looking back, sure he would follow.

America. From her, there was all this talk of America. There were other things to talk about as the train clattered along, but this *free country* seemed constantly on her mind, often on her lips.

And so strong was her assumption that they would go to America together that he let it go unchallenged for now. He reasoned with himself that he ought not to burden this new relationship with a disagreement. Later, he would discourage this foolish notion of travel to some unknown country by giving her the more reliable information about her *America.*

"Jadwiga is coming. With a soldier, Jadwiga is coming." The children passed the word.

Edmund Wdowiak had stayed ashore this day, expecting her. It wasn't worry, not even concern. She could handle herself, he knew. If he had been unable to teach her sewing and the finer points of preparing meals, he had at least taught her to handle herself. He couldn't tell her all a young woman must know of young women's things, but he told her what she must know of young men. It wasn't worry. It was just a matter of being there for her return. He walked the shore road toward them.

She ran ahead to him, leaving the one in the Prussian uniform answering the questions of the curious children who gathered about him. He expected her to career into his arms and spin him around with the force of her greeting as she had done on the few other occasions when they were separated for more than a day. But it was not so enthusiastic, and he knew before she spoke that the soldier was more than a passing matter.

"Papa, I found him—the one in my dream."

"Well, Jadwiga, it shows in your eyes."

"He has ears like you. Eyes, too. He is very handsome."

"He wears Bismarck's colors."

"He is Polish, Papa."

"But a German uniform?"

"They chose him for the ceremonial marching."

"In the uniform of the Prussians?"

"He was a substitute. He normally wears the grey."

"He is a good Polack, then?"

"Papa, he is the one. The one in my dream."

"But in his heart, Jadwiga, is this one a German?"

The soldier had bent his knees to squat among the children. Edmund Wdowiak saw that even as the young man answered the questions of the bold ones who crowded close, he involved the shy ones with a wink or a question of his own. He even raised one to his shoulders, and gave his hat to another. To yet another, he gave up his jacket.

It was a surprise to Paul—that her father came to meet them.

By the time their train had arrived in Gdansk and they had walked most of the distance along the shore to Gdynia, he knew much of the community in which Jadwiga had grown to such appealing maturity. Through her words, he knew her friends. And he knew about the fishing life on the Baltic at the Bay of Gdansk. He heard the bitter cold of winters and the gentle roll of summer waves in her voice.

Yet it was a surprise when suddenly they were surrounded by a dozen young children who shouted her name and asked questions about him.

Yes, a soldier, she told them. *No, he doesn't have a gun. No, there are no other soldiers coming, only this one.*

He saw that she picked the questions to answer. "Will the soldier be your husband?" was one she ignored.

When Jadwiga stooped to pick up two of the smallest girls who insistently pulled at her dress, he lifted two young boys, one to his shoulders, the other into his arms. The youngest, they were the least afraid of his uniform and most curious about soldiering.

But it was a surprise when her father approached—it had to be her father—walking along the shore road coming to meet them. She put the little girls down and ran ahead to him. Paul thought it best to stoop down—to busy himself with the boys who insisted he must have a gun in his pack.

Father and daughter held close for a long time, as though they had been separated far longer than the few days of her absence in Poznań. There was something good between them, and it was allowed to show.

"Paul." She reached into the group of children and pulled him up.

The father's hand, extended in a greeting, seemed the size of a bucket.

Edmund Wdowiak was not larger than Paul. But there was the deep color of a face well-acquainted with the sun and the small lines beginning to spread from mouth and eyes that demanded respect, and there was a largeness about him that transcended measurement in size and suggested bigness of spirit, and depth of experience.

"Welcome." By instinct of training, Paul almost saluted the authority in his voice, but instead he extended his hand, too. The father's grip was easily more commanding than any officer's.

"My welcome is for you, not for your uniform."

Paul didn't know what to say to this. He knew a proper response wouldn't occur to him until later, so he said nothing.

"Paul is from near Kalisz," Jadwiga said. "He has just completed his compulsory service." She emphasized *przymusowy—compulsory*.

True enough, Paul knew, there was great resentment of the Prussians as there was of the Russians and Austrians in those sectors of divided Poland. But it was the way of things. No one his age had known any other. Here in Gdynia, nearer the Prussian border, there would be even more hostility. But he was not ashamed of the blue uniform he had come by chance to wear. Rather, he considered himself fortunate to have been chosen, and pleased with himself that he had marched well.

At the beginning, he had resolved only to make the best of a bad situation in serving his two years. But in his determination to make a positive experience of it, he had found real security in German discipline. He liked knowing what he was to do and when, and having a firm standard of behavior and performance. He was a good soldier, they had told him, and it was true. He felt he could wear this uniform with pride.

He stood all the straighter.

They began walking now, Jadwiga between the men.

"Your parents are farmers?" the father was asking.

"They are, as were my grandparents. And Jadwiga tells me that you are fishing people."

"Here on the Baltic, there is only fishing, and a little commerce. But the commerce is in Gdansk, and here we are merely providers for the stomachs of a vast region."

"I'm eager to see your boat."

"Oh, it isn't much. A working boat. More than see it, you will sleep on it if you can stay with us a few days. It is not mine, of course. We operate it under contract for a German Baron who has fishing rights. The Germans control this as they control everything."

"Papa, you should have seen the parade in Poznań, in the great circle. The flowers were beautiful. The uniforms and the drums…"

"Bismarck sends the goosesteppers to show us we are his chattel, Jadwiga—to show us the consequences if we resist as they do in the Russian partition. This is not something to be admired."

Paul swallowed. It was indirect, but he felt attacked along with the Prussian army he had served. It wouldn't be proper to argue with the older man, but perhaps a time would come to speak of the positive aspects of the army.

"Yes, Papa." Jadwiga was only closing the subject, not necessarily agreeing, Paul could tell. "Tadeusz Stawicki sends his greetings. He says that in two summers, he will send his youngest son to you to learn fishing."

"David?"

"Yes."

"He has no more land, then?"

"No, no more land. The older sons complain that it will not be enough even for just the two of them to work together."

"What of his daughters?"

"Both married, both last year."

"To the Rogulski twins."

"Yes, how did you know?"

"I talked with Tadeusz's sister some time back, and it seemed that would be the way of it."

The children lost interest now that Jadwiga and her soldier were occupied in adult matters. Gradually they dispersed, mostly through the hedges to the beach. The late afternoon sun pinholed through the overarching willows and oaks, their leaves rustling in the breeze coming off the bay.

Already, the Germans had been mentioned three times. The uniform, the fishing rights, and by implication, the land insufficient for the third Stawicki son. The older man was probing for his true feelings about the Germans. Because he made no response, there was an awkwardness Jadwiga tried to dispel with talk of unimportant matters.

Finally her father approached the matter more directly.

"You have been a soldier for how long?"

"Two years, sir. The required service."

"It is over, then?"

"Yes. Although I can re-enlist."

"Your uniform. It isn't the Polish uniform."

"I was in the Engineers—a Polish company. I wore the grey. This uniform is an accident, really. I wore it only for the marching in Poznań, when we were mustered out."

"The Prussians are not appreciated here."

"No."

"Do you have other clothes to wear?"

"Fatigues, in my knapsack."

"We will find you some clothes to wear. The blue of the sea is beautiful, but among our people, the Prussian blue isn't welcome. There could be trouble. Antagonism."

Before Paul could answer, Jadwiga darted ahead to walk backward. "You must come fishing with us, Paul, and you will need other clothes for that. And I will wash your uniform for you."

"But it will be for your own protection that we will give you other things to wear ashore, as well," said Edmund Wdowiak. "Even though you are Polish, in these parts you could become the target of much ill feeling toward the Germans."

"I believe I can defend myself," Paul said.

"No doubt, no doubt. But there is no need to inflame feelings, is there? The people in this region are still very Polish, despite the many years of occupation."

"*Poland has not yet perished*," Paul said, quoting the patriot's hymn. He half-meant it to be ironic, but it was not taken that way.

"No, not yet. As long as there are speakers of the Polish tongue and men and women who dance the mazurka and the polka together, there will always be a Poland."

"And a Polish people. Yes, sir." Paul had no desire to offend Jadwiga's father. His own feelings about the successive divisions of Poland by predatory neighbors were very Polish, yet overtly neutral as a practical matter. First-hand, he had seen the might and discipline of Bismarck's forces. He knew it was futile to resist. Indeed, he had found opportunity in accepting the situation.

"I learned much from the Germans," he said tentatively.

"Yes, of course. There are two things they teach you. They teach you to be strong, perhaps even to lead. And they try to teach you to be German, not Polish."

He paused, but Paul made no comment.

"It's good to learn the one lesson. But not the other. You are Polish. They are the Prussians. They don't belong here. It is our country, not theirs."

"I made the best I could of my compulsory service," Paul said. "I didn't bring the Germans here. But I have learned much from them."

"But you have not learned to be German instead of Polish, so we will find you something else to wear."

Edmund Wdowiak slapped a hand across Paul's back in closing punctuation of the difficult conversation. Jadwiga decided she would help.

"Paul, come down to the beach with me. Let me show you the beach!" She glanced at her father for permission to go, which he gave with his eyes.

"Here," he said to Paul, "let me take your pack." Paul took it from his shoulder and handed it over. Jadwiga gave him her shoes. "And Paul..."

He looked at the older man.

"Paul, welcome."

"Thank you, sir."

Sunset was already near as Paul and Jadwiga walked the salt-wet sand toward the Wdowiak shack. In an ebbing tide only fingers wide, shore birds with spindly legs worked the thinned edge of waves to find the tiny creatures that made their meals. Along the beach, there was the soothing sound of sea against shore to distract him, and with it, the sound of Jadwiga's voice.

"My father feels strongly about the Germans, doesn't he?" She looked at Paul, waiting to judge the strength of feeling in his response.

"He expresses himself strongly."

"He means no harm. I have even heard him say that were it not for the Baron's schooner, we would have a difficult time making a living from the sea. Then, at other times, he resents the quota we must meet."

"I myself have little quarrel with the Germans," Paul said. "But your father is right about the one thing."

"What?"

"I am Polish."

She smiled at him and he saw that she liked it, that he was Polish before he was anything else.

"I'm Polish, and though the Prussians may rule here long after we are gone, they cannot make me a German. I am Polish."

He thought of the German officers pretending to teach the Polish officers to goosestep. He knew now that they had been making fun, playing games of bumping the Poles, ridiculing their gait. It wasn't only that they couldn't take his Polishness away from him. They didn't really want to make him German. Obedient, yes, but not a German.

"You will wear other clothes, then?"

"Of course. Even if I chose to be stubborn, I could not wear my uniform constantly. It does need washing, anyway."

"You must save it, Paul. It will soon be threadbare if you wear it all the time."

"There's no need to make excuses for wearing something else. I am not on duty here. Unless I reenlist, my army service is over. While I visit, I will wear the clothes people wear here."

As she had on the parade ground at Poznań, she snapped her hand loose and turned him to look up into his face. "You are the one," she said, and she put her arms around him and kissed him. Clinging to one another, they lost balance when a wave washed footing away. They fell into the receding water, still kissing and holding tight to each other.

Chapter 4

On Wednesday Paul met all of Jadwiga's friends and many of their parents. Apart from the stories of his arrival in a blue uniform and his service to the Germans, he was well-accepted among the fishing people. Only Władek and Zdenek, the helpers, were a sullen exception. With Jadwiga's young friends, there were playful wrestling matches and foot races at the edge of the water. Some of the girls even flirted with him when Jadwiga wasn't looking.

Yet, the matter of the uniform and Paul's supposed Prussian leanings hung unresolved like a discarded fishnet gone stiff in the sun. It did not help when, that afternoon, Paul was teaching young boys to march, and Edmund Wdowiak heard him using German words of command.

At supper, it was plain that Jadwiga and her father had been talking about Paul and his military service. When she spoke to the elder Wdowiak, it was a continuation.

"In America, Papa, it won't matter what language one speaks, if one learns the American language, too." Getting no response, she added more: "And the Americans will not care in what army a man has served, as long as he is willing to serve in the American army if the time should come." Paul glanced at Jadwiga's brother Konrad, who was doing little to hide his awkward feelings.

"Papa," Jadwiga continued, "in America we will be judged by American matters."

"By other Poles in America, you will be judged by how Polish you are." This was plainly intended as much for Paul as for her. "Even there, Poles will hold bad feeling for those who divided Poland. Even there, the Congress of Vienna will make a bad taste in good Polish mouths."

Paul finally spoke. He labored to be polite, trying without success to smile. In his voice, there was poorly concealed anger as he addressed Edmund Wdowiak.

"What would you have me say?" Jadwiga's father stopped eating and looked at him. "Would you have me say I denounce all Germans and Bismarck, too? Am I to forget the discipline and strength I was given in my compulsory service? Yes, I am Polish. I have the good tastes of a Polish mouth. But I don't hate everything German. I take the good, I reject the bad. I tell you again that I did not bring them here, and as much as I might wish for Poland to be united and free again, those days were gone long before I was born, and I can't change it back." He paused to take a breath. All eating had stopped. "My hating the Germans wouldn't change it back. The good I learned from them I will have in my heart and my mind forever, and I couldn't change that if I wanted to. But I am Polish. As much as any Pole, I would have my country free of the outsiders. But I have made my peace with a bad situation."

As Paul stopped speaking, eyes shifted to the older man.

"You are Polish," Edmund Wdowiak said, as though asking.

"Yes, I am Polish."

"Yet you teach Polish children to march to a German tongue."

"Marching is marching. The commands are what I know. It was play for them."

"The games children play become the beliefs they defend when they are grown."

"They are not damaged. If they learn to march to German commands and the day comes when they must march against the Prussians, the better they will know their enemy."

"And would you march against them?"

"Could we win?"

"Would you march against them?"

"To win, yes. Not to lose and be enslaved all the more. But to win, Polish men must learn what the Germans know of militarism and combat. We defeat only the enemy we know."

"They are the enemy?"

"They are the enemy of all the Polish people while they hold our land for themselves. But they cannot hold our hearts as they hold us in military service."

"They are your enemy?"

"They rule us. They are the enemy. We all must make our accommodation until better times come to Poland."

Paul's reference to accommodation—the Wdowiak fishing contract with the German Baron—brought a charged pause to the conversation.

Jadwiga broke the tension. "Paul is a good Pole, father. He is a good Pole as you are, and Konrad is, and Konstanty. In America, there will be no bad Poles, only bad Americans and good Americans."

Paul felt an impulse to address this crazy business of America, too. But he reached for self-discipline. Better to put matters at peace with one's elders, as difficult as it might be. He resolved to do so, and spoke directly to Edmund Wdowiak, quietly.

"Sir, if I am not truly welcome here because I happened to come in a German wrapping, I will leave. And no bad feelings. But the fish you catch from your German Baron's boat don't care that they are hauled aboard a German's boat in the nets of a Pole. The learning I took from the Germans knows no nationality. The few German words I speak are adaptation, not embrace."

The father's face was dark, unexpressive. It angered Paul that he was so unyielding. "And I am Polish." He became aware that his voice was rising, and resolved to control it. "By God, I am Polish..." Involuntarily, he stood. "Polish, whatever you might think of me for serving in their army..." He had to catch his breath. "A good Pole and I love my country." He realized, suddenly, that he was standing. "And you offend me by suggesting I am anything else."

Paul was alarmed. The words were true to his feeling, but the tone far more sharp than he intended. He was embarrassed to discover he was shouting at this man in his own house. Quietly, he said, "I did not mean to shout. I apologize that I shouted." Then he turned, walked to the door, opened it, and walked out, taking deliberate care to restrain himself and close the latch quietly.

"Papa." Jadwiga looked at her father, her expression a mixture of pleading and exasperation, but his eyes would not meet hers. He looked across the table, into the space between his daughter and son. Time, at once racing and plodding, was measured in Paul's strides. Finally Edmund Wdowiak spoke:

"You'd best go after him. He has forgotten his uniform."

Jadwiga didn't move. Tears appeared in her eyes. Finally, he looked at her, and suddenly there were tears in his eyes, too.

"All right...He has forgotten his uniform, but he will make you a good husband, too."

"A good Polish husband," said Konrad.

"Yes, a good Polish husband."

Jadwiga leapt to the door. "When I bring him back, you will make peace with him."

The elder Wdowiak nodded a casual assent, as though it were a trivial matter, and Jadwiga was gone.

"If he will come back," Konrad said.

"She will bring him back," Edmund Wdowiak said.

As he walked down the beach, Paul had no destination—no plan. He had not intended quite so much fire in his own defense. He sensed vaguely that he had allowed his own words, as much as the older man's, to bring him to anger. He felt ashamed that he had lost discipline. But it was done. He couldn't go back now.

Then, through the hiss of waves on the beach, he thought he heard Jadwiga calling his name. Abruptly, he stopped, not because he thought the call was real, but because the sound of it inside his head distracted him from argumentative feelings and made him think of losing her—leaving her behind over a crazy political argument with her stubborn father.

And then he knew that it was really her voice calling to him, and he turned.

She ran full speed into his arms, crying. He had all he could do to stay on his feet, catching her.

"Paul, you must come back."

He looked at her, incredulous.

"Come back? Why? For what purpose? To apologize further? Because I'm not Polish enough for your father?"

"No..."

"He thinks I'm not Polish because I learn things from Germans. He thinks a Polish bucket turns German if it carries their water."

"It isn't that..."

"He is not a reasonable man, Jadwiga. Your father is..."

She put her fingers on his lips, gently but firmly. Her voice stopped him in mid-sentence.

"Yes." A pause. "Yes, it's true. It is true that my father is too much a zealot in these political matters. But this wasn't a matter of politics, anyway."

"What do you mean?"

"Paul, it was a test of strength. He is a zealot, but...Oh, he doesn't even see it, but...You don't...Oh, Paul, all my father really wanted was to see that you are strong enough for me. You had to challenge him for me, and you did. And now he gives you respect for this. Come back. It will be he who will apologize. Please come back now."

He thought for a moment. "Jadwiga, let's walk for a while."

"They'll think I'm running away with you."

"Would you? Would you run away with me? Would you leave them?"

She held him more tightly, but wouldn't answer. "Come back with me. Finish your supper."

"I'm not hungry. Walk with me."

Together, they walked toward the pier, hands held tightly. Neither spoke. She knew he would come back. He knew he would. He wouldn't lose this prize over trivial politics.

Paul finally broke the silence.

"Jadwiga, you speak so often of America."

"Yes."

"Even tonight, you were saying to your father that in America..."

"Yes."

"You want so much to go to America."

"Yes."

"Why?"

"Poland..." She paused in thought.

"Paul, Poland has become a marching ground for foreigners—a place where even good Poles use the languages of others to give orders." She glanced at him now, to be sure he was not offended, then continued. "Where children know they're Polish only because their parents say so, not because the land is owned by their countrymen. Opportunity in Poland now goes only to those who occupy, and only to those who will be their servants. We must be free of all this—go where *our* children can be Polish. We must have our freedom, and they must have theirs. America is a free country."

"Perhaps not so free as you think, Jadwiga. There was talk in the army."

"What talk?"

"Of America and what has happened there. There was a great war among the Americans. Some fought to set the black ones free. The others fought to keep them slaves. Those who wanted freedom for the black people won. Now they need new slaves in America. If we go to America, we will be the new slaves."

"Paul, this is only army talk. Some have gone already, even from Gdynia, and they have written back about America. There is good pay for good work in America, even enough to save. And good land you can buy with what you save. I'll show you the letters."

"But how do you know they're truthful?"

"They come from people we know, and others known by friends."

"I'll read the letters."

"Come back, now, before my father thinks we've run away."

"He knows you wouldn't run away."

"But he's not so sure you would come back. He thinks I will bring you back, but he isn't sure. Come back now. He wants to apologize."

"We could wish to keep Jadwiga here with us forever," Konrad Wdowiak said to his father. "But we cannot."

"What has this to do with anything?"

"It has to do with how difficult it is to accept another to whom she gives her heart, Father."

"You think I am jealous of the young soldier, then?"

"Not jealous. But when you see the man who will take her away, it is difficult to accept. Isn't this true, father?"

"My argument with him was not over the feelings Jadwiga has for him. It was over his German leanings. He's Polish, but sometimes he looks more German to me."

"But Jadwiga is right. In America they will be judged by whether they are good Americans. This must be true."

Now the older man spoke slowly, thoughtfully.

"It is as much a question of character, Konrad. Integrity."

"I believe this one has character."

"Yes, I think you are right."

"He may have too much character. If he's half as stubborn as a Wdowiak, it may be too much for Jadwiga to bring him back."

"Perhaps."

"Perhaps we should go after them. Perhaps she will bring him back only if we..."

"I should. It was my quarrel with him. I'll go."

When he found them on the beach, they were holding one another in the sea breeze.

"Paul," he said, "there are some good Polish fish out there waiting to be caught by some good Polish fishermen. Jadwiga must stay on the beach tomorrow. Will you come fishing with us?" He extended his hand.

Jadwiga still in his arms, Paul took her father's hand, then all three were embracing.

The next day, it came clear to him why Jadwiga stayed ashore. It came in a flashing moment of understanding with the first protest from his stomach: Jadwiga was ashore to spare him his seasickness being witnessed by her.

And he was sick indeed. The waves beyond the shelter of the bay were unpredictable in an irascible spring wind. He was caught concentrating too intently on a tangle of line and net. Almost before he could realize what was happening, he had to spin to the rail to vomit.

Edmund Wdowiak seemed not to have noticed from his position at the helm. When the first episode was over, Konstanty slapped him on the back. "It catches everybody, Paul. Don't be concerned. Keep your eye on the horizon for a while."

He tried to smile. He was grateful Jadwiga was ashore.

The next day, Friday, Edmund Wdowiak sent his daughter back onto the water, and he walked Paul to every shack on the beach, introducing him to all the other fishermen's wives and their children and any fisherman found ashore for the day.

Paul had already met them, but they indulged Edmund Wdowiak, so he did, too.

Chapter 5

In his euphoria, Paul had little patience to think through the helpers'
hostility. Clearly, they wished he would go away. But Jadwiga told him
she had given neither Zdenek nor Władek any encouragement. And it
was obvious that each, though part of the working family Wdowiak,
was held at arm's length when it came to inner family matters.

Early on, there had been the friendly challenges—the spirited
wrestling matches that seemed more than just spontaneous fun. At first,
it was only a testing, but then offense was taken at an innocent remark,
and there were more serious individual tussles.

Paul proved the equal of each.

But after the Saturday night dance at Gostomski's Hall, when Jadwiga
walked home amid the three of them but preferring Paul's arm, there
came the most serious incident.

Lingering in his arms before going into the Wdowiak shack just up
the slope of the beach, Jadwiga was contentedly happy, relaxed, and
trustful in his embrace. Their kisses were long and warm, but the choice
to kiss instead or talk was hard to make, and they were soon laughing at
themselves in their awkwardness of choosing.

"You danced many times with Rysiu," Paul said.

"He is a good friend. Were you jealous?"

"Oh, no. I was pleased because it gave me ample opportunity to
dance with his sister. She didn't seem to mind my uniform."

"She is a good friend. But her parents, too, would frown upon your
uniform."

"So she said—that she is a friend, I mean."

"What else did she tell you?"

"That Rysiu should have proposed last year. She thinks it is too late,
now."

"He did ask last year. He asked me if he could send the *swaty* and the bottle."

"He asked, and then he changed his mind?" It was his little tease, pretending to assume she would drink to Rysiu with the proposers. In turn, she pretended to be hurt.

She turned in his arms, breaking away. "I told him I was waiting for the one in my dream," Jadwiga said. "But it's foolish to believe faces in dreams belong to real people."

"What about this one in your dream? What does he look like?" Paul gently turned her toward him, so that he could look in her eyes.

But she looked away. "He's handsome." Her hands were on his chest as though she might push away at any moment. "He is tall." She turned her face toward him but closed her eyes as though to think very hard. "He is very straight, and his eyes are the color of the sea." Now she opened her eyes, and there was a tear in one.

"This sounds like one you will never find."

"No, because the one in my dream is kind, too, and gentle, and sweet. And he will take me to America."

"You're fortunate to have dreams that show you the way so well. As I told you in Poznań, I could never dream so well."

"Dreams aren't real. My mother said that to dream too much is to hope too deeply for something which may never come."

"So the one in your dream may never come?"

"Perhaps never." Now she was teasing him.

"Now that you know the one in your dream will never come, perhaps it's time for someone else to send the bottle and the men."

"Perhaps. But Mother would also tell me that dreams shouldn't be given up so easily."

"How would one persuade you to dream a different dream?" Now there were more tears as she looked up at him, into his eyes. "Suppose I told you the one in your dream is one I sent long ago?"

"You sent?"

"Long ago."

"Why?"

"Perhaps it was so that you would tell Rysiu you were waiting." With the flat of his thumb, he caught a tear that threatened to roll down her face. "Perhaps I sent the one in your dream to hold a place for me."

She rested her head on his chest, waiting.

"Perhaps you no longer need the one in your dream."

She remained still.

"Perhaps I should speak to your father, since the one in your dream will not be coming."

Now when she turned her face to his, tears were flowing beyond any hope of capture.

"Oh, Paul, you *are* the one. I *told* you. The one in my dream." She stroked his face as though to confirm that he was not an illusion.

And now tears came to his eyes, too. They tried to kiss, but what the feelings did to their faces made it hopeless, and they just held one another very tightly.

When finally they parted Paul had a seizing moment of panic mixed with his feelings of excitement and love. Why did he let these conversations run away with his mouth? *He had suggested marriage, and she had accepted.* It was more than he had intended just yet, but as he walked toward the pier, the pounding of his heart told him that he had happened upon the right course—that he was too much in love not to follow through.

Then he became conscious of a movement behind him, was alarmed, and crouched, turning as he went. The first blow was thus a glancing one. In the clouded moonlight he sensed it was Władek or Zdenek, then he realized it was both. In a split-second of sickness he felt certain they had been outside the Wdowiak shack—listening to his talk with Jadwiga.

The second blow, from behind, caught him squarely across the shoulders, and he crashed to the uncertain ground of rocks and sand and beach growth. Now one of them was kicking at his ribs. He began, finally, to defend himself. He rolled over and scrambled away from the chopping boot, feeling the pain of a damaged rib, trying desperately to get a sense of where they were.

As he tried to get up, one was behind him locking his arms to hoist him up. Grasping for stability, his hand closed on a jagged rock just as he was raised upward. Dazed, caught without footing, he was unable to defend himself as the other man began driving fists into his stomach.

Paul raised a leg, trying to fend off the blows. A fist struck his kneecap squarely, the next blow was less forceful, and he knew the man was hurt.

But he knew he would have to break loose to mount any real defense. He raised both legs and lashed out with a foot. His boot raked across the face of the man in front of him. Then he drove the rock in his right hand downward into the groin of the man behind him, and he was free.

But there were two of them, both strong, both working to damage him. He turned away, not to run but for time to recover, and tripped over a boulder. The pain in his ribs and stomach shot through to his back as he broke his fall with outstretched hands. They were on him quickly, trying to hold him face down while they hit him in the small of his back.

But they did not work together well. Both had been holding just one of his arms, and suddenly neither was holding it. It gave him enough freedom to spin and lash out with his feet. There was a loud crack and a groan as his boot again caught some part of a head. With the free hand, he swept the sand around him for another stone and found one just a bit larger than a hen's egg. With an open hand, he slapped it into the head of the one grasping for a hold on his other arm.

No words had been spoken, but now he yelled at them. "What is the cause of this? Why are you doing this?"

No answer.

They recovered too quickly for him to get out of the way, and now they were on him again, this time holding his back against the ground and pounding his stomach. Quickly, in pain and in the exhaustion of resisting two strong men, he became unable to fight.

When they had beaten him so that he truly hurt and was beyond half-consciousness, one of them hissed down at him, "She is not for you."

The other said, "Leave us. Go back to the Germans."

Then they hit him again, and walked away.

When gathering wind blew a wave against him, minutes or hours later, he awoke wet and in searing pain. But he realized with surprise that they hadn't hit him in the face—then realized they must hope he would keep silence about the attack and simply take his leave. Suppose he did, he wondered. If he did, what would Władek and Zdenek do to resolve their own conflict over Jadwiga? As retching tore painfully at his ribs, he resolved they would not have the chance.

The blue uniform now reeked of his vomit.

In great pain, he staggered to the schooner. He made no attempt to mount the hammock in which he had been sleeping, but curled into a ball on the deck. Then he was unconscious.

Chapter 6

As though a Sunday had never been missed, the Wdowiak household prepared for the journey to St. Teresa's. When their guest didn't show his face at his usual time, Edmund Wdowiak went to the pier to invite him to go to church, taking clothes for him to wear.

"What in the world happened to you?" he asked the sleepy figure on the deck of his boat.

"It was nothing," Paul said, feeling a thrusting pain in his stomach even as he rolled to help himself stand. "Little more than a contest of strength that became too enthusiastic."

"After the dance."

"Yes, sir. After the dance."

"With whom did you have this contest of strength?"

"I heard no names."

"The priest told me of this sort of thing," said Edmund Wdowiak. "Did this have to do with Jadwiga?"

"No, sir. No. It was merely a bit of fun that became more spirited than intended."

Paul wouldn't think of naming the helpers as his assailants. They were more a part of this Wdowiak family than he. He was only the newcomer, brought for a visit.

"We are going to church, Paul. I've brought these for you to wear. Perhaps they objected to your uniform?"

"It could be. I wore it for the dance. I wanted to wear it for church." Paul was still struggling to get up, and he took the hand Edmund Wdowiak offered.

"We don't dress so formally for church. Anyway, the priest would scold over it. If you think I dislike Germans, you know nothing of disliking Germans until you've heard the priest."

"Yes, sir." Paul found that as he tried to stand straight, there was pain around his ribs. Rather than reveal it, he quickly sat on the rail, jack-knifing his body.

"We must leave for church soon. It's a long walk."

Walking was more than Paul wanted to contemplate. He thought of begging off, and Edmund Wdowiak caught the hint of desperation visible in his eyes. "How are your ribs?" he asked.

"Not so good."

"You wash and shave. I'll fix something for your ribs."

Twenty minutes later, Paul had shaved and bathed in frigid water from the cistern aboard the schooner. From fishnet and mending line, the skipper had fashioned a wrap, which he cinched with rope, from behind, as Paul clung to the schooner's mainmast and winced.

"You may have more than one broken rib," Edmund Wdowiak said.

"I think so."

"This must have been a powerful opponent."

"He had the strength of two," Paul said, nearly laughing over his little joke, but caught short by pain.

The older man gave a last pull to tighten the makeshift support, and grunted. "How does that feel?"

"You should be a healer instead of a fisherman."

"Finish dressing now, and come to the house. We must leave very soon."

"Sir, before you go..." With difficulty, Paul started pulling on the trousers the elder Wdowiak had brought him.

"You need help."

"No."

"With your pants."

"Well, I can use some help, yes. But I wanted to speak with you."

He felt ridiculous. How could he ask Edmund Wdowiak for his daughter in marriage while the man was helping him put his pants on? In his few moments of lucid thought between bouts with pain, Paul had thought about how to ask this question. He would discuss his prospects as a farmer, he thought, and perhaps—depending on the older man's mood—mention the offer to become caretaker of his lieutenant's lands in Poland. Now, being careful not to hurt himself as he cleared his throat, he tried to catch the father's eye as the man pushed a trouser up his right leg.

"I want to marry Jadwiga," he said.

He hadn't intended it to come out this way. It just did. There was no reaction from Edmund Wdowiak, who simply continued to help with the trousers.

"Sir, I mean to say that I would like you to consider…I love Jadwiga very much. I believe she and I…"

The man wasn't reacting. It was as though he heard nothing. Paul pulled the borrowed trousers up to his waist, still trying to catch the father's eye.

"Sir, I do not mean to offend in my way of asking. I have no family here, no *swaty* to send. I…and I realize I'm not clever with words." Paul scoured his brain for something to say—something right.

Edmund Wdowiak handed him the clean linen shirt he had brought to the schooner. He looked at him with his usual half-smile that could be hiding contempt or anger or curiosity or joy. Then, finally, he spoke.

"Two conditions, Paul."

"Sir?" Paul struggled to get the shirt on so he could look at the man, and listen.

"Two conditions."

"Yes?"

"No German names for my grandchildren."

The pain of putting his arms into the shirt had Paul at a disadvantage, but he struggled to follow. It sounded as though the Wdowiak man had been listening after all. It sounded as though permission were about to be… "No German names. No, sir…"

"And for the wedding, you will not wear the uniform."

"The uniform, for the wedding? No, of course…" Finally, the shirt fell into place. "Then…?"

"Then unless Jadwiga has changed her mind since a few minutes ago, I believe you are betrothed."

Both men broke out in smiles, then into laughter, Paul wincing in pain. Edmund Wdowiak extended his shovel of a hand and Paul clasped it in a grip that sent more pain through his shoulder to his neck. The pain didn't matter. But when the joining of hands became an enthusiastic embrace, suddenly it did matter. Paul moaned.

"I must be more careful," said Edmund Wdowiak. "We must keep you in one piece. At least until after the wedding."

"I'll be all right. Sir, thank you. Thank you. I promise I…"

"Make your promises to Jadwiga, Paul, not to me. Be good to her, and you need keep no other promise to me."

"Yes, sir."

Together, they stepped from schooner to pier. His ribs hurt again.

"Paul..."

"Yes, sir?"

"Paul, there's another thing."

"Yes, sir."

"The helpers sleep under the pier on Saturday nights until they know whether we are to fish or go to church on a Sunday morning. I stopped this morning to tell them they could have the day off."

"Yes?"

"Paul, since you plan to take my daughter away from me, I will need Władek and Zdenek to help me fish. Do you think you can restrain yourself? Perhaps you could leave each of them in one piece?"

Together, they had a good family laugh.

St. Teresa's was a simple church much like the one Paul knew from his childhood. The services, so familiar, took the usual course, the kneeling and standing and sitting again a routine any churchgoer, even a casual one, would know.

But the priest showed himself to be a different man than others Paul had heard.

"Let us pray today for the revelation of Lech," said the priest as he stepped away from the altar. "All good Polish children learn the story of the White Eagle, but there is a lesson for all God's people in this legend of the first great defender of the Polonia.

"We may remember him for his defenses against hostile tribes. We may remember him as the one who united our tribes in mutual respect and the strength that allowed good people to till the soil without worry that their land would be taken from them before the harvest moon appeared.

"We may remember him for his love of learning.

"But today, we remember him for a mistake. We remember him for his love of falconry and his illusion that he might steal a young bird from the nest of the noble white eagle, and make of it the best hunting bird of all the land.

"But the white eagle defended her nest, as Lech defended his people and their lands. Even struck by his dagger, the blood of life flowing across her white feathers, she defended her nest and her young.

"From this, Lech learned shame—shame to think that he could take the young eagle from its mother—shame to think that she would not defend..."—and now the priest's voice rose in volume and determination—"…would not defend her home and children just as Lech was the defender of his people and their lands.

"Let us pray today for the revelation of Lech, the first Duke of Poland—the man who placed the white eagle on the crimson field of the Polish flag. Let us remember him, and the dedication of the white eagle, and the teaching we may find in the threads of this story."

After mass, Paul and Jadwiga waited outside to talk with the priest. Edmund Wdowiak sought out Alfons and Lilianna Posienko.

"I now know the part I didn't know before," he said to them.

"The tall one is to be the groom, then," Lilianna Posienko said. "He is very good-looking. It will be a beautiful wedding. Your daughter will be a beautiful bride."

"And when will this ceremony take place?" asked Alfons.

"Soon," said Edmund Wdowiak. "It will be soon." He put a coin in Alfons Posienko's hand. "The priest will set the date. It will be soon. But this part is now the secret part: They are going to America."

As Edmund Wdowiak walked away to join Jadwiga, Paul, and the priest, Alfons turned to Lilianna, pointing to his head.

"They bounce on the waves," he said. "America!"

At the Wdowiak shack early that evening, when the leavings of supper had been cleared, there was a toasting by the Wdowiak men, father and sons. To long life and a happy marriage, to many strong children, and to wisdom and understanding between man and wife.

When Edmund Wdowiak approached his daughter with the tangled silk thread, at first she laughed, remembering friends taking this test of patience for the trials of married life. But it was a mother's place to have this traditional moment with a betrothed daughter, and Paul saw that tears came to Jadwiga's eyes, keeping her from manipulating the thread.

"It isn't fair," he said. "Jadwiga is a fisherman's daughter. Any fisherman's daughter who can untangle line and net can easily manage the untangling of a simple ball of thread. It isn't a true test for her."

The others, who couldn't see Jadwiga's tears, showed puzzlement.

"It is I who must take the test of patience," Paul said. "I am not so good with line and net, and it's a test more fair for me."

On his knees now, he joined Jadwiga. Together, they sorted out the tangled silk.

Chapter 7

Paul Adamik's parents were amazed. Of their three sons, they had been sure that he, the youngest, would be the last to marry. He was the first. They were sure he would marry a local girl from their farming community. Jadwiga Wdowiak lived in a world apart, among fishing people. They had thought he might re-enlist in the army, or that he would find some way to settle into farming, even though their land was hardly sufficient for their two older sons. Now, he gave some appearance of an interest in fishing, of all work.

But more than any of these things, they were amazed by Jadwiga. It was not just that she made them the king and queen of her world along the Baltic beach. It was not just that she was pretty. Or personable. Or so in control of everything about her. Or seemingly lively and bright every moment.

It was, instead, the entirety of her. She was vivacious and solicitous. And a planner—she had prepared everything.

"I can now understand how this could happen to him so quickly," father said to mother.

"And to her," mother said to father. "Let us not underestimate our Paul."

While they knew their son, coming to know his bride was all the focus of their trip from Kalisz to Gdynia—that and, of course, the wedding itself.

But so much had been arranged in so short a time. At every home on the beach, there was vodka and a cookie. Then, down the beach from the Wdowiak home, the Rogulski home became the temporary home for Wojciech and Oleńka Adamik. Their home could be spared, the Rogulskis said, for all their children had flown. They were present only briefly, and then away, staying with others. But before taking his leave, the elder Rogulski told Wojciech Adamik, "This will serve as your home and the groom's home, and welcome. It is humble, and perhaps less than you are accustomed to enjoying, for which I apologize, but it has been a happy home for us, and for the young ones, for their first night, it will make a good start."

Paul's father was overwhelmed by this consideration. It was not that he wouldn't do the same for a couple in special need back home in Kalisz, but he had not expected this from complete strangers. From the things in his luggage, he presented a pigskin money envelope to Franciszek Rogulski. "This is sorely inadequate as a gift in appreciation for your great generosity," he said. "It is of my personal fashioning, from an animal I slaughtered last year, and made with an even number of stitches, so that your riches might grow within it." Oleńka gave Maria Rogulski a small velvet pillow filled with horsehair. "From our hardest-working puller of the plow," she said. "On this pillow, your shortest nap will be more refreshing than a night of good sleep."

Then the Rogulskis were gone. Even so, there was too little time for overdue conversations with their son. He had stories to tell of his time in service to the Prussian army, but they had little interest, for they had read his few letters over and over. They wanted to know more about Jadwiga, her father, her brothers, the fishing. The questions were endless.

Paul was momentarily embarrassed when he could not answer some basic questions. How old were Konrad and Konstanty? Older than Jadwiga, he was able to answer—and then he added, "The same ages as my brothers." While he was not altogether sure, he thought some answer was better than a display of ignorance.

"Your own brothers will arrive in two days," Oleńka told her son.

"It is the custom here that a *stary* go among the homes of those to be invited for the wedding," Paul said. This is a role for Timoteusz, as the younger of my brothers. But I also will require a man to attend me, and this will be Walenty. Jadwiga has others, here, who would take these roles, but I would rather these things be done by my brothers.

"In two days they will be here," Wojciech assured his son.

And they were. They arrived in late afternoon, carrying their own valises and hauling additional ones with clothing for their parents, packed for their stronger young bodies to bear.

Walenty and Timoteusz were welcomed warmly among the families of the beach. Jadwiga charmed them, and they chided Paul for his temerity in setting a standard, in his choice of wife, which they said they could never match. Time for making acquaintances was short, but they looked around among the unmarried daughters of the fishermen for others like Jadwiga. Several of the young men made proprietary gestures, suggesting claims upon certain of the girls, but the girls themselves were joyfully flirtatious with the brothers of the groom. And when it became clear that both young men would be returning to Kalisz soon to give needed attention to farming matters, and that they were therefore little threat of future competition for the smiles of the girls, they were welcomed even among the young men.

The young Rajmund Racek, in fact, took it upon himself to draft Walenty for the wagon, and then to explain, at length and in excited detail. "On Monday night we will pull the Vladowski's fish wagon—it is the biggest one—with four black horses, to the home of Jadwiga. I will ride the lead horse, and you the one behind. Each of us will carry a whip. At the Wdowiak house, we will unhitch the horses and lead them—we must do this very slowly—lead them to the grove of trees for water and feed. While we do this, the guests in the house will come out and steal pieces of the wagon. If we catch them before they get back into the house, we must give them a whiplash or two." He paused to fill Walenty's glass with more beer.

"But why...?" Walenty asked.

"It is the custom."

"...why a wagon?"

"Oh, because the next morning, Jadwiga's *przędanki* will load all her bedding upon the wagon to haul it to the Rogulski house—the nuptial house—but only after the horses have been decorated."

"But if the guests take parts of the wagon...?"

"Oh, no, you see, the next morning they must confess what they have taken and return each piece in exchange for wheatcakes and *gorzałka*. They must say, 'I confess I was the thief, but you have a long road awaiting you, and I therefore return this for your journey.' Then we will hitch the horses and go to the house of the groom. Only then can the *przędanki* prepare the marriage bed so that it may be ready for Jadwiga and her husband when night falls."

Walenty was aware of the last part. "Yes, and make it smoothly, with no wrinkles, so that married life will supposedly proceed calmly into the future."

"On the way, of course, there will be the brigands blocking the way. We must pay in vodka and walnuts for the wagon to pass. It's great fun."

"Some of this is different in Kalisz," Walenty said.

"Of course. But here, in this Kaszuby region, one must take a bride the Kaszuby way. But I will tell you a secret. You must tell your brother that, on the wedding day, at the church, he must be the first to see Jadwiga—before she sees him. If she sees him first, it is said that she will be the one to rule their lives. If he sees her first, he will have all the privileges of the husband, then he will be in charge. Tell him." Seeing that Walenty was amused, Rajmund added, "If you think this is a tale of silly old women, just take the time to inquire of my father."

So it was that Walenty Adamik was recruited into participation in the joyful ceremonies of the wedding wagon.

For Jadwiga and those attending her, the days leading up to the eve of the wedding were filled with anticipation and good humor, and a meticulous taking care that all would be as it should be. There were the gloves—the *rękawice*—to be presented to Walenty and Timoteusz and Paul's parents, and some in reserve should other Adamik relatives appear for the wedding. And for Paul, an outfit—shirt, trousers, stockings, and gloves, with a neck kerchief and a second kerchief should his nose require attention. There were gloves for the priest, and a gift of Silesian cloth for the mother of the groom—a thousand details.

To all these things, the *gospodyni* Lilianna Posienko paid the strictest of attention, lavishing sweetness upon Jadwiga and her father, gently guiding the bride in all the matters a mother might otherwise supervise. She was solicitous, indulgent, with a knack for courtly authority when circumstances required, but in the background when matters could proceed without her involvement.

To the Adamiks, however, she was worse than any Prussian commander—fussy, demanding, unsatisfied. "Are we but players upon her stage?" Wojciech Adamik asked, but Oleńka was more understanding. "She knows the customs here, my love, and she is concerned that we make no mistakes. It will be this way only until Tuesday. Then she will be gone."

When Alfons Posienko presented the fur hat he said Paul must give to Edmund Wdowiak, and mentioned its price, Wojciech's jaw dropped, but Paul was ready with the necessary funds from his mustering-out pay and the matter was settled before his father could raise an objection. Then there were the cloth hats for Konstanty and Konrad— "You should consider yourselves lucky that there are no more brothers of the bride," said Alfons, "and no sisters to receive the lengths of black cloth. It is only once in your life that you will do this, and it must be done with every detail correct." Wojciech thanked fate for his son's mustering-out pay, and uttered a quiet prayer that Walenty and Timoteusz would find no brides among these Kaszuby fisherfolk.

Alfons provided, without further charge, the long black coat Timoteusz would wear in reciting invitations to the wedding, and then rehearsed him in the speech:

I invite all of the members of this household,
Because I come to this doorstep with greetings this day,
Not just from anyone, but from two young people who are preparing to
    enter into the holy state of marriage,
Because this married state was not begun by us, nor does it end with us,
But God Himself joins together the many types of pairs.

Once Timoteusz had memorized this much, Alfons gave him the bad news—there was more:

Just as each birdling, darting among the clouds, searched for the other of
    its pair,
So did these two young people dance, party, and search until each found
    the other,
As they are mutual in their appeal, the faster the better to get to the state
    of matrimony.
They have chosen us their starsi *to announce their plan, to invite the*
    maidens and cavaliers...

"You must know this well," Alfons cautioned Timoteusz, "for by the time you reach the last house you will no longer have command of your tongue. At each house, you will be given strong drink in celebration, and you must drink at least a little, in a toast, you see. But keep your wits about you. There will be many houses to visit. Fortunately, the bride's *stary* knows the town and will make sure you leave none out."

Concerned that he carry out this duty with precision, Timoteusz suggested there should be written information, in the event some family might not be home.

"No, no, they will all be waiting. There must be no written invitations. It is the rule. They will be ready for you. They all know."

Alfons Posienko also explained to Timoteusz that, on Tuesday, he would precede Paul and his parents into the church, holding his red cane high— "You must not worry. I will be playing the organ, but my

Lilianna will tell you when you must walk into the church, and she will make certain that you are followed by the *przędanki*, and then the bride's party. Only see to it that you are not too intoxicated and that you keep your raiments as I have arranged them."

Then, before a command that Timoteusz recite the *stary's* invitation yet again, Alfons assured him that all would be as it should be—that he, Alfons Posienko, as a *gospodarz* of long experience, and his wife, Lilianna Posienko, as a *gospodyni* of high reputation, would see to all in the ceremonies to come. "For you, it is only to know this speech of invitation," he said, "and in the rest we will guide you at each turn. After that, all you have to attend to is the enjoyment of this special occasion for your brother and his bride."

Wojciech and Oleńka soon fell into the spirit of things. Apart from their eager concern to do well by their brother, so did Walenty and Timoteusz.

Paul, however, was like the frayed end of a severed anchor line on the Wdowiak schooner. He felt like a puppet, pushed this way and that, manipulated by Alfons, commanded now and again by Lilianna. Worst of all, Jadwiga had abandoned him. She had her own preparations requiring attention, and she was kept from him by Alfons and Lilianna and by her *przędanki* and by circumstance. "You will do this only once," Walenty told him in an effort at reassurance that failed completely. "Only once," said his father, "and only with Jadwiga, and after that these arrangers, these overbearing managers will be gone, and you will be in charge."

That conversation reminded Walenty that he had yet to warn Paul that he must catch first sight of Jadwiga on Tuesday. But there was much to do in preparation, and he told himself he would remember on the wedding morning.

Tuesday morning came with a burst of wheat-yellow sunshine crashing through the windows of the Rogulski home. There was no rooster crowing to herald the arrival of the morning as it would at the Adamik home in Kalisz. The odors of the bay were different from those of the farm. But minds stirred awake with a shock of first realization that this was the day that had been the point of so much attention and concern. Heads reeled, at first, with the hard drink of the night before. But then there were duties to be performed and customs to be observed.

As his brothers watched, stifling the telltale yawns of too much celebration and too little sleep, Paul brought his parents to chairs at the

Rogulski dining table, turned so that they might face him as he knelt before them. As they sat and listened, Oleńka brushing an insistent tear away, he reached deep within himself.

"I was a difficult child for you, my mother, and a stubborn student for you, my father," he said. "I have not done my share. What I have done, I have done badly. I have been a burden unworthy of the kindness and care you so generously gave to me. I regret that I was so often a disappointment for you, unappreciative, headstrong, attentive only to my own pleasures, and unseeing of the pain I brought to you. On this day I take a bride, I humbly ask that you forgive all these shortcomings in my nature."

Wojciech then bid his son to stand in an unspoken command supported by a gesture from Oleńka, whose tears flowed freely now.

"My son Paul," Wojciech said, speaking from his chair with his head bowed in lieu of the customary kneeling, "the failings were mine. You came to us in innocence, a gift from God, and it seemed that only days passed before you became a man, and I had wasted all my chances to be a loving father, kind to you, worthy of your respect, the gardener of your dreams. I ask your forgiveness for all my shortcomings as your father."

As Paul offered a hand to his father, Oleńka began to speak. "It is the custom that the mother be the source of nurturing for her children. For such a loving son so ready to please his mother..."—and now she sobbed— "I was a mother blessed beyond my abilities to deserve. Your days with us were too few, and now they are gone, and I ask that you forgive"—another sob, and a pause as Oleńka composed herself— "I ask that you forgive my many failings from which now I can never be redeemed."

Paul reached for his mother's hand, and now mother and father stood to face their son, all their hands joined. There were tears in Paul's eyes.

"As God in His heaven knows, I could not ask for parents more worthy of what little joy I may have given. In all these things, let all our memories be only of the happy times we have had together."

Now Wojciech and Oleńka spoke together. "Good son of ours, may the Lord be with you and your bride in the new life you begin together this day."

Then Walenty and Timoteusz put their hands into the circle and repeated the words. "May the Lord be with you and your bride in the new life you begin together this day."

All then converged in a tight embrace. All five understood the significance of this moment. Paul, especially, was conscious of the change about to take place in this family. Never again would this close circle of shared blood be as it was in this moment. From today onward, it would include Jadwiga and, through Jadwiga, her father and two brothers. From today onward, there would be a new family—his own. It would not be long before the events of the day would launch all of them into new and changed relationships.

By day's end, Paul knew, he would have one more thing in common with his father. Both would carry all the joys and responsibilities of a designation new to Paul—*husband*.

Chapter 8

There was a moment, outside St. Teresa's Church, when Paul was distracted with a last-minute brushing of his shoes to remove dust they had accumulated on the road. He was assisted by Walenty, who carried a spare kerchief just for this purpose. Alfons Posienko had reviewed the groom's party and satisfied himself that he had done all he could to make them ready for the ceremonies about to begin. With some primping of his own, perhaps by way of example, he had brushed sand and dust from his own fine shoes and had pointed, in a hint, at Walenty's and Paul's.

As they stood straight again, shoes clean, Paul turned for a last moment of conversation with his father and mother, and he was caught in the distant beam of Jadwiga's broad smile. From the middle of her bride's party, just arriving, she had seen him, and her eyes were again flirtatious and possessive.

Only then did Walenty remember Rajmund Racek's caution about the groom being the first of the betrothed to see the other on their marriage day. But he, too, was captivated by Jadwiga's smile, and somehow it no longer seemed important that Paul be warned. Anyway, it was too late, and anyway, it was a belief only among these Kaczuby.

When Paul and Jadwiga stepped before the priest in a formal request that he join their lives in marriage, the man solemnly agreed to do so as the *przędanki* dropped coins into the basket at the altar. This was a Tuesday on which no other couples were to be joined in marriage, as Edmund Wdowiak had wished, so the wedding party gathered, standing, behind Paul and Jadwiga, all facing the priest, who began, slowly, to intone his wedding homily.

Paul was moved, but not by the words of the priest, which he barely heard after the first moments. Jadwiga was beautiful. He would expect any girl to be beautiful on her wedding day, but he had never seen any bride so radiant. She had chosen cobalt velvet for her vest and skirt. Her white apron was short, only a token by comparison to others he had seen. The vest was embroidered in the traditional gold and six other colors. Her hat, azure blue, covered by a crocheted white overlay veil, took nothing away from her hair, now braided and wrapped at the top of her head, so that the back of her neck could be seen.

He stood straight, as though on a parade ground, taking pains to look relaxed, and then became aware of the priest's continuing words. "The Lord awaits. On this day, the Lord awaits as you give yourselves to each other, and to him, in the sacred ritual of marriage. For you, the Lord has arrested the sun in its passage across the sky, and he has stayed the rain, held the clouds, stilled the birds, quieted the wind, so that forever may this moment be remembered as the moment of union of Paul and Jadwiga."

They knelt now, for their special communion, and for the first time in the ceremony, their hands touched lightly. For Paul, it was a charged moment. *This Jadwiga, this treasure, was giving herself to him forever. How could he be worthy of such a prize?* To him, it seemed that time had stopped, indeed.

But then they were standing and the priest was speaking the words and they were repeating them. And, in just the smallest moment, they passed from a state of being sweethearts to a state of union in marriage.

At a nod from the priest, Paul removed the crocheted white cover from Jadwiga's hat, and now, she was his wife, wearing the hat of a wife, and the wedding party mingled behind them just before opening a path so that they might be surrounded by everyone and hear their words of joy and congratulation.

There was the moment, at the center, when Wojciech and Oleńka Adamik and their sons, and Edmund Wdowiak and his sons, surrounded Paul and Jadwiga, arms interlocked at their waists, in a kind of protective ring broken only where Helena Wdowiak would have stood, between the Skipper and Oleńka, whose hands touched. But no tears issued from the eyes of Edmund Wdowiak, despite a pressing awareness of his wife's absence. For him, this was a day of finishing, of climax, of completion. Now his daughter, who would forever belong to him, belonged also to another, and he felt his family richer and stronger, and saw his daughter as no longer the small girl he had allowed to fall asleep on the warmth of his chest, but as a woman. For him, his Helena was present, her spirit embodied in Jadwiga.

At Gostomski's hall, the music was perfect, not a note out of place in polka or mazurka. Married women, who until now were absent from the ceremonies except for the *przędanki*, finally joined in the celebrating.

There was a formal dance, begun to music of deliberate cadence, without percussion, in which Edmund Wdowiak and his daughter danced, apart at arms' lengths, only their hands touching. Then they were interrupted by Paul as he replaced the Skipper as Jadwiga's partner and the drums again became part of the music, the tempo increased, and they held tightly together in a dancing embrace.

There were cheers, then, and livelier music as Jadwiga's brothers and Paul's brothers chose partners and danced around their parents. Oleńka and Wojciech, conscious of the absence of Edmund's wife, joined hands with him in a circle. They circled the opposite way, dancing more slowly to only half the beats of the music.

For Skipper Edmund Wdowiak, these were the moments in which his Jadwiga became a married woman. There were the further frivolities of a wedding, of course. The newlyweds stole away while guests pointedly ignored them in favor of bad jokes told by men whose skills with humor were so lacking that they themselves became the target of laughter. The guests then pursued the newlyweds, lagging behind, as they escaped to their wedding abode. And when the wedding party demanded entry, there were the newlyweds' calls out through locked doors: "If you are not *cudzy*, if you are not Germans or foreigners, give us some sign." Slips of paper were then passed under the doors and through windows open only a crack, and voices were raised in the traditional songs of the marriage day. Only then were the remaining wedding guests admitted for a final toast and treat of cake.

But for the Skipper, there was that moment at Gostomski's Hall when Jadwiga became his married daughter and Paul became his new son-in-law—that moment when the music hesitated and his daughter passed into the arms of another, the drums took up the tempo, and the dance of life quickened.

Chapter 9

"We'll carry clothes in seabags," Jadwiga said to Paul. "Mostly in seabags, but I can wear two or three dresses—perhaps even four."

For a week of heaven, of falling more and more deeply in love with her, he forgot ever hearing of this crazy notion of travel to America. When it crossed his mind, he dared hope she'd forgotten.

"We must go soon to make application for passage. There's a long wait. We'll have to wait weeks, maybe months."

She caught him off guard, in a state of ecstasy, and his new world threatened to come apart.

"The lists grow longer by the day. We must register."

His silence wasn't assent, he told himself. He was preparing his arguments. The unvoiced disagreement towered between them, a barrier more impassable by the day.

Finally he spoke, taking care not to appear arbitrary in his exercise of the authority of husband.

"Here in Poland," he said, "I have prospect and promise. There is the farming and the potential for my father's farm to be shared among all three sons rather than just my older brothers. There is the offer to manage my lieutenant's lands. I could even re-enlist in the army. I would rise in the ranks."

She pouted. "You promised we would go to America," she said. "You promised me in Poznań, and at Stawicki's farm, and on the train, and here."

He couldn't remember promising. True, he had let her speak of it as though it were an agreed plan. He had avoided dispute. He had promised to look at the letters.

The letters. "Where are the letters of which you spoke?" For the moment, perhaps he could smooth things over by diverting to the letters.

"We'll go see the Stanieks tomorrow," she said. "They have the letters."

"Good."

"They live in Gdynia. While we're there, we can go to make application for passage."

"No, Jadwiga. This requires much thought and consideration. To make application without consideration..."

"It costs only a little to make application. Maybe there is no cost at all."

Now she was her child-self again, pleading with him as though for a ride on his shoulders. If happiness were to return, application would have to be made.

"We will make application, then. But only..."

Now she threw her arms around him and kissed him again as she had before the wedding, like a child finding a lost toy. There was again a newness in their loving.

The next morning, she woke him with the sun for the walk into town.

The letters were genuine enough, it seemed to him, written by people the Stanieks said were reliable. The letters told of work for all, and of good pay. Of churches of all kinds, Catholic included, and of authorities who did not busy themselves with the law-abiding individual. Of land at fair prices, of schools for all children, of opportunity for those who would take it.

These were generalities Paul distrusted with a soldier's anguish over ambiguity.

The Stanieks, who were older people, explained that they themselves were not candidates for such a voyage. But they knew where to go to make application. They walked there with Paul and Jadwiga.

Paul heard his best news from the passport counselor: "There is a wait of some months for so-called steerage class," the man said. In Polish very good for a German clerk, he said it was a matter of when the ships returned from their trips, and how long this would take. "In second class more places are open and there is not so long a wait." Paul's inclination would normally be to apply for second class, but he was relieved when Jadwiga made the decision that would give him more time.

"Steerage," said Jadwiga. "We apply for steerage."

To Paul she said, "We must save most of your mustering-out money for a start in America."

For him, the argument wasn't class of passage or the uses of muster-ing-out pay. Later, away from the Stanieks and the passport counselor, he would take up the larger issue with her. Once and finally, he would tell her. He would speak firmly, with the voice of the husband: *We will stay in Poland*, he would say.

There would be difficulty over this, of course. Tears and silence. But he was the husband, and it was the husband's place to decide. He had decided. He would tell her. He would be firm.

But she would not yield. The conflict went on for weeks. She insisted he had promised. He maintained he had not. Her father stayed out of it, but not because he didn't care. It was a matter of letting his new son-in-law and his daughter work things out for themselves.

As though his decision made no difference at all, Jadwiga spoke daily of what they would need on the trip: They would take dried fish for the train trip across northwestern Poland to a German port with access to the open Atlantic. She would need a washboiler, Jadwiga said, for wash-ing clothes, and a good washboiler would be useful for carrying some things.

Paul kept silence. He didn't want to be drawn into a discussion of how many layers of clothes they could wear or whether seabags or nor-mal traveling trunks were appropriate for such travel. He had agreed, he reasoned, only to make application for passage—not to go.

But with Jadwiga, there was no question. "The waiting list is long. You must go to Gdynia and be sure the passport counselor understands that we intend to go. It could be he will have an opportunity to put us on an earlier crossing. If he sees you, he'll know we're eager and can be moved to an earlier ship."

Once, only to pacify her, Paul did go to see the counselor. He was bid-ing his time until he could have a serious discussion with her. But again, the unvoiced difference threatened their closeness.

Walking with her on the beach one breezy, sunwashed afternoon, Paul spoke as husband to wife.

"I have thought a great deal about this question of travel to America."

Jadwiga, who had been expecting this, said nothing.

"I have decided we will not go." He hadn't intended to say it this way. He meant to reason, explain, and discuss his doubts. It just came out. No matter: It all came to the same thing.

She became cold and unsmiling as she stopped to look up at him, accusing. "This is not as we discussed, Paul."

The promise again. She would say he had promised.

"I did not promise you, Jadwiga."

"From the first, we talked of going to America."

"You talked of it. I said nothing."

"You said nothing. Was this to deceive me?" She turned to continue walking. He followed.

"No. I said nothing…"

She turned on him now, angry, tears threatening. "Did I wait until after we were married to tell you I wanted to go to America?"

"No."

"Did you wait until after we were married to tell me that you did not want to go to America?"

"I said nothing at first because…"

"Because you wished to deceive me."

"Jadwiga, I wished to do no such thing. I wished for us to be happy."

Now she smiled and her eyes widened as they always did when he said sweet things. "We will be happy in America." She took his arm and clung to him as though needing support to walk in the sand. "More happy than here."

He was disarmed. It was as on the parade ground at Poznań when she had made him forget. He had to concentrate to maintain his resolve. On this, he would not be charmed into forgetting.

"I am not certain the Stanieks are truthful people, Jadwiga."

"What do you mean?"

"It could be the letters are not genuine. Perhaps they're being paid to get passengers for the shipping company."

"No. There are other letters, too. Letters from good people."

"This troubles me greatly."

Now there was silence between them. They walked, their shadows reaching farther. Shore birds flew up as they approached, then settled behind them. Paul thought of his prospects in Poland, and marshalled his arguments.

But it was Jadwiga who ended the silence:

"Paul, America is a free land, better for us than here. In America, there is no Bismarck, no Czar, no Regent. The letters are from honest people. They wouldn't write of opportunity in America unless they found it to be so. This has been my dream for many years, and I've listened to all I could hear about America. I've read all the letters I could find. I believe what is said, and there is nothing that is bad."

She hardly paused, but it didn't matter, because when she started this way it did no good to interrupt.

"We aren't like the Stanieks, who have raised a family here and have their children near them. We're still young, you and I, long lives before us. In America, the prospects are better for us."

Now she stopped walking again so he would turn toward her. "And better for our child."

"Our child?"

"Yes."

"Jadwiga, what are you saying?"

"I think I am carrying our child. It is perhaps just a bit early to tell, but I am quite certain now."

"Jadwiga, this makes me very happy. But how do you know?"

She was being unfair. She was raising this matter of a child in the middle of these discussions of America to distract him. She said it would be another week before she would know with certainty, but even now she felt sure. Then tears came to her eyes, and she made him hold her.

"Paul, the thing I want most in the world is for this child to be born in America—to be an American child born away from the stomp of the Prussian boot, in a free country where there is opportunity and good pay for good work, and a future filled with promise rather than question and doubt.

"Here, there is only doubt. Everyone speaks of freedom, but this land has been under the foreigners since my father was born and nobody has been able to change it. There has been only repression and death for trying. And each new year of Prussian rule makes it the less likely that change will come. In America, there are no foreigners who rule. In America, the people are all from other countries, and they all rule together. In Poland, our only prospects are subject to the rule of the Germans here, and the Russians and the Austrians in the other parts. In America, the Americans decide these things."

He thought to turn away in his confusion of reason and emotion, but she touched his face in the way that she knew would capture his attention. "Most of all, Paul, I want our child to grow in freedom and in a country where there is true prospect."

She hadn't yet used the worst of her tricks and already he was feeling defeated. The worst of her tricks would be to pout and refuse to talk with him, and refuse to be near him. And her reasoning, after all, was perhaps not so wrong.

"We will come back to Poland if America is not all you say? This is a question only. I am not yielding. I haven't yet decided."

"It will be."

"But if it is not?"

"If it isn't, we will come back."

"It will be how long before the child comes?"

"It will be February, Paul."

"I will go to the passport counselor again the day after tomorrow. But before it is decided, I must give it much more thought."

The next day, out on the water, Paul spoke with his father-in-law. "Jadwiga wants so much to go to America."

"Yes, she does. Since her mother died it's been her dream that one day she would go there with her husband to live. She has dreamed this dream so much that she has no other."

"Do you believe what is said about America?"

"Much is said, much written. There are the few who are unhappy for one reason or another, or for a while. But most of what we hear is good. And we hear enough that it is difficult not to believe."

"But do you believe prospects are truly better there?"

"I believe that is the case. America is a big country, being built day by day by strong young people like you who have gone there seeking opportunity. In Poland, there is no building. There is only the taking by the foreigners to whom the Congress of Vienna gave our land. I believe things must be better there. Better than here."

Paul's troubled mind wandered over these questions as he hauled nets. As he considered the alternatives, he reached a conclusion that such an adventure as Jadwiga wanted was surely a mistake. He knew there would be no peace with her until he settled it.

Near sunset, as the schooner leaned in a reach toward the pier, Edmund Wdowiak spoke to him again.

"Paul, if you and Jadwiga decide to stay in Poland, there is prospect for you if you wish to be a fisherman here with us. We don't live like royalty, but we exceed the Baron's quota with ease, and this brings enough for all of us. And I'm sure there are other prospects for a determined and disciplined man such as yourself. But all of what I say of the opportunities for you here is even more true in America. I don't believe you would make a mistake to go there. But if you stay, Jadwiga will be a good wife to you and a good mother to your children. You both will be happy. She knows she must follow where her husband goes. This is a matter you must decide."

The Skipper, it was clear, would support him in any decision he made. They could go to America, and if it turned out to be a terrible mistake, they could return and he would cast no blame. But without question, Edmund Wdowiak thought it would be better for them in America.

That evening, after the schooner returned to the pier, Paul went to see the widow Brusnicki, of whom it was said that she had a copper wash-boiler for sale. He took it to Jadwiga, and she held him and cried in happiness.

BOOK TWO

Chapter 10

The morning frosts of November were gripping with chill when Jadwiga, Paul, and her brothers woke early for the long walk to Gdansk. The time had come, and there was none to be wasted. Even so, last goodbyes of father and daughter ceased only when breaking day gave warning they must start.

"Take care of my daughter and my grandchild," Edmund Wdowiak said in a last farewell to Paul Adamik. As the father and son they had become in the months since the wedding, they embraced firmly.

It was time to go.

In the rail center, all was tumult. Men of mission and destination walked with deliberate stride, knowing the why and wherefore of their movements. People with packages and bags pushed and milled. Everyone hurried. Everyone was going somewhere.

In this purposeful milieu, Paul, Jadwiga, and her brothers were hardly noticeable. Paul's sky blue uniform was no longer a mark of individuality. Nor was Jadwiga's pregnancy a point of differentiation, for it was barely visible under her accumulation of clothing worn to spare the burden of yet another parcel.

Paul felt a rushing helplessness. Soon Konrad and Konstanty would put down the luggage they carried and bid farewell. He and Jadwiga would be required to turn themselves over to the jurisdiction of the shipping company.

Turning back would be all the more difficult.

But Jadwiga had no thought of turning back. Far from it. She babbled excitedly when numbers on a corner building matched those on the official envelope. She was child-like again, as though discovering a playmate in hiding and wanting more of the game.

Inside the big doors men of book and pencil worked in an enclosure of official window-glass, wood, and thin iron bars. With hardly a word, Paul and Jadwiga were being marked down and checked off and passed along and their papers stamped with official markings. All this had a feeling of finality about it.

Now, like others around them, they were saying their last farewells. Konrad and Konstanty shook Paul's hand enthusiastically and then there was new crying as Jadwiga and her brothers hugged each other. The brothers even turned to leave but came back for yet another hug from the sister who was leaving them forever.

Just for a moment when the huddling of the Adamiks and Wdowiaks finally broke apart, contemptuous eyes fell upon the blue German uniform. Others, also waiting, turned their backs.

Then the brothers were gone.

Paul and Jadwiga were left in dimness. It was a small warehouse littered with a bewilderment of men, women and children, each burdened with bag, box, or crate.

In this cauldron of close disarray, each family could be distinguished from the next by the attention to children and by the confinement of conversation within each small group of related people. Between families, there was the caution of luggage carefully stacked and children held in check.

One official now came from the cage to quiet the talk and call names to see that all was as it should be. Seeing that it was, he signaled for the opening of massive sliding doors, and there was an immediate spill of people and baggage onto a loading platform that extended into the alley behind the building.

A big freight wagon pulled by two strong horses had been drawn up so that an open side met level with the platform. At a word from the counselor there was bedlam. Children were held atop luggage to keep them from harm. Men pushed and elbowed, each to provide for his own.

"Go with the Polack bastards," a big German drayman growled at Paul in taunting German as he secured the sideboard of the wagon, pushing men and women with the same inconsideration he applied to baggage.

Paul tried desperately to ease the jam that pressed Jadwiga against the staked sideboards, but he was at the disadvantage of standing atop her copper washboiler. It was humiliating. He resolved that if one day she bore him a squeezed or crippled child he would tell her, *It was only for my army money to take you to America that you married me!* He had thought about this as their day of leaving approached and the feeling of finality came upon him.

He felt humiliated and angry as the wagon began moving and Jadwiga was squeezed again. This was only the first step in this crazed journey, merely over the cobblestone streets of Gdansk to the railroad yards.

Here he was, not waiting for a regularly scheduled train in a depot with regular traveling bag and valise in hand, but in a freight wagon on a washboiler of the household laundry category. He had been a soldier—an officer, even—in the world's strongest army. Now he was like a fool—a town character who had somewhere scavenged a uniform—like one in a band of gypsies being chased from a community.

But it was senseless to grumble. He had promised Jadwiga he would take her to America and that was that. And let it be that the pledge was made under duress of a dimpled smile and deep blue eyes. He would be a man of his word. He would make the best of this crazy venture and surely she would tire of hard travel. Surely she would wish to turn back before they boarded the ship at Bremerhaven.

Even as he thought it, he knew it would not be that way.

Yet, grumbling could only make matters worse. Children, standing now in the cinder path of the freightyard, were cold and becoming hungry. They began to fuss in the monotony of a long wait. The clatter and clang of freight cars being shuttled from track to track made for worry, for there was no one to tell this wagonload of people how they might fit into the comings and goings of trains.

There seemed to be ten families. Paul counted thirty-nine heads as wait plodded into longer wait and the fuss of children became the contagion of crying, and men began to ask each other if perhaps they should be getting on one of the passing strings of cars. There was a sudden concern that a train just pulling out might be the one to which they were assigned.

Some of the men maintained that the freight agent, a toothless Prussian whose chin and nose nearly touched to part his long mustache squarely in the middle, had motioned from the freight house that they should stand just as they were. Some of the women thought they belonged aboard a bright red boxcar on another spur of track. Still others thought the agent must be an incompetent who had forgotten them. They were without counsel.

It was plain to Paul that there was a need in this group for leadership. These were migrating people, strangers to one another, clutching bag and baggage in reserved distrust. This journey, now by rail, later by ship, would be under the jurisdiction of German shipping—German words. Paul could call forth German words. He had been an overseer of men, a sergeant, qualified to lead, to bring order forth from this chaos.

Thus it was that he stepped forth in the formality of stiff military gait, going up the steps of the freight-house platform to clarify once and for all the disposition and assignment of this group of people.

The snap of hobnailed army shoes and the click of heels startled the freight agent, who turned with a jerk from his chore of checking barrels and crating. He looked at Paul with the ragged deportment of an arrested and frightened individual.

"Is it that we are to wait longer or do we belong on a train already?" Paul asked with German words.

The response came with such an irregularity of gulps that Paul had to search in the hollowness of the man's mouth for an answer. And even then he could not salvage enough to piece the words together because they were muffled amidst chomp of chin and nose.

Watching and listening from the cinder path, the other men found it amusing that this young one without as yet even a single child had appointed himself to get information for them, and now could fetch no meaning from the mouth of the toothless worker.

Meanwhile, some of the women were fearful that the one in uniform had scared the toothless one out of his wits as well as his speech. But the freight agent began to stammer again, this time in Polish.

"You are to stand there and if you frighten someone again you will not be getting on any train," the freight agent yelled. Among the other travelers there was amusement at the comeuppance for the self-appointed interrogator of freightyard workers. Now they agreed: the agent stammered Polish words and German ones with equal impairment, so he must have had practice in this deficiency of speech. It was a relief that his affliction hadn't come just because of this young upstart among them.

"When one travels, one sees much," someone said, and laughter among them brought a feeling of harmony.

Only as darkness approached was the railyard monotony of squeaking wheels and spasmodic puffs broken by a deep whistle blast from a bigger locomotive on a main line of tracks at the head of a long stretch of cars.

This signal of readiness could not be mistaken because the freight agent stirred again, his eyes fastened on them as he came down the steps. With a motion of his arm he led the way across the rails to a car at the middle of the long train—a sooty green flatcar with makeshift sides erected waist-high to the average man. It was a lumber carrying car, seemingly pulled at random from a siding of empty cars.

Now they all made way for an elderly couple with a genuine traveling trunk, and a withered old man dependent on a pair of crutches. But from then on bag, box and kettle were thrown into the car and children were yanked and tossed so there would be no delaying of the iron beast that hissed its impatience. They were at last en route to Bremerhaven and the tension of their long wait now gave way to conviviality. Food taken from washboilers and traveling boxes brought satisfaction to stomachs. Then families nestled under woolen blankets in a bustle of bed-making, cuddling against a November cold that threatened all the more with darkness and gathering speed.

It was a difficult night of clickety-clack and sway as the train labored over low hills, sped across plains and through forests. It meant a bone-freezing sleeplessness, contending with a wind all the more frenzied for the race into the Baltic darkness.

But, families reasoned among themselves, it would not be cold and wet forever. At long last they were on their way to America and there was a satisfaction among them.

Chapter 11

As the bitter insult of night grudgingly gave way to an indifferent advent of day, a cold drizzle came to make teeth chatter.

But morning and the train droned on, and at last a new warmth of sun pierced the last remaining clouds of heavy color. The travelers came from their family huddles where bedding had become drenched. Blankets were hung over the side of the car to dry in the buffeting air surging past the boxcar ahead.

Like the others, Paul and Jadwiga had the difficult choice of removing outer layers of wet clothing so they might dry, or leaving them on as shield against the stabbing wind. Paul found it remarkable that Jadwiga remained in good spirit despite the wetness and cold. His hope—that hardship of travel would persuade her to turn back—was fading with the growing light of day.

Food was brought out to subdue the anger of stomachs denied too long. Cold meats and buttered bread eased the anxieties of children tearful for want of something to be chewed.

As the last of lingering wetness passed, the flatcar took on the attitude of a Sunday picnic—a mingling of people from various parts of the land. Children became playful, and there was occasional crying from those who had their bottoms whapped for running the length of the car, disrupting people.

With this scolding of children came meeting and visiting, one family to the next, the next to another. Soon, Juliusz and Maria Sczepaniak came all the way from the other end of the car to meet Paul and Jadwiga. They were nearly the same age, and they, too, had the anticipation and the anxiety of pregnancy. Maria was a month further along, but in all other ways was smaller than Jadwiga. She had a rounder face and timid eyes. Her step was not as bold as Jadwiga's on the moving car, and in being introduced by her husband she was shy. Jadwiga said something complimentary about her brown hair, swept back and tied beneath a shawl, and they were soon holding hands and telling each other their ages and from what part of the country they came.

Like Paul, Juliusz was tall. But he was a funmaker who flitted from group to group in a quest for laughter. He grinned and patted Paul's shoulder while shaking his hand, but then left him with their wives in a counting of months. Thus it happened that Paul was left alone on the outer rim of the congregation and handshaking of men.

It left him not so much with the wives as with the children—more than a dozen. Paul liked children—especially the boys who realized he was a soldier and asked questions about horses and guns. Anyway, he preferred their company: they had common sense and didn't babble constantly of America.

But even without children demanding his attention, Paul reasoned, he would hardly beg a friendship of anyone, or grovel to abate the incident on the freight platform of Gdansk where he'd made an ass of himself with his few German words. True, he was no longer in the army but he could still stand straight. He knew he had a bullheadedness about him that kept him from getting into the spirit of merriment. But he sensed that the others shunned him. Some even turned their backs in a pretense of reaction to the air whipping past, even while clammy-warm in layered clothes.

Even the children were heavy with extra clothing, so big and round that when they fell in the playfulness of running, they rolled unhurt. Now and then Paul righted a little boy or girl.

He liked one boy in particular—Franek Dominiak, nearly seven, who told his name and age without having to be asked more than once. He was smart. Handsome, too, with big, searching eyes. He was the most settled of the children, so bright that when Paul asked how many brothers and sisters he had, he held up four fingers. And to demonstrate he brought his three sisters from between people and luggage so Paul could see for himself. Then he brought his brother Konrad, who had to be carried. His sisters, he said, were Pelagia, who was four, and Magda and Manya, both two years old.

Franek seemed to be aware that it was unnecessary to explain that Magda and Manya were twins, inasmuch as they were the same age and identical of size and face. Paul was careful not to question this, lest he make a fool of himself again—this time to this exceptionally smart boy. Neither did Paul question Franek about his parents, for they stood nearby with some of the others and looked from time to time with smiles of pride that their son spoke so brightly with a stranger. The parents looked like a set—both broad and strong. The man, especially, had the carriage of a bull.

"This car," Paul explained in answer to one of Franek's many questions, "is littered with chips of wood and bark from trees because many times it has carried loads of timber from the forest to mills where boards are cut to make houses, barns, and more flatcars like this one."

"We aren't in a car with a roof because a boxcar has no windows for air and light. And with doors open, someone might fall out."

"I had no horse. I was in a company of engineers—special soldiers who build things—things like bridges."

Jadwiga, meanwhile, went with Maria Sczepaniak to the forward end of the car to meet a Russian family, Piotr and Ursula Jakubik and their sons, Voytek and Vicek. Word had been passed among the women that Ursula had experience at midwifery, and it gave Maria peace of mind to meet her. Jadwiga was interested, too, except that her baby would come after arrival in America and she would be attended by an American midwife—a proper professional one with authoritative notice on her house.

But their meeting with Ursula Jakubik was short because Ursula's husband and sons hadn't the tact to go away and leave women to talk of women's matters. The sons, especially, who were eighteen and twenty, stood speechless, eyes and ears open.

"Those two are like mules with their big ears in the air," Jadwiga whispered, and Maria giggled in agreement. Shoulder to shoulder, like twins in their pregnancies, they flitted from family to family, meeting people and talking as though they had known each other all their lives.

But with Paul, there was still only Franek, boy asking, man answering. Paul encouraged the questions, none of which were childlike. Why this, why that, Franek asked.

"Why must you kiss your way into a sergeant's uniform? Why don't you just don it as I don my coat and pants?"

This time, Paul couldn't answer, for Jozef Dominiak had heard his son's question and was coming swiftly to whap his son's behind, his arm already swinging. The man was big, far bigger even than Paul, and his thick mustache twitched in sudden anger.

Hardly thinking, Paul pivoted around Franek, deflecting the father's blow. It was a casual move that could even be taken as a mere accident of timing, but the big man could not stop, and he staggered, off balance.

Franek, slow in turning, didn't know what had happened. "Why did you do that? Spin around me?"

Leaning over the boy, Paul said, "Enough questions for now, Franek. Go to see your mama for a while." Straightening, he patted Franek's behind to send him on his way, and again deflecting the boy's father, who was reaching for his son in a strengthened determination to punish. Franek was still unaware of his jeopardy. But this time, to the others watching and to the elder Dominiak, it could be no accident.

"Pig!" shouted the bigger man, and now even more of the men turned to see what the commotion was all about. Now Jozef Dominiak prepared to charge again—this time at Paul.

Already, he was *Big Jozef* to the other men, and the immediate favorite in the fight about to start. Paul knew why. The others had only contempt for an upstart in a Prussian uniform with leanings to the Germans. They thought he had kissed German behinds for his promotion to sergeant. They were sure he was about to be thrashed.

Now he sidestepped and tripped Big Jozef, putting him off balance so that he tripped again while trying to avoid falling on people's crates and boxes. His head hit the flatcar's sideboard smartly, and he blinked momentarily with insensibility. Then, snarling in anger, teeth clenched, he began to rip off his long overcoat. He was ready for a serious fight.

But two of the men, thinking better of encouraging a fight between Poles on a German train, stood before Big Jozef, raising their hands to urge calm. Then more joined in, and though none touched him, by grouping before him, they held him in check.

"Stop this madness!" an elderly man yelled. "You will jeopardize us all! Stop!"

"Since when is it that a man cannot whip his own child?" Big Jozef yelled, directing his shout at the older man while glaring at Paul.

Paul yelled back to make himself heard over the train's rumble. "Whip your child if he does wrong. But not from behind when he is only asking! This is a smart boy you have. A boy who wants to learn. If you hit him when he is only asking, you will beat the smartness out of him."

"When I hit my boy is no concern of yours, or of your army!"

Already responding, Paul didn't hear the last of his words. "You are right, of course. You are right. But you were going to hit him because of what is said about me, and that is my concern."

"I didn't say that about you!"

Standing a bit closer now, Paul spoke with less force. "Well, then, let's find the man who did. Make him explain to your boy. Pounce on that man for speaking. Not...not on your son for only hearing and asking. He is a smart boy. Punish him for doing wrong, but not for his wondering and for repeating something about me. He is a smart boy. He asks only to learn."

Whether inarticulate with rage or swayed by Paul's argument, Big Jozef Dominiak did not immediately respond, and the elderly man spoke again. "Now shake hands, you two! You must shake hands."

Delfinia Dominiak, who at first had cried out with alarm when Big Jozef hit his head, now joined the men trying to pacify her husband. She touched his face, trying to capture his attention. Jadwiga, meanwhile, picked up Paul's blue army hat and put it back on his head.

Paul approached the bigger man. "This is a smart son you have." He still shouted, but now only over the noise of the train, and in a tone more reasoning than scolding. "I will be proud some day to have a boy who listens so well and asks such smart questions."

Big Jozef glared only a moment longer, then gave a small nod, and the others could see that he was pacified. The old man spoke again. "Shake hands now, both of you. You must not fight. There must be no hard feelings over the questions of a child. You must shake hands."

Paul tipped his head to the side, smiled weakly, and extended his hand to Jozef Dominiak. The big man's muscles lost tension and he extended his own hand, gripping Paul's tightly, capturing it firmly in a demonstration of strength. "It is a matter for me, with my boy."

Paul returned grip for grip, even while glancing down at the man's hand, which had the power of a vise. "It is your matter. Of course." Only then did Jozef relax his grip, and Paul managed something more of a smile. Jozef did not smile, but his face became more placid. Around them, the other men relaxed.

Jan Poglicki, who had been among the first to restrain Big Jozef, patted the men's shoulders as they shook hands, and made a confession.

"I was the one the boy heard talking," Jan said. "I was in the army, too. You know how soldiers talk behind the backs of officers. Jump on me now, if you must, but it was nothing and I did not mean to stir up this trouble." Jan's face was thin, his build slim, and he was sure-footed despite the rocking of the car. He wore a black sweater from his ears to his hips and a stockingcap of the same thick wool.

Juliusz Sczepaniak, sensing a role for the funmaker, winked broadly at Jozef and Paul. "Instead of trouncing this Poglicki for his flapping tongue, the two of you should each hold him by an ear and make him explain to Franek about this business of kissing and uniforms."

Jan stepped back in mock fright. "But I would not know how. I wouldn't know what to say. Perhaps you could do this for me and spare my ears such a pulling."

"It is so simple," said Juliusz, taking center stage among the men. "I can show Franek, and all of you, too, how Paul must kiss his way into his uniform.

"First, he must take off his jacket and give it to his wife to hold. Franek, you come here where you can see. He moved about like a director of actors on a stage. Other children, sensing a game being organized, broke free of mothers and followed Franek into a semi-circle of audience.

"And now you, Jadwiga—you hold your husband's army coat for him. But don't let him get even the first arm into his sleeve unless he kisses you. Then he must kiss you again or he cannot get his other arm in."

Jadwiga caught on quickly and she was coquettish, smiling.

Awkwardly, Paul turned, blushing, to kiss her. Such playacting was hard for him. But he sensed this foolishness would serve reconciliation, and quickly concluded that a small barter of his military dignity for peace and acceptance would be a trade well made.

In his mind a balance was struck, and he did his best to perform his role in Juliusz's skit.

Chapter 12

Now Paul felt better. He had made the acquaintance of not only Big Jozef Dominiak and the funmaker Juliusz Sczepaniak but also of Jan Poglicki, who now looked to him in respect, rather than turning his back. Even as Juliusz's impromptu pageant wore to its close, children reenacting it in play, Jan was already showing off to Paul his own Stanisław and Katrina, ages two and three, and comely wife Estella, who was chubby like Delfinia Dominiak.

The elderly peacemaker of stern voice and velvet-lapeled overcoat was Kazimierz Steck. He and his wife Salomeya, both distinguished, were owners of the genuine traveling trunk with a leather handle at each end.

Salomeya had about her an aura of serenity, a peacefulness unbroken even when her Kazimierz shouted during the fighting. She was dressed neatly in an overcoat of gray wool and a skirt bought new at a clothes mart, and she was draped nearly to her ankles in a dark gray shawl of fine and fanciful weave. Everyone courted the favor of these two gray-haired ones. It had become known that they already had two grown sons in America. With genuine American sons, perhaps they would be the ones to take by the hand upon disembarkation.

But the oldest traveler was Bolesław Kradzinski. *Old Man Kradzinski*, as he already was known, wore a tattered rabbitskin coat and, around his head, a woman's shawl. Like Paul, he had served in the German army, and he told his story readily: Recently, he had received payment in compensation for bones broken years ago when an army wagon toppled on him and pinned him in the mud, leaving him on crutches still. Though a tired old man, he carried his weight in his own family of emigrants, for the army allotment had bought passage for his daughter Viktoria, his son-in-law Tadeusz Murak, and his little grandsons, Jan and Jakub, four and two years of age. Tadeusz and Viktoria were already well into their thirties, having married late.

Now, instead of being on the edge of the introductions, left out, Paul was the one to whom others were coming to introduce themselves. Jadwiga stood with him, even though she had already met most of them in her flitting about with Maria Sczepaniak.

There came the bespectacled and amiable Stanisław Krulik, who had been one of those to restrain Big Jozef during the fighting. He was going to America with only the male half of his family, Władek and Lancek, fourteen and twelve, leaving behind a wife and two young daughters until he and his sons could earn enough American money to send for them.

With the Kruliks came a shy couple with a four-year-old girl holding hands between them. They were quiet and slow to respond as Paul gave his name and Jadwiga's. Jadwiga stooped to ask the child her name.

Child and mother answered at once, but child and mother disagreed.

"Teresa," said the girl.

"Franciska," said the mother, then she was immediately flustered by the discrepancy.

"I am Ludwig Karpczinski," said the husband. "My wife is Polka."

"The little girl likes to call herself Teresa," said Polka. "But she is Franciska."

Franciska's father looked at Stanisław Krulik, who had listened to these awkward moments. Stanisław shrugged, then nodded. Shifting, Ludwig moved so that Paul and Stanisław and he formed a triangle separate from the women and child. "We are traveling as the Karpczinskis," he said, "and that must be the name by which we are known. Ludwig, Polka, and the child Franciska."

Paul looked confused, so Ludwig continued. "Our friends the Karpczinskis received their papers for America but they heard some things and they decided not to go. It is also said that the American authorities are getting more strict about newcomers. We decided not to wait."

Stanisław and Ludwig looked at Paul, seeking a sign of understanding, perhaps not yet fully believing they could trust a man in a German uniform. Paul sensed this, and spoke forcefully in reassurance. "So this is who you are. The Karpczinskis—you are the Karpczinskis. Ludwig, Polka, and Franciska. This is who you are."

Ludwig was relieved. He patted Paul's shoulder, nodding and smiling. Stanisław smiled, too. There was now an understanding among them, and a sense they could stand together.

Now Ignatz Ran introduced himself to Paul and Jadwiga. He was already the object of good-natured sportmaking among the others for having a wife a head taller than he—yet the same number of children as Jozef Dominiak, the tallest and strongest. Ignatz's powerful wife was Kostanta, and their brood stepped down gradually from seven to one and a half years of age: Bernadina, Monika, Bolesław, David, and Mikal.

With such congeniality, all misunderstanding and uneasiness soon passed. As darkness came, the elderly Salomeya Steck called upon all to pray together in a mass kneeling. She led them in not just the Lord's Prayer but also the litany of all the saints so that all in heaven would hear them and keep them safe.

The prayer asked especially that the train would soon stop somewhere, anywhere. Anywhere, as long as there would be a creek or spring, for they had gone without water all that day and much of the day before. Food was plentiful, but the children cried and begged for water.

Twice during the day the great iron engine had stopped in respite. But the first time it was in a hamlet where people pointed, called out unfriendly words about Gypsies, and boys threw stones. Later it was in a forest where trees had dissipated the drizzle of the night before. The men talked of getting off the train to look further into the forest but there was a dread that the train might start without warning, and leave them behind.

Mothers pampered their children and pacified them with buttered bread and promises that if they went to sleep there would be something to drink when they woke. With each promise they themselves swallowed hard from friction at the throat. But sleep finally overtook the children, brought on by the monotony of the rumbling train and the warmth of all their clothing.

Fathers of the youngest tots stayed awake into the night with pails or kettles at hand, peering into the darkness. But when the train stopped again, nowhere did the shine of the moon reveal a ditch or puddle.

Then it was moving again slowly, then faster and faster, leaving behind all but a hope that somewhere, perhaps at daybreak, they would stop again.

Somewhere, the locomotive would have to stop.

Chapter 13

Jadwiga and Maria Sczepaniak, already inseparable friends, snuggled together at the trailing end of the car, despite the wind, away from the others where they could talk. Paul and Juliusz talked too, standing nearby.

"Tell me," Paul said, "why did you consign yourself and your wife to this travel in the open of freight passage?"

"Any other way would cost too much," Juliusz answered. "And you? Why are you traveling this way?"

"To save money, too. I wanted to change to second class, but it would put us at the bottom of another waiting list. Jadwiga wouldn't hear of it. She wants to have her baby in America."

"My Maria is too far gone, I think. She will bear our child aboard the ship," Juliusz said. In the clouded moonlight, Paul thought he could see nagging worry pass across the face of this jester.

"What do you know about America?" Paul asked.

"Our neighbor has a letter. It says that for the work you do in America you get not just produce and use of a stove and bed and a measly *złoty* or two for clothing. It says you get pay in American money—sealed in an envelope. Enough to buy food and clothing and pay rent, and there's even some left at times. If you save you can even pay toward land to build your very own home."

"We must hope this letter is not a falsification."

"The letter had a genuine American stamp and the address on the envelope is the same handwriting as the message."

"Let's just hope it's not false."

When their wives had settled, Paul and Juliusz went to warm them by sleeping at their backs. But still they talked.

"Look, Jadwiga," Maria said, pointing. "What do you suppose…"

What they saw were the Jakubiks, standing in a corner at the forward end of the car. Piotr and sons stood and stared into the darkness while Ursula stood behind them. After a moment she edged out of the corner so that now Piotr was hidden. Then Piotr did the same so that a son was concealed.

"Jadwiga, what are they doing? Why do they move in a circle?"

"Maria, go to sleep now," Juliusz said.

"Let us settle," Paul said. "Leave the Russians to their business."

"Water. That's what their business is. They have water," Jadwiga said. "They waited so they wouldn't be asked to share it."

Even in sleep, there was constant awareness of nagging thirst and the unrelenting movement of the train. When it was sidetracked, the slowed tempo of clickety-clack brought men to their feet. They even saw the glint of precious water in the fields at trackside, but when the train stopped they found it was oily and the air stank of rotting apple and grape pulp. Before they could search, a speeding train passed. Immediately, their own train moved again, and they had to scramble aboard. Thirsty children, awakened by the sudden roar, cried again in thirst, and the men gathered in council, a deepening desperation in their voices.

"When we stop again we must go to the Germans who drive this train and tell them," said Ignatz Ran. "They must stop where we can get water."

"Paul, you can go forward to the driver of this locomotive and speak your German words for us," said Stanisław Krulik.

Several of the men—those with the youngest children who were most pitifully thirsty—remained awake, watchful for any opportunity to get water. When dawn began to suggest itself, they saw first signs of community life. This brought new hope for a stop.

The signs of life gradually became a small city of angles and lines just so—a big German city so well-established that a uniformed lampman, stepladder across his shoulders, walked from one crossroad to the next putting out the flames and cleansing each lamp of soot.

But as the train slowed and rumbled into a large railyard, there were no other signs of life. Windows of trackside buildings were dark, and wisps of morning smoke rose from only a few distant homes.

Among the men with children, anxiety over lack of water quickly became a frenzy to take advantage of this opportunity. Coats were thrown into a heap. Pails and buckets were taken up.

"Look there, between the buildings," Ignatz Ran said to a small group around him, "we can go to the houses." They were looking over the right side.

Paul heard this. "I can ask one of the railroad workers," he said to Ignatz, but he was ignored. The men were pointing and talking among themselves, and as the train slowed there was an eagerness to be the first over the side. The nimble Jan Poglicki led the surge.

"Let me ask the yardman," Paul yelled at Tadeusz Murak. To all of them, he yelled, "Stay together. If you scatter, only one or two may get water. Let me ask!"

"This isn't the army," Tadeusz yelled back. "The Germans will treat us like Polack tramps. Ask if you want."

Jozef Dominiak yelled, "The first to find water, shout for the others." And then they were all over the side, running pell mell for houses and shops.

On the left side, as the train brought them past a yardman, Paul and some of the women signaled with gestures of cup to mouth. The worker ignored them, but when the train stopped, he mimed drinking to show that now was the time to get water. He pointed to large buildings at the edge of the yard, warning by his gestures and motion that there was little time.

Carrying a pail, Paul went down the ladder. Jadwiga started to follow, but he snatched her pail away. "No, Jadwiga. It is not for a woman carrying a child to climb and run," he scolded. The last of the pails gone, Jadwiga stayed with the other women.

To make certain of the direction, Paul went to the yardman. "There?"

"Go, hurry," the yardman said, pointing across several pairs of tracks at the freighthouse and speaking careful German. "Over on the other side. A horse trough and pump." He gestured with an up and down motion of hand-pumping. "Through there. Hurry!"

Paul ran, pails in hand, and leapt onto the loading platform. He tried one of the sliding doors and found it locked. He pounded, but there was no response. He pounded on the next and kicked at the next, but none opened.

He ran back to the yardman, who was signaling the reassembly of the train. But the man only looked at his timepiece and said "Go back. They're just coming now. Hurry."

He ran back to kick doors again. This time there was a stir behind one, but it opened only part-way. A clean-shaven young man stuck his head out, but he slid the door shut in Paul's face. Then he yelled from behind it: *"Raus! Raus Polack! Raus Amerika!"*

Paul yelled back. "*Nur wasser, nur wasser. Für mich, nicht. Für kinder...Bitte, für kindern.*"

If there was an answer, it was lost in a bang and roar from the train, rammed by another string of cars. Paul jumped off the platform, fearing the train was about to leave, but there was more coupling to be done. He climbed back onto the platform to kick doors again.

It wasn't until he reached the end door that there was a stir—the click of a hasp, then the resisting squeal of metal rollers. Someone edged the big door partly open—just enough to pop out a dingy derby hat and small head.

"I ask only for water," Paul said in German, "water the yardmaster said I can have from a pump." He realized he was shouting, as though his voice still had to penetrate a door. More softly, "I beg of you, Herr Freightmaster."

The freight worker, an older man, looked both apprehensive and puzzled. Paul realized his German, spoken in panting gulps, wasn't clear. He put his pails down on the platform and reached into his shirt for his army discharge papers, hoping they would qualify him for water.

But the man had no interest in credentials. Seeing by the pails that water was the need, he struggled to slide the big door open, but Paul, thinking another German was about to shut a door in his face, had it jammed in its track with the toe of his shoe.

"*Dumkopf!*" the worker shouted, again putting his head through the small opening. His hat went askew upon his head, revealing a shiny baldness. "If you want to get through for water, at least let me open the door!"

Now Paul helped him, and with the added force the big door broke free, taking the German with it, except for his hat, which toppled from his head and went rolling on its rim in the scatterings on the freighthouse floor.

Paul chased after it, picked it up, and handed it over. This alone widened the German's eyes in surprise, but when Paul came to attention and saluted smartly, the man stepped backward in alarm. Just before he recovered enough to laugh, Paul ran through an open door to another loading platform on the other side of the building. A hand pump and long trough for watering horses were just steps away.

He jumped from the platform and ran to the pump. He jerked the handle up and down, first with one hand, then with both. But the pump required priming, and there was no time, for just then there were two short whistle blasts from the locomotive. There was time only to scoop water from the trough. He was clumsy with haste.

Now he began retracing his steps. At the platform he put down the pails. He climbed up, grabbed the pails, ran through the freighthouse, slipped on sawdust, and spilled much of the water. "*Danke, danke.*" He nodded his head in appreciation to the German worker, who stood open-mouthed at this performance of a thirst-crazed Polack.

Already, the train was moving, just starting. He steadied the pails and jumped from the platform. He ran frantically, but clumsily, as though on stilts, trying to preserve the water while negotiating the hostile footing of rail and tie, stone and cinder. From the flatcar, Jadwiga was yelling at him, but he couldn't hear her.

The train thumped and groaned at its couplings. He easily caught up, and found he could stay alongside at a brisk walk, but he couldn't climb aboard, helpless with a pail of precious water in each hand, None of the women could reach down far enough to take the pails. He simply stayed abreast of the car, walking faster as the train took on speed.

"Where are the men?" he yelled to Jadwiga.

"All running back on the other side!"

He could, at worst, toss away one pail. He needed only one hand to grip an iron rung to get aboard the train. But all the water was needed, even if the other men were bringing some. He had to change from a fast walk to a slow run, but he kept both pails, waiting for one of the men.

Finally, Jan Poglicki came, but he couldn't reach low enough, either— the train was high on the rails while Paul ran low on an uncertain cinder path. Holding a pail high, he even spilled some of the water in his face, just as the awkward position brought cramps about his ribs.

The situation was getting serious. The locomotive was puffing faster, easier, and for him it was harder.

"Go to the end of the car," Paul yelled to Jan. Get on the rungs where you can reach me!" He slowed to drop back to the iron ladder.

But Jadwiga was already there, lifting her skirts high as she climbed over the side to the ladder. She stood on the bottom rung, clutching a higher one. She grabbed one pail and passed it to Jan, then snatched the other. Then she quickly climbed up to make way for Paul, who by now was keeping up only with the help of a hand on a rung, the train pulling him. With the last of his breath, he hauled himself onto the rungs, paused to fill his lungs, then climbed up the ladder and over the side, letting his body flop onto the car.

The last of the others were still returning. One by one, empty pails jangled into the car. In the rows of houses, they had found no one to give them water.

But at least there was some. The two half-filled pails were given to Salomeya Steck to measure for the children. There would be only a little for each, but it would pacify them, and the mothers were grateful. But when Ignatz Ran regained his breath, he chastised Paul. "You were to call us upon finding water. Why didn't you yell?"

Tadeusz Murak joined in. "Why didn't you fill the pails? Why did you bring only half-pails of water?"

Ludwig Karpczinski and Piotr Jakubik seemed about to add their voices to this harangue, but Stanisław Krulik saw anger spreading across Paul's face and he interrupted.

"I'm thankful that Paul brought water for the children. Let's not criticize without first showing appreciation."

Big Jozef Dominiak, a fist doubled, sided with Stanisław. "Ignatz," he said, "shut your whining mouth." The sight of the outsized Jozef holding out a fist at the smallest man of them all was at once alarming and humorous. "Paul tried to organize us to go together and we didn't listen." His voice grew louder with each word. "You didn't listen, I didn't listen, everybody didn't listen. Now you should be embracing him in congratulation and gratitude instead of yelling at him." Now he glared at Tadeusz, too.

"I only asked…" Ignatz started, then thought better of it.

Stanisław and Jan, who only the day before had helped to restrain Jozef from his attack on Paul, now stood astonished at his exaggerated defense of Paul—threatening the diminutive Ignatz.

Kazimierz Steck stepped in. He fastened his eyes on Jozef's. "Jozef," he said quietly, "we all thank Paul. Next time, no doubt, we will surely listen to what he suggests. We will be less frenzied, will we not?"

Big Jozef relaxed his fist, nodding agreement.

Both Tadeusz and Ignatz took advantage of the moment, slapped Jozef on the back, and the confrontation was transformed into harmonious agreement.

Peace made, Paul left this gathering, angry at the criticism, embarrassed at Jozef's vehemence in his defense. He took Jadwiga off to the side for a moment of privacy where the noise of wheels on tracks shielded their words.

"Jadwiga, let the men climb over the side of the car when it is moving. This is not for you to do, and you must…I forbid you to ever do it again with your big belly," he said sternly, even while still short of breath.

"Don't be cross," Jadwiga said, and she kissed his cheek. "I'm so proud that you are my husband. Only you could get water for the children. You will be a good father."

He had in mind to scold some more, but she made it difficult. It crossed his mind that in speaking to him, she was like Kazimierz Steck talking to Big Jozef, using her deep eyes and soft voice to tame his anger not only with her, but even what he felt toward the men. He thought he must not be so easily diverted.

"I know you can climb masts and jump from boat to boat," he said to Jadwiga. "But you must not take our child with you in such craziness. Climbing on a moving train for pails isn't so safe as stealing a hat from a goosestepping soldier."

With this talk of their child and of hat-stealing, and in his exhaustion, tears came to his eyes and she held him.

Chapter 14

Fresh now, the locomotive gathered new speed, its line of cars coursing straight through open fields. A cold wind snapped around the boxcar ahead and snarled down across the flatcar. Women gathered children for protection, making nest-like huddles against the left sideboard of the car. The men gathered against the other side, forming an unspoken apology by making Paul the center of their talk. But there was little real planning, for there was little they could do. They spoke mostly of the speed of the train, which made it apparent there would be no stopping for some time. Before long, they huddled, as well, for refuge from the relentless chill.

This was not as he would have planned it.

Long before now, his Jadwiga would have been comfortable in a stone cottage on the lands of his German lieutenant in Poland. Instead she had to squat to the floor of a speeding freight car, thirsty, buffeted by moving air that gave no quarter. By now Jadwiga could be running through field and forest, taking clear water from cold springs and bringing him a lunch basket of beer and chicken as respite from the mending of fences. Instead her only taste of water was from a horse trough, gotten at risk of life, limb, and unborn child.

He would have been responsible for a country estate, a keeper of game and lands, earning a roof over their heads, perhaps supervising workers and using skills learned as a leader of other soldiers. Instead he ran like a fool to beg water of freightyard workers, and was expected to answer for getting too little.

He was heartsick. This was not as he would have planned it.

He looked at his wife amid the boxes and bundles and felt his heart beat more heavily. She was happy despite the cold and misery, comforting the timid Maria, talking brightly, girlishly, of babies and America. He shut out this scene with hands over his eyes and scorned himself for being so in love with this woman as to have made her this foolish promise of America in a moment of weakness, under duress, distracted by beauty that took unfair advantage.

He took his hands from his eyes and his mind from these thoughts suddenly when he sensed that the men who had been squatting near him were gone. Simultaneously he became aware of a slight slowing of the train, a line-up of all the men looking over the side of the car, and a stone bouncing off the sidewall near him.

The men stooped behind the sideboard of the car, except for Big Jozef, who stood shaking a fist and shouting. He yelled. "*Psia krew niemiec,*" over and over.

Standing, Paul saw well-dressed German boys throwing stones and shouting insults. It was Sunday, and these were the children of church-going city people—boys who otherwise would have been at work or school.

He squatted again. Salomeya Steck began leading Sunday prayer, and he found it a refuge.

"Jesus, have mercy on us. Jesus, save us."

This was not as he would have planned it.

As thirst hounded and afternoon threatened to become night without reprieve, the men talked again of the need for water, and Ignatz Ran turned to Paul. "You, Paul," he said, "Why can't you go with your German words to the iron horse and ask the men who command it to stop this train at the next village?"

Stanisław Krulik joined in. "You can walk on top of the cars as the trainmen do," he said. Jadwiga noticed the focus of conversation on Paul, and came across the car to listen.

"Trains have schedules," Paul said. "The engineer can't stop unless it's in the schedule or there's an accident or emergency."

"It is an emergency," Ignatz insisted. "We need water."

Paul thought for a moment.

"For the children."

All the men were looking at him. He saw that he must agree. Jadwiga said nothing.

"I'll try. But I don't think they'll stop. I'm sure they won't." He took his army papers from the inside pocket of his overcoat, which Ignatz took from him. The men patted him on the back and spoke words of encouragement as he went forward to straddle the endboard of the car and then to climb on the iron rungs to the top of the boxcar ahead.

But he merely stood there, looking forward, bracing himself against the wind. Suddenly he turned about and came down.

"There's no need for me to run on the train," he said excitedly. "We're going to stop soon—in Hamburg!"

"How do you know?"

"I could see a big city and a bridge over the Elbe River. I was in Hamburg once on an army train. All the trains stop."

Already, authoritative lettering spread across a broad masonry building told them they had reached the railyards on the edge of West Hamburg. Soon, they passed a railcar repair shop, then a water tower, and then the train stopped abruptly in a shudder of couplings.

Now, such plans as had been made when the train was moving were cast aside. Most of the men scrambled from the car to run back to the water tower. Only Big Jozef, Jan Poglicki and Stanisław Krulik, with his sons, remembered and stayed with Paul. Their locomotive had been uncoupled and it was puffing along a parallel track toward the water tower. "We'll be here a long time," Paul said. "We can save our breath."

So it was that they walked while the others ran. The others reached the water tower when Paul's group was only half the way there, and went directly to a faucet at the end of a pipe clamped to one of the huge legs of timber.

A worker, sitting on the funnel to direct its flow into a locomotive, yelled at them in German and motioned for them to get away from the faucet. Ignatz Ran shouted back in Polish. "We must have water too. Not just you and your *lokomotywa!*"

Running back to the flatcar, they yelled "Hurry!" at the group with Paul. But Paul persisted in asking. He stepped up to the water tower briskly, as though presenting arms with the pail he carried.

"Herr Trainmaster! We ask your permission to take drinking water." While walking calmly, he had worked out the words.

"Not here. This is river water, contaminated with sewage. I'll show you where to get well water."

Even as the man spoke, Paul saw the sign: *Flusse*. He said to Władek Krulik, "Run as fast as you can. Leave your pail. Tell the men they have bad water. Don't let anybody drink it, not even a drop. It's mixed with filth." Władek glanced at his father, who nodded, and he was off.

The trainman, having finished his chore of tank-filling, got off the funnel to send it skyward, pulled by the counterbalance of iron weights on a cable just inside the supporting trestlework. Then he slid down the coal chute connected to the locomotive's tender car and came down the iron stepladder from the cabin carrying his own oak bucket.

"Come with me," he said to Paul.

"Herr Trainmaster, I thank you."

The man led them across several sets of tracks and around some idle sections of trains to a long, red, windowless shed on a spur of tracks near the edge of the railyard. It stood high on pillars of brickwork for cars to be unloaded at the level of its platform, and it smelled grandly of farm produce. They walked under the building on wooden planking, a well-worn shortcut to the other side where there were loading platforms for wagons. There was a well with a watering trough for horses, and a pump of the new kind with a crank handle.

"I thank Herr Trainmaster," Paul said again. Solicitously, Jozef Dominiak took the trainman's bucket to fill it for him.

"I'm a fireman, not a trainmaster," the man said. "The trainmaster is in the cabin asleep. He has a long night of work ahead."

Paul then pieced together German words to ask how long the trip to Bremerhaven would take. The trainman pulled a railroad timepiece from a pocket and pointed to show that the hour hand would complete a 12-hour half-cycle.

Paul was so enthusiastic at learning this that he couldn't help saluting in appreciation and gratitude. This drew a grin from the man, who even returned the salute as he took his filled pail and turned to go back to his duties.

Now there was real joy. Despite their own thirst and their eagerness to take water to their women and children, they moved deliberately, with composure, to cup their hands and catch the water and drink. While cranking for Paul to drink, Stanisław Krulik tried to explain the workings of the pump to his son and Jan Poglicki, but Jan was more interested in a joshing argument with Big Jozef over whose turn it would be to crank next.

But just as Jozef took up a pail to fill it, a group of workers came from the freighthouse—five of them, one in the lead. Each one carried a metal tool. The leader waved a hand at the emigrants to warn them away from the pump. In German, he shouted at them all. Only Paul understood his words, but they all knew what the man meant.

"No water for train passengers," he said. "Payment first." He was a big man, the muscles of years of lifting showing under his jacket. "Pay first," he said, looking to see if anyone understood him.

The Poles backed away from the pump. There was no choice. They had no tools to use as weapons, and the workers were crowding them.

"They want money? For water, they want our money?" Stanisław asked.

The big German took the crank handle from the pump and held it in crossed arms, saying something to the effect that if these Polack water seekers had the money to travel to America, they must also have money for water.

Paul didn't answer immediately. He searched his memory for German words. As he did, Jan Poglicki suggested that by himself Big Jozef could probably beat the entire crew of the warehouse, let alone just these five. Jozef was ready. "We'll just take the water," Jan said, "and bash them if they try to stop us."

"Wait," Paul said. "First, let Lancek run for the other men while I talk with this one."

Stanisław said to his son, "Go. Hurry."

"*Guten morgen, mein Herr*," Paul said. The man's eyes, which had been darting among the group of them, now fixed on Paul. There was clearly some surprise at the crisp German. Though Paul's German carried an unmistakable burden of Polish, the sharp edges of military pronunciation were evident. But the man made no reply.

"Do I understand correctly," Paul asked, "that you wish to collect money for this water?"

"Yes," the man said as Paul approached him.

"You will be forgiving of me, please, if I speak your language poorly." His mind raced. He had no idea what he could say to the man to get the water without paying, much less how to say it in German. He could only stall until Lancek fetched the others. "Would you allow me..." He spoke hesitantly and with great deference, lowering his voice, "...to speak with you over here?" Paul gestured to indicate a place away from the two opposing groups.

Shrugging, amused, the man walked the few steps with Paul.

"Allow me to explain something of our circumstances," Paul began, mimicking a phrase he had practiced after hearing Lieutenant Shubert use it many times, though always sarcastically. This helped him fall into the rhythm of the German language, but he still groped for the words he needed. "These men, and their wives, and their children, have all been aboard a train, without water, for over a day. There is a great need for water."

"Then there is a great need to pay," the man said loudly, glancing back at his fellow workers.

"*Verstehe*," Paul said quietly. "Let me find the words," Paul said. "You wish money..."

"The pump belongs to the shipping company for which I work. Not to the railroad. Those from the train must pay."

"Yes, you want money. Excuse my request, but would you be so kind as to look at the papers I carry?" Stiffly, with exaggerated ceremony, taking as much time as he could, he reached for his discharge papers. Deliberately, he went to the wrong pocket, then the right one. He took the papers from within the envelope, and in an attitude of great deference and exaggerated care he smoothed them against his uniform before handing them to the man. He even clicked his heels. For a fleeting moment, he allowed himself to hope the man couldn't read.

But after a moment the man looked at him with a mean smile beginning to creep across his mouth. "These papers are nothing more than..."

"Yes," Paul said. He took the papers and began folding them. "Nothing more than discharge papers from your army." Now he found he was speaking almost without thinking. "That's all, it's true. But the others, your comrades, don't know this. I would only suggest, begging your pardon, that a good ending of this question of water for thirsty women and children is—might be—Is the word correct?—might be that you tell your friends it is a German army matter—that I carry an official paper. I suggest this only because I can see only one other possible ending to this disagreement, which would involve fighting." He was surprising himself; he had never before spoken so many German words at one time, without a rest. "I don't believe these men will allow me to pay you for water. But they will not go back to their children without water."

The man stiffened and began to uncross his arms, tightening his grip on the pump handle, drawing himself up threateningly.

Deferentially, Paul held up a hand, asking for a moment longer to reason with him. "It would be well to end this without fighting. You see, just yesterday I myself fought the big one, and I can tell you it took all the others—nine or ten men—to keep him from...from crippling me. He is the one you personally will have to fight." Now, from the corner of his eye, he saw the others coming at a run. "And if you will look to the place I look, you will see that we will not be fighting alone." Without moving his head, he showed with his eyes where he wanted the man to look.

When he looked back, the man was not so stiff.

"Now, *mein Herr*, I extend my hand, hoping you will take it in friendship and tell your men they must not stop fathers who need water for children. It is an army matter. Say that to them. But if you don't take my hand in friendship, try instead to hit me with that pump crank, and the fighting can begin with us. And the big Polack will make you a cripple."

Those from the warehouse were now outnumbered. Even with the tools, the odds were against them. Glaring, the man shook Paul's hand, saying nothing. Then Paul stepped back, clicked his heels, and saluted. He then reached out for the pump handle, which the man let him take.

To his gang from the warehouse, the German spoke sharply, too quickly for Paul to understand every word, except that he heard *army* and *army paper* and *army matter* and *permission*. The men backed away.

Paul stepped up to the pump, inserted the crank handle, and with a grand gesture, invited Big Jozef to turn it.

"What did you say?" Stanisław asked.

"Merely that Big Jozef would kill him," Paul responded. Jozef laughed and smacked Paul on the back. Stanisław laughed, too, and it caught on in the larger group.

Now tension abated and joviality returned, but the emigrants worked quickly to fill their pails before there could be more trouble.

Someone noticed that Jan Poglicki was missing. Whether or not he had filled his pails was uncertain. "It doesn't matter," Paul said. "We have enough water. We'll be in Bremerhaven in the morning."

Now they surrounded him in a circle moving toward their flatcar. "How do you know this?" Tadeusz Murak asked.

"I know from talking with the one from the water tower," Paul said.

"Tomorrow already we will be on a boat?" asked Ignatz. Paul shrugged his shoulders, but such was the jubilation that Ludwig Karpczinski took him by the nape of the neck and kissed his forehead. "May the Lord bless you," he said.

Now they hurried. Now they had more than just water to bring. There was good news, too. There would be an end, finally, to this clatter and jam of freight train travel where people were expected to be only as thirsty as boxes of machinery or bags of grain.

But it didn't take good news, or even the water they brought, to transform the day. When they returned, there was a kind of picnic in progress aboard the flatcar. Apples were being passed around. One was handed to Paul as he set his feet on the level of the flatcar. The children ran, jumping in excitement, taking theirs from a bundled shirtful at the middle of the car. Adults passed two pails around, selecting and polishing and biting zestfully.

Only the Poglickis and the elderly Stecks were exception to this new joy of a fruit rare enough at home, but totally unexpected in the midst of freight-car travel. Kazimierz and Salomeya stood near their traveling trunk talking seriously, quietly.

Jan and Estella were off by themselves in a corner of the car, away from the celebrating, also talking. Suddenly Estella yelled.

"You thief!" she shouted. "You gave me your promise. We are not yet in America, we are not even aboard ship to America, and you break your promise to me and the priest. You stealing fiend!" She was beginning to cry now, waving her arms at Jan, as though to hit him, but really in frustration.

Jan backed away from her anger, looking at the others. He was embarrassed, and at a loss for words that might somehow restore the party spirit he had created with his stealing. Estella sat heavily on a box, giving herself to tears of anger.

For just a moment Jan seemed about to sit with her to reason, but he gave up the thought when she looked up at him and shouted again. "You thieving..." She didn't finish. Most of the others turned away, to pretend they hadn't heard.

Jan left her crying and walked toward Paul and the men who had just returned. Pleading his defense to them, since she wouldn't hear it, he said, "There are a thousand bags of apples and I opened only one. And that one won't be discovered for a week—I covered it with other bags." Then, hands extended in a gesture of helplessness, he said to Paul, "What else am I to do when they leave the doors open and stop their work to demand money for water?"

Paul didn't respond with word or expression. He simply looked down at the apple he'd been given, and put it in Jan's hand and turned away. Other adults slowly covered theirs with a fold of arms or a rearrangement of coat or jacket.

Jan stood in awkward silence. Paul turned back to him. "Only you will go to jail if this is discovered."

Kazimierz Steck now moved to them. "Jan," he said, "this is a serious matter. We are all together here. We all want to go to America. If this is discovered—if we are found with apples, there will be questioning. We would be interrogated by the railroad Germans even while our ship sails away. People would have to choose between missing their passage and giving you up to the authorities." Jan started to look around, but then lowered his head.

"Jan," the old man continued, "these others might be proud and stubborn and they might shield you. They might chance missing their places to America, perhaps to save again and go another time. But I am an old man, and I am not so proud, not so stubborn. I want to see my sons again, in America, before I leave this earth. Jan, if they were to discover this thing and take us all to be questioned, I would tell. I beg this of you. I have never betrayed a comrade. Don't put me in such a position now."

The old man's eyes fastened on Jan's. He put his hand on the younger man's shoulder, and even the railyard sounds seemed to pause in gentle insistence of response.

"That would not happen," Jan said. "I would confess. But I understand. I understand I cannot put everyone in jeopardy. I understand."

Except for Estella, still sobbing where she sat, this eased the tension. Jan turned to look at his wife, then slowly walked toward her. But passing Paul, he paused.

"You must not be surprised if, before this journey has ended, a skill at filching from Germans will be more prized than a skill with their words."

Chapter 15

As daylight faded, a wet snow began to fall, and the iron horse stirred again. A whistle stabbed its warning into the convening grey. A shudder of steam gave notice of powerful pulling to come. Coupling strained at coupling. The emigrants were again a moving community.

This was a big city they were leaving. It had big wealth, with many lamplit surreys drawn by beautiful and well-appointed horses. The buildings were big, wrapped in giant eddies of snow. It was a city of big minds, for there were no stones thrown where rail crossed road, no shouted insults. The people were of big thinking and there was only staring. It was even safe for the fathers to hold the smallest children in their arms so that they too could see what it was like to travel. Many streets were wide. Some were straight and long, testing the limits of the eye. There were many post lamps, being lighted one by one. Their light glinted from cobblestones, caught by jewels of snowmelt.

Hamburg was a city to be remembered by a traveling people.

"When I was a little girl," Jadwiga told Maria, "there was all this talk of America."

They stood together, best friends holding hands, watching the passing scenery. Paul and Juliusz were occupied with building a tent—a simple affair of blankets sloped between sideboard and floor of the rail car, wedged into place with sharpened scraps of wood. It was Stanisław Krulik's idea. The slope would divert falling snow so that Maria and Jadwiga might sleep dry. Paul and Juliusz would sleep dry, too—inside the Adamik seabags.

"In those days," Jadwiga continued, "everyone was talking about America. I remember everything. We were to go—our whole family. I remember thinking how strange it would be to leave Gdynia and have to find a husband elsewhere—in a new country, even. But my mother always said I would have my pick wherever we would go.

"But then there was a war in America, and people stopped going. And then my blessed mother was taken up to heaven by the Lord God." She crossed herself. "So I waited for Paul."

"Juliusz told me that, were it not for Paul, the men would've had to fight for water." By expression and tilt of head, Maria was asking if Jadwiga knew more of the incident about which the other women gossiped with fragments of information from their husbands.

"Delfinia—the Dominiak woman—said Paul talked the Germans out of charging money for their water," Jadwiga said.

"Is this true?"

"I don't know, Maria. Paul has told me nothing about it. Nothing. He isn't talking. He just thinks." Maria giggled at this, so Jadwiga explained. "He only thinks how much he doesn't want to go to America."

"Doesn't want to go?"

"He goes for me. It's because I want to go. He goes only because he promised me…because he loves me. He is a good man, my Paul, but he doesn't understand about America. He hopes I will change my mind before we sail."

"Oh, Jadwiga, you won't, will you?"

"No, of course I won't. I want my baby to be an American baby—born in America."

Maria was relieved. "With us, it's Juliusz. He wants to go. I know almost nothing about it. It is said there is work and better opportunity…more money…"

"And no Germans. No foreigners with their armies. A better place for our children."

"But Paul doesn't want…"

"No. He doesn't want to go. He never really thought about it until we met. My father said I must help by pointing the way. So I am helping him. Now my Paul thinks only of what he leaves behind. But in America he will see what lies ahead."

"Jan and Estella are going for a new start. He promised the priest he wouldn't steal any more. He promised Estella, too." Jadwiga was thoughtful now, but Maria was talkative. "The Dominiaks go to get away from the Russians. They came all the way from the Russian partition. Delfinia said she and her Jozef were brought together by their families. They only met each other the day before their wedding. Jadwiga?"

"Yes, Maria, I'm listening. I'm sorry. I was thinking about Paul. I wish he wanted to go like your Juliusz."

"Jadwiga, do you suppose we will be on the same boat? You don't suppose…"

"Yes, I think so, Maria. Ignatz—the little one with the big wife—Ignatz Ran," she remembered the name, "he knows a relative of the passport counselor. They make a contract to fill all the third class space in a ship. Steerage class is what he called it, though."

"Steerage?"

"It's the bottom of the ship where the steering machinery is on the new ships with steam engines to help the sails. But we will be on a sailing ship. At least I think so—hope so. All that fire is dangerous."

Maria giggled. "That little Ignatz man used to stand on his Kostanta's shoulders to pick apples. It was faster than using a stepladder. She said it gave them time to…Jadwiga, how did you meet Paul? He isn't from your village."

"I dreamed about him," Jadwiga responded, enjoying the smile of curiosity this brought to Maria's face. "I dreamed that he would take me to America. And then I found him in a parade of soldiers."

Maria looked uncertain whether Jadwiga might be making fun.

"It's true, Maria."

"Juliusz's family were neighbors. It was always expected that we would be the ones for each other. I think we've always known it. Both of us are the youngest in our families. One of my brothers is married to one of his sisters, too. But it is good—our parents didn't push us too hard. In the end, we were the ones to decide together."

"You make an attractive match, the two of you."

"But no more than you and Paul." Maria glanced at Paul and Juliusz, who were now arranging bedding inside the tent. "He must love you very much, Jadwiga, to go to America even though he doesn't…well, just going for you."

Jadwiga was quiet and thoughtful. She didn't answer. Then Paul and Juliusz came to them, and their conversation had to end.

Paul felt a jolt. Death-deep in his disconnected sleep, a German officer was shouting at him as he lay unmoving on his bunk. It was an incomprehensibly quick string of German words that he could scarcely understand, though he knew he was being called to task. The officer's words meant two things simultaneously. He was not standing at attention, he was being yelled at for this infraction, and he was being asked to answer for his disloyalty in asking for a transfer. He couldn't find words with which to respond, but it hardly mattered for he had to stand before he could speak, and he couldn't stand because the blankets of his cot were so tight over him that he couldn't move. And even if he could stand, he was sweaty and he smelled from this struggle to come to attention when he couldn't even move from his bunk.

And now the officer was bending over him, shaking him, and the whole bunk jolted beneath him, and he knew there was terrible punishment about to come.

"Paul. Wake up."

Light flooded into his eyes and the German officer was gone but Ludwig Karpczinski was there, shaking him.

"*Meine Frau...*" he said, but the words were slurred and incomprehensible. Then he realized he was responding to the questioning.

"What?" Ludwig asked.

"What time is it?" Paul blurted, becoming conscious of a tired strain in the muscles of his arms and back. He had been struggling against the confines of his seabag, striving to stand at attention against the constraint of canvas and oilcloth made to contain and protect a schooner's suit of sails.

"It's morning. You can still sleep. But you were struggling in there so I woke you up. Jadwiga says we are in Bremerhaven. It's a railyard. You can sleep some more if you want. We'll wake you up if we need you to talk to Germans for us."

"No, no. I'll..." Paul wriggled inside the sailbag, trying to free his arms to get out of it, and feeling foolish. He remembered Jadwiga and Maria laughing, making Juliusz and him helpless with the bags.

Nearby, Polka Karpczinski was talking to Jadwiga. "How do you know we're in Bremerhaven when there are no boats?"

"I can smell it," Jadwiga said. "I smell the sea." Then she saw that Paul was awake and went to him with a morning kiss. "Paul, we are in Bremerhaven." She stooped to help with the seabag, stripping it away as quickly as she skinned a fish. "I can smell the water," she said. "Can you smell it?"

The odors were merely railyard odors—smoke hanging low and heavy with the wetness of a fine morning drizzle, ripe animal manure, rotting produce, the metallic burn of steel brakes on steel wheels. And the stench of his own body. To his sleep-soddened brain, the scene and the scents seemed the work of a deranged devil's apprentice. He smelled no sea, but Jadwiga was bright with her discovery of salt in the air.

Ludwig, amused by Paul's befuddlement but wanting to rescue him from it, said, "From the top of the boxcar you can see—there are many lines of cars. The unloading will take a while. The freighthouse is some distance away. You have plenty of time for sleeping."

Jadwiga took his arm. "Take my place in the tent, my sleepy husband. You must be at your best with your German words to be sure we get on a boat."

The tent was inviting and warm where she had left her odor moments earlier. He imagined holding her. At last, he thought, this would be a chance for real sleep on a stilled train.

Outside, Salomeya began a morning prayer. "Jesus have mercy on us. Jesus save us." Renewed sleep came quickly.

Waking briefly some time later, Paul found Franek Dominiak asleep beside him.

When he awoke again, sensing it was much later, it was to the sound of the youngest children crying deep, unhappy wails of hunger. He emerged from the tent into the passing drizzle, wanting to hold and comfort them all at one time.

There were the Dominiak twins, Magda spelling Manya's breaths, Manya spelling Magda's, so that there was a continuous keening. The young Ran brothers, David and Mikal, joined in, and there was danger of Katrina Poglicki and little Franciska Karpczinski becoming part of the chorus. All wanted something to eat, and it didn't help to tell them that all the packed food was gone—that the next meal would be aboard ship.

But Jozef Dominiak and Ignatz Ran had an unexpected reserve for this crisis of hungry children. Each had two apples. And when these were produced, it developed that Tadeusz Murak had also saved one, as had Ludwig Karpczinski and Old Man Kradzinski.

The eighteen and twenty-year-old Jakubik brothers also produced apples but had no intention of turning them over to relieve the crisis among the small children. Piotr scolded in a whisper. "We will not have these Polacks looking down on us. You are old enough to go without so the young ones will stop crying."

Soon, each child who was awake had some part of an apple and the crying abated. But Jan Poglicki could produce no apple for this sharing among children. He turned to his wife and spoke in anger.

"So, Estella, it is wrong to provide for the children by taking apples from those who would deny us water. Is it now wrong to have these apples in reserve to stem this flow of tears? Why don't you carry on with these men who are heroes with their children at the expense of your husband?" He walked away, but turned to point a finger at Paul.

"What do you say now? Now who will take the punishment if this thievery is discovered? Will it be the one who provided for the hungry children in the first place? Or will it be those who perform these heroic deeds of producing food from hiding?"

With a quickness flowing from anger, Jan spun away from Paul and before there was any sense of what he was doing, he vaulted over the side to the cinder path below. "Don't leave the car," Paul yelled, but Jan's feet could be heard crunching the cinders at a run. At the sideboard, Paul saw only that Jan was headed toward the freighthouse as he skittered under cars of the adjacent train. He checked an impulse to chase him without quite knowing why, then rationalized that one man loose in the railyard, missing from their car here in Bremerhaven, was already too serious an infraction of the rules.

Delfinia Dominiak shook a finger toward Estella. "This time when your husband comes back, maybe we should tie him up. What do you think?"

"What is it with your Jan?" Jadwiga asked. "Was he born for trouble?"

"Jadwiga, he promised me he would stay out of trouble. It is just very hard for him. He is a good man. Good to me, good to the children. He promised me. It's just that whenever there is trouble..." Estella lost her voice. Tears came to her eyes, making Jadwiga and Delfinia regret their cross words, so they sat her down on some baggage to comfort her.

On the next track, another string of freight cars moved an eight-car distance, pulled by a distant yard engine. Pelagia Dominiak, the four-year-old whose cough was getting worse, awoke hungry, calling for her mother. But Delfinia had her little Konrad in her arms and was involved with Jadwiga and Estella. "Go to Franek," she told Pelagia. "Wake him up. He's saving a piece of an apple for you."

An oddly mixed attitude settled over the flatcar. Here they were in Bremerhaven—all felt sure of that, since they were amidst lines of freight cars being unloaded. It was good to know the rail travel was over. Yet there was a feeling they should pick up their belongings and go—go to the freight depot, go to a ship, go to a wagon—do something to continue on their way. But all knew they were only to wait. It was a curious time of uncertainty, yet anticipation, a mood complicated by Jan Poglicki's running off.

It was apparent the train on the adjacent track was being unloaded faster. It moved still another four-car length toward the freighthouse.

When the noise of the moving cars ended, a distant music could be heard—the reedy wheeze of an accordion. Men, women, and children went to the sideboard to lean out and look backward along the tracks.

But it wasn't until a half-hour later, when the drizzle had finally stopped and the adjacent string of cars rolled forward again, that they knew the source of the music, which was a boxcar. The song was *Katrina Polka*, and there were harmonicas, too, and a fiddler.

This provided a lively break from the tedium of waiting. Before the song ended, there was even some impromptu dancing, but mostly there was the passing of greetings between the new-looking boxcar and the bedraggled flatcar.

These men, Galicians from the Austrian partition, were now invited aboard the flatcar. They too were going to America, to the free country, they said, and now there was much to celebrate. Not only were they at last in their port of embarkation, but now they had discovered countrymen going to America, as well.

Their music set the rhythm of an exuberant acquaintancing. The musicians piped their companions aboard with a spirited mockery of some remembered pomp. Some men among the hosts formed a kind of reception line, and at its end Viktoria or Jadwiga or Maria gave each visitor a welcoming twirl in time with the music.

These visitors were mere youths, most of them, an even two dozen. They were without wives or children or trouble or care, clean and dry despite the morning's weather, and they made a light-hearted contrast to the families of the flatcar. Even the sun now began to appear, as though in response to their presence.

They were talkative, sure of themselves, even annoyingly so. They were warm and dry, they bragged, for their car had a roof. They had benches for sitting out the hours of freight travel, and straw for bedding. Every time America was mentioned, they cheered and pantomimed the raising of glasses in a toast.

Imitating a bandmaster, Franek conducted their music, giving this up only when Pelagia insisted he dance. Other children joined in, encouraged by fathers, mothers, and Galicians alike. Everyone was alive with the music. It lifted the corners of mouths soured by open travel. It seemed even to hasten the drying of clothes hanging wet on bodies chafed raw. It incited a spontaneity and harmony of movement not seen before in this group of dissimilar people. The music brought them together and transformed their mood.

Many of the visitors gathered around Kazimierz and Salomeya Steck, as though to adopt them as grandparents. Solemnly and respectfully, they introduced themselves to Old Man Kradzinski, as well.

Stanisław Krulik, meanwhile, undertook to learn all he might from the small group of the visitors, while Paul, Ludwig, Jozef, Jan, and Ignatz listened and occasionally asked a question.

"How does it happen you are all going to America together?" Stanisław asked.

"We are to be under contract, an American contract," one named Stefan said proudly. "We go free to America. Our passage is paid by the American company."

They all knew of this kind of arrangement. The youths were under a two-year contract as laborers. Supposedly, when it was over, they could remain in America or return to Galicia, whichever they might choose.

"All the arrangements have been made by the American representative." Stefan was a giant, broad-shouldered, young, unmarked and fair. All the Galicians were strong, as though each had passed a test by lifting three of the others.

Speaking in a confidential tone, Stanisław put an arm around the youth. "Stefan, my boy. You look to me like the smartest one. Perhaps you can tell us more about this American agent," Stanisław said.

"He wears fine clothes and he has a mustache and he said he would speak well of us in America," Stefan said.

"Did the American say that everyone must have a speaker of good words in America?" Paul asked.

"He spoke only of us. He said we already have work, and he would speak well of us to get us into America. He said in America the laws are becoming more restrictive because undesirables have been getting in. He said none of us will have this worry. He said we will go right to work. We have jobs waiting for us."

The string of cars moved again on the adjacent track. Some of the Galicians were concerned that they not become separated from their car. But as before, the cars stopped after eight had rolled past, and there was no cause for worry.

But it had called attention to their car, and one youth suggested in jest that perhaps the Stecks would like to leave this gypsy travel of the open car and join them in their boxcar for freight travel of the first-class category. This led to some remarks being exchanged about means of travel—paying like respectable people, or going in bondage. A flow of happy conversation threatened to become a jealous confrontation.

Salomeya Steck rescued the mood by asking the musicians to play a hymn—the hymn that recalled military heroism—the hymn used at the end of masses in all of Catholic Poland. All sang, and there was a renewal of feelings of brotherhood between the faction of the flatcar and the faction of the boxcar.

Jeszcze Polska nie zginela	Poland has not perished yet
Póki My Żyjemy.	So long as we still live.
Co nam obca przemoc wzieła	That which alien force has seized
Szablą odbijemy.	We at swordpoint shall retrieve.
Marsz, marsz, Dabrowski!	March, march, Dabrowski!
Z Ziemi włoskiej do Polski!	From Italy to Poland!
Pod Twoim przewodem	Let us now reunite the nation
Złaczym się z narodem.	Under thy command.

Just as the singing ended, Paul caught a movement in a corner of his eye and looked up to the trailing boxcar. A yard policeman, a club tightly gripped in his hand, stood looking down on them. His eyes darted from one man to the next. Then he shouted at them in German. He waved an arm, pointing with his club at all of them and at the Galicians' boxcar.

Quietly, Paul summarized. "He's angry about people being on the wrong car. It would be best to go back to the boxcar." The Galicians began to leave as the watchman scolded. In the midst of this another worker came along on the cinder path, official leather notebook and loose papers showing him to be a man of authority and responsibility. Standing on the ladder of the flatcar, he interrupted the flow of Galicians. He was counting.

Now the policeman yelled to him in German. "Half these Polacks belong on the other track. I don't have time to straighten them out. I'm looking for a sneak thief."

"I'll take care of it," the second German yelled back. Speaking to those aboard the car, he asked "Does anybody here speak German?"

Paul answered. "I do, sir. Sir, it is only that the Galicians joined us to celebrate arrival in Bremerhaven. Nobody intended to break rules."

"It is nothing," said the freightmaster. "The watchman makes a large fuss over any small matter today just because he's having trouble with a trespasser. Are all your people here?"

Paul hesitated a moment, thinking of Jan Poglicki, then responded. "Yes, sir, all are present." As habit dictated, he stood at attention in giving this report.

"Please come with me," the freightmaster said, and he waited while Paul hurried to the ladder.

Jadwiga rushed to him, concerned, and Paul realized that only he had understood the conversation. "Don't worry, Jadwiga. This man just wants my help because I speak German." To Big Jozef, who was the man nearest him, Paul said, "When Jan comes back, keep him here. They are looking for him, and I vouched that we are all here."

The man's office was in a corner of the freighthouse—a makeshift affair furnished with attractive fine wood furniture that was slightly damaged. Open at the top, it collected noise from the activities of men moving crates and boxes from trains to the warehouse.

Paul found it remarkable that the man didn't object to the stench that rose from his body like an evil fog. More than anything now—more than an end to this crazed journey, more than staying in Poland, more than food or water—more than anything, he wanted a bath.

The man looked down at papers on his desk, motioning to a chair where Paul should sit. Without looking up from his work, he began speaking.

"It is likely that the man the watchman is chasing is from your car, or from the other car—the men from Galicia." He flipped his hand to show that he didn't care. "If he's caught, and if he's stolen anything, he'll probably be taken away. Or if he hasn't, he may be allowed to go with you. But if you get him back, don't let him or any others get away from your group. Getting you all to the ship and aboard will be easier for all of us if the people match the papers. Do you understand?"

"The group is to keep together," Paul said.

"Good."

The man leaned back in his chair now, and for the first time looked directly at Paul.

"Why the uniform? Were you in the army?"

"Yes, sir."

"And now you go to America?"

"Yes, sir."

"You should stay here."

"Yes, sir."

"I mean it. Right here we need somebody who can talk to the Po...your people for us. A lot come through now. More every week."

Paul wanted to seize on this opportunity immediately, but he could say nothing. He had promised Jadwiga. Perhaps later, back at the flatcar, he would discuss this with her.

"Well, your ship will sail the day after tomorrow at the earliest. So there is no hurry. We will move all of you to the ship today, but there is no hurry. I will depend on you to bring your people here, in small groups. No more than six or eight at a time." He held up as many fingers to be certain Paul knew the numbers. "When you get them all here, you should line them up according to the list of names on this paper."

Paul saw that the names were alphabetized and nodded understanding. The German, satisfied he could read, reached to his desk drawer for a stack of lettered pasteboard tags, each with a string. Gesturing with the tags, he continued.

"Keep your people clear of the workers. They can be troublesome. There is always a casualty when Poles come through. Be especially careful of the workers.

"Each person must have his tag with his name on it around his neck before you all go on the wagon to the pier. Keep the tags. Don't pass them out until everybody is here. Don't lose any. You'll need one around each neck to board the ship at the pier. And then every man, woman and child must have a ticket hanging from his neck for the authorities to read in America.

"And in the event that anybody is sent back it will simplify matters if he has his ticket. It will get you passage back to where you came from without cost or argument.

"Do you understand?"

"Yes, sir."

The man handed over the blue paper of lading and the pasteboard tickets, and Paul understood that he was dismissed to go about the assigned tasks.

Sent back. Passage back. As he returned to the flatcar, the German's words haunted him. He wondered why the idea of being sent back troubled him. Especially because, from the beginning, he didn't want to go.

Chapter 16

"Jadwiga, do you smell a ship yet?"

Everyone on the wagon laughed together at Juliusz Sczepaniak's little joke, even Jadwiga, who stood at the front looking ahead, watching through a renewed mist of rain, for signs of the sea.

Paul laughed, too, though less than the others. While his wife played community lookout in eager anticipation, he sat in mid-wagon, adrift in thought. The others had become a light-hearted band now that the difficult period of rail travel was over, now that the misery of the flatcar was behind them. Even though they were again crowded on a freight wagon, now they would be on a ship where they could wash, where food would come, where it would at last be dry, where they could at last settle instead of constantly changing from one conveyance to another.

Paul's reluctance to join in the community of satisfaction and anticipation had to do with his worries over the wisdom of this trip he had promised Jadwiga. It would not do, he thought, to stand by such a promise if it would mean lives of misery from then on. But here they were, already on their way. And she would insist, he knew, and it would be hard to be firm with her. And he lacked proof that this crazy surge to America was a mistake.

On the other hand, it was clear that this ragged group of emigrating people needed help—someone to guide them past those like the German cartmen in the freight depot who made sport of migrating Polacks—a need for leadership.

And more than anything, there was the need to keep his promise. In the end, whatever else might come, as long as Jadwiga wanted to go through with this madness, he was bound by his word. Bound, he was, by the foolishness of a promise given when his guard was down.

And Jadwiga was giving no sign of turning back.

They had become a large family, he thought. Standing, he looked around at them.

The Stecks, Kazimierz and Salomeya, were like grandparents, wise and steady, peacemakers, thoughtful and open to the love and caring of their fellow travelers.

Old Man Kradzinski, feeble, requiring constant care and attention lest he fall from his uncertain crutches and break something important inside his body...the old man whose name was already just *Old Man* to everyone except his grandchildren Jan and Jakub, who were routinely assigned to keep him warm at night.

With him, Tadeusz and Viktoria Murak, constantly giving the special attention, leading him to the privy on the moving car three and four times a night.

Juliusz Sczepaniak, funster, the clown who could not get enough of making people laugh, and of laughing himself.

Juliusz's Maria and his own Jadwiga—like young sisters, each awash in the glow of a child on the way, both spirited and enthusiastic, the quiet Maria the more so in the company of Jadwiga's gritty boldness and innocent readiness to challenge any obstacle.

Jozef Dominiak, *Big Jozef*, already everyone's big brother, all muscle and misplaced emotion, now ready to defend anyone in the group—even those who had earned his wrath. Back in the freightyard, there had been an incident when a worker tried to take Ignatz Ran's crate. Laughing, Big Jozef had lifted the worker over his head just to frighten him.

Ignatz, the littlest man a source of comedy just by standing next to his burly Kostanta, who might have flattened the worker herself, had Jozef not gotten there first.

Ursula Jakubik, the community's self-announced midwife, ready to serve Maria when her time of need would come. And if Jadwiga's time should come early...but Paul banished that thought from his mind.

The couple with the secret, the Karpczinski's, who really had some other name they were leaving behind. And Franciska, the child whose real name would always be with her.

The black sheep, Jan Poglicki, the stealer making trouble, perhaps forgiven too easily when his thievery could be excused as deserved by the German freight workers. Readily forgiven, it seemed, by all but his wife, Estella. She was more watchful of Jan than she was of their two-and three-year-olds, Stanisław and Katrina—even though Katrina had begun to cough and wheeze.

And the other children:

Franek Dominiak, who lifted their spirits with his intelligence and winning eyes. His sister Pelagia, everyone's concern when she coughed long and dry. The twins, Magda and Manya, together in weeping and crying, together constantly at either side of Delfinia, together at the directionless play of two-year-olds. Konrad, the creeper, an angel of quiet in Delfinia's thick arms.

The Ran children, stair-stepping from Bernadina's seven—by right of age in charge of any game played by more than one—down through Monika and Bolesław and David to Mikal, just finding his tongue at one and a half.

The Krulik brothers, Władek and Lancek, quick of mind like their father Stanisław, the thoughtful middle-aged intellectual who admitted to being good with machines, who had devised water-diverting tents to keep women and children dry aboard an open train.

Around him there was community talk, the laughter of a group that already had its small history of shared experiences: The stammering yard-man who was equally inarticulate in both German and Polish. The great chase, when the men nearly missed the train failing to get water. Paul himself, running with pails overhead, giving himself a bath. The carefree Galicians, led by Franek in music and marching. The stupid railyard policeman so easily baffled by the confusion of too many people aboard a car. The sight of Hamburg in the snow at dusk. And the moment when a clumsy freightyard cartman had tried to ram Tadeusz Murak's baggage, but missed, ending up an embarrassed and angry jumble of arms, legs, wheelbarrow, and pain.

With these things shared, he thought, they were now a moving village of people. They were all the more a community for their flaws.

These were good people, after all, Paul thought as he looked around—people with whom he could willingly cast his lot, given that they had this difficulty of a sea journey ahead of them, under German command. They would surely need his knowledge of the language to see them through.

So it was that as their wagon drew closer to the docks of Bremerhaven, Paul Adamik finally let go of his hope that Jadwiga would lift from him the burden of the mistaken promise to take her to America.

BOOK THREE

Chapter 17

The horses turned now, and with them attention turned to the wagon's new direction of travel.

"Jadwiga, does the teamster take us right?" Juliusz yelled. "What does your nose tell you?" The answer was evident, for it was a cobblestone road extending onto a planked pier.

Even before the wagon stopped, Jadwiga was bubbling with excitement. "The Frederika!" She turned to the other women. "This is a good ship…This is one of five sister ships Bismarck built years ago to name after his wife, Juliana Frederika Charlotte Dorothea…something…I've seen the drawings many times on big calendars in the fishmarket. They're fast. They've crossed the Atlantic many times in just thirty days."

There was no mistake. The teamster grunted and motioned at them to get off his wagon, sweeping his whole arm to show he meant baggage and all. Then he went up a wide gangway into the belly of the huge vessel, carrying the official papers of lading.

Truly, this Frederika was a magnificent ship. Heads had to be flung far back to look straight to her top. She was big, stable, heavy in the water. At rest, the tip of her masts traced hardly an arc in the sky. Sails furled, her rigging made a spider's lattice against the grey. To Jadwiga's eyes, she was power at rest—a surging orchestra restrained to quiescent wood and rope.

While the men passed baggage from the wagon to the pier, the women herded the children into a group to be watched and kept safe from the dangers of this new place.

Wagons came and went, pulled by teams of powerful draft horses. Cartmen more purposeful and disciplined than those of the railyard wheeled load after load into the belly of the ship, each one checked off a list in the hands of a calmly efficient loading master. Crates of machine parts went aboard, then hay and straw. There were pigs, chickens, and supplies of food in clearly marked bags, barrels, and boxes.

It was hard to know where to look next. It was taken as a good sign that a special group of cartmen moved only the baggage of certain passengers, and from the things being carried it was evident that moneyed Germans would be passengers. There was a new and pressing impatience to go aboard—to be part of this new world where there would be food and bathing water, a privy, and a place to rest. But a hawk-eyed officer with silver stripes on his sleeve looked down at them from the deck, and it was clear they were to wait.

Nearby, a worker watched a group of four cows, temporarily penned with ropes and waiting their turn to board. Some of the children were delighted to see two powerful workhorses, reddish-brown coats newly brushed, being led into the hold. But Franek Dominiak was transfixed by the ship, and Jadwiga was soon holding his hand, answering his questions, pointing at sections of rigging.

"The three big sticks? They're the masts, Franek." She smiled at his way of asking. "They are called 'masts.' And you see the pieces that go across on each one? They're called 'yards.'"

"Yards," Franek said, fixing the word in his memory.

"The sails are on the yards, tied up close. See them?" Franek nodded. "When it's time to go, the sailors will open up the sails to catch the wind. The yards can be pulled this way and that with the ropes—the ropes are called 'lines'—to turn the sails to best catch the wind."

"Lines."

"That's right."

Some of the Frederika's lower yards were 60 or 70 feet across. Jadwiga imagined the power and she envisioned the grand ship, all sails set, thrusting through waves. Her own experience, all with fishing schooners, had been mundanely practical. But she felt the tradition of wind-beaten sails flowing in her family blood. She knew of the traditions of the sea, and of the vaunted new clippers, racing passengers and cargo on routes around the world.

She sometimes felt a sadness, knowing more and more shipowners favored the new vessels of iron and steel, with steam engines and smaller sails. It was shock enough when she learned that some of the great sailing ships had ribs of steel, even though clad in wood. But ships dressed in metal made her think of pear trees bearing brass fruit, lacking understanding of their reason for existence. And a sailing ship shorn of the better part of its rigging and sails, smokestacks sticking out instead, suggested a beautiful princess with her hair burning away.

But on this day of boarding such a magnificent living thing for the journey to America, her heart was full of awe for the God-given power to capture the breezes blown down from heaven and use them to traverse oceans. There was the essence of miracle in this, she felt sure—a miracle like the brightness and curiosity of the little boy whose hand she held or the new life growing within her.

Impatience brought on a conviction that boarding was imminent. The Stecks were urged forward. The general agreement was that they should board first, just as they should be first to disembark in America, for they were the oldest, the rightful ones to go first.

But the Stecks hesitated. "Paul must go first," Salomeya said. "He understands even the Germans of book learning. And Jadwiga knows about ships. It is best for all of us if they go first. In America we will go first where we know the two American sons who will be waiting for us." Kazimierz nodded his agreement, and it was decided.

Jadwiga hugged Salomeya and kissed her.

But still they had to wait.

Their teamster came from within the hold of the ship. Without a word to them, he climbed upon his wagon and spoke to the horses and rumbled his wagon away off the pier.

And still they had to wait. Nearly an hour passed, and even Paul grew restless. He stood near the gangplank, taking upon himself the duty of keeping his fellow travelers clear of it, out of the way of the sailors who came and the workers who went. He yelled in German at Juliusz. "You! Stay clear!" Maria giggled. Her funmaker husband had strayed intentionally just so Paul would have an excuse to yell so the Germans would know that one among this group could speak their language. Jadwiga frowned at such foolishness amid so much seagoing purposefulness, but when the others laughed, she relented. At least Paul wasn't making a last-minute speech to her about staying and his prospects in Poland.

But the officer watching from the deck wasn't interested in language facility among passengers; his concern was the loading. The loading master appeared to be about to call for the milk cows to be boarded. But the officer signaled his determination that first, it would be the turn of the people. The loading master shouted something at them in German and gestured. The procession began.

So it was that Paul and Jadwiga were first up the gangplank past the scrutiny of the officer, who cared only about the tags around their necks.

Paul even saluted, but Jadwiga could forgive him even that in the same spirit she forgave the funmaking and yelling in German at Juliusz. She could forgive him much this day, she thought, for they were at the point of no turning back, and he didn't hesitate or lecture. He even smiled as he boarded, and there could be hope that he might leave behind his fits of deep and distracted thoughtfulness.

When they left the light of sky and free-blown air behind and gathered in a dim gangway between rows of second-class cabins, the travelers were the odiferous exception to a strong scent of soap and cleanliness everywhere. When the wealthy Germans came from their cabins to see what it was the ship was swallowing now, some of the women even shielded their noses behind the children they carried.

But Jadwiga stood proudly. She shined with a smile of anticipation. Her washboiler was copper-bright with a recent shine. From it, she took a red shawl that she spread across her shoulders. Even the buttons shined on her overcoat, bought by her father, new, at the clothes mart in Gdynia, not from a peddler of used goods. And yes, she carried herself with pride because she had a smart husband who knew how to deal with Germans in their unending stream of officious function. And because she had chosen a tall one, he even looked down on most of them.

Now an officer of lower rank motioned them into a widened gangway at midship. Under a large ship's lamp, he looked down to see what they were bringing aboard. Behind him, a seaman waited.

After a cursory inspection, the officer pointed out an area under the light where he wanted only the men to stand with the bags, boxes, and washboilers at their feet. "Women and children out of the way," he said.

Now the officer pointed while the sailor confiscated. They went from bag to box, washboiler to crate, taking lanterns, lamps, and candles. They even looked into small containers—pitchers, dippers, and sewing baskets—to take away all means that they could find of making fire.

Finally each man had to step out of line, take off his overcoat, and turn out his pockets. Most wore an extra layer of pants, and they removed the outer ones, leaving only the inner pair.

The young sailor felt through their clothes with searching fingers for anything they might be hiding inside their underclothing. The men found this embarrassing, but they knew it would do no good to protest, and they understood the need to take away fire-making materials.

But the sailor found no more contraband. When he reached Jan Poglicki, who had contrived to be the last inspected, he felt hard through Jan's heavy sweater, then motioned for him to take it off. He stepped back and gestured in accusation to his superior, forming a pistol with his hand.

But the things under Jan's belt were only a pair of flat-nosed pliers and a harmonica. He spoke Polish to the sailor in pretended explanation. "The harmonica isn't a lethal weapon except when played by a Galician, and the pliers are unusual only because they disappear when the railroad men of the wheelbarrows make trouble for Polish travelers."

This cocky admission of pickpocketing drew a restrained laugh from some in his own group, but only a shrug from the seaman, who was interested only in orders spoken in German. The officer in charge turned away with a grin on his face, amused by a passenger's concealment of such disparate objects. He went forward and up a wide ladder of steps leading to topside and the first-class deck. It meant they had passed the examination—even Jan Poglicki.

After the women helped with repacking, the young sailor signaled them all to follow him on a path of fresh sawdust leading to a large hatch held open by a counterbalance of pulleyed weights and strong springs. He led them forward, through the hatch, down a wide hard-wood ramp toward the bow. He negotiated it with quick, light steps to the base of the main, midship mast where it met the keel. He waited there, patting the two work horses.

They stepped carefully on the ramp lest they spill all they carried. Even watching their feet, they saw that the gangway running forward over the keel was lined on both sides with bales of hay and straw stacked nearly man-high almost to the crosstimbers supporting the second-class deck overhead.

This straw was a welcome sight, for now a warmth washed over them. Their noses were greeted by a pleasant patchwork of odors: the horses, bags of oats and barley; straw, hay—and still, the strong soap. Even the manure had a hearty freshness preferable to their own sweaty stink, and there was a satisfaction at the prospect of settling.

With both hands, Jadwiga held Paul's arm and looked around. An amber glow from two lanterns contributed to the sensation of warmth, flickering playfully on hues of wood, straw, burlap, horses, and people. As the emigrants gathered at the bottom of the ramp, they felt wrapped in a fabric of order here in the contented belly of a ship now ready to sail. Jadwiga rested her head on Paul's shoulder, and showed how pleased she was by tightening her grip on his arm. In response, he tightened the arm against his body. There was a new feeling of being in this adventure together.

When finally Tadeusz and Viktoria had helped Old Man Kradzinski all the way to the foot of the ramp, the young seaman coaxed the horses to one side, murmuring at them. Then he waved to them to follow him again, and walked past the hay and straw, past stanchions waiting for cows, to yet another hatchway, this one upright, farther toward the bow. It had a top and bottom double-door leading to another compartment. The sailor opened it, and waved them through, up a pair of steps.

Past the door, it was darker. The odors were darker, too, less of hay, more of sea water and fresh water and soaked wood. Calves were just inside the hatchway on either side. And the pigs were there, too, with their paired pungencies of swill and new manure.

Paul, still leading, paused. Just a few steps forward of the hatchway there was a small pile of manure, and it was evident why the hatch had a double door—for manure from the cows to be shoveled through the upper half into this pig pen compartment. He pointed so Jadwiga would see, and she pointed for Delfinia Dominiak, and so on as each found the way around the pile, then around a large wooden rainwater vat, then around the base of the forward mast, then into a larger space between the mast and a framework of bracing at the bow. Here, the gangway became a slatted drainage deck, spread over the contour of the ship's keel.

Again, they stood with their possessions. Many of the men and even some of the women had to stoop or stand with their heads placed between the crosstimbers.

A ship's lantern with a copper base and brass handles gave light. As their eyes adjusted once again, they could see the pig pens, mounted on the ship's ribs, raised above the drainage decking. Overhead, there was the sound of water trickling in hardwood troughs that led to the rainwater vat.

"No soap in the water barrel," the seaman said. He barked out the German words, and to make certain they understood, he held a cake of soap and pointed to it and the water barrel, shaking his head, then motioning with his arms that these two things were not to be mixed. "No soap in the water barrel," he said again.

Then he turned, spit into the manure pile, and slipped quickly through the hatchway, not looking back. Paul followed, expecting more instructions and wanting to ask questions, but the German slammed the hatchway hard in closing punctuation of his encounter with these Polacks.

Paul wasn't so much angered as unpleasantly surprised, feeling tricked into a box and trapped. He was certain the sailor had seen him following.

But this was just the sort of place they had prayed for all day. The rainwater was stream clean and there were many cakes of soap on a shelf screwed to the crosstimbers near the rainbarrel. They could wash, and the dirty water and soap would drain through the slatted flooring and flow away beneath them. Forward, lengths of rope tied between every other crosstimber would serve as clotheslines.

Eager to wash, the women were already hanging the wet blankets to screen themselves. Little was said. Everyone knew the women would begin the cleansing and housekeeping, and the men must make way. Their turn would come after their wives had washed the children, then themselves.

They gathered around the manure pile, backs to the calves, aft of the water vat, which would further screen the women.

There was consternation. Paul was quiet with it. Stanisław Krulik patted him on the back. "Only the young and most stupid of the Germans turns away from you, Paul. I've been watching. You get farther with the smarter ones—the older ones of high office."

There was anger. Big Jozef, who was holding his little Pelagia because she was too sickly for a cold water wash, said "Paul, I wish for the day I will meet this one who slams the door in your face. Perhaps it will be on an American pier where I will slam *him*—down to the ground."

There was uncertainty. "Is this to be our part, then? With the pigs?" Ignatz Ran asked. "He didn't say anything, the German. How are we to know?"

"It will be best if we resign ourselves to the pigs and the low ceiling," Stanisław said. "If there is a change for the better, we will adapt."

There was hunger. "I could resign to almost anything if I could only have a big plate of goulash right now," Ludwig Karpczinski said.

Stanisław shrugged. "We've paid for food aboard this ship. The Germans will bring something soon, I should think."

They stood with their backs to the warmth of the calves. Big Jozef put Pelagia stomach-down on one. She coughed less, and she could sleep. He had only to cover her with his sweater and hold her so she wouldn't slide off. Anyway, there was the understanding among the men that the sturdy calf would absorb some of the little girl's sickness.

Partly so she might sleep, but mostly because there was little to be said, the men talked only fitfully.

After a while, Jan Poglicki said, "If I were you I would not worry about this German who slams doors, Paul." But that subject was no longer of interest to anybody, and they were quiet again. Nearby, behind the blankets, children shrieked, protesting cold water.

Ignatz Ran said, "Perhaps it is only because we're dirty that the German shut us in with the pigs. When we have washed away whatever bugs we've brought into this boat, maybe they will open the door for us."

"We should resign ourselves," Stanisław said.

"Everything about this place is clean," said Kazimierz Steck. "It's well scrubbed, all of it. You can smell the soap. Anyway, if we can run the gauntlet of the freighthouse workers, this is nothing for us to deal with."

They laughed at the mention of the railyard wheelbarrow pushers, except for Ignatz, who said, "You know, I really thought I was a dead man when that fellow came after my crate. Jozef, I thank you again."

"Jozef, what was it that kept you from breaking the man in half?" asked Tadeusz Murak.

"It was only that Paul suggested that it would be more useful to borrow the man's wheelbarrow as punishment for his ignorance. But now I think I should have smashed him anyway."

"The one who bothered me took enough punishment for both when Paul feinted him over the edge of the platform," Tadeusz said. "It may be they're still trying to figure out what parts are his and what parts go with his wheelbarrow."

Now there was laughter at the image of the worker trying to crowd Tadeusz and being force-fed his own medicine. And in the midst of this good feeling there was yet more laughter when Magda and Manya Dominiak toddled toward them, bouncing with the excitement of being clean and fresh. They ran to their father to be dried from their bath. Their teeth chattered from the cold rinsing, but Big Jozef rubbed them with their towel until they were warm. While he did, Kazimierz Steck watched to see that Pelagia would not slip from her place on the calf.

Other children came squealing to their fathers, clean and chilled. Both Jozef and Ignatz soon had hands full, so Paul and Juliusz, as yet without squealing young ones of their own, assisted in drying and warming child after child.

When his daughter came from behind the blankets, Ludwig Karpczinski squatted down and held out his arms and yelled, to her delight, "Look at my Teresa!" Then he caught himself. "Franciska! I mean Franciska! Look at my Franciska!" And there was more laughter all around.

The children brought out their feelings of love, and there was this small happiness among them.

Chapter 18

Behind the blankets, Salomeya Steck was washed and combed and pampered by Jadwiga and Maria, who by now had fully adopted her as their grandmother. Thus she was first to emerge from the washing, smiling and still serene, to be welcomed warmly by all the men.

The other women followed one by one. Without hesitation, the Jakubik youths went immediately to Ursula, who stood while they combed and braided her hair, one on each side. There were glances among the men, but they took care that Piotr not see.

Some of the women were a surprise. Where layers of clothing had given them a bulky appearance on the train, Polka Karpczinski and Viktoria Murak now turned out to be of unexpectedly handsome proportions. More of Polka's face showed, and it was striking for its character—and for a deeply dimpled chin.

Jan Poglicki's Estella emerged wearing a pleated light brown Sunday dress of her own making—one she would show to American employers, she told Viktoria, in seeking work as a seamstress.

When Jadwiga and Maria joined their husbands at the manure pile, the soot of train travel was gone, their hair was combed and clean, and cheeks showed red from scrubbing. Juliusz nudged Paul broadly. "Who are these pretty girls? Perhaps we can get to know them before our wives come out!"

Kostanta Ran and Delfinia Dominiak came out last, and now each was all the more a contrast with her husband—Kostanta because of her great size as against Ignatz's smallness, and Delfinia because she was so short standing next to Big Jozef, and smiling amiably where he had shown little of his lighter side.

The children and all the women now had a clean freshness about them. They smelled of tallowed naphtha so that even in the confinement of the Frederika's forward hold the spirit was that of a picnic moved into a barn to escape a sudden rain. But the men were out of place, still burdened with wet clothing, faces still streaked with the grime of rail travel, beards dirty and uncomfortably unkempt. Even those who had joined in a pact to let beards grow all the way to America agreed there would be ample time later. They all wanted to shave.

They left the women and youngest children at the manure pile, but they were quickly disappointed to discover there was water enough for only two or three to wash. Stanisław Krulik suggested Paul should bathe first. "He'll have to talk to the Germans of this ship for us when they come. Anyway, it's still raining outside, and the barrel will soon fill again."

So it was that Paul was behind the blankets, washing, during the incident of Maria, Jadwiga, and the hunchback.

Leaving the children to the women, the men now explored this dim place with little headroom. Though sold as steerage class, the term exaggerated the merits of the space. Where crosstimbers supported the deck above, the taller men had to take care not to bang their heads, a condition progressively worse nearer the point of the bow. There, past the pigpens, there was a repair—a reinforcement of the very point of the Frederika with a cross of hardwood studding. At angles to the horizontal piece of this cross, two more pieces of hardwood reached to the curvature of the ship's keel. Boards formed a kind of triangular platform raised to waist level. Below it, a tattered sail was stored or forgotten. Above, it was spacious enough for Jan and Juliusz to crawl in for a rest while waiting for water. The rest of the men leaned or sat on the brim of the pigpens, their backs to the warmth of the animals.

Tadeusz Murak tried to encourage conversation between Kazimierz Steck and his father-in-law, Old Man Kradzinski. Despite their ranking as the most elderly, the two old men had very little in common, and Tadeusz found himself carrying the burden of a conversation going nowhere.

The Krulik and Jakubik boys talked together, and this left their fathers, Stanisław and the Russian Piotr, with Big Jozef Dominiak. But Jozef participated only when Stanisław spoke directly to him. In the way he stood, putting Piotr as much behind him as possible, it was clear he wanted no involvement with the man. Before long, Stanisław gave up and attended to an animated conversation between Ludwig Karpczinski and Ignatz Ran.

Sitting together, Ludwig and Ignatz were counting piglets suckling at six of the eight big white sows. Some were newborn, some near weaning.

To Ignatz's practiced farm eye, a plan was evident: their young weaned, one by one the sows would go to the chopping block once the ship was under way.

From this plan for systematic propagation of pork, Ignatz calculated that the Germans were prepared for a crossing of six to eight weeks. Depending on how soon the two remaining sows would yield, it could be even longer, he explained to Ludwig. With these figures in mind, each man cast a measuring eye past the rainwater vat to Maria and Jadwiga, who stood together at the double door, ears pressed to hear anything from the other side.

While Maria watched, Jadwiga tinkered with the latch on the top half of the door. She easily discovered how to open it, even though it was constructed for opening from the other side. But the door itself was stuck, the wood damp and swollen. Only when Jadwiga and Maria pushed together did it spring free.

But it didn't swing far. It stopped with a resonant thud, an unexpected sound which immediately gave way to a bellowing. Then the door was pulled open and suddenly Maria screamed, backing away from the hatchway.

Jadwiga didn't scream, but she too backed away, startled by Maria's scream but also startled by the spectre rising from behind the bottom half of the door.

It was a mass of scraggly black hair shooting off in every direction, with wild eyes and an open mouth from which emitted the bellowing, and now cursing. The beast had a hand brought up to the place where a forehead might be hiding, then a second hand, and it wheeled about in the pain of having been struck there by the careering door.

When it pivoted this way and that in pain, it could be seen to be a man. A strange looking one, to be sure: a hunchback, German by his profanity, a hairy apparition made the more ferocious by the pitch and intensity of the cries.

Instantly, Juliusz was off the triangular perch at the bow, running to see what so terrified his wife. Maria, barely catching her breath, turned and ran blindly into his arms. Others were coming, too, jolted into action by the sudden commotion.

"What is it? What's happening?" asked Polka Karpczinski.

By now Jadwiga's surprise was becoming nervous fascination as she watched the hunchback, who still pirouetted in pain and bluster. "It's nothing," she said. "Only a peeper at the crack of the door." Unable to hold back, she began to laugh.

Paul, naked and unable to come out from behind the blankets, yelled, "What is it out there?"

Nobody knew what to say. All they knew was what they saw and heard: a prodigious leaping about and an uninterrupted abundance of German syllables. Jadwiga couldn't answer. She was laughing. Others began to laugh, too.

The hunchback's rage needed no translation. He was infuriated—a pretty young girl screaming at the sight of him, another in a sputter of giggles at his pain. And now a crowd gathering—Polacks yet, laughing at him. He took one hand from his head and reached out to the open half-door, and slammed it with all his force. But he slammed so hard that the latch didn't catch and the door merely rebounded.

He stormed and yelled something more. They realized he thought one of them had pushed the door back. He slammed it again. But Jadwiga, amused by the notion, pushed the door out again.

"Polack bastards!" the man yelled in German.

"Blood-of-a-dog German!" Jadwiga yelled in Polish.

Twice more he slammed the door. Twice, more boldly each time, Jadwiga pushed it open. The man was all the more angry, seeing her so playful.

His pants finally on, Paul came charging out from behind the blankets, half-shaved, half in lather, just as the German turned away from the door, letting Jadwiga have her way with it. Despite the smear of soap, Paul's face showed futility in his effort to understand the situation from the fragments he saw.

"*Psia krew niemiec!*" Jadwiga yelled again.

"Jadwiga, stop this! What are you doing?"

Ludwig and Ignatz and Polka and Big Jozef all started to answer at the same time while Jadwiga simply enjoyed her triumph.

Paul could see through the open hatchway that a ship's officer was just coming down the ramp, interrupting whatever it was between the German and Jadwiga. It was the one who had scrutinized them just hours before to make certain each had a ticket. Now it was he who bellowed in German, pointing a gloved finger into the face of the hunchback, scolding wrathfully. So intense were his phrases that Paul couldn't grasp all the words, but he gathered a serious infraction had been committed a second or even a third time.

It seemed like minutes before it ended. In his hand the officer waved pasteboard papers three times the size of tickets. The hunchback said nothing, simply standing meekly for the reprimand.

Now the officer turned toward the Adamiks, who stood at the fore of a gathering of astonished passengers. It appeared he was about to give another scolding, and Jadwiga was again on the offensive.

"Tell this one," she said to Paul, "tell him in your German words about this miscreant who peeks and slams. Tell him. Tell him he frightened Maria, who is with child. And tell him we all are hungry!"

Paul squirmed. He had no intention of telling the man anything of the kind, but she wouldn't let up. "Hush, Jadwiga, so I can tell him. Hush." Then, in German phrases assembled in greater haste than he would wish, he said to the officer, "There appears to be a dispute."

"Ah, you're the one who speaks German. Good. I couldn't recognize you with all that soap smeared across your face." Gesturing toward Jadwiga, who stood hands on hips, fire still in her eyes, he asked, "Is this your wife?"

"She is, sir."

"My compliments."

"Sir?"

"My compliments to you for your selection. She is not only beautiful, she also has a good spirit."

"Thank you, sir."

Then to Jadwiga, Paul said, "The officer says this kind of thing, whatever it was, is not to happen any more."

"What about food? We have already paid for food. When will we eat?"

"Jadwiga, please. Let me talk with the man. It is hard enough in German without all this help you give me."

The officer smiled at her, and Jadwiga settled back from her toes onto her heels.

"You were wearing a uniform earlier. Were you in the army?"

"Yes, sir, a sergeant of Bismarck."

He handed Paul the pasteboards he carried. "Good. Please hang these on the mast. They are the rules and conditions for steerage, one in German, one Polish. If you abide by rules here as you did in the army, and if your people do, we will have no quarrels, you and I."

"Yes, sir, Herr Shiffmeister." Paul saluted.

The officer returned the salute before turning to leave, and Paul was pleased. Jadwiga frowned at him. She knew he hadn't asked about food.

As Paul turned to hang the pasteboard cards of rules, he saw that Maria Sczepaniak was half sitting, half lying on the drainage deck near the rainbarrel. Juliusz stooped next to her. Salomeya Steck knelt, left hand on Maria's pregnancy, right hand raised in prayerful entreaty.

She prayed aloud: "Jesus, save us. Jesus, deliver this child from evil.

"Blessed Mary, give this mother peace and a straight child of good health."

The women all lowered their heads in prayer.

Chapter 19

It was women's business, Paul knew—this matter of the jeopardy to the straightness of Maria's child. The grandmother Salomeya Steck and the midwife Ursula Jakubik had knowledge of these things. He didn't entirely subscribe to the belief that now haunted these wives as they prayed to Holy Mary. But he didn't know to a certainty. It was best, he thought, to allow the women their ways.

From what he heard, Jadwiga hadn't screamed. Going by what he saw, she certainly wasn't frightened by the hunchback. But it seemed to him a natural thing when Jadwiga knelt with Salomeya while the old woman prayed for her child, too. Prayer couldn't hurt, he thought.

But he felt awkward, standing with bowed head, naked above the waist, half-shaved, soap drying on his face. Furtively, the other men glanced at him occasionally as the grandmother beseeched saint after saint on behalf of Maria and Jadwiga and their babies. But they stole glances at Juliusz, too—glances that suggested pity—and Paul didn't like the feeling. But he realized that, like Juliusz, he should be at the side of his wife for this supplication to the Almighty and His saints, so he went to them and knelt, too, next to Jadwiga.

He gave his hand to comfort her.

She gave a little squeeze to tell him not to worry.

Her child would be a straight one, she knew, strong and smart and tall like him. A brave child, like her father who went to the Baltic day after day, year after year, bringing fish from sea to market through high waves and cold storms. A good child, like her blessed mother of memory, who lived now in heaven with Jesus. A clever child, good with his hands, able to tie nets, perhaps, like her brother Konstanty. A gentle child, like her brother Konrad.

An American child.

Jadwiga realized tears were flowing from her eyes. They were tears of happiness thinking of her baby, and tears of goodbye for her father and her brothers—tears she had let go only partly in farewells at Gdynia and Gdansk.

She knew she must stop these tears lest they worry Paul, who needed nothing more to trouble him, so she called to mind something funny— the bellowing hunchback at the doorway. Immediately, she had to suppress that thought, lest she laugh while Salomeya prayed.

Better to concentrate and pray, instead of the sacrilege of laughing, even at the hunchback. She turned her mind to listening to Salomeya, and her eyes to Maria. Maria had been frightened by the hunchback, true, but now she was all the more alarmed with the weight of prayer Salomeya gave to making straight children against the threat of a bent back.

Poor Maria, Jadwiga thought, so disposed to fret, so in need of a big sister to hide behind. If only they could have been sisters before now, when she might have taken Maria to sea to fish and be bold even while being careful.

The praying ended just in time, as a new odor fought its way through the collage of scents in the air. Through the hatchway, two young German galley helpers carried a heavy iron cauldron of soup smelling grandly of ham. One took a basket from a shoulder and handed it to Lancek Krulik, who hurriedly passed out its contents of bowls and spoons.

Everyone hastened to arrange baggage as tables or sitting places. They did so quietly, for the air remained dense with the seriousness of prayer. The men, who had followed the lead of the women in solemnity, remained hushed waiting for the women to be first to ease the covenant of quiet.

But the arrival of food lightened the hearts of the children. They came to Estella Poglicki, who acted in substitute for Salomeya. It was understood that Salomeya would normally portion the soup, but she was weary from the burden of praying.

Franek Dominiak, whose eyes had been wide with wonder, brow furrowed with questions during the praying, was the first to speak when he handed his sister Pelagia the bowl of soup he fetched for her.

"Be careful, it's hot. Don't spill it."

So earnest was Franek in his role of big brother that almost everyone laughed softly, and the sharp edges of tension went dull. Gradually, they began to converse, carefully avoiding the subject of the hunchback.

Before finishing his shaving, Paul helped Salomeya to the framework of repairs at the bow, and with Jozef lifted her into it so that she might rest. With a boost from Jozef, Kazimierz joined her. Jadwiga spoke quietly with Maria, and together they took soup to the Stecks. It was a relief that Maria was not stricken in any serious way.

Quiet groups of conversation formed—the Stecks with the Adamiks and Sczepaniaks at the point of the bow, the Poglickis sitting on the edge of a pigpen platform with the Rans, the Dominiaks with the Karpczinskis on boxes in the middle of the drainage deck, Stanisław Krulik nearby with his sons and the Muraks and Old Man Kradzinski.

It happened that Piotr and Ursula Jakubik and sons Voytek and Vicek were part of no group except their own. In the cramped quarters, there was no circulation from group to group, so the Russians appeared to be outcasts kept apart. All the adults noticed but, remembering the incident of water unshared aboard the train, none troubled to solicit the company of the Russians.

When he reached the bottom of a bowl of soup, Paul remembered the pasteboards of rules the officer had given him. He took out the one printed in Polish.

> *There will be a penalty of only bread to eat and water to drink throughout the voyage for anyone caught even touching a ship's lantern.*
>
> *On penalty of having the water barrel sealed with cover and padlock, water is to be used for bathing only when the barrel is full above the red line (more than two-thirds full).*
>
> *The ship's doctor is to be called in the event of sickness, particularly fever.*
>
> *Two bales of straw for bedding are provided at the start of travel, and one each week thereafter.*

At night, the rules went on, the straw was to be spread over the canvas provided; in the day, the canvas was to be hung from the timberwork, straw inside, away from the lantern.

While Paul read, the hunchback appeared at the door, hefting a bale of straw up to the top edge of the lower part. Paul thought it odd that the man didn't open the bottom half to make it easy, until he pushed the bale through to land squarely in the manure pile. Then he did the same with a second bale, taking care that it hit the first bale to mash it down even more. Then he swung his head around from its normally bowed position to look in at the Polacks, to be sure they understood who it was they had offended.

As the supply of soup was gradually exhausted, thought turned again to rest—sleep to recover from the tiredness imposed by a day of transition from flatcar to freighthouse to wagon to pier to ship, a day of anticipation and waiting, of disappointment and worry, but a day of satisfaction in the start of this last leg to America—the boarding of a ship.

The Krulik boys went about collecting the bowls and spoons. There was discussion of whether they were to be kept by each family, or kept in a common place. But Estella Poglicki suggested the Germans would collect them, and Jadwiga said she thought this might be the case, since it would conserve fresh water to wash them in one place.

But for tonight, Jadwiga said, it would surely be all right to wash them, for there would be no strictures on the use of water until they were at sea.

"We're not at sea yet?" asked Maria, surprised.

"We're at dockside," Jadwiga said, surprised by Maria's question.

Jadwiga started to get up, to take the eating implements from Viktoria Murak, with whom they had been deposited. She understood that she and Maria would do this washing; they had no children to tend, and they were the youngest among the women. But with a gesture, Polka Karpczinski told Jadwiga not to trouble; she would do it. Jadwiga, after all, was with child and she had been victimized by the hunchback. It was a day for exceptions. Then Polka asked, too: "You mean to say we aren't sailing yet?"

"When the Germans put her to the weather, you will know we are sailing."

Polka and Viktoria together began the washing, on the floor at the rainbarrel near the mast. The other women joined them to listen to this talk of ships and sailing by the fisherman's daughter who knew of such things. Children listened too, particularly Franek Dominiak, attentive as always when questions were asked and answers given.

The gathering of the women at the water barrel cleared a space for bathing by the men for whom there had been no water earlier. Ursula Jakubik didn't join the women, and Piotr seemed to be waiting his turn to bathe.

"How will we know?" asked Polka.

"Well, you will listen to the ship, for one thing. She will speak to us."

So that Jozef Dominiak might wash, Paul held Pelagia to warm her. He studied the pasteboard of steerage rules, giving particular attention to the rule about sleeping arrangements. By precedent of the last night on the flatcar, there was an expectation that Stanisław Krulik would endeavor to organize the sleeping, but Stanisław wanted to share the responsibility with someone.

"How does the ship speak, Jadwiga?" Kostanta Ran asked.

"The noises. The wood will rub and creak." She put her ear to the mast. "You can hear it."

"What does it say now?" Franek asked. "Does it speak like the Germans or like the Polacks?"

"Poles, Franek. Not Polacks." Delfinia smiled at him. "That is a bad word the Germans call us. We are Poles."

"Papa says 'Polacks' sometimes. So does Bernadina's father."

Kostanta glanced at Delfinia, and saw that it was all right for her to respond. "Yes, my husband Ignatz and the other men say 'Polacks' sometimes, but it is when they wish to express that the Germans have contempt for us."

"Or sometimes it is because to say 'Polack' among themselves makes the men feel more together, more united," Delfinia added. "It is a word that is used in special ways, Franek, some very bad and some perhaps not so bad. If you listen carefully you will learn when it is not so bad to use it."

"Like talking to God," Franek said.

"Yes, like talking to God."

Franek hadn't forgotten his question of Jadwiga. "What does the boat say now?"

"Listen."

As Jadwiga had done, Franek pressed his ear against the mast. His eyes widened.

"It sings. Hums."

"That's right."

"It only knows one note."

Jadwiga laughed. Several of the women pressed their ears against the mast, joining four-year-old Jan Murak and seven-year-old Bernadina Ran, who had followed Franek.

Paul glanced up from his reading of rules just as Stanisław Krulik and Ignatz Ran came from their washing. A puzzled smile spread across each man's face, and Paul realized how odd this must look to someone who hadn't heard the conversation: Three young children and four grown women pressing the sides of their heads against this giant piece of furniture.

"The boat is singing," Franek said to them. "It is, really." He stepped aside as his way of suggesting they listen.

They did. Both men put ears to the mast. Paul, seeing it all through fresh eyes as Big Jozef returned from washing, laughed quietly.

"See?"

"Yes, Franek, it does sing." Stanisław winked at Ignatz.

Franek still pressed Jadwiga. "But what does it say?"

"It tells us some wind has come to blow the rain away. You can hear the wind in the mast."

Franek listened again.

"But when they put the sails on the masts, there will be a different sound to tell us that we are sailing. You will see."

"Does it have more notes then?"

Jozef Dominiak watched his son of seven years asking questions of Jadwiga. Children, it seemed to him, were a tightly wrapped bundle of such questions, constantly coming unraveled. Answers didn't help. Answers just mated with the questions and bred more questions. A child could ask, and ask, and ask some more, until answers and questions alike made the head sore.

But he had been like that, too, though not so much as Franek, whose questions Delfinia encouraged. His own parents had discouraged questions, so he more often asked his big sister. But even she wasn't as patient as Delfinia, who almost never shut off the flow.

A man could give answers only so long. It would be well, in America, to be the provider again. To have the pride of work and the appreciation of wife and family for food brought to the table. There was work in America, and payment in good money. Perhaps it would be as the Galicians claimed, that a contract would be necessary, but there would be work to be the provider, he felt sure.

Jozef saw that Paul and Stanisław had their heads together at the pasteboard of rules, which now hung on the mast. He looked down to read it, while Ignatz Ran stood immediately in front of him, looking up to read it.

"The canvas is the one below the timberwork up front, I think," Stanisław said. "It's an old sail."

The last of the men had finished washing and shaving, so wet blankets now were hung off to one side. Dry ones were folded. Baggage was moved to one side. Jadwiga climbed into the bow cribwork to sit between Kazimierz and Salomeya and watch preparation of the sleeping space.

When spread out over the slatted deck between the water barrel and the reinforcement of the bow, the canvas made an adequate sleeping area for everyone. "This is particularly true," Paul said to Stanisław, "if the Stecks sleep up in the cribwork. Each night, we'll help them get up there."

"And I believe Big Jozef and Jan will be holding their sick ones on the calves, at least tonight. They will probably sleep in shifts." Then Stanisław spoke to his sons. "Władek, Lancek, bring the straw. Clean off the manure. Leave that part behind for the twisted German to sleep on."

With the straw spread on the canvas, families looked to Stanisław and Paul to suggest a sleeping order, and it was quickly seen that men back to back, women back to back, children between man and wife, would be the best arrangement. There were the exceptions of Jozef and Jan with their daughters and the calves, and Stanisław with no wife, but when places were assigned, it worked out nicely.

The Adamiks and Sczepaniaks would be nearest the bow, Juliusz with his back to one of Stanisław's sons; Ludwig and Polka Karpczinski next, Estella Poglicki next to her, the Dominiak children except for Pelagia, then their mother Delfinia. Viktoria Murak, her children, and husband Tadeusz would follow next in order, Ignatz Ran to Tadeusz's back. After the Ran brood there would be Kostanta back to back with Ursula Jakubik and finally would come the three Jakubik men, Piotr and his sons of manly age next to the rainbarrel. Old Man Kradzinski would sleep with the Murak children, as usual, in the space between Tadeusz and Viktoria.

Now Piotr Jakubik, who had been quiet and apart with his wife and sons through all the praying and eating and socializing, raised an objection. "This isn't right. You put my family next to the rainbarrel where it is lowest and coldest. There are younger ones who can better keep warm there."

Stanisław, who throughout the trip had not yet uttered a word in anger, responded quickly when his fairness was challenged. "You want the young and pregnant ones to trade with you? Is that what you have in mind?"

"You have two grown boys and no woman," Piotr shot back. And it is plain to see you have placed yourself in the middle where it is the warmest, back to back with Juliusz where I belong."

Paul defended Stanisław. "Since when is it that you should pick this warmest place for yourself?"

"Since Sczepaniak's wife is pregnant and my Ursula is a midwife. They will need us. Not tonight or tomorrow, perhaps, but the need will come. And it may be that your wife, too, will need us one night." Ursula set her head back, chin out to punctuate what Piotr said.

Jozef Dominiak straightened, glaring at Piotr. In the cribwork with the Stecks, Jadwiga's back stiffened and she braced herself with her hands, prepared to jump down to join the argument. Salomeya restrained her with a hand on her shoulder.

Ludwig Karpczinski saved Paul from having to challenge the Russian over the matter of midwifery. "Because your Ursula is a midwife does not mean that you will hold this over our heads, or over the heads of the pregnant ones."

Big Jozef still glared at Piotr, fists clenched. Piotr saw it. Unvented anger reached across the space between them, and the atmosphere seared with friction. Delfinia watched Jozef closely, and appeared ready to hold him back from a fight.

In the repairwork, Kazimierz spoke quietly to Jadwiga. "I know what you want to say to Piotr, Jadwiga. But don't. Think of Maria. Don't antagonize Ursula. Jadwiga, say something that will change this bickering."

Jadwiga turned her head, considering this radical suggestion. Salomeya nodded to encourage her. She jumped down. "Paul and Stanisław have tried their best, and it's all good, but there is one mistake. But this is understandable because the German army doesn't travel in the holds of ships."

The argument stopped. Jadwiga had everyone's attention, and now she spoke slowly to let feelings of grievance give way to curiosity.

"Near the bow it will be coldest and loudest once the ship is under way. That's why the bow has been repaired. It's taken too many hits of the waves already. It isn't the best place. Kazimierz and Salomeya will do well tonight while we are at rest, but after that, they should be the ones to sleep in the middle, for warmth and to be away from the rumble.

"So the Krulik boys should be in the box of repairwork after tonight. And it might be that we will want to do some other changing around once we see how the Frederika goes."

There was a new texture to the tension in the air, a softening—compromise. Piotr, who saw that he had all the others arrayed against him, took the last words.

"It is settled," he said.

Jadwiga glanced at Kazimierz and Salomeya. Smiling barely perceptibly, both nodded their heads to her. On the drainage deck, Jozef took his eyes from Piotr only when the Russian turned away to spread a blanket.

"Jozef fought beside Romuald Traugutt in the Dziadkowicki Forest," Delfinia told Jadwiga late that night after children were asleep. "In the January Rising in 1863?" She paused to see if Jadwiga knew this bit of history from the Russian sector. Jadwiga nodded.

"He was decorated, even," Delfinia said proudly. "He fought the Russians because of the decrees about the church—that to be Catholic is to be a revolutionary. And while he was away his brother helped us with the family.

"But Traugutt was betrayed, and others with him, and they were put in Pawiak Prison. There was a mistake—the Russians made a mistake—and Jozef's brother was taken instead of Jozef. There was torture. There was nothing that could be done. His brother sent word out to Jozef asking, as a final request, that Jozef leave Poland. Jozef carries his written message. It says, 'My brother, this is a fair sharing of our fight for Poland's freedom: You have done the fighting, and I will do the dying. But you yourself must be free even if our country cannot be.' Jozef wanted to stay—to find some way to free his brother, but there was nothing...The last we saw of him he was shackled in a long line of others—all the best young men—being walked to Siberia. We will never know what finally happened to him."

"This is why Jozef hates the Russians so much."

"Yes. Everything Russian. But there isn't a Pole in the Russian partition who doesn't hate them, Jadwiga. Muravyev, the Hangman, has seen to it that in all of Lithuania there's not one family that hasn't been touched by exile or torture. There was no law. Our village was destroyed—reduced to a nothingness. We moved to another village, and it happened again. Jozef takes his promise to his brother, made in a gesture of farewell when we saw him in the line of shackled men, as a sacred obligation.

"We will never see Poland again."

Chapter 20

It was a curious thing, thought Jan Poglicki. The hunchback, with a whole hay-filled compartment to himself as his quarters just to watch horses and cows, had the luxury of a king. And yet, the man was abusive.

Jan stood with his head bowed, listening to Salomeya slowly invent a bedtime prayer. From the dark corner where his Katrina and Jozef's Pelagia slept on the backs of calves, he could see that the hunchback moved about the midship compartment with ease, despite vision restricted by the hang of his head.

He was abusive with peeking and bad language to pregnant women and sleeping straw thrown into manure. And then, when the Russian youths had been looking out the hatch admiring the horses, the man had chosen just that moment to throw manure through, just so he could catch them, mouths agape, square in the faces.

A good thing Piotr had been involved in the argument over sleeping arrangements. Had he not—had he seen his gawking sons splattered with the cows' first shipboard leavings, the hunchback's body would by now have a bend or two more.

But that would have been trouble, real trouble. Even while tied up at shore there must be some terrible punishment for attacking a member of a ship's crew, Jan was sure. It wouldn't matter, really. The Germans were in control and there would be no attempt to assign proper blame for any incident. Automatically, the Polacks would be at fault.

Anyway, the hunchback's abusiveness called for a punishment more subtle and long-lasting than the knob that had grown on his forehead or even having his back broken in yet another direction.

Salomeya's prayer went on. He himself would say a little prayer, Jan thought, that Salomeya would have an attack of quick speaking and short-ened praying. It wasn't that he didn't believe in the Holy Church and the saints and the rest. It was just that people went on so about it. Surely God had plenty of prayers to listen to. Better to save the elongated talks with Him until there was something really important to discuss—perhaps the maiming of the unborn child of Juliusz's wife. Perhaps like that.

The hunchback shambled about the midship compartment, sticking to the gangway between bales of hay where the going was easiest. He was carrying something toward the forward hatchway—something heavy. He paused, hearing the praying. Quietly, he opened the bottom half of the hatchway, and put two buckets through.

Swill. Swill for the pigs. The leavings of the meal of crew and upper-deck passengers.

At least the man had respect for prayer in progress. At least he didn't burst in sloshing hogwash about. Perhaps if Salomeya could save the long praying for just these times...

When the prayer ended, Big Jozef came to check on his Pelagia, and held Katrina, too, while Jan went forward to pour the buckets of slop into the troughs. The sows immediately made a noisy meal of it. He set the buckets down on the other side of the hatch for the hunchback to pick up. He suspected the man had in mind to wait until people were asleep, then to make a boisterous business of hog feeding. He would find only the emptied pails.

"I'll watch first," Jozef said, gently rubbing Pelagia's back. "You sleep."

"No, I can't sleep so early. You sleep first."

"Did you hear the Russian?"

"Yes."

"He is big, and he thinks he can scare us. I was about to break open his throat for him."

"He isn't worth it, Jozef. Wait until America."

"He shows his contempt for us."

"It doesn't matter. He's only one Russian, strong only when the Czar's armies march behind him. They beat us with better guns, but we are better people. Don't bother with him."

"Damn him." His fist doubled, the big man clung to his feelings for a moment. "Wake me, then, when you get tired. If she wakes up, just rub her back." Jozef went off to join the others.

Jan took over the rubbing. He could rub the back of only one child at a time, precarious as it was atop these calves. His Katrina slept well, so he rubbed Pelagia.

Poor Pelagia. She sounded so hollow when she coughed, as though something were eating out her lungs a day at a time. Jozef already had so much to contend with, he thought. Why did he look for fights, too? Retaliation could be so much sweeter if done with finesse. And less a risk.

The hunchback approached on the midship gangway again, this time looking from side to side at the hay. As time went on, Jan realized, the hay would dwindle, layer by layer, until it would be at waist level. Then it would be good sleeping space, perhaps.

The hunchback took something from a pocket—something larger than his hand. Going to his knees, he pushed it deep into the crack between two bales of hay. Then he took something more from another pocket and pushed it into the same place. Again, another pocket, and this time Jan saw a bottle of whisky.

Whisky was probably forbidden for ship's crew, Jan thought, unless issued on captain's orders. This would be the hunchback's private supply, or part of it.

The German rose and studied the hiding place, counting, memorizing which crack between bales held his treasure. Then he again walked toward the hatchway, and noticed the empty buckets left outside. He peered into the forward compartment, eyes searching through the dimness. Jan stood dead still.

Seeing nothing, the man turned and walked away. Shifting position just slightly, Jan watched him go aft toward the center mast, near the horses.

Past there, it was hard to follow his every movement because the horses stood crosswise of the ship, obstructing the view of everything aft of the mainmast. To make it all the more difficult, the man wore dark grey, and there were times when he disappeared.

Now he was appearing and disappearing behind the horses, carrying a step-stool. He placed it in the center of the gangway and disappeared again. When he emerged again, he carried a big bundle—a roped piece of canvas he untied and unfolded in the gangway. It was a strong length of canvas fashioned into a hammock. The hunchback moved about, hanging it between crosstimbers above the horses, just forward of the mast, above and across the gangway.

A good idea, Jan had to admit. The hunchback would have the warmth of the horses steaming up from below—something to consider for his Katrina and Jozef's Pelagia. And while awake, the hunchback would have a full view of the midship gangway from his perch.

The man was systematic. Plainly, he'd done this many times before. He climbed the stool again, steadying himself against a horse, holding a rope in his hand. He took a drink from a bottle in the other hand, rolled into the hammock, pulled the stool up behind him and hung it above between two crosstimbers, ready for morning.

The Krulik boys had left the four lengths of baling cord from the sleeping straw hanging on the end post of one of the pigpens. Steadying the girls on the calves, Jan left them for just a moment, and fetched it. Then he slipped out of his dark sweater. Watching the girls carefully, he quickly tied the sweater ends with two of the baling cords, then stretched it diagonally between the corner of the nearest pig pen and the post of the calves' stall fence.

Katrina was the lighter of the two, so he put her into this first hammock. It sagged just enough to put her backside in contact with a calf's back. It would do for this one night, he thought, and tomorrow a blanket might be used instead.

Leaving Pelagia carefully balanced, he retrieved a hanging blanket, nearly dry. Pelagia's calf cooperated by standing still, and in only a few minutes he had another hammock. He wrapped the ample blanket around the girl and secured it with his belt, which would also serve to hold her in place should she move in her sleep.

He padded about the forward compartment quietly. Everyone was asleep. Then he leaned on the bottom half of the hatchway door, listening, slipping off his shoes.

The hunchback wheezed. It was a half-snore—only the one part. When it became regular, Jan lifted a leg over the half-door. Wheeze by wheeze, he brought the other leg over, then pushed himself off to land softly on the midship gangway.

Surveying, he heard that the hunchback still slept. He went quickly, in quiet stealth, to the hiding place of the whisky. He reached deep into the crevice. His arms were longer than the German's, and he quickly verified that there were three bottles wedged between the bales. He left the closest one in place, and pulled out the others, which he hid in another crevice. Then he rearranged the straw so there would be no evidence of his visit.

The German still wheezed in his hammock.

Jan decided to explore some more, and made a foray to his right as he faced forward to confirm his memory of how the cows were held in staunchions. He saw that if everything remained the same, it might be possible, were the need to arise, to milk a cow one night.

The wheezing continued. He considered a further exploration aft of the mainmast, but it would require passing close to the horses and the German. He decided not to take the chance.

He went quickly back over the half door and back into the forward compartment. He hadn't made a sound.

The hunchback still wheezed.

Chapter 21

With just a little squeezing, three of the men could lean on the half-door to look through the hatchway. When the doings on the other side were especially interesting, three or four more could crowd behind, being careful not to step back into the manure pile.

Such was the case this morning of the first full day aboard the Frederika.

"It could be he's dressing for a woman," said Ludwig Karpczinski. "if we're to sail today as Paul says, she may come to say goodbye."

"There does not exist a woman of such stupidity," Big Jozef proclaimed conclusively. "Not even among the Germans."

"If she did," Ignatz Ran added, "she would not have the wits to find her way to the pier."

"Yesterday, he looked like a twisted black sheep," Jan Poglicki said. "Today he looks more like a doll the devil would knit from the wool of such a sheep." The men laughed softly, not wanting to reveal themselves.

There was a difference. Yesterday the hunchbacked German, dressed in black sweater and black stocking cap, had looked like one continuous scraggly mass. Now, by contrast, he was perversely handsome. He had attracted all this attention from the forward compartment early in the morning when he came with mash for the calves and swill for the pigs—wearing an expensive suit of dark blue serge, clean and neatly creased.

"There'll be an inspection before we sail, I think," Paul said, leaning on the center of the door. "He's getting ready." Stanisław, crowded just to his left, nodded agreement with that possibility.

"First he took a swig of whisky. Then he cleaned under the horses and cows," Jozef Dominiak recounted. Now at Paul's right, he had been first at the door in the morning when he awoke to relieve Jan Poglicki in tending their daughters, only to discover that Jan had slung them in hammocks, and had been sleeping all along. "Then he took a swig of whisky. Then he took out his dress blues. Then he took a swig of whisky. Then he combed his mustache. Then…"

"Then he took a swig of whisky?" Ignatz Ran was leaning on Jozef's back.

"No, then he went to the privy."

"Then he took a swig of whisky?" Ignatz asked again.

"No, then he cleaned under himself," said Juliusz, whose leaning place was immediately disrupted when Stanisław laughed.

"Then he *needed* a swig of whisky," Ludwig said. And they all laughed again.

Now the German was braiding his beard in tight plaits steered at the bottom to line up with the two rows of buttons on his coat.

From behind all of them and behind the manure pile where he stood with Old Man Kradzinski, Tadeusz Murak joined in. "If the bunch of you aren't careful, you'll get a surprise. It may be that he puts on this show to lure you so you'll line up at the door to be his next target."

They laughed again, as Jan's description of the Russian youths' encounter with the hunchback's manure-slinging was called to mind.

Ludwig stopped leaning on Paul for a moment and looked around. "Don't say anything in front of Piotr. We'll have a dead hunchback to answer for."

"Well, he expects someone, the way he keeps looking up the ramp," said Ignatz.

The hunchback topped off his outfit with a blue seaman's cap and looked himself over in a small mirror. Cautiously, he touched the lump on his forehead.

Forward of the mast and rainbarrel, the women kept children occupied with the task of gathering the straw bedding into the center of the canvas, then hanging it from the timberwork away from the lantern. Periodically, Jadwiga put her ear to the mast.

"Jadwiga, did Paul say we would go today for certain?" Maria asked.

"He said that the freightmaster said today at the earliest. But I think we'll definitely sail today. Something is happening topside."

Kostanta Ran and Viktoria Murak helped Kazimierz and Salomeya Steck out of their sleeping place in the repairwork at the bow.

Among the men gathered around the manure pile between the mast and the hatchway, interest in the hunchback's activities had waned.

Conversation drifted to speculation on the question of the likely length of the trip to America.

"Jadwiga says this ship has made the crossing many times in less than thirty days," said Tadeusz Murak. Old Man Kradzinski nodded.

Ludwig shook his head. "In the summer, probably. I think it must take longer in the winter."

"That could be the time when the winds are stronger," Jozef said.

Jan Poglicki joined the conversation. "But the winds are mostly from the west, aren't they? It could be the thirty days is for the other way—for coming back."

"All this speculation is useless," said Stanisław Krulik. "We should ask. We can ask the Germans. Paul will ask next time an officer comes from topside."

Paul shook his head. "I would ask this one who primps and preens if Jadwiga had not offended him," Paul said. "She gives way to her impulses so easily."

"Paul, there may be an opportunity to make a friend of the hunchback," said Stanisław.

"Or at least engage him in conversation," said Juliusz.

Jozef made a pushing motion with his arm. "The hunchback is a lunatic who waits for an animal to ooze with manure to throw on us."

Stanisław persisted. "It may be that nobody has ever spoken a pleasant word to the man. Paul can try."

"It's worth a try. Don't you think so, Paul?" Juliusz asked. Paul shrugged. Juliusz continued. "If we need information or help from topside we may need the hunchback."

Paul glanced out, where the German again had his bottle in hand. "If such help is needed, I will just go to the deck to ask. It wouldn't do to depend on that man in an emergency, the way he sucks on that bottle."

"We would do well to depend only on ourselves," said Jan.

Juliusz's voice rose. "Jan, your wife isn't going to have a baby on this voyage. If Paul can make a friend of the cattletender, it cannot hurt."

"And it might help," Stanisław quickly added, looking at Paul.

"I will give it my best try the first opportunity," Paul said.

Juliusz and Stanisław both patted Paul on the back in encouragement. Ignatz, who was on the other side of the manure pile and could not pat Paul's back, simply nodded in encouragement. Then he spoke quietly, as in raising a new subject.

"It is well to do so," he said. "We have eight sows in this compartment. Six have dropped their young."

Big Jozef was growing weary of the conversation. "What interest do we have in pigs?"

"Listen," Ludwig started, his hand up to urge attention to Ignatz's words.

But everyone took him to mean they should listen to what suddenly was happening in the midship compartment. There was a burst of noise that drew all the men back to the open half-door.

Ignatz, who lost out in the rush to the door and could not see over Big Jozef, demanded information: "What's going on out there?" He heard sounds of revelry tumbling down from the second class deck. They were the herald of a near-tumble of people—and now it became clear what the cattletender had been anticipating.

It was a new contingent of passengers, not filing down the midship ramp one at a time, but coming informally in small groups; not dangling pasteboards from each neck, but with heads of families holding them in groups; not sweaty and beaten by hard rail travel, but flushed with celebration.

The manure-heaving hunchback now became the gracious host, extending a welcoming hand to each man, bowing to each woman. Despite their reception by this curious creature, the passengers—all German—played their roles as gracious guests. To those who came with drinks in hand, the seaman raised his own glass in a toast of welcome. He showed each head of family the stacked hay and straw as though ushering honored guests to their quarters.

Some who carried baggage put it down to have a look around; others gathered in the gangway. Because the Germans milled about, the Poles watching from the forward compartment were unable to maintain an accurate count, but it was a smaller group than their own—a smaller group with more space, and bales of straw.

As more of this new contingent of passengers gathered at the bottom of the ramp, the revelry of topside was transplanted to steerage. There seemed no end to the toasting, nor to the supply of whisky and wine. The toasts of welcome gave way to toasts to the ship, then to America.

"With so many Germans on this ship it's plain to see why they pushed us into this hole," Tadeusz said.

"They all have genuine traveling containers," Ludwig said. "Washboilers and bags, but no boxes or crates."

"And new headwear and big feathers on the women," Big Jozef said.

Farther forward, word had been passed among the women of the arrival of midship passengers, and there was even some talk of elbowing a position at the double door to observe them first hand until Jadwiga began dancing about with something of even more interest.

Darting from mast to bow and back to mast, listening at each, Jadwiga told everyone at once: "We've been pushed away. We're being towed out!"

Some of the children felt the subtle movement and held out their arms to assist balance as they stood or walked. After a flurry of mild excitement, there was a hush of anticipation, feeling out the new footing. Franek Dominiak ran to the mast to listen.

Among the men braced in a clutch at the open top of the hatchway, the sensation of movement wasn't enough to distract their attention from the revelry in the midship compartment.

There, one of the men untied a horse, and an older boy gave short rides to younger children, fore and aft on the gangway. At the farthest point forward in one ride, one young child chanced to see the men looking out through the forward hatch, and though startled in the middle of a gleeful cry, said nothing. When the hunchback noticed that the horse was out of place, he interrupted excitedly and retied it at the mainmast.

The creaking of wood against wood insinuated itself into the forward compartment like an old chair receiving a body for the first time in years. But it was just an opening syllable in an argumentative dialogue. Jadwiga, her arms around the forward mast, looked up.

"Now stay with it this time, you German bitch."

There was a wretched twist of wood and of strain from mast and keel. A lantern was left behind in the beginning of a grand arc of the ship to the left, then swung its own following arc. Water sloshed from the rainbarrel. The Frederika pulled forward.

Among the women, only Jadwiga instantly found her feet when the lurch came as the Frederika heeled to port. Estella and Viktoria, sitting on a starboard pigpen rail, were toppled into the pen amid offended sows. Several women staggered or squatted to avoid falling, but Polka, Delfinia and Viktoria were unable to catch themselves and with unison worthy of marching soldiers, they plopped on their backsides.

Aft of the rainbarrel, the men grabbed the door, posts of calf pens, overhead crosstimbers and each other to keep from falling. Only Old Man Kradzinski lost footing when a crutch skidded from under him. From dead center in the manure pile, he smiled at the others to show he was unharmed.

Chapter 22

Among the Germans amidship, revelry quickly gave way to a cascading sickness as man after man yielded up the liquor he had consumed—and more. Even many of the women, who had taken less to drink, became ill. Their children were immediately infected by the suggestion carried to their noses, and there was more vomiting.

"We should be grateful the Germans, not we, were celebrating this morning," said Stanisław. He reached for the top half of the door and pulled it closed. Turning to Juliusz, he said, "It's best to leave them to their sickness."

"Let's hope they're still sick when we arrive in America," Juliusz said. "We can walk right past them and be the first to the authorities." As he turned, he gagged. The others left the Germans to their sickness and Juliusz to the manure pile.

In the forward compartment, the lantern hung at an odd angle, deviating from apparent vertical. Shadows moved capriciously. Men and women alike sought the difficult compromise hidden in the conflicting information reaching their senses.

Mothers had anticipated the danger of seasickness, and they now sought to stave it off by organizing a game. They played along with the children. Around a circle, they passed two spools of thread in opposite directions. Any player caught holding both was a loser, and there was much laughter and shrieking among the young ones as they competed to pass the spools more quickly than their neighbors.

Jadwiga met the men retreating from the hatchway and manure pile. "Paul, at last we're sailing—sailing to America."

"The other compartment is filled with Germans," Paul said. "They're all sick—most of them, anyway. They were drinking topside."

Jadwiga looked the men over. She said "Ludwig, join in the game. Encourage the children to play. Keep their eyes off the heel of the ship. You too, Jan."

But Jadwiga was already too late. Saying nothing, Jan simply wheeled about to join Juliusz at the manure pile. Quickly, Ludwig joined the game circle, trying to concentrate on the movement of the spools, but he became fascinated with the strange movement of shadows, looked at the lantern, gagged, and went the way of Jan.

After the wedding, Paul had made many fishing trips on the Baltic with Jadwiga and her father and brothers. He felt himself past the early stages of seasickness, but he wasn't altogether certain he would avoid vomiting. He studiously oriented himself to gravity, stood at the appropriate angle to the mast and side edge of the rainbarrel, and told himself all was well. It was a different experience aboard a big ship, in the hold, no waterline in view. On the Wdowiak schooner, he'd been able to use the horizon for orientation, thinking of the boat as a moving platform under him. Here, that experience was proving helpful, but his senses wanted more convincing that he was standing upright when only the lantern and the hanging canvas of straw agreed with his idea of upright.

It brought to mind those first moments of half-wakefulness when deep sleep is disrupted and the head keeps demanding information about orientation that the senses cannot yet provide. Looking at the children playing the spool game, Paul felt grateful that his comrades in travel had spent the extra day at rest, learning to cope with at least some small movement of the vessel.

His confidence that he wouldn't become ill grew, and he urged himself on with exhortations that he must not, because it could reduce his hard-won standing among his fellow travelers.

Old Man Kradzinski was helped in a change of trousers by Tadeusz, and then he joined the Stecks in the bow cribwork, where all three looked down on the game of spools.

The others, except for Ludwig, Jan, and Juliusz, seemed to have matters under control. Women elbowed each other in pride and smugness that none of them became ill. The children seemed not yet to know there was any sickness, though they knew the ship had set sail.

Jozef and Delfinia both played the game with special effort. Delfinia gave exaggerated praise to their children whenever entrapment by the converging spools was narrowly avoided, and Jozef imitated her. Ignatz

Ran played, but his Kostanta held both her own Mikal and Delfinia's Konrad, who napped in her arms. In turn Delfinia gave special attention to Bolesław and David Ran, encouraging their efforts in the game.

With a glance and jerk of his head, Stanisław Krulik invited Piotr Jakubik to play. Following the example, the Krulik boys brought the Jakubik boys into the circle, too. No one spoke of sickness, hoping the children would remain oblivious.

For her part, Jadwiga was totally unaffected, so much so that she still flitted about, listening to the sounds at both mast and bow. "It's an off-shore wind, quartering," she told Paul, "we will lean to port for a while, then to starboard, then back." Paul nodded, pretending to understand while he sorted out the words. Port, left; starboard, right. Quartering, coming to the sails from behind, but at an angle.

"It's not yet a strong wind," Jadwiga said, "but we are making way steadily." Others, listening to this wife-to-husband chatter, nodded in satisfied understanding. Franek Dominiak, listening a bit too closely, found himself absent-mindedly holding both spools as the other children squealed in delight.

The movements of the Frederika proved a challenge this first day at sea. Just steering a course from Bremerhaven's sheltered harbor, she would turn, presenting less sail to direct wind as it passed behind, rolling to the opposite lean and slowing abruptly. Then there would be another surge forward and a creaking movement into the full lean. One of the Jakubik sons had to go to the manure pile. The youngest children were persuaded to nap. Their older brothers and sisters played the same walking game as on the flatcar, and were spared discomfort.

Adults, seeing the advantage of the hammocks Jan Poglicki had devised for his own Katrina and for Pelagia Dominiak, set about making them for all the children. Rope, badly worn but still strong enough for hammock-making, was found under the bow repairwork where it appeared to have been discarded. Blankets were sorted to choose those best for supporting a child, and shared among the families.

Tadeusz Murak decided to make a hammock for his father-in-law. "I can tie it from corner to corner over the pigpen to get enough length. You'll take the sewing scissors with you," he said to Old Man Kradzinski, "and just cut a hole in the blanket where it will fit you best." Both Viktoria and her father looked puzzled, so he explained further. "This way you won't have to get up even once at night." They understood.

Jadwiga became the teacher of hammock-making and knot-tying when she objected to the crazy variety of knots being used by the men. "You'll have to cut the blanket or the rope every time things must be redone," she said. "There's only one proper knot."

The knot she showed the men was easy for them. But some of the children wanted to learn it, too, and this led her into the demonstration of knot-tying Paul had seen before. At one point, a glint of lantern in her eye, she described one knot as being of particular interest to German officers, and she exchanged smiles with Paul as he watched.

Hammocks were made for Stanisław Poglicki and for Franciska Karpczinski, too, even though their fathers were still occupied at the manure pile. Jadwiga promised Lancek Krulik, whose brother Władek was also at the manure pile, that she would show both how to make full-fledged rope hammocks without canvas or blankets, when Władek was able to watch.

In a misguided moment of curiosity about the Germans Kostanta Ran opened the top half of the hatchway. She was immediately repulsed and she closed it quickly. "The cows and horses are not so lucky," she said to nobody in particular. "These pigs are the fortunate ones."

The meal that afternoon was a great satisfaction, particularly since there had been no breakfast. They were given more cooked ham and cabbage than they could eat. Listening to the conversation between the galley workers who brought it, Paul realized that many passengers were refusing food.

The newness and excitement of hammocks for sleeping made the children unusually eager for bedtime. Parents, grateful they'd won a battle against seasickness, were happy to indulge them. Viktoria Murak proved to have a fine singing voice, and started a community songfest that lulled the children to sleep despite the early hour.

With the children in hammocks, mere tiredness of young ones no longer dictated sleeping hours, so the adults remained awake late into the night, most simply enjoying the quiet and freedom occasioned by children occupied and out of the way.

When finally Juliusz Sczepaniak was able to leave the manure pile, he came to flop beside Maria in agony. "Say what you like about your sailing ships, Jadwiga. I'd rather make this whole trip by train."

But they were on their way to America. In this, there was a satisfaction.

Chapter 23

Sleep was uninterrupted until a late hour of the morning when the yelp of a sow in the first pen on the starboard side woke the older Ran children, seven-year-old Bernadina and six-year-old Monika. Ignatz had placed his older ones there, explaining to the other fathers that when the sow yielded, it would be nothing unusual or worrisome to them. As he had been at their age, they were well-accustomed to such happenings on the farm.

Bernadina and Monika remained quiet, but each reached out a hand to shake the hammocks of their brothers, four-year-old Bolesław and three-year-old David, so they could watch, too, in the dim light from the lantern.

As much as she watched the sow, Bernadina also watched her brothers and their reactions. In her memory, David had never seen this birthing of animals before. Bolesław had seen it only once, and then it was not a sow but the girl-dog of the labor contractor, who became so upset when Bolesław took one of the boy puppies to show Mama. The man hadn't known it was missing until Bolesław returned it.

David's eyes were open wide. At one point he almost flopped out of his hammock trying to see better. He looked to Monika, who was his favorite older sister, perhaps because she was so often assigned by mother to be the watchful one. Monika's smile reassured him, and he watched more comfortably.

Bolesław looked at Bernadina and mouthed the words "Like the dog." Bernadina nodded. She could tell he was troubled, so she said, very quietly, "Don't worry. They'll be all right."

The contractor had drowned about half the dozen puppies in the horse trough, Bolesław watching, terrorized, thinking it was because of what he'd done. This was what was bothering him. Or he could be remembering the kick of the contractor that made his leg and backside blue with hurt for many days. Or the loud argument that followed when father and mother objected to such treatment.

It had been a frightening episode all the way around, Bernadina recalled, counting the tenth piglet as it was born. She played the vivid scene out in her head, even though she could not remember all the words: Both mother and father yelling at the contractor and the contractor yelling back the grown-up words that children, girls especially, weren't supposed to use even though her mother sometimes did.

But the words had not been so much trouble as the part where her big mother, all the bigger because she had Mikal inside her then, held the contractor's head in the horse trough while her father smacked his hindmost with a barrel stave. That part was the real trouble—the smacking part.

But then it had been fun living with Uncle Rysiu and Aunt Maryan until it came time to leave for America. Bernadina would miss the cousins very much until one day they, too, would come to America.

She wasn't sure about this place called America, except that all the grown-ups said it was very good to be there instead of under the heel of the Russians or the Germans or their Polack favorites. She knew there would be a school, and that she might not be allowed to work sorting apples until she was older.

Franek would go to school too, Bernadina thought, wondering if they would be together. His hammock was swinging oddly, and she saw that he was lying there, bringing his hand up to his head, saluting.

As his first activity of the morning, Paul stood over the manure pile wondering what might be done to lessen the stink that made even the water taste bad, so he heard the conversation between the two Germans even before they opened the hatch.

He positioned himself so he could stand upright, his head between crosstimbers, quickly gathering some German phrases with which to start a conversation. It was the hunchback's voice. And someone else.

"I can help you carry the basket topside," the someone else was saying. "Better even, if you like I will get more help and you can just supervise."

"No, no," the hunchback responded. "There are rules."

There was noise from the latch.

"Herman, there is a rule that you have to break your back every morning to get rid of cow manure and pig shit? I have a better rule..." The door opened. "My rule..." The man stopped, stock still. "My God, there is a man here." Then, looking around, "There are people here. My son was right. There are people here."

"Only the Polacks," the hunchback said.

"*Guten morgen, mein Herr,*" said Paul, extending a hand to the unbent one. "*Ich bin Paul Adamik.*"

"My God, there are people here. Herman, why didn't you...Good morning. Yes, good morning. My name is Hoyt Gruenberg...Why didn't you tell me there are people here, Herman?"

"Only Polacks."

The big German shook Paul's hand vigorously, straightening, minding his head. Recovering from his surprise, he even managed a small smile. Absent-mindedly, he continued to shake Paul's hand while he looked around to get his bearings and take in the faces of the Poles who started to gather.

In Polish, Paul said to Stanisław Krulik, "They've come for the manure."

"They've come for the manure," Stanisław said to Ludwig and Juliusz.

"We'll do it so Paul can talk to them," Juliusz said.

"Don't hurry."

Jozef stepped up to take a manure-collecting basket from Hoyt Gruenberg. But as he extended his hand for it, the German grasped it in a handshake. "My name is Hoyt."

"This is Jozef Dominiak," Paul said in German. Then, in Polish, "Big Jozef." In German again, "Jozef will collect the manure for you."

"Oh, the basket. Yes. Herman, these men will..."

The hunchback grumbled and nodded grudging assent, left out in the banter between the friendly German and the eager Polack. Their talk was talk in which he had no interest. His forehead still showed his wound.

"Herr Shiffmeister," Paul said in practiced German phrases he'd rehearsed quietly, "by your leave I wish to report that the first sow on the starboard side came forth with young ones last night."

This was of interest to the hunchback, and he immediately went forward to count the litter.

"So, you go to America," Hoyt Gruenberg said.

"Yes," Paul said. Striving to keep a conversation flowing, he asked, "You, too?" Then he realized it was a foolish question.

"We are twelve families. My son said there were people up here, but I didn't believe him. How many families?"

"Ten."

"But more children than we have, I think." He saw Magda and Manya, the Dominiak twins, who came around the rainwater vat with other children and some of the women, who were curious to see what the hunchback had brought with him that was of such interest to the men. He squatted to behold the spectacle of identical girls. He smiled, spoke to them in German, and started counting: "*Ein, zwei.* Hmmph. *Ein, zwei.* Look at these two, like two little paintings. My, my."

Neither understood his words, but both smiled, then laughed, responding to the friendly gleam in his eyes. When he reached out, Magda and Manya were willing bundles of giggles as he stood up to do a little dance with them.

"Delfinia, Paul must talk with this man," Jozef said, and Delfinia tried to take the twins from the visitor. But he would have none of that, nor would the twins, who clung tightly.

"Herr Gruenberg, this is Delfinia Dominiak, wife of Jozef and the mother of the twins."

"I must be called Hoyt," he said. "Please tell her I now can understand why Jozef's daughters are so comely."

"Yes." To Delfinia, Paul said, "This is Hoyt Gruenberg. Hoyt, he wants to be called, he says. He says the twins are very pretty."

"It's because they take after their dimpled mother."

"He says it's because you are so pretty that they are, too."

Delfinia blushed, smiled shyly, and glanced at Jozef, who stopped shoveling manure to smile proudly.

The hunchback finished counting piglets, then found he was in the midst of the socializing, and the sour expression returned to his face. He watched Juliusz and Jozef, who had made little progress in moving the collected manure from its pile into the basket.

"He is impatient," Paul said to Jozef in Polish. Then, in German, but still speaking to Jozef, he said "*Schnell, schnell.* We must not keep this important man waiting. Quickly!"

Jozef looked confused, but he and Juliusz hurried the manure collection anyway.

Hoyt Gruenberg poked the hunchback with an elbow. "Don't be such a grouch, Herman. They delay so that we can talk." To Paul, he said, "Herman scrambled his brain with liquor yesterday. Once the ship started moving, the drinkers abandoned their bottles. Herman made sure they didn't go to waste."

Herman grumbled. Paul extended his hand. "Herr Shiffmeister, my name is Paul Adamik."

"Don't stand on formalities, Herman, shake the man's hand." The hunchback reluctantly put a hand out. "Herman, before this trip is over you may have all of us trained to do your work for you. How is it you live such a fortunate life?"

Herman grunted, shaking Paul's hand without looking him in the eye. "I am not properly called *Shiffmeister*," he said.

"*Jawohl, mein Herr*," Paul said. He had promised Juliusz, so he would make the effort with this surly cattletender. But he felt he was lowering himself, and it was distasteful to him.

As Juliusz and Jozef finished the collection of manure, Hoyt Gruenberg stooped to deposit Magda and Manya back on the gangway and took the basket by one handle. He motioned for Paul to take the other. But the hunchback reached more quickly, shaking a finger.

"Herman has to instruct me," Hoyt Gruenberg said, winking. "Another time perhaps you can help." He turned to go through the hatchway, and as Herman made an elaborate show of closing the lower half to indicate that the Polacks were to stay in the pig pen compartment, he added, smiling, "If you have no plans to go out, perhaps I'll return later for a visit. Tell the little girls their Uncle Hoyt will come back soon."

Paul smiled. Juliusz and Jozef, standing next to him, also smiled and they waved goodbye, too.

"This is a good one, this German," Jozef said.

"He calls himself uncle to the twins."

"The hunchback is a bitter mouthful," said Juliusz.

"Let's call him Herman," Paul said. "Let's use his name. He's difficult. It will take some time to patch things up with him. Maybe never." Then seeing that this distressed the worried Juliusz, he added, "But we'll all work at it—all of us."

Still standing by, Stanisław added, "I think this Hoyt will help us make a friend of the cattletender. Juliusz, at least he's someone else to talk to if we need help."

Juliusz spoke earnestly to Paul. "Next time you talk to him, find out if there's a midwife among the Germans, Paul, please. And if not, ask him to find out about the rest of the passengers—if there is a midwife elsewhere."

Only then did they notice: Piotr stood in the shadows past the men at the rainwater vat. Hearing Juliusz, he turned from them and walked away.

Chapter 24

When three days, then a fourth and fifth, passed without the Germans of the galley organizing some regularity of providing meals, it was no longer possible to excuse this as a reasonable consequence of first days under sail. One day, there would be no breakfast, but a midday meal would come early. Another day, children would be kept awake until late, awaiting the evening meal, but it would not come.

Meals that came were lacking. When the quantity was such that Salomeya could be generous with the ladle, it was soup so thin that hunger was more stimulated than satisfied. When it was rich or thick, there was too little.

They were hungry. To a man, to a woman, to a child, they were hungry.

Paul, comparing notes with Hoyt Gruenberg in one of their frequent conversations at the door, learned that the problem was nearly as serious among the families midship, but there seemed to be no correspondence between the two sections as to time or schedule of service, which meals were missed, or what was served. Both Paul and Hoyt found it a mystery without reason or rhyme. Paul asked no questions of the galley workers who came with the food, for they were mere youngsters. Hoyt tried, but learned nothing from them.

They were hungry, and food was on their minds.

"I've already been wanting strange foods a lot," Jadwiga told Maria in their days-long conversation. "At the fishhouse, the women said it's my baby asking as it grows."

"If there's too much of this, the child will be a demanding one," Maria said. "This is what my mother explained to me. It's best not to give in, but when I could get cream, I couldn't help it. I just wanted it so much."

"I was a demanding child," Jadwiga said. "My mother used to say that all the boats on the Baltic could not bring enough herring when she was carrying me. It was the same with my brothers when they came before me."

Maria's thoughts had gone to her family. "Jadwiga, my mother cried so much when Juliusz and I told her about going to America. I thought she would die of a broken heart. My father, too, but it wasn't so bad with him. I think Juliusz discussed it with him even before he told me."

Jadwiga thought of smoked fish and her stomach called out to remind her it was past mealtime. She saw that children felt the same. Mothers were trying to distract them, but it was a losing battle.

Jadwiga knew that Paul and his big German friend also talked about food, and that there was thought of making a complaint. She suspected there was a relationship between the plodding progress of the Frederika and the shortage of food: Whatever provisions were aboard had to last through the voyage. But her own hunger was already near the point of being unbearable, and she knew Maria's must be worse: Maria was due sooner, and she was less robust.

"Do you miss your mother, Jadwiga? I miss mine."

Jadwiga made the sign of the cross. "My mother has been gone for many years. Since I was twelve. Even before my monthly times started."

"Oh, that's right. I'm sorry. You told me on the train. Then...then you've been keeping house for your father and your brothers for a long time."

"Yes. But I fish with them, too."

"Who keeps the house now?"

"It isn't settled. My brother Konstanty will marry soon. Then there will be a woman in the house again. Or it may be that Konrad will bring home a wife. They all fish together, anyway."

"Didn't your father want you to stay at home to help?"

Jadwiga found this a curious notion. She knew of daughters staying at home to keep house, but usually it was because there was no one to marry or because parents were very ill or feeble or because the son didn't marry a woman to bring home.

"My father has always known I would one day leave for America with my husband. He has always said it would make him sad. But happy for the new life his grandchildren would have. It was understood—I would keep house, yes, but then I would go to America with my husband."

In their hunger, they looked to Salomeya for fairness, and in truth none doubted her, though there were the unavoidable grumblings as the days wore on with too little to eat.

There were the times, such as when Piotr or Ursula or their strapping sons grouched that they weren't getting the food for which they had paid, when Salomeya could have passed the ladle to someone else on an excuse of tiredness. But she knew that to do so would open her replacement to even greater challenge. She did give fair portion to the smallest of the children, lest they become too scrawny to be acceptable in America, while giving just a bit less to those who had the heft of past indulgence on their bones. It didn't help to quiet the grumbling of the Russians that they all belonged in this latter category, mother and sons bulging with fat, father with muscle. With a practiced eye, Salomeya judged the needs of each family, and it was understood that from that point on each family could redivide if husband wished to give something extra to wife or child. There was the extra amount given to any child who seemed to be growing ill. It didn't help, in the worrisome antagonism between Piotr and Big Jozef, that Pelagia Dominiak was constantly ill with her cough, always needing the extra consideration.

And no one doubted that Salomeya favored the pregnant ones just a bit, even though each was further favored by her husband with an extra portion from his own allotment. Both Maria and Jadwiga were nonetheless hungry all the time.

Except for the Russians, there was a confidence that Salomeya's distribution of the food made it stretch beyond what could reasonably be expected.

They were beset by tiresome routine.

As hunger gnawed at the stomach, boredom gnawed at the spirit.

First to succumb were the children. They strained at confinement, longing to run and jump, to burst forth with a joyful ring of laughter that had no reason to come here in the dark hold of a sailing ship. There was whining.

When children were allowed to find their own amusement, too often it involved noisiness or running that tried the patience of the men. There were attempts to compromise the nature of play and to restrict the hours during which such disturbances would be permitted. This confined the children all the more.

The men were next to go. Unaccustomed to spending time with their young, let alone those of other families, and accustomed to time in the open sun through the day, most surrendered quickly to an irritability with one another and their situation. Even Juliusz seemed to lose the capacity to draw some enjoyment from making fun.

Among the women, the challenge of keeping children amused with limited resources preserved their own interest longest, yet confinement and lack of options overtook them within days, poisoning their patience.

Most able to withstand the dreary sameness were those without children. Salomeya's patience was endless, and for Maria and Jadwiga, there was still a freshness in entertaining young ones. These attempts, often with games new to the children, held off a bit longer the moment when each would give way to fidget or whine.

But they succumbed.

The men took to tending the pigs. The hunchback began to leave the food for the animals just inside the hatchway, knowing that one or another passenger would rush to do his work. The men vied for the task, even gambled to win it as something to provide a moment's diversion. Pigs became a center of interest.

Despite the lack of light, women became eager to comb the hair of others, trying varied styles. Some sewed. A few worked in yarn. Polka even unraveled a sweater to start a new project, saying she would turn one big sweater into small garments for the expectant ones.

Some men took childlike delight in the challenge of hand-wrestling. Even after it was clearly known who the winners were likely to be in these regular contests, they made odds and placed bets, looking for surprises that seldom came.

The monotony of prayer was a relief from the monotony of nothingness. After a few days, Salomeya Steck was no longer inventive, but it didn't matter for there was still a certain unpredictablity in the question of what she would repeat. Even the few men unlikely to trouble with churchgoing when ashore became willing worshippers.

Washing became a special treat. There was constant interest in the level of water in the rainbarrel, and in the strict rotation of turn-taking established more or less by chance in the first days. Women guarded their privilege of bathing the children.

Now and then there was even some pointless bickering.

Piotr and Jozef wore a mutual distrust into a worrisome antagonism. The other men were conscious of a need to keep them separated, even as they felt a good fight would be diverting.

Maria and Jadwiga grew closer day by day. Time on their hands, they compressed the acquaintancing of a lifetime into days. Pregnancy their mutual condition, they spent hours together sharing what they knew about this matter of bearing a child. Other women, wanting to share this excitement of anticipation, volunteered their knowledge, and there were sometimes gentle arguments over conflicting pieces of advice.

The men, keeping it secret from Juliusz, gambled on the date his child would be born, and on how many piglets would arrive in the next yield.

But there was little seasoning for a diet of boredom.

There were the hunchback's visits in moods that ranged from unpleasant to surly. He never tired of counting the piglets and waiting for each of the sows to yield its young.

Keeping his scheming from those who might object, Jan Poglicki involved himself and others in a plan to steal a piglet. When the next sow yielded, but before the cattletender could make a count, one newborn, perhaps even two, would be transferred into the litter of a sow whose young were nearer weaning. The men would see that it wasn't nosed out for the suckling. Piglets would be transferred, then, sow to sow, so the hunchback would never know of the uncounted extra one. Sooner or later, there would be an opportunity to slaughter and dress the fattened animal. In the meantime, there would be a distraction in the endless debate over how an animal, or its parts, might be preserved and cooked in the confinement of the forward hold.

For Paul, there was at least the diversion of the German men who came to the hatchway. Themselves bored, they soon tired of rearranging bales of hay for the housekeeping of their wives. They could spend only so much time bamboozling the cattletender by pretending that each shovelful from cow or pig was a full basket to be lugged to the deck for dumping. They came to the half door for their own diversion of a talk with Paul, who wrote down new words and phrases. His German consequently improved day by day. He even taught Franek Dominiak some of the words and phrases, and discovered that doing so helped him remember them.

Hoyt Gruenberg came most often. He was the most friendly, and Paul grew to like him. Hoyt had once served at sea on a big ship, and he was sensitive to the Frederika's moods. From him, Paul learned much of German ships and German words. When Juliusz heard the big German's deep voice, he always came around the rainwater vat. He always asked the same question: "Has he found a midwife?" Hoyt soon recognized the Polish question, but the report didn't change.

"There are none among our women who profess to such experience," Hoyt told Juliusz through Paul. But he had taken to sneaking topside when Herman wasn't alert, he said, and he would try to spread the word among the other passengers.

One day, when Juliusz was especially worried because Maria was growing weaker, Hoyt responded to his distress with a suggestion.

"Paul, there is a doctor aboard, you know. Does Juliusz know?"

Paul translated, but Juliusz shook his head. "This would not be proper," he said. "Maria wouldn't allow it."

"I gather he thinks it would be wrong," Hoyt said.

"That's right."

"Tell him: In Germany it's more and more the custom to have a doctor present." Paul translated.

Juliusz shook his head again. "No, no. Then it would be better to hope for the best with the Russian woman."

"We have a midwife among us in this compartment," Paul explained to Hoyt. "A Russian woman. But Juliusz is concerned that the woman will...won't...Well, her husband said some things. Juliusz will feel better if he knows there is another midwife."

"But your wife is also due. How do you feel about..."

"Jadwiga isn't due until after we arrive in America."

"But it will be soon after."

"Yes."

"Do you have arrangements? Where will she have the baby?"

"No arrangements. We'll consult a priest. I've been concerned about this, but Jadwiga wouldn't delay the trip. She wants the baby to be born in America."

So Paul had the diversion of conversation with the Germans. One who came more and more after the first two weeks was named Fritz Adenauer. He was more friendly, more solicitous, than most. But his German was heavily irrigated with the sloshing sounds of southern provinces, unlike the officers whose voices bristled with crisp precision. Paul found it difficult to grasp his meaning quickly, and the talk seldom rose above casual amenities. Anyway, Paul found the man hard to like. All the features of his face—the wrinkles of his forehead, elongated ears, the lie of his hair, the set of his mouth—all led in a singleminded point toward a long, slender nose. Paul couldn't avoid Fritz Adenauer, but he didn't prize his visits.

Chapter 25

And for the children, there was at least the diversion of Salomeya's stories.

It may be that you are wondering, she said one bedtime to the gathered children, *how it is that there are so many different kinds of birds that fly in the sky. There are the crows, and the birds of prey, and the gulls, and the spindle-legs of the shore, and the swallows. There are so many kinds of birds that one must ask and wonder, from where have all these come?*

I can tell you how this came to be, she told them.

We all know that Our Lord Jesus and His Mother and His Father lived for many years in Poland, hiding from Herod, who searched and searched for them over all the lands until he died, never having found them.

Jesus loved to play, just like you, Franek. And just as you have done, Bernadina, Jesus loved to make little pies of mud. His little Polish friends made pies, too. The girls made things of mud that looked liked cakes and dolls, and the boys often made little soldiers and wagons and horses.

But Jesus made little pies of mud that were different from those any of the other children made. They were all the same, and they all looked like little swallows.

But one day Jesus decided he was going to show off to his little Polish friends, and when he had finished a whole row of his special little mud pies, he took a great, deep breath, and one by one, he breathed into them, to give them life. All the children were delighted to see the swallows dance in the air and fly about.

The Blessed Mother was not pleased with what Jesus had done, and she scolded him. "It is not for you to give life," she said, "it is for God to do this."

Now this made Jesus sad like any little boy is when his mother scolds him, and he knew that he would have to do something to atone for this playfulness and showing off that he had done with God's powers. So he decided that he would teach each of his little Polish friends how to make mud pies as lovely as the ones he had made.

And so he did. But what do you think happened?

Of course, each child's little pies were just a little different from the ones Jesus had made, and each child's little pies were just a little different from those of his friends, for each child put some little part of himself or herself into each of the little mud birds he made.

Well, I can tell you what happened. All the children wanted their little pies to fly, as well. Wouldn't you want yours to fly?

So just as Jesus had done, each child took a long, deep breath, and tried to give life. Of course, nothing happened, and each of their pies just stayed there where it was, and this made the children sad.

It made Jesus sad, too. So he asked his Mother, "Couldn't I just breathe life into these birds my Polish friends have made?"

Blessed Mary was about to say no to Jesus, but we all know that sometimes things happen to make parents change their minds. Just then, the swallows Jesus made the day before gathered around her head, swooping and singing and showing how happy they were to be alive, and so Mary spoke quietly to Jesus. And what do you think she said?

The Holy Mother told Jesus he could breathe life into the little birds the other children had made, but only after the children went away, so that he wouldn't be showing off.

So Jesus waited, and when all his friends had gone away, he took another deep and long breath, and he breathed life into each of the little mud pies that looked like birds.

And when the children returned, how happy they were to see the air filled with their creations, flying and singing their own special songs. Each boy and girl picked out the bird he had made, and gave it a name.

And to this day, each of the birds is known by the name given to it by the little Polish child that day.

And now you know how it has come to be that there are so many different kinds of birds, for there is a kind of bird with his own special shape and song for every Polish child who played with Jesus on that day.

After her story, when it would be time for all the children to sleep, Salomeya would chant the song of the watchmen of Lubownia:

Zapierajcie swiatlo, ogien,
A idzcie spac z Panem Bogiem!

Dim the fires, put out the light,
And may God keep you safe this night.

Chapter 26

As the days wore on, Maria spent more time asleep, encouraged by Jadwiga and the other women, who saw that there was a need to conserve her strength. Jadwiga spent more time with Paul at the hatchway.

Their love was still new. In him, she still saw the straight, strong and kind soldier whose roots sprang from soil more interesting to her than the Baltic beaches she had known since childhood. He saw in her not just an incredible beauty and strength of spirit, but a wisdom and a keenness of mind he'd never seen in other women.

True, he wished of her that she would be less demanding—less eager to have her way with the important decisions of their marriage, such as this emigration to America. She wished he had less militaristic reverence for Germans and more willingness to raise a challenge on this matter of insufficient food without waiting for Hoyt Gruenberg's lead.

But they were truly in love. So overwhelming was this feeling that other feelings, by comparison, had hardly a hint of presence in their lives. When they were together at the hatchway door, the others left them alone in a privacy to be interrupted only by the German men who came to talk, or by the occasional child allowed to walk about the forward compartment.

Jadwiga was constantly worried about the Frederika's headway. She was convinced, as was Hoyt Gruenberg, that the handling of the ship was less skilled than it should be. Her concern focused on the race between the baby growing within her and the travel toward America: The Frederika didn't seem to be trying to win.

She also worried about Maria—a more immediate concern.

"Maria's getting weaker, Paul. Estella thinks it may just be that her time is getting nearer, but she isn't getting enough food. I'm worried that she may be sick with something when the baby comes."

"And you? How do you feel today?"

"Hungry, as usual. I've been wanting carrots all day."

"Carrots? I thought you didn't like carrots."

"I don't, particularly. My baby must like carrots."

Paul chuckled. He and Jadwiga had talked about this business of the baby's hungers, and he didn't know what to make of it.

"Or if there were prunes..."

"Perhaps we'd better talk about something else, Jadwiga. Perhaps about names?"

"I am wary of this subject, Paul."

"Because of what Viktoria said?"

"My mother said the same thing. It was long ago, but what Viktoria said reminded me: the child named before birth is a temptation to fate."

"It's hard not to think about it."

"If we both think about it, when the time comes we'll be able to decide easily. Anyway, we won't know until the baby comes whether we will need a name for a boy or girl, so let's not decide now."

"Fine."

In Jadwiga's attitudes, Paul found an odd blend of women's beliefs he had heard in childhood, and new ones he thought must be special to the Poles of the Hel peninsula, or perhaps to fishing families. She was practical, a fisherman's daughter who could tempt fate daily on open water. She had learned, he thought, that her own resources, and those of the men who sailed with her, were the important consideration in surviving...that the superstitions of the sea meant little. Yet she deferred to an old wives' tale about the naming of children.

And sometimes she didn't know when to let go of a subject.

"It isn't that I really believe in this saying," she said, ignoring the fact that he thought he had closed the subject. "It's just that when it is unnecessary to do so, there is no good reason to tempt fate."

"Fine, I don't disagree," Paul said.

"Maria doesn't believe in it, and I don't try to persuade her that she should wait. So you see I don't really worry about it. It's only that for our child, because there is no reason to do so, I prefer not to decide early."

"I understand," Paul said. "It's fine."

"Maria told me today that Juliusz has agreed: if her baby is a girl they will call her Jadwiga."

"For you?"

"Yes, for me." Inexplicably, Jadwiga suddenly had tears in her eyes, and Paul held her to keep away the sobs that might follow. After a time, she continued. "Juliusz will speak to you about our being Godparents. There are to be Godparents in Poland, too, but in America, we are to be the Godparents."

"This is a great honor, Jadwiga." She was still weeping. "It may be that we should be prepared to ask them for our child."

"It's like the naming," she said. "We will wait."

He would indulge her in this, of course. And in anything else. It was enough that she was carrying his baby. Let alone that she was carrying it aboard a ship that didn't seem to know how to go on the ocean. Let alone that with little complaining, she was carrying a baby without enough food to eat.

One mid-December evening, Fritz Adenauer came to the half-door to interrupt their conversation. Ordinarily, it would have been an unwelcome interruption, but this time he carried something with him.

"This is for Jadwiga if she would like it," Fritz said, and he held out a generous chunk of cheese. It was a part of a much larger portion, which could be seen by the fact of its size and the absence of cheesecloth around most of it.

"Fritz, thank you," Paul said. "We were just talking about how women with child have such hungers." He took the cheese from Fritz and handed it to Jadwiga. "Fritz brought this for you, Jadwiga."

Jadwiga's face brightened. She thanked Fritz, looking to Paul to translate her words, and bit into the cheese without a breath between. Looking at Jadwiga, Fritz nodded his head just slightly to acknowledge her thanks.

"This is so good," she said. "Where did he get it? Was this in his traveling trunk? Does he have more?" she asked. Without pausing for translation or response, she quickly added, "I must take some to Maria. Paul, find out—please find out if there is any more." She said another thank you before disappearing around the water barrel.

"Jadwiga," Paul called. She came back, poking her head around the rainbarrel in an attitude of curiosity. "Jadwiga, be discreet. The children…"

"Yes, of course." She hid the cheese in her clothing, and she was gone. Paul laughed, and Fritz did, too.

"You're very kind to share the extra food you've brought along when you and your wife must be very hungry like all the rest of us," Paul said. "Thank you very, very much. You've made this a special day for Jadwiga."

"Where did she go?"

"Her friend also carries a child. Jadwiga wants to give some to her."

"She is also very kind. I don't know that I would share."

"It's just that she's worried. Her friend is due soon, very soon. Jadwiga thinks she's becoming ill. She wants to help her any way she can."

"Commendable."

Even feeling gratitude, Paul disliked Fritz's demeanor. It took effort to hide the feelings. "Of course, she had no more than seen this cheese for a moment than she was asking where it came from and if there is any more."

"You can keep a secret?"

"Of course."

"It—this cheese—it's from the store of special foods for the officers and first class passengers. It's all in a large closet right back there behind the big mast, under the gangway ramp. Herman has a key. He has lots of keys. There is one he never uses, and it may be that it doesn't even fit the lock. But Hans Koenig is a machinist. He got a look at the key the mess helpers use, and then he saw the one like it among Herman's keys." Fritz was excited, as though the cleverness had been his own. "He borrowed Herman's key when Herman was drunk and then—from a handle on a tool in his toolbox he filed a copy. He finally got it to work just last night."

"This will be discovered, won't it?"

"I don't think so. Not for a long time, anyway. We took from the bottom crate."

"Now or later..."

"It may be. It doesn't matter. We're all so hungry. With some luck, they will never get to that crate before we are off this damned ship in America."

Paul felt a disruption in his stomach, knowing Jadwiga was eating stolen German cheese.

"Even if they find out before we reach New York, they have no way of telling who took it," Fritz continued.

Paul wished Fritz hadn't told him any of this. He was wishing the cheese had never appeared. Raised with an ingrained certainty that wrongdoing would inevitably be punished, he found it hard to believe Fritz and his accomplices could put naive faith in their act going undiscovered. Perhaps they had taken so little, he thought, that the missing cheese would be too little to matter...that it would be assumed to be a matter of how the crate was packed.

Suddenly, Jadwiga was back. "Does he have more, Paul? Will he sell us some?"

Paul wanted to put Jadwiga off with a promise that he would tell her about it later, but he knew that wouldn't work.

"Jadwiga, it's stolen. We mustn't say anything. I promised."

"Tell Fritz we want to buy some more," Jadwiga said. "Tell him we will pay a fair price."

"We'll talk about this later, Jadwiga."

Jadwiga pouted a bit, but she knew that the best way to change Paul's mind was to let him have his way, at least temporarily, and then to catch him at a moment when he would be responsive to her suggestions. So she held her tongue, except for saying another *danke* to Fritz, who this time smiled at her.

Minutes later, when Fritz left them, she was back on the subject.

"Where did he steal the cheese? From another passenger?"

"No. Worse. One of the others found a way to get into the stores. If it's discovered, there will be punishments."

"But if they're going to steal food, it should go into Polish stomachs as well as German ones."

"We could be questioned. We should stay clear of it. I wish I didn't know."

She was silent, then, but it wasn't agreement. He knew he would hear more of this.

Chapter 27

It started the next morning.

She whispered. "I'll go crazy if I don't have more of this cheese, Paul. The hunger was bad enough when I had to endure it thinking there was no choice. Now that I know there's food I could have, it's all the worse. I must have a brick of it so it will last and I can eat from it as the baby demands it."

Paul wanted no dealings with thieves. He wanted not even a flirtation with dishonesty while aboard this German ship.

"And Maria should have some, too."

His conscience was offended by the idea of encouraging thievery by buying from the thief. He couldn't stand the thought of being in the position of begging the purchase of stolen goods from a man like Fritz, even though Fritz seemed more than willing to sell.

"Your child must be a strong and smart one. Your child must have the food it needs to grow strong and smart even before it comes into the world. It is your child asking, not me. Your child will not be corrupted, be made a thief, by this cheese—not any more tomorrow when we know how it was gotten than yesterday when we didn't know. Your child is asking, and one day you will tell your child of this journey and your child will know how hard it was to provide."

His father and mother, he thought, would chastise him just for listening to this pleading that he become an accomplice to theft. His upbringing of straightness and honesty in all matters was something that would stay with him despite all adversity. The temptation was momentary, he knew, and succumbing to it fraught with guilt and danger.

"Your child is asking, and you hesitate. You are more loyal to these Germans who sail this ship so badly, these Germans you have not even met, than you are to your own baby and to me, your wife."

To yield would serve to stop Jadwiga's pleadings only temporarily. To yield would reap a harvest of disgrace in one's own mind if not before the world. Satisfied for the moment, Jadwiga would not forever be satisfied, and there would be the problem of how to satisfy her hungers the next time, and the next.

"One day it will be asked of you, Paul Adamik, what it is that you did for your child before your child was born."

He knew he couldn't do this. He could not yield.

"You have already been a good father. You are already taking your child to America, where there will be opportunity, and where you'll be able to provide. Now isn't the time to hesitate to do what your wife and your child need. The hunger is very great, and your child's need is great."

He couldn't.

The deal was made two days later. It came with the understanding that Fritz was involving himself in a double theft. With his partners in this business of stealing from the ship's first-class stores, the plan was to hide whatever was taken, so that each could then take from the total to consume. This way, there would be far less chance of an individual being discovered with stolen food in his possession. But Fritz said he would also be stealing from his partners—from the cache—to sell to Paul.

"Further," Fritz explained in whispers that made his German all the more obscure, "it has been agreed that if the thefts are eventually discovered, the four of us will accept the responsibility and there will be no allowing blame to fall on others. Only we will be punished, and for this risk we are receiving good payment from the others.

"But there is agreement that no one outside our section is even to know of this, let alone receive from what we take. Thus I will be taking an even greater chance by selling to you—a chance of discovery either by my comrades or by the officers of the ship. Do you understand?"

Paul nodded that he understood. He wanted to walk away. He resented having to listen to this lengthy preamble before being allowed to do something he would prefer not to do.

"Furthermore you must understand that this is not a matter simply of asking for something and my getting it for you. I don't have the key Hans made. Even if I did, I couldn't risk using it alone, because I would need a lookout both to keep me from being caught by my friends and by the authorities."

"I understand. You can sell me only what you have." "And that there is extra cost for this risk."

"Yes."

"Very well. There is some cheese left, and I am willing to sell you one brick for two marks. Is that of interest?"

Paul nodded again. Within, he was wincing at the price, which was so far beyond merely unreasonable that he found it hard to believe that Fritz could demand this much. But he had promised Jadwiga. And it was needed because without it, he would have no peace.

Then he spoke the German sentence he had worked out: "My wife has hope for some cheese for her friend."

"Even if this were possible, what would she say about its source?"

"I don't know. I will buy only for Jadwiga."

"I'll get you some cheese tonight. Have the money ready. With extra, just in case. Maybe I can bring two bricks for you."

Paul nodded again. He couldn't see that he had any choice. Buying from a thief meant doing business on the thief's terms. He resolved he would buy all he could this time, but then persuade Jadwiga that the price was exorbitant and the risk excessive.

That night, the meal brought by the Frederika's galley help was cold. Until then, evening meals had been at least warm.

"They've quenched the fires," Hoyt Gruenberg told him across the half-door. "Cold meals at the end of the day are a sure sign. The captain fears a storm. There must be no chance of a spill of hot coals."

Paul was waiting for Fritz Adenauer to arrive with the cheese he had arranged to purchase, but he couldn't tell Hoyt. Lurking within sight of the hatchway, Fritz was already growing impatient. Jadwiga was waiting for the cheese. Paul became so distracted with this worry that he was having trouble putting German words together. Hoyt noticed, then noticed Fritz.

"Is he selling food to you?" Hoyt asked abruptly.

Paul pretended he didn't understand. Hoyt wasn't fooled.

"Listen. Those three are courting trouble," Hoyt said. "They're selling to almost everybody, so much it's sure to be noticed. They're like the drunkard who thinks one more swig won't be noticed, until he has taken so many swigs that there's nothing left in the bottle. If he's selling to you, make sure he understands your payments are for his taking the risk—*all* the risk."

Paul nodded, then looked away, not wanting to meet the German's eyes.

"I'll go away now so you can talk with him. Be careful. He's not to be trusted." He poked Paul's shoulder as he left; Paul took that to mean that he understood.

Fritz hardly waited until Hoyt had crawled into his own space in the straw. He had the cheese with him, wrapped in a butcher's apron, but he withheld it.

"Did you tell him?"

"No," Paul said. "No, nothing." Nervous, wanting the conversation over, he found only his simplest German words. "I told him nothing."

"See that you don't. I don't trust him. He knows. All the men know, and most are buying from us. But he must not know I'm selling to you or even that you know what we're doing."

Paul nodded. He wanted the transaction over—to be away from Fritz's moment of control over his life. Glancing furtively into his own section, Fritz passed the cheese through to Paul—two bricks, and received Paul's four marks, which he immediately pocketed.

"Tomorrow night, or the next night, we'll get something else, maybe some dried fruit." He said it with an assumption that Paul would want to buy. Not waiting for any discussion, not even saying *Guten Abend*, he walked away.

Mercifully, Jadwiga did not thank him effusively, which would only have intensified his feelings of shame. She took the cheese and tore off a large portion, which she began eating immediately. After a first mouthful she kissed him on the cheek. "You will be a good father," she said.

By that time, Maria and the others were asleep. After eating much cheese—too quickly, Paul thought—Jadwiga quietly slipped into the row of sleepers.

As she did, he felt the ship heave in response to a heavy wave crossing the bow. The storm was beginning. Lost in thought, feeling unclean, he remembered something his father once said to him: *There is only one unbearable hardship: Being untrue to yourself.* On the other hand, he reasoned, perhaps he could never understand the needs of a woman with child. His part was to provide.

When he joined Jadwiga, sleep came uneasily and fitfully. He was in it now, with Fritz. The exorbitant prices would be demanded until all his army pay would be gone and, for it, his only purchase would be shame. Half-awake, half-dreaming, he remembered Kazimierz Steck's warning to Jan Poglicki aboard the train—and then, Jan's words: *You must not be surprised if, before this journey has ended, a skill at filching from*

Germans will be more prized than a skill with their words. But he could smell Jadwiga's hair, and his heart was torn.

When the storm in its fullness hit the ship, it was sudden and instant. There was thunder, and the Frederika twisted, as though spun by a giant hand. With the movement, a deep-throated *crack*. Then, almost immediately, the ship's timbers reverberated as something heavy crashed to the deck above.

Almost as one, the row of sleepers sat up in alarm. In the midst of a half-dreamt argument with a German commander, Paul heard Jadwiga's voice: "The mast. The *mainmast*. They've lost the *mainmast*."

Chapter 28

By the reckoning Maria recounted to Jadwiga, it should have been many days past Christmas that her baby would arrive. This intimate knowledge, shared among the women, gave the illusion there would be time to prepare.

But such was not the case.

There was soft singing and praying at bedtime. Maria, feeling unwell, didn't participate but listened, eyes focused on a distant scene. She said her thoughts were of home and how things would be among her family on this eve of holiday. Salomeya held her hand. Jadwiga stroked her hair and cheeks as she lay amid extra straw gathered in provision for her special situation.

There was a sense of the ordained.

It was the middle of the night when Maria awoke in great pain and clutched at her Juliusz.

It was Christmas eve.

The men cleared out, going aft of the rainbarrel to the manure pile to stand with the worried Juliusz to wait out the birth of his child. Only Jozef Dominiak lingered for a moment, to move the lantern. The women put up the blankets for privacy.

Within the enclosure, the midwife Ursula Jakubik and the grandmother Salomeya Steck attended Maria. Jadwiga stood ready to do their bidding, as did Estella Poglicki and Viktoria Murak, the two of fewest children—the two who could be spared, perhaps, until their children would wake and call for motherly attention amid the worrisome events of the night.

There was immediately the apprehension that something was not right. It was not just that Maria was too early; there was the irregularity of the pain and her gasping for breath.

Among the men, there were no words said to ease Juliusz's mind. It was no time for the pretense of reassurance. He stood among them, yet alone; with them, yet apart from them by great distance, shuddering with the cold, a stranger to compassion. He could only wait.

There was a sense of the ordained.

Thus there was an unvoiced understanding among the women that the still child was not the fault of the Russian midwife. There was, in any case, the immediate matter of Maria's continuing difficulty and time enough later for recriminations.

Jadwiga stood, crying quietly, saddened, then knelt in a silent entreaty to God, terrified beyond her ability to feel, while Salomeya Steck prayed aloud and Ursula Jakubik looked on in helplessness. And while her best friend, Maria Sczepaniak, yielded in her struggle and died.

It was Jadwiga, going to Paul for comfort, whose tears brought the sadness to Juliusz. No words were needed. They stood together, arms now finally encircling Juliusz in uncontrolled sobbing. Jadwiga cried as Paul had never heard before, and he silently shed tears in quantity she had never seen before. The other men stood helpless, weaponless in a lost engagement with disaster. There was the awkwardness of no place to go and nothing to do where they were. Juliusz, Jadwiga, and Paul were alone, anyway, in the isolation of transcendent grief.

It was Christmas Day. And it was not Christmas Day.

It was a December 25 forever to be distinguished in memory by the singularity of the death of Maria Sczepaniak and her child, and the extraordinary grief of Juliusz, husband and father of departed mother and child.

Because a portside pigpen had been emptied by the taking of a sow, baggage had been placed there. There, the Stecks' trunk provided a place, lifted from the discomforts of mundane life, where Maria and her child could be at rest. Before Juliusz saw his Maria again, she was dressed in the wedding gown the women found among the meager accumulations of their short life together.

The baby, dressed in the only garment it ever would wear, was placed in Maria's arms upon her breast, and the cross was put into her hands.

When the cattletender came to the hatchway for the first time that morning, Hoyt Gruenberg came, too, and with them there was a face new to this forward compartment of the Frederika's hold.

Hoyt spoke softly to Paul over the murmur of praying.

"I passed the word topside about the need here for a midwife. I'm very sorry, but the ship's physician heard of this today and he has come…I told him no man would be welcome, but…If Juliusz and his wife could just talk with him…"

"Mother and child died in the night," Paul said. "It was too early for the child to come."

There was a flash of astonishment on the doctor's face, then anger and despair, then resignation.

"I am Doctor Hoffmeister," he said, offering his hand. "You are Herr Adamik?"

The doctor was a younger man than one might expect, taller and more handsome. Though his features were Germanic, they were softened by a demeanor more gentle than one might expect of a ship's official.

"The deceased must be buried soon," he said to Paul. "By the end of light today."

Paul nodded.

"Then tomorrow I will examine all the people in this section. The children, the women, the men, everyone."

Paul nodded understanding.

"Is it true your wife is pregnant, too?"

Paul merely looked at the doctor.

"I must examine her, as well. This is no place to give birth. We will take her to the sick bay when the time comes."

"She hopes the baby will wait until after arrival in America."

"If so, all the better. But we must be prepared. You should resign yourself to the possibility of birth at sea. This ship is not as fast as it once was, and we've had bad luck with weather…several days at calm, several in difficult winds making little real progress…"

"Is it certain the baby will come before we reach America?"

"I can't answer that until I examine her. What do you understand to be the date?"

"In a month, perhaps."

"We will prepare for birth at sea."

Paul's mind raced, searching for a way of handling this with Jadwiga—and with the others. He reached within himself in a conscious effort for calm. There was time to think it through, he told himself, and he said nothing.

"For now, there must be plans for the burial. By four o'clock you must choose the bearers—four men sure of foot. If the weather remains safe, they and the husband may come to the deck. Do you understand?"

Paul nodded.

"Now I must examine the body."

Paul led the doctor to where Maria and her baby lay amid prayerful sorrow. All the women and many of the men prayed; most of the children copied them. Kazimierz Steck knelt with Juliusz, who still sobbed.

The examination was cursory. It seemed to Paul that the doctor wanted only to verify that Maria was dead. When they returned to the hatchway, the doctor spoke to the hunchback. "I'll send the plank. You bring the stone and line. Be prepared by four o'clock, but give these people some time. Wait until later."

A young seaman brought a smooth hardwood plank with carrying handles to the hatchway, where Paul waited to receive it. Helped by the seaman and Hoyt Gruenberg, Herman brought a squared-off ballast stone, which they placed just inside the hatchway with a coil of rope.

There was the quiet murmur of the rosary. From time to time, Salomeya Steck prayed aloud. And there was Juliusz's sobbing.

At 2:30, Paul caught Jadwiga's eye and she left the community of prayer. He tapped Big Jozef's shoulder to get his attention, but spoke to Jadwiga.

"Jadwiga, the doctor told Herman to prepare Maria. He brought this stone and line. It will be best if the hunchback has no part in this."

"Nobody will tie the stone except me."

Alone, Jozef carried the stone. Paul took the plank, Jadwiga the rope, and they went forward to Maria. Tadeusz Murak and Ludwig Karpczinski rose to help, and they transferred the body to the plank.

Juliusz became apprehensive. Paul went to him, and spoke quietly. "Juliusz, the doctor says that Maria must be buried today, but there is still an hour. You will go to the deck, and there are to be four bearers. Do you want to choose the bearers?"

Juliusz shook his head.

Following Jadwiga's gestured, unspoken instructions, Jozef placed the heavy stone on the plank, at Maria's feet.

Paul went to Kazimierz Steck. "There are to be four bearers," he said, and Kazimierz understood he was to make the selection. He pointed. The bearers were to be Paul, Ludwig Karpczinski, Big Jozef, and Stanisław Krulik.

Jadwiga did her best to lose herself in the tying of the knots. She knew that if she gave in to her pain she would be unable to do it. It went slowly.

She knew that if she didn't tie the knots, an ordinary seaman might do it. She had no experience with German seamen on big ships, but she knew the tendency was to use a clumsy grab knot that could go slack and allow a body to tumble independent of the weight. These were special knots, tied reverently for the stone, but especially so for the body. Stone and body should become an entity that would slip cleanly into the sea as though stone alone.

Her first experience tying these knots had been with her dog—the family's, really, but the first with which Jadwiga had a special bond. She recalled her father guiding her hands in practice, and then in the tying to the animal.

Securing the rope about Maria's stone, she recalled how she came to understand the need for it to be her to do the tying; it brought understanding that this was the last she would see of her pet. There was resignation and release in this preparation of a body for the sea.

She gathered the skirt of Maria's wedding dress to tie it with the line so it would hold securely during the plunge to the water.

In doing this she had to pause to allow a new flow of tears.

It had been a May afternoon.

There had been the knowledge that Helena Wdowiak would die. The same illness had taken another woman in the small fishing community, and the wait for death had been difficult.

The bravery of Jadwiga's mother was even greater than that of her father, who stayed at her bedside through the last days, holding her, praying with her, allowing himself to cry softly when sleep would come briefly to relieve his Helena's suffering.

Just at the end, when there was no more time and no more hope, her father brought Jadwiga to stand near her mother and then to hold her hands and then to hug her and kiss her goodbye. And Jadwiga's mother quietly slipped away in a soft sleep that took her last breath.

Her brothers were at sea, fishing with the helpers, and Jadwiga met them at the pier to tell them their mother was gone. One of the helpers went for the priest, and at nightfall, just as the sun slipped into the sea, Helena Wdowiak went to her final resting place secured to a stone with knots tied by husband, sons, and daughter.

Jadwiga had been only twelve. Her brothers, though older, had cried as much.

But afterward, it was Jadwiga who missed her mother the most. As she went about doing the things her mother had done, she learned over and over that she should have asked, so many times, how this was done or that was done. There were the neighbor women, but Jadwiga by then was not inclined to ask.

She grew closer to her father and brothers than ever before, now that they were mother to her, as well.

She would remember forever the tying of those knots—the gathering of her mother's wedding skirt about her ankles, the manipulating of the rope, and the deep passion of despair.

Now she was feeling it again, this time for the little sister she hadn't known until just a month of precious days before.

At 3:30, Herman again came to the hatchway, this time dressed for an occasion on deck amid officers. Hoyt Gruenberg was with him. But Paul met them, blocking the way. "She has been prepared," he said. "The knots have been tied." When Herman looked doubtful, he added, "My wife is from fishing people. She knows the proper tyings."

"Then bring her out so I can see. If it's wrong, I must answer."

"Yes, very soon." As much to Hoyt as to the hunchback, he added, "It's best if you wait here." Hoyt understood, and he turned so as to encourage Herman to turn with him and wait.

Forward, Paul nodded to the other bearers, giving a special tilt of his head to Jozef so that together they could take the stone end of the plank, where the greatest weight was concentrated. Ludwig and Stanisław took the head end. Estella Poglicki began to tie Maria's wedding cap to her head with a white ribbon, but Juliusz objected through gasping sobs, and it was understood he wanted it as a remembrance.

Juliusz following, the bearers made their way through the pinch of the hatchway and past the Germans in midship, who stood with bowed heads. The scaling of the midship ramp was awkward for Jozef and Paul, who, going first behind Herman, held their end of the plank low so the stone wouldn't get away from them. Behind, Stanisław and Ludwig held their end high to keep Maria level.

It was awkward for Juliusz, too. He couldn't move in any one relationship with the procession. He had to follow through the first hatchway, but then his help was needed on the ramp. It was just to steady his Maria's corpse, with the baby tied in her arms, but Paul thought it was more than should be asked of him. The hunchback, leading the way but trying to examine the knots, was no help.

There was a burst of unfamiliar sensation as they emerged into daylight. The air was scythe sharp with December cold, its freshness an assault on the lungs. Though the sun was blood red and low in the sky, its light burned to the back of eyes accustomed only to a lantern's glow. The sight of a horizon at variance with the deck brought a momentary threat of nausea.

Shivering, they waited while Herman went for the necessary ship's personnel. They were long minutes in coming. Juliusz knelt beside his Maria and their child, as though to shield them from the wind.

As their eyes fought to accommodate the light, the other men began to look around. Paul could not look at Maria. He looked instead into the rigging at the damaged mast, a ragged break interrupting its reach for sky. The squared sails on foremast and mizzenmast were only partly filled with breeze, not straining with power the way calendar pictures promised. For a moment, he willed air into one of them, and drew America nearer by inches, but then the breeze failed and will gave way to worry over the coming of his own child.

The cattletender returned with the doctor and an officer. The officer gestured, and the bearers raised their burden to waist level. Juliusz clutched Maria's body, making it difficult, while the officer examined the knots. "Sehr gut," he said to Herman, who acknowledged the compliment but avoided Paul's eyes.

Now the officer led the burial party toward the aft starboard rail, showing by example that they must be careful on the outsloping tilt of the mist-iced deck. They found it difficult to level the body to the horizon, coping with the uncertain weight of Juliusz, who still held Maria.

With a gesture, the officer had Paul and Jozef place the foot end of the burial plank on the rail. With a hook of his head he signaled that Jozef should stand ready to pull Juliusz away. He held up three fingers to Ludwig and Stanisław as indication of a count, and then there was a short wait as he read softly from a small Bible in his hand.

He looked up at Jozef, who pulled Juliusz away as gently as necessity would permit.

"Ein, zwei, drei," he counted. Stanisław and Ludwig lifted.

Maria's body, holding her child, slid gracefully into the frigid air and straight down. Looking over the rail, Paul saw the ocean cooperate in this difficult moment by heaving low with a wave to receive the bodies as they entered in peace with only a dip and the softest of sounds.

Paul couldn't look at Juliusz. He wanted to rush to Jadwiga, to hold her, to know she was there.

Chapter 29

Viktoria Murak, who once had dealt with a man of medicine, explained to the children that they would be asked to hold out their tongues for the doctor to see, and that he might look into their eyes, too. It wouldn't hurt, she said, and they should do what the Adamik man, speaking the doctor's words but in Polish, would tell them.

In spite of these assurances, there was apprehension. The coming of the ship's doctor would have been a welcome event to give respite from routine had it occurred under circumstances less bound to the grief of the day before. As it was, there was the worry the children felt over death and their understanding that a child, too, had died. And now this man of the ship who concerned himself with the sick and dying was coming to see them, and things were being said to calm them. To the children, this was disquieting.

The visit was later than Paul had expected when he told them of it the night before. The doctor, who next to Hoyt Gruenberg was the kindest and most soft-spoken German they'd encountered on this trip, even took a few moments to pay his respects to Juliusz and say consoling words for Paul to translate.

The children were examined first, and though the doctor spoke of starting with the youngest, his plans changed when Bernadina Ran and Franek Dominiak decided they would set an example and stepped forward holding hands. Bernadina giggled, but Franek stood at an exaggerated military attention, except for his tongue being out.

No one could help it, and there was a little laughter. It was a tenuous but welcome rip in the cloak of grief over the compartment. Furthermore, it settled the minds of some of the other children. Four-year-old Jan Murak stepped up behind Franek, starting a queue of boys.

Katrina Poglicki rushed to be second of the girls, beating Monika Ran, who pulled Pelagia Dominiak with her. Apprehension disappeared in a burst of competitive spirit, and the crying from Bolesław Ran was not in fear of the doctor, but in pique at being last in line.

Examination of the children became routine after the first two. The doctor's assistant needed no instruction for holding the lantern, and Paul simply repeated the sequence of instructions for each child.

The doctor talked, nonetheless. He looked at the children, speaking soothingly, but his words were for Paul: "Herr Adamik, because it is late today we will put off the examination of your wife until tomorrow. I'll give you a pass to come with her to the sick bay at eight o'clock."

"Show the doctor your tongue," Paul said to Katrina.

"Am I speaking too quickly?" the doctor asked.

"No, sir."

"Please stop me if I speak too fast or if my meaning is unclear," the doctor said, and then he continued.

"I know that there is great suspicion of having a man attend a woman in childbirth. And that some of the people with you here may even consider it very improper. Ears, please."

"Let the doctor look in your ear, Katrina."

"I know this is the case. I want you to understand that my only concern here is that we have no more death aboard this ship. We've already lost three—two in the crew and…"

"Now the other ear."

"I don't say your wife will die in childbirth without my help. Only that this hole is no place for a child to be brought into the world. It's unclean and that alone represents a danger to both mother and baby. Please tell Katrina she has been a very good girl and ask her if I can have a kiss on my cheek."

"Katrina, the doctor says you're very nice and were very good. Do you have a kiss for his cheek?"

Shyly, Katrina kissed the doctor, then ran to her mother. The doctor turned now to Paul, and spoke directly to him. "I hope that when her time comes, your wife will come to sick bay, bringing with her a woman of her choice—the midwife or another—and we will extend to her the best circumstances possible for a birth. If there are any difficulties, we are equipped far better there than here. Who is this next one, what is her name?"

"This is Monika."

"*Guten tag*, Monika."

"Show the doctor your tongue, Monika."

"Mind the lantern, Bruno. Lower, please. I can't promise you it will go better for your wife than for the one we put into the sea. But I can help her and the baby. Chances are better in sick bay. I don't ask you to agree, just to understand what I say. Do you understand me?"

"Yes, sir."

"It's up to you to speak with your wife. There will probably be great opposition from the other women. I don't expect you to persuade everybody. I only hope that your wife will have the courage to ignore what the older ones say and take this opportunity to have her child in cleaner conditions and with professional assistance."

"Ears, please, Monika."

"Tomorrow I hope we find there's nothing to be concerned about. But there is no way of predicting all that might go wrong, and we are better prepared to deal with the unexpected in sick bay."

"*Ja, Herr Doctor.*"

"You must tell your wife that she is not to be worried because of her friend's death. It is likely all will go well for her. But do what you must to persuade her to have her child in sick bay, please, for her sake."

The doctor finished examining Monika and looked at Paul. "She is not to be concerned. You will be nearby, and if she wishes another woman can come with you."

"Yes, sir, I understand," Paul said.

"Which is the mother of this one?" the doctor asked, having come to Pelagia.

"Delfinia," Paul said, gesturing toward her.

"How long has she had the cough?"

"Since before the trip, Herr Doktor. Delfinia, when did Pelagia's cough start?"

Delfinia looked at Jozef, who answered: "Many months…a long time ago." Paul translated.

"This bears watching. She is not a healthy child. I will send down some medicine with my assistant. The mother should give it to her at bedtime, and perhaps once late in the morning if she is coughing. Please tell her."

Paul translated. Both parents thanked the doctor.

"Now before I examine the adults and then the infants, please introduce me to your wife. She must see that I have no horns."

Paul looked at Jadwiga and beckoned her to come to them. The doctor, who had been sitting on a traveling trunk while examining the children, stood, being careful to fit his head between crossbeams.

"Jadwiga, Dr. Hoffmeister has asked to be introduced to you. He wants to examine you tomorrow, not today, but he wants to meet you now."

"*Wścibski.*"

"Jadwiga, please don't. He will ask that I interpret your words to him."

"No matter. He is a snoop."

"What's she saying, Herr Adamik?"

"Hello. She says hello."

"Please tell her I'm pleased to meet her and that I want to help her. You can tell her the other things later."

"Jadwiga, the doctor is glad to meet you. He only wants to help."

"Herr Adamik, let us understand something between us."

"Yes, sir."

"Tomorrow, I'll have many questions for your wife about how she feels, about how she's sleeping, and so on. It's important that you interpret accurately, conceal nothing, and give me the best meaning you can. It's important to my understanding of her condition. Understood?"

"Understood."

"Tomorrow you will be accurate to the syllable?"

"Yes, sir." Paul was embarrassed. He had no idea whether the doctor had understood Jadwiga's comment, but he was embarrassed that she called him a busybody and that he was caught concealing the meaning of her words.

"Now, please ask the adults to respond to questions as a group. Ask first if anyone feels any nausea other than seasickness. Upset stomach or dizziness."

For another few minutes, Paul interpreted the doctor's questions for the adults. Juliusz, who lay with his back to the group, was not pressed to participate. There were no responses that would call any individual to the doctor's attention, except when Ignatz Ran started to speak of his aching hip. He was quickly discouraged by looks from the others. Attention turned to the Stecks and to Old Man Kradzinski, with questions appropriate for people of advanced age. Bolesław Kradzinski followed the lead of the Stecks, and said nothing of any special aches or pains. The doctor commented that for old people, they seemed to be holding up quite well.

There was no way to be alone. No privacy. No place to go. Only the Stecks had any semblance of privacy, but that was in the bow cribwork at the cost of proximity to the cold of the sea which reached through straw and clothing to suck heat from the body. Although Jadwiga said the Stecks should have a warmer place, Kazimierz and Salomeya wanted to stay where they were. It was above the slatwork, away from playing children and somewhat free of the intrusion of casually roving eyes. It gave them, at least, a way to be alone.

After this month at sea, wanting to be alone was a compelling urge that rivaled hunger in nagging at the mind.

It was harder for the men, the women agreed. The men weren't accustomed to the children playing underfoot. They weren't used to the constant proximity of other families, of other idle men. Jozef and Piotr, in particular, found their uneasy truce all the more wearing for being rarely out of the sight of each other.

When there was enough water in the rainwater vat, bathing provided brief respite from the constant presence of others. Even shivering in the cold, one could linger just a moment or two longer than it took to become clean, and bathe in the aloneness before once again having to emerge into the open of the compartment.

There was one other place, aft of the bulky rainbarrel, near the manure pile, at the hatchway door. There, a person or a couple could be away from the rest. Others passed by going behind a screen of blankets around the manure pile, so it wasn't perfect, but it was the closest thing.

For the others, the hatchway was a place to be for short times during the day. But at night, they gave it over to Paul. At first the benefit was conversation with Hoyt Gruenberg and a harvest of gossip. But now that they were relying on him to deal with Fritz Adenauer after the other Germans were sleeping, there was all the more reason Paul should have the leaning place of the hatchway half door to himself after the evening meal.

Days before Christmas, it had become the evening custom that the German passengers would sing a hymn, then pause while the Poles in the forward compartment sang one. Then the Germans would sing another, then the Poles, and so on. The voices would waft softly through the open top half of the hatchway door, eventually putting the children in both sections to sleep. It would end when a German woman with an extraordinary soprano voice sang *Ave Maria*, the other Germans humming.

This made it a welcome place of refuge for Paul and Jadwiga on the night of the day after Christmas, for there was much to be talked about. But for a long while, Jadwiga wanted only to be held while she cried.

"It is so wrong." This was all she could say. "It is so wrong."

Paul said nothing, feeling that nothing was so fitting as silence. He felt like crying, too, except that there were more immediate concerns distracting him.

He was concerned about Juliusz, who was deep in bewilderment and grief now, but whose response to this tragedy seemed somehow incomplete. Paul wondered what it was he expected of Juliusz, then realized what it was: anger. Paul was feeling anger, but there was none yet from Juliusz. Paul's was vaguely directed at God, but without full conviction that he could blame God. Juliusz wasn't showing the rage he must feel.

Even in these thoughts, Paul was distracted by another concern—the thefts and his role as go-between. He was no longer so uneasy with the dishonesty: Kazimierz had lifted some of the guilt by saying that his own family and his own people were the proper concern of first weight. What troubled him now was the inconsistency: Fritz made claims of double-stealing but then had little difficulty satisfying the quantities requested. Paul took this as evidence that there was no double-stealing—that Fritz's partners were fully aware of what was going on. He was reminded of a comment of Tadeusz Murak's that Fritz was probably selling to the forward compartment because he could, without stigma of gouging his own, charge many times more than a fair price.

But more troubling than anything else was his concern over Jadwiga and his own child. This overriding worry stole his capacity for orderly thought and sensible analysis. It was particularly difficult because he found Jadwiga unpredictable at best and quite unreasonable much of the time. His own thinking was that having the assistance of the German doctor in bringing their child into the world was only prudent. The impropriety could be forgotten if only mother and child were healthy and survived. It need never be mentioned again. Surely the others would be understanding and forget this once all disembarked in America, but even that didn't matter. He cared only that Jadwiga and the baby would be well.

But he doubted his ability to persuade her even to consider it. It was, after all, women's business. But he would try.

"Jozef was whispering," Jadwiga said long after her sobs had subsided. "He was whispering that if Juliusz were to take his hammer from his tools and kill all the Russians, it would be a simple matter to have them disappear with the manure."

"He didn't say this to Juliusz, did he?"

"No, to Ludwig. Ludwig told him not to say it to Juliusz."

"We must be watchful of Juliusz."

"Yes." Talk of incidental matters, important as they might be, was Jadwiga's way of letting go the silence between them. She knew Paul wanted to talk.

"Jadwiga, I must tell you what the ship's doctor said today."

"He wants to be the one to bring the baby."

"Yes."

"Paul, if the baby comes while we are still at sea, it might be best. Would you object?" Paul was astounded. "I will ask Salomeya her views on this," she continued. He had expected resistance. "I must ask Salomeya about Ursula's midwifing. I don't know if Ursula was at fault in Maria's difficulties, but even if she wasn't, I wasn't reassured. She wasn't calm when there was trouble. I've seen many animals born, and difficulty in birth, but I don't think Ursula has seen difficulty such as Maria had. I will ask Salomeya."

"But in the meantime, tomorrow morning, the doctor wants to examine you."

"Yes, I know."

"He gave me a pass and he wants us to come in the morning."

"Yes, that's fine." Paul was astounded a second time. "You will be with me all the time?" He nodded. "I still hope my baby will come in America. There is still time."

"Time until when?"

"February."

"But when in February?"

"The middle. But the baby could be late, or it could be early. But February is it, of that I'm certain."

"You said the Frederika has crossed many times in thirty days. We could be in America."

"I hope so."

"I thought you might be unwilling to have the doctor examine you."

"He is a snoop, as I said. *Wścibski.*"

"No. I believe him when he says he wants to help."

"Oh, I believe that. He was very good with the children. But I don't know that it is correct for him to help, especially if there is a midwife. He wants to help, but he's also a snoop."

"But you're willing to be examined?"

"Yes. Anyway, if he asks something that I don't care to answer or wants me to do something improper, we will just walk out. By then I will have seen the sails and how the ship goes."

"Oh, that's it, then. You want to go topside to see the damage."

"And you must ask him where we are, Paul. It will help me judge whether we will be on the ship or in America when the time comes."

"He will want you to agree to the sick bay."

"We'll tell him I must ask Salomeya."

"He may want agreement tomorrow."

"There's time. If he knows anything about babies coming he will know that. Anyway, I can agree and then simply not go to him when the pains start. But we needn't worry about what to say until tomorrow, and then when you're translating for me, we can talk it over if he asks something I feel is wrong."

There was scheming in Jadwiga's voice, but Paul was grateful that no argument was required to get her to the doctor for the examination.

"Anyway, if Ursula is not a good midwife, it may be that the doctor will be better. We will hear what he has to say, and then I'll ask Salomeya."

He held her gently in gratitude. But within moments, the German woman's voice rose above the creaking of the ship, singing *Ave Maria*. Jadwiga's tears flowed again, and he gathered her closer.

Chapter 30

The wind had sharpened teeth. Paul tried to stand upweather to protect Jadwiga, but she moved about the deck freely, relishing the scratch of December across her cheeks. This was like a Sunday outing for her—a chance to see light of day and things of the Frederika not seen in Bremerhaven.

The deck shimmered with frost, testimony to the wetness of wood and chill of the air. A luster of sugarmelt on coils of rope told its tale of rigging unchanged overnight. The sky held no bright spot of sun; instead a sunrising yellow-grey challenged eyes fresh from the dark hold. In the air there was a suggestion of snow to come. The topgallant of the main-mast, stripped of its yards, was lashed to the starboard rail. There was exhilaration in the surge of the ship, but sadness in seeing her wounds.

"They've lost most of their mainmast sail area—the high part that gets the best air," Jadwiga told Paul. "They're carrying more sail than they should on the foremast, trying to make time, I suppose. But they can't ride as high on the wind without the main sheets. They've crippled this ship."

"What speed do you think we're making?"

"No better than half what we should. But even worse, we're tacking without enough mainsail, too shallow to the wind. We should be chal-lenging it more, like this." She plotted a course with her arm, cutting tighter to the flow of air. "Speed means nothing when the ship is out of trim, so flat to the wind."

Despite this bad news and the obstreperous wind, Jadwiga was happy to be in the open. They were early for their visit to the doctor just for this reason. It was too cold for first-class passengers to be on deck, and only a few sailors were required for this period of steady going that demanded no changes of sail. They were virtually alone.

"I'm afraid Hoyt's right," Jadwiga said. "This is an old wheezer of a ship. They're saving the mainmast to show the wood was weak with age and perhaps parasites. They'll claim the mast should have held, but it's fortunate it gave way. We could have been pushed far over to the side. We would take the backwash of waves through the hatches."

After they had walked the deck around, stopping often to examine rigging and relish the sweep of Atlantic around them on all sides, Paul asked a seaman for directions to the sick bay, then suggested to Jadwiga that they should not be late.

The doctor's office presented a crisp Teutonic orderliness. There was a clear intentionality to the arrangement of each implement and item of furniture. Here, years ago, the cabinetmaker's craft had been practiced with love in a tradition of shipwrighting that had made the Frederika a great vessel. Clean edges, doweled joints, and shine were everywhere. Surprising to Paul, there was even glass in some of the cabinet doors, and everywhere the brassy gleam of keyholes. Even to noses contaminated by pig-pen travel and recently assaulted by fresh salt air, there was an odor of tenacious cleanliness.

Pointing, the doctor's assistant directed them to sit on a bench to wait. He sat at the doctor's desk, but on a sidechair, occasionally writing on the top sheet of some papers.

"Ask this one if he knows our position," Jadwiga said.

He was about to ask, but the outer door opened. It was the doctor. The assistant stood, and Paul did, too.

"Ah, the Adamiks. Welcome. Bruno, take the Adamiks' coats. It's not so cold in here as to require outerwear."

"Jadwiga, he'll take your coat," Paul said.

Jadwiga took off the coat, revealing a large dress that Paul recognized as a loan from Delfinia Dominiak. She had outgrown her own clothes—even an overlarge dress brought to wear in the final weeks of pregnancy. Paul was surprised but said nothing.

"Now, Bruno, there are breakfasts for the Adamiks almost ready. You will go for them, please." As the assistant left, the doctor spoke to Paul. "I have nothing to say about meals served to passengers. But I know you're not receiving full ration. Here in the sick bay I do have my say, so I have arranged a good breakfast for you while you're here."

"*Danke, Herr Doktor.*"

"To the extent you wish to do so, Herr Adamik, you may set aside any part of yours and take it with you for your wife to eat later."

Paul noticed again that there was something different in the doctor's German—something not unpleasant, but he couldn't take the time to contemplate what it was. To Jadwiga, he said, "Some breakfast is coming for us."

"Good. This will be at least one good meal we will have this week."

Now the doctor settled into a casual posture on the edge of his desk. "Please translate."

"Herr Doktor, Jadwiga sometimes speaks with a sharp tongue..."

"Translate the sharpness as well as the words."

"She comments that this is at least one good meal we will have this week."

"Rations are always a problem. This is only my third passage, but it was the same last time. They say it's never good. This trip is particularly bad because progress is so poor. The mate has ordered rationing for an extended voyage—even longer than originally expected as the longest possible transit."

"I understand," Paul said.

"What did he say, Paul?"

"I'll tell you some of it later. He says the meals are small because our progress is slow."

"And birds have feathers."

"Jadwiga, please hold your tongue. He insists that I translate exactly."

"Good. Ask our position and how many days we are supposed to survive on these stingy rations."

The doctor looked at Paul inquisitively.

"Sir, can you tell us how many days of sailing are left?"

"Was that her question?"

"Yes."

The doctor looked at Jadwiga. "We haven't yet covered half the distance. It could go well, and we could make New York in another 25 to 30 days. That's longer than we would like, but there was an accident with the mast. Did you notice?" Paul nodded when the doctor glanced at him. "But if we have another storm or if the winds don't hold...Well, then we will have a longer time."

Paul translated for Jadwiga, who sniffed in disgust at the answer.

"Please ask your wife, Herr Adamik, when exactly it is that she expects the birth."

"She has told me..."

"No, please ask her."

"Jadwiga, the doctor asks exactly when you expect the baby will come."

"On the twentieth day of February."

"So exact?"

"Yes, February 20."

When Paul translated the doctor cocked his head thoughtfully. "It's just possible we'll make New York before the baby comes," he said, then looked at Jadwiga again. "Frau Adamik, we will serve you and your child best if we prepare for arrival on the ship." He paused now, after each sentence, for Paul to translate. "So much the better if we are ashore first. But as much as we might hope for this, we should prepare for birth at sea. Do you agree?"

Paul translated. "Tell him yes," Jadwiga responded. Paul thought fleetingly of Jadwiga's father. Jadwiga could have responded for herself, with the German *Ja*, but she would not allow the language to soil her tongue.

"Aboard this ship, I am responsible for the health of all the passengers, the officers, the crew. I am responsible for seeing that you have the best care possible, and your child too."

When Paul had translated, Jadwiga nodded.

"You, or some of the women in your compartment, may wish that it were otherwise, that I wouldn't be involved in the child's coming. It's not a matter of choice—not for you, not for me. Do you understand?" Again, Paul translated.

"Tell him I understand, but not that I agree to this."

"Herr Doktor, Jadwiga wants to be clear that she does not yet agree that you be present for the birth. She intends to ask advice of the older woman traveling with us."

"I understand. Herr Adamik, please help me to be as persuasive as possible in your interpreting of my words. I ask you to do this because I know you want a healthy child. I assure you the birth should take place here, and not in steerage."

"Yes, sir."

"Do you, at least, agree?"

"I believe you, but it will be Jadwiga who will decide this."

"You, at least, have no concern about my presence during the birth— about my attending your wife?"

Paul's German became labored. He didn't want to offend the doctor.

"It is an idea which takes some considering, Doctor, but I will not oppose anything Jadwiga decides, and it is my hope that she will have the baby under the best conditions. If the women from our contingent..."

"Yes, one or two should be present, of course. Well, let me—let us—explain this to your wife."

The doctor spoke thoughtfully of birth procedures, starting with emphatic reassurance that any one or two women Jadwiga might choose could be present for the birth. He paused for translation, now and again answering Paul's questions about difficult words. Twice, he consulted a list of words on his desk. Sometimes, Paul was embarrassed. It made for a strain in his translation, but if it bothered Jadwiga, she didn't let it show.

As this continued, the assistant returned with breakfast carried on a single large tray, and the strong smell of the room was quickly replaced by the enticing odor of hot oatmeal, hot buttered rolls, and sausage. The doctor mumbled something to the assistant to send him away, and the young man disappeared through curtains into another part of the sick bay.

"Jadwiga, I'll save my rolls for later when you're hungry again. Eat my oatmeal and yours, too. Any of the sausage you don't want now the doctor says we can save for later."

"You eat some oatmeal, too." He tasted it to satisfy her.

"Between now and the time we arrive in New York," the Doctor continued, "I want to examine Frau Adamik once each week, and she must report any changes in her condition."

Paul translated, and Jadwiga looked at him with the expression that meant she was scheming.

"Will there be food each time?" she asked. Not so reluctantly now, Paul translated.

"Yes," the doctor said, "as long as I can manage it. Good food is good medicine. Please ask Frau Adamik if she's having any discomfort."

"My only discomfort is trying to sleep in the cold when we are not given enough straw and I cannot keep my baby warm."

"She has no discomforts, she says, but says that it is too cold in steerage and she finds it hard to keep her belly warm."

"I'll send Bruno down with an order that you be given extra straw just for your wife. And I have some extra blankets you can take." Paul translated, then the doctor continued, addressing his remarks directly to Jadwiga. "From now on, for these last six weeks of this pregnancy, it will be very important to keep healthy. You must not be ill when the baby comes. Any sign that you have of feeling unwell you should come to see me immediately, or send for me. Herr Adamik, of course that's the case for you, as well, or for any of the others."

Translating, Paul realized what was different about the doctor's German. It wasn't the language; it was his respectful use of *Herr*—it was attitude. Jadwiga finished the oatmeal and pushed the tray further onto Paul's lap to indicate she was finished. The doctor stirred from his informal seat on his desk to hand Paul a small oilskin pouch and a piece of paper large enough for wrapping the sausage.

"You can use this pouch if you'll return it when we dock," the doctor said, and he returned to his desk. Without waiting for a response he said "I would like to judge the size and shape of Frau Adamik's abdomen…" Paul didn't know the German word for abdomen and looked confused for a moment. "I want to judge the size of her belly," the doctor said. "Then I can see progress when you come again in a week."

Paul started to translate, but the doctor interrupted.

"Before you finish, please let me clarify. What I would like is for Frau Adamik to stand at the wall, and for you to stand behind her, and to use her shawl to draw her skirt to her. There is no need for touching."

Now Paul translated again, and when Jadwiga heard what the doctor had in mind, she appeared relieved. She stood and went to the far wall where Paul had indicated, handing him her shawl as she went.

"Herr Adamik, when you're talking about this later, please tell her that as her time draws nearer it will be best if I touch her abdomen— belly—to judge the size of the baby and its position. I also want to show her what to watch for when it is near time for the baby to arrive. I leave it to your judgment to tell her this when the time is right. I don't want to alarm her by discussing it now on this first visit here. Understood?"

"Yes, Herr Doktor."

"Please draw the shawl tightly. Please ask her to stand as tall as she can comfortably. And when you drop the shawl away she should remain still so that I can fix the drape of her garment in my memory. She should wear this same dress the next time, as well."

There were more questions, more answers, more explanation—so much that Paul's mind became weary with translating talk about a subject of which he knew little, to and from a language still a challenge to him. By the time they left the doctor, carrying blankets and the sausage in the pouch, he felt exhausted. It was near noon.

Jadwiga asked Paul to tell the doctor's assistant that the straw, the subject of the note he carried, should be held back until she would be ready for it. The assistant shrugged to show he didn't care.

Outside, snow was falling. Jadwiga commented that the sails had gone more slack and were flapping.

Chapter 31

Everyone had a question.

"How far have we come?"

"Is the mast really damaged?"

"What did the doctor want?"

"How does the ship go?"

"What is the weather?"

"How much longer to America?"

"Where is the new baby?" Franek expected a surprise.

They were welcomed like long-absent family members. Everyone gathered around. But Jadwiga was preoccupied. She asked Big Jozef to help Kazimierz Steck down from the repairwork in the bow so she could talk with Salomeya. Paul, meanwhile, started by answering Franek's question about the baby. Only then did he sit in the circle of men and women to tell them what had been learned.

"I am old and I know only the ways of my youth."

In the cribwork, Salomeya held Jadwiga's hands in hers, speaking slowly and softly of private matters.

"It was the same with my mother. She knew only the ways of the times when she was a young girl. These things she taught to me so that I, too, would know them. But there were many things I did not learn well, because I could not always see, when she spoke, that they would one day matter to me.

"And there were many things she could not teach me."

There was a pause now, as Jadwiga wiped a tear away with the back of her hand.

Jadwiga turned in the cribwork to face Salomeya more squarely. "What things?" she asked.

"Those I had to do for myself. I could not know from my mother that I should go to America. I can only follow my husband when he follows our sons. From her I learned that I should follow my husband, but I have not always done this. There have been times when I have chosen, and he has followed me."

"America—I can understand that. But what other things, Babka?"

"Those things which one must discover for oneself. You know of these things better than I, Jadwiga, for you had not so much time with your mother to be told and to ask. You have made your way well, have you not?"

"I learned from my father and from my brothers and sometimes from a neighbor or a relative. But it is true that there were many things I learned alone because I had no mother to teach me."

"Jadwiga, do you know how you have taught the women to judge the going of the ship?"

"Yes."

"This is something they did not know until you taught them."

"Yes."

"You are the youngest, but you are not the least wise."

"But I haven't had a baby, Babka."

"And you are concerned that you might make a mistake."

"I...I am concerned to do the right thing."

"And you would have me tell you what is right?"

"Yes. You must know."

"I do know. I know that what you do will be the right thing, Jadwiga."

Jadwiga felt distressed and showed it, like the child being tested but not understanding the subject and expecting to be punished for wrong answers. When she started to speak, Salomeya touched her lips.

"So often, I have seen that it is the young who teach the old. There is a time, my lovely young friend Jadwiga, when the older ones have less to teach the young than they have to learn from them. Not all perceive this to be the case, but it is so.

"When I was young it was for parents to find the ones their daughters would marry, and it was always the case that the eldest daughter must marry first. My parents believed in this. Everyone believed in this.

"I was the oldest of the daughters, but when I had passed my twentieth summer, my parents had as yet not chosen for me. Or perhaps they had chosen, but without reciprocation. I was coming to think that if I ever married, I would by then have the down for one hundred pillows for my husband's head.

"But my sister Basia, who had reached the age of eighteen, was found by a young man from the next town and she wished to be betrothed. She showed him to our father in church. But my father and my mother would say only that first a husband would be found for me, and then if the young man would still be free, he could be considered as a suitor.

"This made for discomfort between Basia and me, for though we loved each other very much, I was keeping her from betrothal.

"I did not wish to become a bride of Jesus, as much as I revere the holy sisters. But neither did I wish to cause unhappiness to my sister. I spoke with my mother, and she with my father, and after a time it was agreed that the custom would be broken, and my sister would become betrothed and marry before me.

"To me, it was a matter of shame, but I wished it to be this way for my sister's happiness and so that there would be no breath of the devil between us. And this was a case, Jadwiga, in which the old ones learned from the young ones, and the old teaching was forgotten in our family."

Jadwiga knew the story was not finished, because Salomeya was still choosing words, remembering.

"It happened then," Salomeya continued, "that at my sister's wedding, the groom's man was a handsome young soldier who took my breath and my heart away." There was love in her eyes as she looked at Kazimierz, who was amid the others listening to Paul tell of the visit topside. "Thus it was because the new way was accepted that I found my husband.

"You see, Jadwiga, I am not one to tell you that the old ways always are the best. It can come to be that there is fortune in listening to the young, and in the changes they bring to the old ways.

"You will decide about this doctor and about your baby. What you will decide will be the proper thing."

Jadwiga hugged Salomeya and kissed her cheek. "Babka, you will help me then, wherever the baby comes?"

Salomeya held Jadwiga's face in her hands, smiling. "You are my daughter, born to another but come to me at last. You will choose and I will learn from you."

When the hymns started that evening, Jadwiga was not at the hatchway with Paul for his dealings with Fritz Adenauer. Instead, she was at the port-side pig pens, where she lifted and sorted the weaned piglets from three pens to two. Then, while others watched, mystified, she carried buckets of water from the rainwater vat, which was overflowing with snowmelt, and washed the floor of the forwardmost pen.

The next morning, she opened the seams of the seabags that were the Adamik luggage, joined them together with their drawstrings, and spread them in the pigpen. Then she told Paul to collect from Herman the cattletender the bale of straw to which the doctor had given her entitlement. She spread some of it, saving more than half, and then luxuriated in the clean warmth well above the slatted drainage floor where the others had their old canvas sail and their straw.

"You will explain to the hunchback," she told Paul, "that the doctor said I must have this straw in a place where I can keep it together and keep it clean."

Chapter 32

Despite circumstances—and because of them—all the emigrants anticipated a new beginning. While this carried with it the worries over how
such a new start would be made, these could be put aside on the special
occasion of the start of a new year.

There was grief, especially for Juliusz, who became withdrawn.
Jadwiga grieved, too, but less desperately; she had the thoughts of her
own pregnancy distracting her. For the rest, the coming of the new year
was a cause for subdued celebration. This was more the case among the
Germans in the midship compartment, because they did not feel the
heaviness of Juliusz's heart, nor were they expected to show continuing
respect for his time of loss. But among the Poles, too, any cause of diversion was welcome. There was drinking among the men and chatter
among the women.

Somehow, Jan Poglicki produced two wholly unexpected bottles of
spirits, quite enough for the ten men. Piotr and Ursula had vodka among
their traveling things, and they joined, though on the fringes.

Stanisław Krulik's sons Lancek and Władek were given their first taste
of adult drink so that they might participate in the quiet toasts to the
past and Poland, and the future and America, offered by Kazimierz
Steck. The Russian boys Voytek and Vicek wanted to toast, too, so
Ursula gave each a small measure of Piotr's vodka.

For the children, there was a special treat of the contraband cheese for
the party, held back for just this occasion. Salomeya divided it among
families, and mothers passed it out with the repeated caution that it was
to be eaten slowly, in small bites, because there would be no more when
it was gone.

For a time, despite their hunger and sadness, there was happiness among them. There was spirited boasting of the special intelligence and agility of each man's child, and of what each would accomplish once in America.

For a time, there was again the joshing with Ignatz over his bringing forth from the powerful Kostanta all these children—five of them. And to Big Jozef Dominiak, there was the suggestion that in light of little Ignatz's accomplishment, it was nothing of which to boast that he himself had but five.

For a time, there was a looking forward in a spirit of optimism.

Exactly what happened was not reconstructed in detail until later when there was time to talk and sort things out. At the time, there was only the yelling, the banging, the scuffle, and the blood, then the men falling upon the combatants to restore sanity and order.

It started on the other side of the rainwater vat away from the parents when one of the Russian boys snatched cheese away from Konrad Dominiak. The other one held the infant, hand over mouth, so that he would not be heard to cry.

It happened by chance that while this was going on Big Jozef felt the need and was going to the manure pile, a smile still on his lips from a story told by Ludwig Karpczinski. No one was sure exactly what he saw, but it ignited his temper and detonated a rage, and before there could be any accounting of his movements, he had both the Russian youths by their throats, against the rainwater vat, and he was choking the life from them. Vicek even fell unconscious to the drainage deck when released. Both were released because their father, hearing the scuffle, came quickly around the vat to launch himself onto Big Jozef's shoulders to pull him away from his sons. He did this with an elbow crooked around the big Dominiak's neck and a knee thrust into the small of his back.

But once Big Jozef released the Russian youths, his hands and arms were free to turn on Piotr. From here on the other men caught glimpses of what was happening as they scrambled to stop it. As though he had no arm at all around his neck, Big Jozef spun around—he was roaring now in his rage—and drove a giant fist deep into Piotr's stomach. This took away all the Russian's breath and doubled him over in pain and surprise.

Just as Stanisław Krulik and Tadeusz Murak were about to pull them apart, just as Big Jozef was joining his hands into one giant fist to come down on the back of Piotr's neck, there was a knife in the Russian's hand, taken from a pocket or from somewhere under a belt as he went down, and then there was blood coming from Big Jozef's leg. Only because Stanisław saw the arc of the knife and instinctively jumped back did he fail to have his leg gashed, as well. Jozef's blow lost some of its force, but Piotr was on his way down anyway.

Even so, and even though he was unable to catch his wind, Piotr was going for another slash at Jozef's legs when a quick-moving Jan Poglicki seized his wrist and pinned it, still holding the knife, to the deck. Paul stepped on the hand. Franek was there, getting Konrad out of harm's way, and he picked up the knife. Paul and Jan held Piotr down, wondering how all this had happened.

Jozef was bewildered at seeing blood on his shin. He hadn't seen the knife. In his surprise, he let Tadeusz Murak and Ludwig Karpczinski pull him off his feet and away from Piotr.

Because Delfinia Dominiak was starting to yell and would be screaming any second, Ignatz Ran hurried to close the hatchway door so the Germans in midship wouldn't see. But he was too late—two were already peering into the half-light at the rainwater vat trying to discover what brought such gutteral sounds of anger from within someone.

"Only a drunken fight," Ignatz said. "Only a fight. Everything is back to normal now." Apologetic when he realized they hadn't understood his Polish words, he shrugged and closed the top section of the door.

Voytek Jakubik, gasping for breath, dragged his brother, who was already coming around, toward the double-door hatchway and away from the fray. Only now did Ursula come upon the scene. At first, she didn't notice her husband being held on the deck. She went to aid her sons. It was becoming crowded aft of the rainwater vat, and none of the other women could get past to see what was happening.

Jozef grabbed one of his shirts that happened to be hanging to dry near the rainwater vat and wrapped it around his bleeding leg to stem the flow. "I'm all right," he told Tadeusz and Ludwig, "the bastard only scratched me."

"What in hell happened, Jozef?" asked Tadeusz.

"Those apes of sons of his took the cheese from Konrad. From the baby! They took the cheese from the baby!" Just for the blink of an eye, it looked like Jozef might get up and go after the sons again, but he was occupied with his leg. "God damn him, where did that knife come from?"

"Let's look at your leg," Ludwig said.

"No, no. Let me keep it wrapped so the blood will stop. It's only that he broke the skin."

By now Delfinia was with them and she was near hysterics at seeing blood on her husband's leg. "I knew there would be trouble with the Russian," she wailed. "I knew it from the beginning! Oh, Jozef."

"Those fat sons of his took Konrad's cheese right from his mouth!"

Now Ursula Jakubik yelled, a fist doubled. "And you nearly killed them with your choking!"

"If they do that again I myself will kill them," Delfinia yelled, and for a moment it appeared the wives, too, might fight.

Paul and Jan, who easily held Piotr down because he wasn't resisting, were beginning to get some idea of what had happened. "Do you have any more knives?" Jan asked Piotr, and the Russian grunted, "No." Even so, Jan ran his hands over the man's legs and around his belt to be on the safe side.

"You will come with us to the other corner, away from Jozef," Paul said. Piotr grunted his agreement, but they manhandled him anyway just to be sure he wouldn't break away to resume the fight.

Kazimierz Steck, who stayed in the cribwork throughout the uproar because there was no one to help him down, was at a loss to mediate, for he hadn't the facts and as yet no one had sorted out the details. Old Man Kradzinski, who was not fast enough with his crutches to get to the scene of the disturbance, kept asking his son-in-law Tadeusz to tell him everything that had happened, but very little was clear.

The only one among the men whose heart wasn't pounding by the time the scuffle was over was Juliusz, who didn't move from his new sitting and sleeping place just forward of the rainwater vat. Virtually nothing would move him, it appeared, until he was reconciled to his loss.

When things settled down, Franek quite formally turned Piotr's knife over to Paul. Konrad was upset and showed it until he finally fell asleep, held and rocked by Franek while Delfinia gave attention to her Jozef.

Voytek and Vicek stayed close to their mother and father, each keeping an eye on the Dominiaks across the slatted deck. Neither parent asked what happened. It didn't matter. They were separate camps.

No one took Piotr's side, and no one was neutral. Right or wrong, it was assumed the Russian was at fault. In any case, the use of a knife in such a fight was contemptible for its surprise and unfairness. Whatever started it, the knife was an unacceptable countermeasure.

There was much gratitude that Jozef's wound, according to Jozef's own report, was only a breaking of the skin. This would make it unnecessary to report it to anyone, and there would be no official record. All were concerned about the effect such violence might have on their acceptance in America, were it to become known to the ship's officers or to the officials who would evaluate the newcomers upon arrival in New York. For the Russian, most agreed, justice for the use of a knife would come after they were ashore in America and everyone was through the official gates of acceptance. Then Big Jozef would make so much Russian garbage out of Piotr.

The men slept in shifts that night, watching Piotr and Jozef. It could be seen that neither man was about to shake hands with the other, and further fighting had to be prevented. Stanisław and Paul were first on watch.

"We will always have to keep them separated," Stanisław said.

"Yes."

"Even if it means a watch through the night, every night."

"That's what it will take—just so the rest of us can sleep without worry that we'll wake up to find one or the other of them dead."

Stanisław shrugged. "Eventually, Jozef is going to kill him anyway."

"But not aboard the ship. Not until we have passed the officials and we are in America. After that they can settle it as they wish."

"Delfinia was right," Stanisław said, shaking his head. "This has been coming from the beginning. Jozef blames Piotr for everything that happened in the Russian partition. And Piotr has known from the beginning that Jozef has this hatred for him. We should have been watching them more closely."

"Stanisław, if this is discovered—or if, Jesus save us, one of them ends up dead, will it hurt all of us for acceptance in America?" Paul asked. He realized, suddenly, that it mattered to him.

"I don't know. We must keep peace."

After a time, they woke Ludwig and Ignatz to take the watch. Paul crawled into Jadwiga's pig pen, wrapped himself in a blanket, and cuddled close to her.

Chapter 33

As days passed, plodding their way into weeks, the dealings with Fritz Adenauer continued, though there was increasing discontent over the prices he demanded. Paul tried to reason with him, but the German simply shrugged, turned his mouth downward and said he should be demanding even more, considering the risk.

Tadeusz Murak, who had replaced Juliusz as the collector for the fund, calculated that by the middle of January the German had collected the price of another full passage to America. Fritz would surely be one wealthy German after disembarkation.

"He could keep going back and forth," Ignatz said. "He could make this a business."

"We will renegotiate these prices in America," Jan Poglicki said. "We will renegotiate behind the first barn."

Juliusz remained withdrawn and unaccepting of consolation. His despair was palpable.

The tension of constant watchfulness over Piotr and Big Jozef was wearying to the men and a worry to the women. Jadwiga was apart from it by virtue of her special place—the pigpen she had appropriated for sleeping in her special supply of straw. Paul was relieved of watch duty by the other men, who wanted him to continue his dealings with Fritz Adenauer. Thus he was less affected by the tension, and with various of the German passengers he was able to practice for greater fluency in his second language.

The increasingly frequent visits to Dr. Hoffmeister became the punctuation of an otherwise routine passage of time for both Paul and Jadwiga. The food they received each time made Paul wish he had never started the dealings with Fritz, since Jadwiga's complaints about hunger dwindled away to nothing. He rationalized with the thought that the stolen food was keeping the children in good health.

Jadwiga gave the doctor no promise that he could assist in the delivery, always repeating her hope that the ship would arrive in America in time. But there was an increasing rapport between them, despite the difficulty of speaking only through Paul. Each realized that Paul took the sting out of Jadwiga's words and the frankness out of the doctor's. The doctor cautioned repeatedly that the Frederika's progress was poor and there could be no certainties.

And there were worries.

There was worry, especially, over Big Jozef. Under the circumstances it was not expected that he would be very social, but he seemed to be lost in a melancholia, a mood unknown to his Delfinia. More often than reasonable, considering the chill of ocean so near through the ship's wooden skin, he was sweating.

By the fifteenth of January, Stanisław Krulik became convinced that Jozef's wound wasn't healing properly. Other men, reluctant to face the worst, insisted that Jozef's own evaluation should be accepted, but Stanisław saw this as a hollow hope: Everyone knew Jozef would minimize the seriousness of his injury out of pride and out of a conviction that whatever befell him, he could heal. Stanisław spoke with Kazimierz Steck, urging him to ask Jozef to show his wound.

"Suppose it is very bad," Tadeusz Murak asked. "What then will we do about it? Cut the Russian the same way?"

"Perhaps it will be best that Paul ask the doctor for some medicine for Jozef," Kazimierz said.

"And then there will be questions," Tadeusz said. "And perhaps trouble."

"But perhaps," said the old man, "it will be better to answer questions about a small wound than to answer them about a dead man. There can be no harm in seeing how serious is his wound, and when we have seen, we will decide what further must be done, if anything."

There was grumbling, but the old man went to Delfinia and Big Jozef.

"My big friend, I worry about you."

"Worry instead for the Russian."

"Not about what might happen, Jozef, but about what has happened. You don't look good to me. You look instead like a man who is not well."

"I will be fine."

"You must show me your leg, Jozef."

Delfinia eagerly agreed. "I've been asking him to see it. Jozef, please show this wound of yours. Let Kazimierz see it. I am so worried."

Jozef looked at each of them in turn. "All right, then, to ease your mind, Delfinia."

The trouble was immediately clear even while the big man's lower leg was being unwrapped. There was a dreadful stench. The wound was not healing. It was getting worse.

"I can't do anything more right now." The doctor angrily brushed the curtains aside as he emerged into his office where Paul waited. "Had you brought him here immediately, things would go better for him. You should have come for me at the beginning, Herr Adamik. You have seen the sick bay, you speak the language, and you should have known that if there was to be help for the man it would be here."

"Sir, he concealed the seriousness of his injury."

"Nonetheless, waiting has made this a more serious matter than necessary. And it is a tragic matter."

"Yes, sir."

"I want you to explain to him. It is not within my conscience to take a man's leg from him without giving him an explanation as to why this must be done. I will tell you, and then you must tell him and his wife. And you must help me to prepare him for this surgery, so that it will go as well as possible."

"Pardon, sir. You did say, 'take his leg'?"

"Yes."

"Oh, my God."

"What did you imagine could be done? Earlier, we had a chance. Now it's a matter of saving his life, not his leg." Paul was shocked by the seriousness of the situation.

"Herr Adamik, if it needs repeating…If there are any other injuries, from whatever cause, or any sickness, you are to notify me immediately. Immediately. Of all the passengers on this vessel you should know this without such a tragic lesson. If there is anything more of this kind, or if any injuries are being concealed in your section, I hold you responsible, personally. Am I speaking clearly?"

"There are no other injuries, Herr Doktor."

"What about the man who did this to Dominiak?"

"There are no other injuries."

The doctor shook his head in disgust. I will explain this simply so you don't have to grope for the meaning of medical terms. Then you must explain it to the big man and to his wife."

"Yes, sir."

"There is rot in Dominiak's leg—spreading. I've had four big seamen in here to hold him down while I scraped at it and cut away at it, but it isn't enough. If this bad leg stays with him, the poison will spread through his system and he will die." Involuntarily, Paul shuddered. "Understand: There must be no promise that taking his leg will save his life. Only a certainty that if we don't, he will surely die. Is this clear to you?"

"It is clear. But..."

"Can you make it clear to the man and his wife? What you must tell them is this—that there is no chance of survival unless the leg is taken."

"I see."

"Then I will need your help. He has called your name. He trusts you. Is this so?"

"Yes."

"He's very strong, and when the seamen have held him it hasn't gone well. It is a difficult thing for them to see, and they grow weak, and Dominiak is so strong...Well, it is just not satisfactory. To cut off his leg, we will put him to sleep. You must persuade him that it is for his own good: you will hold a sponge over his face and he must not resist."

"I will?"

"He trusts you."

"Yes, sir."

"And then you will have to explain what happened to the officers, who will have to make a report of how this thing happened. But that's later. I will send Bruno to bring the man's wife here, and you will first tell her, and then him. She will help calm him?"

"I don't know."

"Whatever the case, she must know."

Below decks, there was a growing apprehension.

There was the alarm of Jozef's injury, even worse than Stanisław feared when he urged that it be examined. Then there was the doctor's reaction when he came to see it, alarming because his demeanor was nothing like the friendliness he exhibited on his earlier visit.

And there was the way he had ordered Jozef taken immediately to topside, to the sick bay, on a litter. This only confirmed the seriousness of the wound.

There was the worry that there would be an official record.

Then, after a long wait, the doctor's assistant had come with the note for Paul to come topside.

And now another note shown to Herman the cattletender. Delfinia, already in a fretful state over her husband being taken away, heard her name called by the hunchback, badly mispronounced but recognizable.

Everyone knew now that it was very serious. There was no room now even for hope that it could be otherwise.

Delfinia looked to Jadwiga and Polka Karpczinski for assurance they would look after the children in her absence. "Franek," she said, "I must go to your papa upstairs. Stay away from the Russians. And take care of Konrad. And don't be any trouble to Jadwiga and Polka."

Franek looked very worried, so Jadwiga took his hand. "Your mama will come back, Franek. But for now, while both your mama and your papa are gone, you must be the strong one, and help to care for your sisters and Konrad."

Franek stood a bit straighter and held back the tears threatening to break forth.

Going forward to get her coat, Delfinia walked part-way across the slatted deck toward Piotr Jakubik and family. "If I do not get back my Jozef, I will kill all of you," she hissed. Nobody tried to keep her from speaking to the Russians, and for a stinging moment, the eyes of everyone were fastened on the Jakubik family. Everyone knew Delfinia's threat was not an empty one.

Chapter 34

There must be no surprise, the doctor said. It would be enough that a man would have to accept loss of his leg. He should not have to do so thinking it was done without his foreknowledge and consent. It would be best, afterward, if at least the man did not have to overcome that additional bitterness.

Paul felt ill-equipped for this duty. True, he could speak the two languages, hearing thoughts in the one and changing them into words of the other. But that did not qualify him to bring a man the news that a leg was to be taken from him.

Becoming a cripple was a serious matter.

It was not simply a question of disfigurement, of looking different. There was more. A man's body was the engine of his family's survival. A man could take his family to a new country only because he had the means and muscle to provide for them. No one would expect to arrive maimed. The tragedy of a limb taken was the tragedy of a family in wreckage without protection, without opportunity. Without work, without pay, a man's family could be cast upon the countryside with constant deprivation the only prospect.

It would be serious enough at home in Poland, where there would be the larger family to help those stricken. There, at least, the taking of a man's leg would be a tragedy shared.

Back home, at least, one's children would not starve. A man's family would be dependent, but it would be understood that were circumstances reversed, the giver of help would be the helped. But for the Dominiaks there were no family members in America.

This was disaster. Nothing Paul had ever done qualified him to bring such tragedy into a man's life. It was hard enough telling Delfinia.

She felt self-recrimination for not having done something better to control the situation or respond to it.

She felt the sudden wish that all this could be taken back...the wanting to hold up her hands against the movement of events. If she could go back to a time before the fight, so that she could be more watchful and alert to prevent it. Or only, please God, to just after the fight, when she could insist the wound be looked after.

But Paul Adamik was telling her through her tears that these matters were not of concern now. What mattered now, he said, was to save Big Jozef's life, never mind his leg. What mattered now, he was saying, was to persuade her Jozef that he must give up this leg willingly, without fighting, so that it wouldn't go badly for him.

She remembered the contests with her brothers, and how it was so much a matter of pride with her young husband that he could match any man's budging, lifting, reaching, carrying. She knew that her Jozef with a leg taken from under him would feel less than half a man.

She remembered him speaking of a man maimed in the fighting in Dziadkowicki Forest. She remembered that he spoke of the man with pity—of how he would forever have to rely on others to do for him and that he would no longer be able to carry his weight, let alone the weight of a family.

She knew how desperately he would hate to be pitied.

Because he had a temper, his immediate thoughts would be of the vengeance already sworn. But then he would quickly be thinking of his family and the responsibilities he would be unable to fulfill. He would be filled with anxiety over how they would be supported. No amount of reassurance would relieve him because their reliance on him was the flame on the candle of life burning within him.

She resolved, listening to this fate that her husband was to be mutilated to preserve his life, that she would be strong, as Paul Adamik was telling her she must be, to help her husband be strong. She would be unable to do anything about her tears, she knew, for she had learned long ago that they were not something she could stop. But she could hold herself from the wailing over this injustice and hurt that was trying to burst from her heart.

And later, whatever else might be necessary for the survival of the family she had made with this gentle and temperamental giant, somewhere within her she would find the means to give him what it would take for him to understand that he meant more to her and to them than out-lifting and out-carrying other men.

So it was that she listened with only silent tears while the young Adamik told her of how they would take Jozef's leg from him.

Paul found this surprising. Before this, she had not shown Jadwiga's command of a situation. He had thought she was all pudginess and dimples and good nature. And he had expected no more than the grand emotional response that had been her reaction to earlier events. From somewhere she was fetching up an inner resource, and for that he was grateful. He found he was hoping that Jozef would have such strength, knowing that he himself would not. Not for this devastation.

So it was that he found himself trying to give strength to the big man.

So it was that Paul Adamik made the promise to Jozef Dominiak.

"Take off my leg?"

"Yes, Jozef."

"Take off my leg?"

"Yes, Jozef. I am sorry."

"To save my life? To save my life? What kind of life am I to have with only one leg?"

"You will be alive, Jozef."

"Better I should be dead than without my legs under me. This cannot be."

"Jozef, I have talked about it with the doctor. It is true. If your leg is not taken, it will kill you."

"Without my legs, how am I to work?"

Delfinia now spoke, trying to hold back tears that would not be held. "Jozef, we will have you alive. We must have you alive."

"Jozef, hear me," Paul said. "There is little time, and you must help if the doctor is to save your life. You must have great courage. It will be as it was in the Forest with Traugutt."

Jozef looked at Paul in surprise that he knew.

"You will have to be brave, but you have no want of bravery. I am to help the doctor, and I will hold a sponge over your face to put you to sleep so that you will not fight the doctor. You must allow me to do this and you must not fight it."

"I fought them by the hundreds in the Forest, Paul, and now they get me with this one cowardly animal who teaches his sons to steal their food from the mouths of infants!"

"Jozef, there is only time now to get ready for the doctor and the surgery. Piotr will pay for this thing he has done to you. But now, right now, we must insure that you live."

"That goddamned Russian. The weapon was brought aboard under his woman's skirts. This I have figured out. My life must be saved so I can take his. I swear to God that he will pay with two legs for my one. My leg! Paul, my God, how will I provide?"

"Jozef, don't think about this now. Your family will not go hungry in America, I make this promise to you."

The big man looked at him with tears and gratitude flooding his eyes. He reached out a hand of friendship and need which Paul grasped.

"You will not leave me, Paul. You will be with me?"

"I will be with you, Jozef. You must promise me that you will not fight the sponge."

"I promise you. I promise this."

He became conscious of a smooth flooring against his cheek and a wetness of urine in his trousers and blood around him. Through a haze of disorientation he realized where he was and why there was so much sunlight. Embarrassed, not knowing how long he had been out, he tried to rise to his feet as though nothing had happened. Around him, things were spinning.

The doctor was gone, and the patient was gone, and there was no need to hurry, so he allowed himself the time on the deck of the doctor's surgery to regain his bearings. He remembered holding the sponge and the doctor pouring the liquid onto it and that the fumes were unpleasant. But nothing else. He had passed out. He cursed himself in shame when he realized he had failed the doctor.

He became aware of voices in German—the doctor and his assistant—at the same moment he heard his name on the doctor's lips. He tried again to stand, and realized as he did that he was very dizzy. The doctor's assistant appeared at the door.

"Herr Adamik, you are all right?"

"Yes, I'm..."

"Your head spins."

"A little."

"The patient will wake soon and Doctor Hoffmeister would appreciate it if you would be at his side when he does."

"He is all right?"

"The patient is...The doctor will tell you. Please come."

"You breathed too much of the chloroform," the doctor said. "It's one sure way of knowing when the patient has had enough."

"I'm sorry..."

"No, not at all. It's not unusual. Do you remember when you went down?"

"I was holding the sponge."

"That's fine. Nothing to worry about. Your big friend has had a difficult time of it. He lost a great deal of blood and when he wakes we must keep him calm. He must not move around or he might bleed more, and we must keep him from losing any more than he already has. Herr Adamik, are you understanding me?"

"Oh, yes sir. I'm sorry. I'm still..."

"No matter. You understand about keeping him calm."

"We have to keep him calm. I understand."

"You must talk to him. He will say some strange things, I expect, and you can ignore what he says and any questions he asks. Just talk with him, quietly, and make him understand as soon as you can that he must lie still."

"Yes, sir. Is he going to be all right?"

"Perhaps. We must guard against infection and further injury now, and we must build him back up. I have never seen such bleeding. It is fortunate he is a strong man or we would have lost him on the table."

Paul looked at the figure on the bed before him. Here was a giant of a man, the ruddy color of his face now lost in paleness, his size and strength lost in the helplessness of lying abed.

He realized it could have been him. It could have been him not because he shared Jozef's hatred for Russians in the same depth, but because in the tight confinement of steerage a man had no place to go— no way to release the hatreds within him—and no place to hide from the hatreds of the others.

He thought of these things and in the man on the bed Paul Adamik saw the reality of his own vulnerability. He shuddered, unable to contain the fright of seeing himself so mortal, so precarious, so close to helplessness.

Chapter 35

He looked, she thought, to have aged some years. The gentle lines of his face had become creases of worry. His stoop was something more than just avoiding the overhead crossmembers. It was a bending to some invisible weight.

Uncharacteristic of him, he didn't come to her first. He went instead to Franek and the other Dominiak children, brushing aside the adults and their questions.

"Your papa is a very strong and brave man, Franek. He and your mama told me to bring kisses to you and Pelagia and Magda and Manya and little Konrad. They love you very much, but they must stay topside for a while. Your mama says you will be a good boy for the women here and that you will help with Konrad and the girls."

Solemnly, Franek nodded.

"Franek, your father's leg was hurt very badly, and it would not work for him anymore. The doctor had to take it off so it wouldn't hurt the rest of him." He paused, she could see, to gauge the boy's reaction—to judge whether he comprehended the nature of this information. He disregarded the adults, who murmured among themselves, some of the men looking forward at the Jakubiks.

"Do you understand, Franek?"

"The doctor took away Papa's leg?"

"Yes, so it wouldn't hurt the rest of him. It was very important to do this, or it would go badly for him."

He was not concealing the seriousness from the boy, she could see. In his demeanor, and in his words, he let the truth out. Yet he was connecting himself to the boy's thoughts, judging, constantly judging.

"So one of his legs is gone now?"

"Yes."

"How will he walk?"

"After a while, he will use crutches."

"Like Jan's grandpa." Franek glanced at Old Man Kradzinski.

"Yes, that's right."

"Where is mama?"

"Your mama is fine. She is staying with your papa to help him. She says she will see you soon."

"Can I go with you to see mama and my papa?"

"No, Franek. They are in a special place where the doctor—do you remember the doctor?—where the doctor can take special care of your papa. You will see them very soon, after a few days, perhaps, or when we all arrive in America."

"What if they can't find us children?"

"We will see that they do. Don't you worry about that. We will see that you are all together. Can you help take care of your sisters and Konrad?"

"Yes."

"Are they being good?"

"Konrad wants mama."

"Perhaps you can explain to him that he will see mama and papa soon."

"Konrad doesn't understand very well. But I will tell him."

This Paul of hers, Jadwiga could see, would make a good father. When he looked up at her, she understood that she was to take the children now, so that he could speak to the adults.

"Franek, come with me now," she said, "into my little house. Bring your sisters and we will all talk together and perhaps after a while play a game." Franek looked at Paul, wanting to stay with him. But Paul's nod of the head told him he should do as Jadwiga asked.

They spoke quietly, not whispering but in lowered voices so as to deprive the Russians knowledge of what they said. They even spoke with a casualness so that the Dominiak children would not hear the seriousness of concern in their voices. Paul showed where Jozef's leg had been taken with an open hand across his own leg just above the knee. Among the men, there were grimaces as they imagined being so cut themselves. Juliusz had no stomach for this and he returned to the place where he had been grieving.

"Will he be all right? He is going to live?"

"He is not yet out of danger. The doctor says he must remain calm now so he won't bleed any more. He lost much blood. And there is the worry over infection. He must not develop an infection. And then we must hope all of the diseased part was taken away so it won't spread."

"Paul, will there have to be a report?" Stanisław Krulik asked.

"The doctor said only that I will have to explain to the officers."

"Damn!" said Tadeusz Murak.

"What about the Russian?" asked Ludwig Karpczinski.

"I don't know," Paul said. "What should I tell the officers?"

"Tell them the Russian attacked Jozef with a knife. Tell them what happened," Tadeusz Murak said. "Tell them exactly what happened. Be sure they understand that none of us were involved except to break it up after the big one already was cut."

"It will go best for us," Kazimierz Steck suggested, "if there is only the Russian to be blamed for this. If anybody is to be sent back, let it be the Russian. Let the Germans understand that there was no provocation."

"He will be sent back for the weapon anyway—for bringing the knife on the ship," Ignatz Ran said.

"All of you must understand," Paul said, "that if anything further happens, it will be very serious." He looked around, at each man, so there would be no mistaking his words. "I hope nobody has intent to do harm to the Russian. If anything happens to him there will then be need to explain not just how Big Jozef was cut, but how and why the Russian was harmed."

"He deserves to go overboard with the manure," said Jan Poglicki. His voice rose, and Stanisław silenced him with a sharp gesture.

"If he does, it will go badly for all of us. Let us be quiet as we talk, and let us not incite ourselves."

Kazimierz Steck spoke again. "It will go badly indeed," he said. "The Russian must arrive in America in one piece so that it will be seen that he alone bears responsibility for this incident. He must arrive in one piece so he can be sent back in one piece. Even if this is the only punishment, the rest of us must not risk the same just to have vengeance for Jozef. It would be more than a matter of one man against one man. It would become an affair for which all of us would suffer." He looked around at each man, individually, caught the eye of each, and received the nodded agreement of each. "Then it is settled. No man here will seek revenge in violence."

"Aboard this ship," Jan added.

"No vengeance aboard this ship."

They put up the blankets, then, so Paul could wash and change his clothes. He had an accumulation of odors about him that exceeded even the usual stench of steerage to which they had become accustomed, and on his clothing there was even some of Jozef's lost blood. He used a second bucket of water. Despite the cold, he poured it over himself slowly, taking its passage over his body as a source of cleansing that removed more than just sweat and stink.

Soon he would have to go back, for Big Jozef was not to be left alone, awake or asleep, lest he thrash about and damage the doctor's work.

He would arrange some sort of schedule with Delfinia. It would be a schedule, he thought, which would give him meals in sick bay, as the doctor hinted. That way there would be food to bring to Jadwiga.

When he was clean and dried and dressed, he went to her special place, the pigpen she had appropriated. With her, there were the children of Jozef and Delfinia, sitting in a half-circle around her, their legs crossed. She was telling them the star story, as he had heard her tell it to the young children on the beach at Gdynia.

"Everyone knows," she said, "that in the beginning the only stars in the sky were the ones God created for Himself and His angels to see. They were very high in the sky, and no one living on the earth could see them.

"But then God, because He is very kind, made stars for people to see, as well. He made special stars for each country, so the French have stars of their own, and the Russians, and the Germans.

"Do you know what happened when it came time for Him to make stars for Poland?"

"Only one," said Pelagia.

"That's right," Jadwiga continued, "God had given the people of Poland so much sky—more than any other nation—that He decided that they needed only one star, because they could see all the stars of all the other countries in their big sky.

"Well, you know what happened to the poor little Polish star."

"Lonely," Magda said.

"That's right. It was very lonely for the Polish star, especially when the stars of the other countries began to act superior because there were so many more of them. It was so lonely that sometimes she cried, but very quietly so that God would not hear. But after a while, it was so sad for the Polish star that she could not shine any more.

"Well, of course God noticed this right away, so he walked over to the Polish star, and they had a talk.

"The lonely Polish star told God everything that was troubling her. About being so lonely, and having no other star to play with, and no one to talk with. And do you know, what she said made God so sad that He cried, too.

"God said to the lonely Polish star, 'You must be patient, little one, and one day you will be given a task to carry out for me that will make up for all your tears.'

"So now the Polish star stopped her tears, and she waited patiently as God told her she must. She was still a sad little star, but she knew that God would remember her, so she wept no more.

"And finally there came a special day when God summoned before Him all the stars of all sizes and nationalities. There was a Great Mission to be assigned. None of them knew what the mission was to be, but all wanted to be chosen. So all the stars crowded about the throne of God, each one trying to outshine the others so as to be noticed by God.

"God stepped down from his throne, and walked up and down the line, looking at each of the stars. They were all very quiet and very good, hoping and hoping that God would choose them. Except that down near the end of the line, there was a commotion.

"What do you suppose this could be?"

Franek waited for one of his sisters to answer, but when none did, he spoke: "The Polish star."

"Yes, that's right. God saw that it was his own special little Polish star, so small that she had to jump about and peek around the other stars to get a look at Him. Well, do you think all this commotion made God angry with her?"

"No," Pelagia said, indignant at the thought. "She was just a little star."

"God went back to His throne, and He took His seat. And then He said, 'You, tiniest little star, little Polish star, you come here to My throne.'

"And God spoke especially to her, but all the other stars heard, too. He said, 'Because you have been so patient, and so good, and have never doubted the promise I made to you, your time has come. The Great Mission shall be entrusted to you. You, among all the stars in My heaven will be the one remembered by all the peoples for all time.'

"'It is you,' God said to her, 'who is chosen to lead the Wise Men to Bethlehem, where My Son shall be born. You will shine more brilliantly than any other star in the skies, and you will be known for all the ages as The Star of Bethlehem.'

"And so now you know," Jadwiga said, looking at each of the children, "why it is that Christmas Eve is special for all the Polish people—because it is the time of their special star that leads them to the Baby Jesus."

He was grateful that she didn't hurry it when he arrived—that she told it all, each thought and word having its own special weight. And that she didn't chase the children away when the story was ended, but instead let the essence of it occupy the air about them. Konrad was asleep in Franek's arms, and Manya was drowsy, thumb in her mouth. But Pelagia and Magda were wide awake like Franek.

No wonder, he thought, with stories like this, that Poles grow up with an unquestioning conviction that God keeps a special watch over their land—a faith that whatever might befall her, the essence of Poland would be preserved, despite partition and occupation. No wonder that the country could bear the weight of armies and domination and the people still keep faith with a better destiny.

Pelagia looked at Jadwiga with sad eyes. "Jadwiga, is Baby Jesus watching over my papa?"

"Yes, little one. And God His Father, too."

When they had gone, he told her more than he had told the others, of how Big Jozef had come out of his stupor talking about Franek, about Siberia, about Dziadkowicki Forest. He surprised himself when he heard his own voice telling her about how he fainted, casually certain she wouldn't think less of him.

He remembered now that it wasn't just the liquid the doctor poured onto the sponge, but that he went to the floor when he saw the cutting and the big man's blood. It was so different a matter, he told Jadwiga, when it was a man's blood rather than an animal's. All the cutting and slaughtering on the farm had not prepared him. Even seeing men who had taken a wound in battle and who could tell of a sword suddenly entering—this was different even than that, when one man, awake, took a razor sharp knife and carefully, deliberately, cut into another man's flesh—a sleeping man's flesh, and then had to cope with a flowing of blood...And that was all he had seen.

"Jadwiga, the doctor is a very good man. He is a German, yes, but he is a kind one and he is being very good with Jozef."

He was preparing her, he realized, for his argument that the doctor should attend the birth of their child. But this was not the time.

"Delfinia will stay with Jozef, and I must go back, Jadwiga. He must be watched all the time, awake or asleep, so that he doesn't hurt himself. If he starts to bleed, he could bleed to death. I must work out a system with Delfinia so that the two of us can watch him. The doctor gave me a pass so I can come and go."

She nodded understanding.

"I'll eat my meals in sick bay, and bring extra food to you at night. I'll have to come down at night to deal with Fritz, anyway. But maybe we can stop buying from him. Maybe now I will buy only for the others. We'll see how much I can bring to you."

With this talk of plans and arrangements, he didn't notice the tear that gathered below one eye and finally rolled off down her cheek.

"Paul, please let us just hold each other for a while now."

They lay close, holding tightly at first. For the first time now, he allowed his body to shudder, and he buried his face in her breasts so that an involuntary cry could finally be allowed to escape its prison within his body. Then he fell asleep, and she decided she would let him, whatever promises he may have made topside. For just a while, she would be his comfort.

Chapter 36

As days passed, Jadwiga came to treasure her private sleeping place in the pigpen. Because it was raised above the drainage deck at the side where the Frederika gathered inward and upward to the bow, there was no headroom, but being unable to stand was small cost measured against the warmth and privacy.

There were the Dominiak children, of course; Delfinia hadn't returned from sick bay. But they were a diversion by day, extra warmth by night, and no trouble. Franek was innocently charming in his imitation of Big Jozef, opening his shirt to warm Pelagia while she fell asleep. Her cough continued, but the doctor's medicine seemed to be helping and it wasn't so severe. Tiny Konrad slept quietly in a blanket-hammock hanging between crosstimbers. Each twin wanted to sleep closest to Jadwiga, but since Manya always fell asleep first, Magda was satisfied by a special conspiracy: her turn, though second, would last through the night.

They all slept soundly. Thus it surprised Jadwiga, one night, to be awakened by a hard kick. With a little laugh, she realized the cause of the disturbance was her own baby, exercising inside her. She waited for more, putting her hands where she would best feel the action of its little legs, but no more came.

She thought it must be nearly time for Paul to come from sick bay, bringing some treat of extra food, and she decided to wait at the hatchway to surprise him. She opened the little gate and dropped her feet over the edge of the pigpen, then sat, letting her eyes adjust to the half-light, peering at the sleepers arrayed across the deck. Even the straw under them was being rationed now. Promised weekly, it came instead at twelve-day intervals.

Everyone was asleep, even the Russians, who had remained watchful for a few days even after Jozef was taken away. It was a peaceful night of gentle lean to starboard; it meant the winds were no better, but Jadwiga disciplined herself to avoid thinking about whether her baby would come in America or aboard ship. God would decide, she told herself. Through her prayers He knew her wishes, and He would decide.

Having verified the path open to her, she pushed herself off the ledge and walked softly to the hatchway. Lanterns turned low in the German section made seeing hard, but the only thing of interest would be the movement when Paul opened the midship hatchway and came forward. He would be surprised to find her waiting.

But there was no movement. Amid the bales of hay where the Germans kept house, at their privy behind the cows, between the horses—no movement. The hunchback's peculiar snore pierced the quiet, rising from his hammock above the horses, but no movement. Jadwiga thought she would fall asleep leaning on the half-door.

Then there was movement.

Among the cows on the starboard side, to the left of the gangway as she looked aft, something caught her eye. It wasn't the simple swish of a tail. It was a larger, more deliberate movement—a person—a man. A German, she thought. A German milking a cow—just finishing!

The figure moved toward the center gangway. He was quick, light of foot, and suddenly turning her way. She tried to move quickly, but leaning, she was unprepared. Starting over the half-door, he bumped into her. It was Jan Poglicki, carrying an empty bucket.

"Oh, God, Jadwiga, you scared me. What the hell are you doing here?"

"Bringing back an empty pail, Jan? You milked a cow and drank it all yourself. None even for your Katrina. Shame."

"The damned cow wouldn't give. Now let me through here."

She laughed. "Jan Poglicki, the great sneak thief, foiled by a cow. Wait 'til the others hear of this!"

"Shhh! No, you mustn't tell, especially Estella."

"I won't. But some day, in America, I'll tell this story on you."

"It's not funny. You need the strength of milk, and so does my Katrina. Pelagia, too. The damned cow wouldn't give."

"She smells the sweat on your hands. You're a thief, Jan, not a farmer."

"You can do better, I suppose? Even a farmer might have trouble at this strange hour."

"Of course I can do better."

"Then you milk her. You'll even have me for a lookout."

In sick bay, Paul woke Delfinia with the good news that Jozef had at last settled into a peaceful sleep, after much talk late into the night. He put on his coat and took the food saved for Jadwiga.

There was a thin creaking from the counterbalancing springs of the midship hatchway as he opened it, holding it against the wind to avoid a slam. Carefully, he lowered the heavy planking and secured it. Across the distance, from the forward hatchway, there was a cough. Someone at the manure pile, he thought.

He intended simply to reach into the pigpen and wake Jadwiga to come to the hatchway and eat some of the beans and pork. But she wasn't there. He discerned the shape of each of the Dominiak children, but no Jadwiga.

It was a puzzle. Perhaps the children had become too much for her and she was back on the deck among the others. He repositioned the lantern to make their outlines easier to see. But she was not there.

In the cribbing, with the Stecks? No. At the manure pile? No, he would have passed her.

There was a moment of panic when it crossed his mind that perhaps the baby was coming and she'd gone to sick bay, but he would have passed her in coming below. He dismissed the notion but couldn't dismiss the feeling of concern. She had to be on her way to sick bay, or at the manure pile. He hurried, leaving the wrapped food on the edge of the pigpen. But at the manure pile, there was only Jan Poglicki.

"Paul, hello. How is Jozef?"

"Jozef is…Jadwiga isn't in her pigpen. She must be on her way to sick bay." He started to go over the hatchway door again, only to meet Jadwiga coming over the other way.

"Jadwiga! Were you going to sick bay? Is the baby…" He saw the pail in her hand. "What's that for?"

"I was trying to milk that Godforsaken cow."

"Jadwiga! If you were caught…"

By then, Jan was with them. "It's all right, Paul. I was lookout."

"Holy Mother of God, the two of you…"

"So, Jadwiga, did the cow smell fish on your hands?" Jan asked.

"Don't be so sassy, Jan. You spoiled her for anybody else."

"What've you two been doing? How long has this been going on?"

"Only tonight. Jan startled her."

"And you did no better, Jadwiga. You're no more farmer than I."

"Paul, you grew up milking cows. If anybody can get milk from her, you can. Here."

He wanted to scold her for stealing, but instead he found himself holding the pail.

"He'll do no better than you or I," Jan said. "With that animal, being a farmer is of no consequence. She will give only for the hunchback."

"You'll see."

"What are you two talking about? I'm not going to..."

"Then, Jadwiga, perhaps a small wager? You have such faith in Paul's ability to get milk from this dry cow. What's your wager?"

"One mark."

"Jadwiga!"

"One mark. Done."

"Just a minute! I have no intention of milking that cow. It's too dangerous. And neither of you try it again. Jadwiga, I forbid..."

"You lose, Jadwiga. He fails to bring forth the milk."

"Paul, am I going to lose a whole German mark because you won't milk that cow? A mark?"

"It's not a ques...One mark?"

"Yes."

A mark—a small ransom, Paul thought. It was wrong, stealing. But these Germans of the ship, starving them, deserved less adherence to their rules, anyway. And a mark, so easily taken.

Or perhaps two.

He looked at Jan. "You wouldn't care to double the bet?"

"Done."

Paul scanned the midship compartment for signs of movement, found none, and went over the half-door. He would do this quickly. He'd take two good Prussian marks from this sneak thief by besting him at his own game and then he'd forbid them to try it ever again.

"Paul will bring milk from that cow, you'll see," Jadwiga said.

"Either way, I win. I have milk for Katrina, or I have two marks."

"If you have the milk, you have it at a very high price."

"I expect to have the money, not the milk."

"You'll see."

"Shhhh. Look." Jan pointed out some movement among the Germans. Both watched for any threat to Paul, but whoever it was seemed not to be headed for the privy behind the cows. It was a man; from his silhouetted profile Jadwiga recognized Fritz Adenauer. He was getting food from a hiding place. Too late, she thought of going to Paul to bring him back.

Jan coughed quietly, but he knew immediately that not only had his warning failed, but his bet was lost. There was the unmistakable sound of milk spattering into the pail.

"I win," Jadwiga whispered.

"Not so easily. He has yet to bring it back."

Now neither knew what to do, because Fritz was just steps away, between the bales, coming to the hatchway to meet Paul.

"*Wo ist Paul?*" he asked. She knew what it meant, but pretended not to understand.

"Jan, you'd better go. This is the one Paul buys from. He won't deal if you're here."

"He doesn't understand Polish."

"No."

"Then I'll go." But instead, he extended his hand across the doorway. "*Ich bin Jan.*" Smiling at Fritz, shaking his hand, patting his shoulder, he switched to Polish: "You're a contemptible bastard. You steal the food our children need so badly, but only for profit. I hope you choke your life away on my money." He left Fritz wondering what he'd said, and Jadwiga holding back a laugh.

The spattering had stopped, but when she glanced toward the cows, there was no movement. She pointed at the bulge in Fritz's shirt.

He held out his hand, doubting she had money, but she reached under her dress and produced some. In return, he showed her the food. It was cheese, and she thought she would never want cheese again. There were round slices of dried apple, and a jar of pears.

She reached for the food, but Fritz held up fingers to show that he wanted three marks.

He was taking a chance, she realized—assuming she didn't know Paul had been paying two marks. She huffed and threw her head back, and waved a hand as though to push the food away. She held up one finger.

"Paul. *Wo ist Paul?*"

She shrugged.

He held up two fingers now. She held out one mark. He shook his head in frustration and held up two fingers insistently. She shook in refusal, and started to move away. Paul was leaving the cow. She wanted to conclude with Fritz so he'd be gone and less likely to see Paul. He caught her sleeve. "*Ja, ein.*" He held out the food. She paid him quickly, took the food, and walked away, hoping he'd do the same. He turned, but Paul was moving quickly, head down, and nearly bumped into him.

"Oh, Paul. Where the hell were you?"

Paul was caught by surprise, no response ready.

"Sick bay again, was it? Bringing back something for Jadwiga? She is a good bargainer, that one, even though she can't speak German. Or maybe because..."

Suddenly, Herman was standing with them. Paul's heart nearly left his chest.

"What are you two up to?"

"Paul is just coming back from sick bay, Herman." As smoothly as he could, behind his back, Paul lifted the pail over the hatchway door and put it on the other side. "What are you doing awake?"

"Not sleeping well—restless. This crossing is taking too long."

"Too damned long," Fritz said.

"I must get some sleep," Paul said. "I'll leave you to talk." He opened the bottom half of the hatchway door as though he'd never think of going through any other way.

"Good night," Fritz said. Herman merely grunted.

Jadwiga was nearly breathless, waiting on the other side of the rain-water vat with Jan Poglicki.

"Suddenly the hatchway is like market day in Gdansk," she whispered. "Why does everybody come around at just the wrong time?"

"Jan, we owe you two marks. You were right. The cow is dry."

"But I heard..."

"You've won your bet. Both of you, listen to me. If you were caught at that, you'd spend the rest of the trip in confinement, with child or not."

"It just seemed like such a good idea," Jan said. "Those Germans are stealing things that will be missed. But nobody arrests a cow for giving less milk one day. Paul, I was sure I heard you getting milk."

Jadwiga put her arm around Paul. "He did, Jan. The cow gave for him. But this husband of mine has a conscience. He couldn't do it."

"It's the risk," Paul said defensively. "The risk is too great."

"Even so," said Jan, "if this trip doesn't end soon, the thievery of the Germans is far more likely to be discovered."

"Let's sleep now, before we wake the others," Jadwiga said.

His heart was still pounding. It was a real problem, he thought, worse every day: The longer the journey, the more likely a discovery of the thefts. From all accounts, there were many days to go.

He ached for it to end.

Chapter 37

Paul carried, unrelieved and secret, the burden of his promise to Big Jozef. Mixed as it was with his worries over the baby coming and over the possibility of being blamed for the thefts of food, it was a confession he had to make to Jadwiga—whatever her reaction might be—however angry at him she might become. He had to confess it, he felt, and get on to the question, still unresolved, of accepting the doctor's help with the baby.

He brought these matters to another of their nighttime conversations at the double-door.

"Jozef is only now beginning to understand that each new appearance of the doctor is not a threat to him," he said, intending it as an explanation for his being away so much. "The doctor thinks he took away all the bad part of the leg, but it still could be necessary to do something more on the table. He has to watch Jozef carefully—to know how he feels. And for Jozef to have trust in the doctor they must be able to talk. This is why the doctor wants me there during the day."

"I understand, Paul."

"For part of the night, I relieve Delfinia, because he still tries to thrash about sometimes."

"But he's going to be well, you think?"

"The doctor says he's as strong as a canal mule. Jozef cursed at him for taking his leg. The doctor says that's a good sign."

"Still, it's an awful thing."

"Jadwiga, I cannot imagine losing a leg. Well, I can, really, now that I've seen it happen to Jozef. But I can't imagine being...dealing with the consequences."

"It changes everything for him...for them."

"All he had to offer in America was his bigness for work. It's all I have to offer."

"But you can learn other things, Paul."

"But Jozef, not so much. He has—had—primarily his strength. And the opportunities to learn other things surely must depend on earning one's way doing the heavy lifting."

She didn't respond, waiting for him to continue.

"Jadwiga, when I was helping the doctor, it was necessary that Jozef be still—that he not fight the sponge or knife. I had to ask his promise that he wouldn't resist. I made him a promise, Jadwiga, because he was so concerned about his family. He thought he might die, and that if he would live he'd be unable to provide."

"What promise, Paul?"

"I promised that his family wouldn't go hungry in America. I promised I would stand by him."

She looked at him but gave no reaction.

"I know I may be unable to keep the promise. You and our child come first."

Still nothing.

"But I hope it isn't necessary to leave them without help. They might not even be allowed to enter if Jozef can't work."

"We can say he is my brother."

"What?"

"Yes. We'll say he's my brother, so he'll be accepted. They'll take us as one family."

"Then, you don't..."

"You're such a good man. I could see at the beginning in Poznań, that you were kind—perhaps too kind."

"But..."

"I understand your promising. And your worry about keeping the promise. But we will try. We'll see what America has to offer and we'll see what can be done. We'll do our best to help them."

She could surprise him. This was one of those times. She was agreeing without his having to make the whole of the arguments. She was even contributing her own idea: She would be Jozef's sister; they would offer themselves in America as a family.

"Later," she said, "after we see what America has to offer, it may be best if they go back where they have real family. But they'll decide that for themselves, I think, if it doesn't work out."

He was so relieved, he almost dared not raise the other matter. He would wait at least a few minutes, if not until another night here at the hatchway.

"Paul, when must you report to the officers about how Jozef was hurt?"

"All day today I kept thinking they would come for me, but nobody came. The doctor has said nothing more. I don't want to ask. I don't want to report Piotr, nor do I want to risk trying to conceal what happened."

"You mustn't. Just tell them what you saw. That won't put Jozef in jeopardy."

"Probably not."

"If they question Jozef, won't it be through you?"

"There may be Germans aboard who speak Polish."

"Tell Jozef to pretend he doesn't understand their Polish. If they question him, let it be through you. You can protect him when you interpret the answers."

"I just hope they'll forget."

"That's not likely. Germans keep records."

Paul thought about this for a moment, then remembered that he wanted to ask about Juliusz.

"It's the same, Paul. He broods. He is hurt so deeply."

"He'll talk with no one?"

"It's been more than a month. He just sits most of the time. He walks around sometimes, but never to talk."

"It's so awful, so terrible a thing." He imagined himself in Juliusz's place and shuddered. It took conscious effort to rescue himself from the feeling. "Jadwiga, I worry so much that what happened to Maria..." He needed to hold her, and she put her head on his chest.

"It won't, Paul. I'm healthy. I've been eating well, especially with the extra from Fritz and from sick bay."

"But there's no midwife."

"No. Ursula cowers with Piotr and their sons at the starboard pig-pens. They move only to go to the manure pile. I wouldn't ask her."

"Who, then?"

"You want me to have the doctor."

"I want you to live, Jadwiga. I want our child to live." Tears came unexpectedly, falling off his face into her hair.

"I'm beginning to believe that God wants our child born on this ship."

"Jadwiga, you must prepare."

"Yes."

"Do you believe it's unholy to have a man...?"

"I would prefer not. I've been talking with the women—Polka, Estella, Viktoria...Kostanta, too."

"And Salomeya?"

"Oh, Salomeya especially. It's just that women know what must be done. A man does not."

"But the doctor does."

"But he's a stranger. He has good intent, perhaps, but he's a stranger—and a German. It would be like having one of the seamen."

"He has assisted before."

"So he says. This may be true, or maybe he just wants to learn. I don't know."

"Suppose you could be assisted by Salomeya or one of the women?"

"He's already said one can be present."

"But maybe he'll let a woman help you, in sick bay, and just be present himself."

"Did you ask?"

"I will, if you'll accept such an arrangement. I just think things will go better for you in sick bay, where it's cleaner, with better light, where the doctor has equipment, and..." She was thinking, so he made no attempt to finish.

After a long time, she spoke. "All right, ask him. I agree about the place. I think it's all right to have him there if a woman assists me."

Now he held her tightly. There were times when her unreasonableness exasperated him, and times when her sense and reason made him love her all the more.

Chapter 38

The doctor and Paul talked over the evening meal.

"I'm young, true—I'm barely a few years older than you, Herr Adamik. I haven't been a physician for a long time. And I'm still learning, yes, but that's true of all doctors."

Paul understood now that his attitude toward Germans was shaped by his time in the army. He confessed to himself that, as Jadwiga chided, he tended to vest command authority in any speaker of the language—at least any speaker of precision and intellect.

"I would learn by attending your wife, to be sure. And one day, something I might learn in attending her might help me attend another woman."

There were exceptions, of course—the cattletenders of the world like Herman the hunchback, and the thieves like Fritz Adenauer. But even they received more of his respect than they were properly due simply because they spoke the language of command. He had to concede this.

"And your wife can benefit from those I have assisted before her. I haven't assisted as much as some midwives, true, but there is no experienced midwife among your people except the one who failed the Sczepaniak woman."

For that matter, he realized, he was all the more obsequious if the speaker of German words happened to be wearing a uniform. But ship's officers who starved their passengers and damaged their ship were not entitled to his esteem, with or without uniforms, with or without their language.

"As to it being improper for a man—a doctor—to be the midwife? I don't want to offend, but that's folk myth…custom taking on the sanction of religious doctrine. There are better ways. Things are changing."

This doctor was different. This was a German for whom one could feel a special admiration. It wasn't rank or age or even the knowledge of a special craft. It was the range of the man—from whimsical humor to decisive action to relaxed contemplation to gentle compassion to the kind of anger that flared now in his eyes behind words spoken with feeling.

"It's when that custom becomes a threat to life that I rail, Herr Adamik. Then I rage against it in sadness and anger. Why?" A dish jumped as he hit the desk with his fist. "Why should life be taken when life can be saved? I feel so helpless that my first attendance to Frau Sczepaniak was after her death. I might have been able to help her. It tears at me. Death is too powerful for us to be helping it with blind suspicion and...damnable ignorance."

While the doctor talked, he concluded he must no longer give special respect to Germans just because they spoke the language by which he had been commanded in the army.

"Please understand I don't predict the worst for your wife. Usually, it goes well. It's when it doesn't that my training becomes important."

The doctor stopped, finally, and after a moment started again to eat his supper.

"What Jadwiga would like, Herr Doktor Hoffmeister, is to be attended, in your sick bay, by one or two of the women. She's willing to have you there. It's only that she's more comfortable with the idea of a woman touching...someone she knows..."

The doctor said nothing, so Paul continued.

"I assure you—this is already a considerable change, to have you present. She comes from Gdynia, where Germans are distrusted and—forgive me—hated. Oh, it's not just that. In talking with the women, she's come to trust their understanding of what is required. It's too bad she can't have such discussions with you. I say that because in what talk you've had, through my clumsy translation, she has come to this point of trust—to have you present. I think she'd trust you more, were you really able to talk together."

"Then she wants two women from your section, and I would be present."

"Yes, sir. It may be that in the time remaining she'll become even more trusting, but it's what she asked last night. Please...I hope it's acceptable."

"It's difficult. I'm responsible for what happens in sick bay. I can't know the skill of these women...Of course, I could step in if there are complications. But I wouldn't want to have to fight them to help her. I'll have to think about this."

Paul leaned back in his chair and looked at the doctor across his desk. Both men smiled slightly. Then, with a jerk of his head, Paul looked down at his tray.

"Here I've been listening to you and eating absent-mindedly and thoughtlessly, doctor. I meant to save most of this for Jadwiga."

"I've had plenty. Take this to her, please, with my compliments."

"Oh, I couldn't..."

"I've finished, except for my beer." The doctor pushed his tray toward Paul. He hadn't really eaten his fill, but wiping his mouth with his napkin made it final.

"Thank you, doctor."

"Well," the doctor said, "I'll think about this proposition. It could serve the interest of doing the best we can by your wife—the best she will allow. I'll think about it."

He shifted in his chair, leaning back in a change of attitude and subject.

"How long were you in the army?"

"Two years, sir. The compulsory time."

"Good service?"

"I was in a company of engineers. The shovel, not the rifle. The Germans—that is, the army officers—don't trust us—Poles, I mean—with guns. They fear more uprisings."

"But you became a sergeant."

"Yes. Just when my muscles became strong enough for the work, I knew enough German to be promoted. Then, of course, I learned even more, being the go-between from Poles to Germans, Germans to Poles. Learning the language was the best part."

"I thought about the army, but this seemed better at the time."

"The ship?"

"Well, I could have learned medicine with an obligation to the army, but I was offered the same arrangement with the shipping company. I have another year to go—perhaps four or five more trips."

"And then you'll settle?"

"I don't know. They'll ask that I stay on—for regular passenger ships. But once out of the emigration ships, it's lazy duty. People who need real medical attention don't travel. On a ship you console for seasickness or give whatever remedy is the current custom for the first few days of a journey...then it's a matter of being pleasant to the first class passengers at meals and listening to the complaints of...Well, I don't think I'll stay."

"Is this an unusual trip?"

"Yes. Less sickness, more injury. Very unusual. The storm really hit us hard. More were hurt than should have been. More death. And treating the captain, of course. He shouldn't be at sea, brought back to work just because he has the papers. They should have left the man on dry land."

"There is talk below decks about the officers."

"That they're not very good, you mean. Yes. It's an old ship, we've had some terrible weather, and command is weak. You'll not repeat this, of course—at least not in the German language while aboard this ship?" Paul shook his head in reassurance. "It's a lethal combination, like a bad recipe."

"Bad...?"

"Bad combination. The weather, the officers, the ship. We'd be fine if any one were better. In combination—*zusammen*—they're killers."

"But we're not in danger."

"Not now. We'll be fine if the weather holds and the stores last. I don't mean to say the first mate is altogether bad. He may be trying too hard. This ship was ferociously clean before we loaded her. No rats. Not one. We have no sicknesses running rampant, which would be the worst...And he is strict with the galley—they don't dare demand money from steerage passengers for food they've already paid for. That's the usual on these ships. And we sailed with a full crew—passengers aren't forced to work. Several signed on—replacements after the storm—but they'll be paid. As emigrant ships go, this one is...There have been mistakes of judgment, but not intent."

"Doctor Hoffmeister, I've been wondering about reporting to the officers about what happened to Jozef."

"Yes?"

"Will they ask me, or am I to make a report without being asked, or...what is the procedure?"

"Are you eager to make a report?"

"No. No, very much the contrary."

"Are things under control down there?"

"Yes."

"How did it happen? How was he cut?"

"Officially?"

"Between us."

Paul told the doctor what he could, leaving out the part about the fight starting over stolen food. Then he added, "But much of this I didn't personally observe. In an official report, I would tell only what I myself saw."

"The other man is no longer armed?"

"No."

"Is the Russian likely to be harmed?"

"Not on the ship. We agreed there will be no retribution here. It's already enough to explain."

"Which brings us to your question about making a report."

"Yes."

"I put down what I knew in the medical log. I gave a copy to the mate. His duty is to make an entry in the ship's log, but first to determine cause and so on. I gave your name as the passenger who reported the injury, and noted that you speak German. From there on it's up to him. Now that I think about it, I'm not surprised he hasn't questioned you."

"Why is that?"

"The mate expected advancement to captain when we return home. With the storm damage...I don't know what his hopes are now. Perhaps just to remain a first mate. It could be that with just the broken mast and the lost crewmen to explain—well, there was the passenger kicked by a horse...Anyway, I'm sure he hopes to have as little of a serious nature on the log as possible. He, too, has enough to explain."

"Will he ignore it?"

"No, that's a greater risk."

"What should I do? Can you advise me?"

"Wait until he calls for you. Unless you want the Russian out of there."

"No. I suppose we'd want him out if this journey were going to last very much longer."

"We have two or three weeks more to sail."

Paul sighed. "Even so, we prefer to minimize it. If the Russian is questioned, he may say things to make it hard for Jozef."

"Just wait, then, until the mate asks you. Then—I think you're right—say only what you know. Tell only what you must."

"I thank you for your counsel."

"You won't repeat what I said."

"No, sir, I will not."

"Good. And if you have other questions, I'm here to ask."

"How does it go for Jozef?"

"The signs are good. Another few days, perhaps, and I'll be able to say there are no complications."

"May I have your permission to tell him that? And Delfinia?"

"Yes."

"Thank you."

The doctor leaned forward. "Paul, while we've been talking I've been thinking about this proposition from your Jadwiga—about the women?"

"Yes, sir."

"Please let me explain my situation. I can't risk blunders by women who don't know what they must. On the other hand, it's not in my nature to confine her in sick bay so that I'm her only recourse. That would be bad, especially if there were problems and then questions raised about my actions.

"So it comes down to my having confidence that the women know what they're doing. And, quite frankly, a matter of their having confidence in me—Jadwiga, too—so if things go wrong, they'll trust me to help or take over."

"Yes, sir."

"So what I want to suggest to Frau Adamik is that we do this her way, but that in advance—starting immediately—tomorrow—the two women and your wife and I talk through the procedures so I can be sure they know what they're to do. And this will give me an opportunity to discuss the possible problems, so they'll understand that I should give direction, or even take over, if there are difficulties."

Paul was disheartened. "They don't speak German, sir."

"No, you'll have to interpret, of course."

"But my German isn't..."

"Your German is really just fine. There will be a few words...It won't be easy, but you can do it." He held up a hand as though to dispel doubt. "When a birth is normal, it's fairly simple. It's only when there are complications that more modern knowledge becomes important. But it's not a difficult vocabulary."

"But to have me present for such talk? It's one thing to have you talk with them. Even that may be a problem, Doctor. But I would be here, and not just here, but speaking the words. They won't accept it."

"Let's try."

"I don't know..."

"Ask your wife, at least, will you?"

"Yes, I'll ask...I'll ask her...but even if she's willing, the others..."

"She needs only two women—or even just one who's willing. Women with experience at birth, of course."

Paul contemplated this counterplan in a state near shock. To be the intermediary in discussion of procedures? He felt awkward and out of place already. But he could ask, at least.

"I'll ask Jadwiga," he said.

Chapter 39

He asked her later that night.

Almost without warning, he was deeply involved.

The questions of propriety were gone. The question of standing aside for women doing matters of women, gone. The worries over how and where this child would be born, gone. Now he was deeply involved.

Jadwiga's choice of Delfinia surprised him. She gave no reason, simply asking that he pass on the request when he returned to sick bay. Delfinia agreed immediately—and would, he thought, to any request Jadwiga would make.

Early in the morning, the doctor showed him diagrams in books—meticulous pictures that prepared him for discussion of things he thought he'd never hear. It was his opportunity to learn the German words and to guess, from his farm experience, what the Polish might be. But the doctor was also trying to spare him at least some embarrassment by giving him a lesson all his own in advance, and he was grateful. He began to think he might be able to face Delfinia and Jadwiga and speak these words, after all.

When he returned to steerage late in the morning he learned that Salomeya had agreed to help, and that surprised him. When he thought about it, he realized his surprise was mostly because of the woman's age. And then he realized, in a moment of shame, that his thinking about Salomeya was more rigid than Salomeya's own thinking about matters far more important.

Jadwiga made no secret of the plan. This led to much interested whispering. No one challenged her right to decide for herself how her baby would come into the world; Salomeya saw it Jadwiga's way, and there was the recent death of Maria to consider. But now there would be talk with the German doctor, all the words to pass through Paul, starting that very afternoon.

There was a good deal more to talk about, wives with their men, husbands among husbands, wives with wives. It made for fresh conversation and a diversion from routine.

Then Jadwiga brought out baby clothes, and he had nervous feelings of imminence. An event that had seemed remotely situated among diagrams and unfamiliar German words now took shape and form and he felt a new, insistent anxiety. She was ignoring him, so he went to the repairwork in the bow and climbed up to talk with Salomeya.

"Babka, this doesn't mean it is already time, does it?"

She smiled at him sweetly. "My good *zolnierz*, Adamik. You are a good man and yet such a simple one. You are at times even so simple as the others. This is only a first sign of readiness. It is only that today, your Jadwiga has a plan in her head. These clothes for her baby are simply part of her plan."

About Salomeya there was always a smile, sometimes even a trace when she was lost in the seriousness of prayer. She was withering with years, but there was a sharpness in her eyes, always glowing with good nature. She was a source of reassurance.

"Salomeya, I'm so afraid for my Jadwiga."

"Don't be afraid, Paul. Think about your feelings and you will see that you fear for yourself more than for her. Is this not true?"

They looked at Juliusz, who sat on the deck in his usual place just forward of the rainwater vat. His knees were pulled up to his chin. Silent, he watched Jadwiga with the baby clothes.

"Perhaps. Perhaps I'm afraid for myself."

"You must not be afraid. You have a good wife. She is sharp in temper and strong with her words, but she tells people right to their faces and not behind their backs. She has made these many days pleasant and interesting for me because of her fearlessness with the ocean and with the Germans.

"Your Jadwiga is strong. When her little *dziecina* begins to fight for the light of day it will not find the mother holding back. She is strong even in her hunger, and when her time comes she will yank me by my hand and I pray only that I can keep pace with her.

"You must not be afraid."

He touched the old woman's face lightly, and kissed her on the cheek. She touched his cheek, and they had a gentle hug.

Then both turned to watch Jadwiga, but there was something else catching the eye. On his knees, Juliusz was rummaging in his baggage and bringing out delicate pieces of cloth. He gathered them together, holding them to his chest, then stood. He walked to Jadwiga, who by now had noticed his activity.

He held out to her those garments which had been intended for his own child, and she took them in her hands. She held out her arms to him, and he fell into her embrace, sobbing, shaking in a release of grief.

The doctor had to take the lead. For all their willingness, Salomeya and Delfinia didn't find it easy to talk openly. It was slow going at first. Paul couldn't help trying to say things as delicately as possible. The doctor's words were delicate enough. Paul's Polish was adequate to the task of translating the subtleties. But he tried to soften the words even more. He wanted Jadwiga to think of the doctor in the most accepting way possible. It went slowly.

But after a time the translations speeded up as the doctor developed a sense of how much should be said before interpretation and became more concise. Paul became less self-conscious. At one point he was startled to find himself intrigued by the similarity between this conversation and another he once translated between a German engineer and the foreman of a gang of Poles working on a bridge. He chastised himself for the thought, but it helped him become comfortable.

He was surprised at the simplicity. There were the technical details, of course, but in overview, what had to be accomplished was remarkably straightforward—at least, as the doctor repeatedly emphasized, when things went as they should.

Jadwiga had more questions than either Delfinia or Salomeya, and she thought nothing of interrupting in mid-translation when one crossed her mind. This led the other women into the spirit of the proceedings and soon a dialogue was developing.

The doctor was asked more than once to defend certain aspects of timing or sequence. Paul translated rhymes that Salomeya and Delfinia quoted—rhymes to help a woman remember the proper order of things in the excitement of a delivery.

The trouble was, of course, that the doctor had different ideas about these things than the women did. This was where the medical reasoning and terminology became harder. Paul's head hurt with the fatigue of so much translation. But it was a successful session, lasting nearly two hours, and it ended amiably with the women each having a small glass of the doctor's wine. Not all the embarrassment was gone, but he made it easier for them.

Juliusz was again talking with the men, though he was not at all the funmaker of the beginning of the journey. He asked Paul more than once about details of Big Jozef's trial under the doctor's knife, expressing contempt for Piotr's cowardly use of a weapon in a man-to-man fight.

Paul found it hard, talking with Juliusz.

Translating was easier the second day, but the subjects were frightening. Jadwiga was interested and attentive, but her questions and comments showed that she believed none of the difficulties of which the doctor spoke would apply in her own case.

The doctor tried to be reassuring, offering speculation and in some cases even statistics to show that while it was good to be prepared for complications, they were encountered infrequently and were not to be a cause for concern.

Paul wasn't reassured. At one point he found himself unable to change the words from German into Polish. He couldn't help thinking of Maria.

Then he saw that his feeling of awkwardness with Juliusz was guilt. He had shunned Juliusz after the tragedy befell him, as though such misfortune could be contagious. Now he wished he could go back to the bad time and be a comfort.

He resolved to be a better friend to the man.

"As soon as we arrive," Juliusz said to him one day, "I must mail a letter back home to tell Maria's family what happened."

When Juliusz talked with the other men, Maria was seldom mentioned. But with Paul, it was different.

"I will send them something of Maria's for them to keep."

Paul asked what he intended to do—whether he would stay in America. Juliusz was surprised by the question, and Paul realized he hadn't thought about it.

"Paul, you're good with words. Will you help me write to Maria's parents?"

Paul agreed to help, though doubting he could. It didn't matter, for in the end, Juliusz wrote it himself. What was important to Juliusz was showing it to Paul.

Many times during our journey, Paul read, *when Maria and I saw something unusual, she said to me that we must tell you about it in our first letter home. She was entranced by the gaslamps of Hamburg and excited by the activity in the port of Bremerhaven. She made good friends among the people in our contingent, and they took her to their hearts. Yet she missed you very much, and this first letter to you from America was much on her mind.*

But I am writing this letter to you without Maria's help, except in her spirit, which remains with me and shall remain with me forever. My Maria—your Maria—our Maria, and her baby were taken by the Lord during childbirth midway in our crossing of the ocean.

Some of her last thoughts expressed to me were of you when she knew she would have a difficult time with the birth. She loved you always, very deeply, and I know that she and our baby are now angels of the Lord looking down upon you as you learn this sad news.

The letter stopped there, as yet incomplete. Juliusz, who had been watching Paul read, had tears in his eyes—tears of resignation as much as of sadness.

"I think it would have gone badly for Maria even back home, just as badly as on the ocean," he said. "I thought we should not make this trip at this time, but she insisted, always.

"She has always been a delicate girl, small..." His voice trailed off, but then he added, "Even the Russian midwife could not make it go better or worse for Maria."

"Juliusz, it's a good letter."

"I may think of other things to write, perhaps not. Perhaps I will send it as it is and then write another letter to them, and to my own parents, when I've decided what I'll do. Maybe I'll go back..."

Paul nodded. Neither spoke for almost a minute.

"Jadwiga is having the doctor?" Juliusz asked. He knew the answer, and it was more a statement.

"Salomeya and Delfinia, in the sick bay. The doctor will be present."

"I'll pray for her, Paul. With the others, I'll pray for her. Maria will be watching over her. It will go well."

Chapter 40

Paul felt the need to think, away from the others, out in the air.

Standing on the Frederika's deck in the late afternoon of February 15, he tried to concentrate. He meant to discipline himself to think only about the matter at hand: The message sent below had asked—no, directed—that he appear before the First Mate to provide information in the matter of Jozef Dominiak.

But his mind refused to cooperate. Like a flat stone skipped across a creek, it leapt from one worry to another: Jadwiga's orneriness, worse today than ever; the growing certainty that the baby would be born at sea; the thefts of food, sure to be discovered.

And now, more bad weather coming. Jadwiga sensed this, and it made her all the more ornery. Paul watched seamen furling the highest, smallest sail on the aftmost mast, momentarily distracted by their display of agility.

And there was the immediate concern over the fracas between Jozef and Piotr. One school of fearful thought held that everyone in the section would surely be turned away from America. Others rejected this notion. Stanisław Krulik, for example, argued that by any standard of reason and justice, only those directly involved in the fight would be so punished. Some reminded him that there were Prussians involved, and talk of reason and justice was thus foolish. The consensus was that much would depend on Paul's answering of the questions to be asked by the German officers.

He turned away to look out over rolling waves. It was true. Making guesses about what the Germans might do was useless. There was a callous uncertainty about it—an unfairness in which a man had no shred of influence over the circumstances of his own life.

He realized he was gripping a rigging line so tightly that his forearm was beginning to cramp.

It crossed his mind, then, that from his earliest memory, others had created the circumstances of his life. First, his parents, and the farm life. Then the Germans and the Army—compulsory service and tightly fixed rules of behavior. Then, Jadwiga. America was her dream, not his. He had chosen to go along with it, true, but he hadn't dreamed the dream himself.

One day, he resolved, he would make himself a promise that the circumstances of his life would thereafter be his own creation.

For the present, there was precious little satisfaction. He did have a special role in the adaptation of his own contingent of people to these shipboard circumstances created by the Germans. But it was degrading: the primary value to them of his facility with the Germans' language was for dealings in stolen food. There was an improvement now, at least; because of the leftovers from sick bay—his own for Jadwiga and Delfinia's for her children—the dealings were mostly for the others. Yet he was still involved.

He could count the satisfaction of being the carrier of some good news. Big Jozef was much recovered, and the doctor had let him pass the word that danger of serious complication was past.

But his greatest satisfaction, he realized, was in having shaped the circumstances under which his child would be born. There would be the careful German cleanliness of the sick bay, and a professionally-schooled doctor who might make a crucial difference for mother or child, or perhaps for both. In this, at least, he was providing for his own.

But the satisfactions were few, the worries many.

He reminded himself, on the way to knock on the door of the mate's quarters, that he intended to be less deferential, less a German's Polack. This made him think of Jadwiga and her conflict with the hunchback, though he couldn't imagine dealing with the mate as she had dealt with the cattletender.

He couldn't help but admire her, as Salomeya did. Her uncanny sense of the particular ship's vocabulary of rocking and teetering, creaking, and groaning, provided a feeling of connection with the goings of the Frederika. She'd become less interested in its nuances once she realized she must be ready for birth at sea, but today she had sensed the coming of a storm. On the deck, going to the mate's quarters, he could sense it, too. Even as he knocked on the door of the mate's quarters, the wind was picking up noticeably, and seamen hurried to change the rigging.

Paul saw a difference immediately. This German, this First Mate, was not like the doctor. His face was ordinary enough, but he held its features in a stern casting that said he was all business and pity the man who would think otherwise. There was no invitation to be seated, no pleasantry, hardly a glance at Paul. The man wanted him to understand that he was an annoyance, speaking the best for it. As soon as Paul identified himself, the officer opened a large book on the desk before him. Paul took it to be the ship's log. From it, the man removed a sheet of paper.

"There is the matter, as you know, of one of your contingent whose leg was amputated."

"Yes, sir."

"I will speak more slowly if necessary."

"No, sir."

"While I could choose to ignore this incident, it is appropriate that I make some entry in the log by way of having complete records."

"Yes, sir."

"How well do you know the individual?"

"We have become acquainted during this journey, sir." Paul felt a flash of anger at himself. His speech was reflexively respectful, as though he had no control of it.

"Do you know anything of the means by which his leg came to be injured?"

"Very little..." It felt unnatural.

"I will read to you an entry I have drafted for the ship's records for the date in question."

"Yes, sir."

"'Left leg of steerage passenger Jozef Dominiak amputated in sick bay by ship's physician Hoffmeister, due to deteriorating condition of infection from a wound, apparently made by use of a knife some weeks earlier. Owing to the passenger's inability to speak German, no ascertainment was possible as to how he received the injury. As the wound appears to have festered for some time prior to medical intervention, it appears the passenger sustained his wound before embarkation.'" Now the officer looked directly at Paul, and their eyes met as Paul looked down at him.

"That completes the reading of the draft entry. Did you understand all the words?"

"Yes, sir, I did."

"You would say, would you not, that this is an accurate portrayal?"

The man wanted him to agree. Paul immediately saw the advantages for both the Polish passengers and the mate.

"I would not dispute this record, sir."

"In your judgment, is it likely to be accepted by Dominiak?"

"I don't believe he will dispute it."

"And other passengers in your contingent?"

"No, sir."

"Fine. In two days, I will complete entry of the record. Before that time, you will kindly make certain that the others in question find this record as I have read it to be consistent with their understanding of the facts." The man's tone made it clear what he wanted Paul to do. "You will report to me before then if there is now, or in the future, likely to be any discrepancy whatsoever."

"Yes, sir."

"Have you any questions?"

"Not on this, sir. But I wish to ask how many more days of travel are before us."

"Three to five. But a storm is coming and it could delay us further."

"Thank you, sir."

"*Danke.*" It was more a dismissal than a polite word of appreciation. Paul thought consciously not to salute, and took care to turn less stiffly than his attitude of standing at attention would have called for.

Just outside the mate's quarters, he allowed himself a deeply drawn breath. All the worry about this interview was for nothing. The German wanted a clean record more than an accurate one. With just days to America, he was hurrying to complete his entries in the ship's log, and finally had to face this question of what to write about Jozef's leg.

The wind had increased substantially while he was inside. On deck, crewmen were rigging rope from one sturdy tying point to another—something to grip in precarious footing if one had to be on deck during the storm.

He was expected in sick bay by now, but decided he would first take below his account of the conversation with the officer.

Piotr and Ursula Jakubik listened as closely as the others while Paul related the mate's intent and the substance of the entry intended for the log. Jadwiga didn't come out of her special place in the pigpen, but he spoke loudly enough for her to hear.

"It's clear," Paul said. "We have the choice of accepting this account as the German has written it, or of offering an alternative account. He wants only an assurance that we will not dispute the entry should there be any questions."

"Who is likely to ask questions?" Stanisław glanced at Piotr, then looked around at the others.

"It is best for all to accept this report, is it not?" asked Kazimierz Steck. "If we make any other account, there comes the question of why we didn't report the incident in the first place. And for the officer, there will be the question of why Piotr was not confined."

"And if this question arises," Piotr said, "there will be the question of why I found it necessary to defend my sons." These were the first words Piotr had spoken, since the fight, to anyone other than his family. The tone was offensive, not properly deferential to Kazimierz. The men were offended just by the guttural sound of his Polish, contaminated with Russian sounds, and they turned toward him, ready to pounce if he moved.

"Then you will not dispute this account?" Paul spoke to Piotr in the same impersonal tone of voice the mate had used.

"Let yesterday be past," Piotr said.

Now Paul spoke more quietly, leaving out the Russians. "It takes two to make a fight. It would only hurt Big Jozef to dispute the officer's entry. It would harm us all if Piotr had the opportunity to bring out that this fight began over stolen food."

"What does Jozef say?" asked Ludwig Karpczinski.

"I go to sick bay next," Paul said. "But Jozef will choose to avoid trouble with the officials, here on the Frederika and when we present ourselves in America."

"Can we then agree," Kazimierz Steck reasoned, "that unless Jozef sees it another way, the account by the German of the ship will be allowed to stand? Can we agree on this?"

Everyone glanced around. "I see no reasonable alternative," Stanisław said.

"Nor do I," Paul said.

"Then it is done," Kazimierz said. "There will be no challenge to the German's writing in the official papers."

Jadwiga had listened with only half an ear. While normally she would have many questions, she had no interest in hearing anything more about Paul's visit with the ship's officer. She was ornery with her aching back and couldn't find a comfortable position. He had to talk with Big Jozef and Delfinia about it anyway, so he left her alone in her disagreeable mood.

The ship's movement in the waves had increased greatly in just the fifteen minutes he was in steerage. Going through the midship compartment on his way topside, Paul used the handhold of a rope strung the length of the gangway along the uprights that supported the deck above. Two seamen were testing the pumps. A third man was cutting lengths of rope from a large coil.

Big Jozef had no quarrel with the plan to accept the officer's account. He wanted to be admitted in America, and wanted no questions about a fight aboard ship. "Anyway," he said, "I want Piotr admitted, too. I have yet to settle with him."

Paul wondered if Doctor Hoffmeister knew the mate's intentions. He found him at his desk, putting away loose things that could be tossed to the deck in the worsening weather. In the days since the amputation, with discussion of birth and medical training and the army and other matters, Paul and the doctor had become friends, at least to the extent their separated stations in life and their conflicting nationalities permitted. Paul enjoyed talking with him and tried to imitate his German, which was even more crisp than army speech, and more erudite.

"As I thought," the doctor said. "He prefers to paint it over rather than account for it. I'm not surprised."

"But he hasn't asked you to accept his account?"

"No. He won't. I would have occasion to see his report only if a passenger made a conflicting claim of some sort." He was thoughtful for a moment. "With the damage, he won't be promoted to captain, anyway. It doesn't matter to me. I'll find a way to avoid sailing with him again."

Paul nodded.

"You see how he overreacts to the coming storm? He has had the men pass out lengths of rope here and in steerage. He wants people to tie themselves in. He wants no more burials on the record. I don't doubt he recorded the woman and child from your section as one death rather than two."

"Food will be cold tonight."

"None at all, I think. It's already past time, and supplies are very short now. Any excuse to skip a meal..."

The doctor was interrupted by movement and sound that shook the ship. His chair tipped and he grabbed his desk to avoid going over. Paul caught himself easily, but images of damage from the December storm flashed into his mind.

"Well," the doctor said, "maybe he's not overreacting after all. Perhaps this will be a good blow. God, I pray there are no more injuries. I still have a seaman with a leg and ribs broken from the last one."

Again, a blow that shook the ship.

"I want to take one look outside before I close up tight," the doctor said.

When they emerged on deck, facing aft, the sky was nearly clear except for the beginning of clouding just overhead. But when they turned to look forward, they saw lightning connect sea to black clouds that bulged with a ferocious turbulence. Below the clouds, a driven rain was approaching the ship. To starboard and port, the wind was driving large waves past the ship, causing the pitching.

The doctor had to yell to be heard in the wind: "Those were the blows we felt—the waves—even larger ones. We're in for a hell of a storm. Let's get inside."

"I must go below to explain about the ropes," Paul yelled. "About tying down."

"Come inside. Tell your friends first. Then you can stay below when you go to tell the others."

It took only moments to tell Jozef and Delfinia they should tie the ropes to give themselves something to grab. He started to show Delfinia how to make a loop around a post, but Big Jozef waved him away and rolled out of his bunk. He immediately had difficulty balancing on his one leg, and showed signs of dizziness. But he shouted at Paul, because now the wind's sound was filling even the sick bay, "Go below. Show the others. We will be all right here." Paul wanted to restrain him, but the ship wrenched again, this time pitching forward to port as though digging into a huge wave. Jozef was steady now, Delfinia helping, so he left them.

Out on deck in the rain, now lashing at everything, a seaman with a bloodied forehead was fighting his way toward sick bay. The man was dazed, and Paul helped him by grabbing his jacket front into a fist and half-throwing him toward the door. It was an effort that served Paul's need to go in the other direction, anyway, but he was having a hard time. The deck was wet and in constant, unpredictable motion, the footing treacherous.

He was caught suddenly by a wave breaking over the deck and swept off his feet. He grabbed at one of the guide ropes but the water propelled him across the deck. He clawed at the wood for a hold. Finally his shoulder, below his outreaching arm, smacked painfully into something solid and he wrapped his arms around it and fought for footing that didn't come. Shocked, he saw he'd been driven to the rail and over it. He had grabbed the last thing available before open sea.

Salt water cascading off the deck tore at him, threatening to brush him off. Rain made everything slick. The eccentric movements of the ship defeated every effort to get his feet on something solid. He hung on in panic and desperation, knowing his strength couldn't last.

Suddenly there was a seaman sliding down the sloping deck, toward him, and Paul thought this man would go over the rail, too. But he had a rope tied around his waist and his wild movement was stopped abruptly. He reached over the rail to grab Paul's pants and belt and started to haul him in like a loose bale of hay. Realizing he had to release his grip on the outside of the rail and trust the seaman's strength, Paul had a moment of heightened panic—immediately followed by a forced surrender to fate.

He felt himself lifted upward against terrible resistance, and flipped to the inside of the rail. For the first time, he saw the seaman's face—it was Hoyt Gruenberg. Paul had a sudden flash of response to the question that had incongruously entered his mind: why was this man risking so much to help him?

Now, a miracle, he was on the inside of the rail, and holding on again, grateful it was over. But Hoyt locked his legs around Paul's waist. He hauled on the rope, pulling them both back toward the safety line. Paul reached, trying to help, but he could do nothing.

Hoyt hauled him by his belt again, and put the safety line into his hands. "Get below!" he yelled, and he was gone, hand over hand along the line, before Paul could speak a word.

He fought his way, skidding, slipping, to a hatchway, assaulted by tall waves that now broke over the deck almost continuously. For a moment, he was afraid to open the hatch, concerned that water might get in. Then he knew he couldn't think about that. He undogged it, lifted it, and inserted himself feet first into the opening like a leather worker carelessly threading a needle. He reached up to fasten it closed and was surprised to see blood on his knuckles.

Midship was a jumble. Paul couldn't immediately see how he would get through it to the forward section. It was apparent, just from the state of disarray, that this storm already was worse than the earlier one. But this time nobody was between the horses getting kicked. The Germans had tied themselves to supports, to mainmast, to cow stanchions—anything stationary.

Forty feet away, the top half of the forward hatchway door banged wildly full open, then full shut. When it opened again Paul saw Jan Poglicki and Tadeusz Murak, looking out into the Germans' compartment, a wildness in their eyes, made the more bizarre by the frantic shadows cast by the swinging midship lantern.

Water was everywhere. Paul was struck behind his right shoulder by a toppling bale of straw and spun around. In a glance, he saw the seamen at the midship pump, working against the pitching motion to evacuate water accumulated to above their ankles. He struggled toward the hatchway over loose straw and a crazed stew of German belongings.

"Get back inside," Paul yelled at Jan and Tadeusz. "Tie yourselves with the ropes!"

The Frederika pitched forward, suddenly, and now instead of fighting his way toward the hatchway door, Paul was thrown against it, his right leg hitting first and collapsing under him, unable to take his weight and the force of the movement.

But he took advantage of the momentum and allowed himself to be hurled over the bottom half of the door, which was holding in its closed position. He cracked head-to-head with Ignatz Ran, who had been behind Tadeusz and Jan and was now pinned against the rainwater vat with them. The vat had been wrenched with the ship; it loosed streams near its bottom.

Jan and Tadeusz were spreading the word about the ropes, but most of the children and many of the women were already tied down. There was fear and yelling, but no panic. Having secured their families, men looked for rope for themselves.

Paul grabbed one length, all he could find, and made for Jadwiga's pigpen. Little Magda—or Manya—he couldn't tell which—was outside on the drainage deck, howling. He scooped her up and looped one end of the rope around her. Coming near, he heard Jadwiga shouting instructions at the other Dominiak children. Inside the pigpen, Franek held Konrad with one arm and a corner post of the pigpen with the other. Pelagia was wrapped, arms and legs, around a pigpen fencing rail, and the other twin held tightly to her. Things were better in the confined space of the pigpen.

When she saw him, Jadwiga yelled at him, too: "Get the lantern."

So frantically commanding was Jadwiga's voice that Paul simply handed the stray twin to her, with the rope, and backed out to go for the lantern. "And the clothesline," Jadwiga yelled.

Paul saw that the Stecks were holding on in the cribwork, confined enough to avoid being thrown about but being pitched, in the far bow, with the ship's wildest movements. And then it struck him, seeing Salomeya, why Jadwiga wanted the lantern and the clothesline.

Now he abandoned all care for himself and lunged for the lantern. He abandoned thought to utter a frightened prayer. He ripped the clothesline from its peg and flung himself back across the drainage deck toward Jadwiga's pigpen. He realized he wasn't being careful enough to keep the fire burning in the lantern and then, for a moment, he was attending only to it when the ship pitched and his legs went out from under him. But he preserved the flame and struggled to his feet.

She was lying on her back, holding a rail with arms reaching back over her head.

"Hang it near my feet," she yelled. "Paul, it's time. The baby is coming."

"I know. Oh, God, I know."

The Frederika rose to the crest of an ocean swell and then plunged to its bottom. Little light remained now that the lantern was gone from its place, and parents grappled for an additional hold on children more by memory of where they were than by sight.

"What do we do now?" Paul yelled at Jadwiga. He was really asking what to do about getting someone to help deliver the baby, but Jadwiga misunderstood him.

"We wait, we just wait," she yelled, and mixed with words of the yell there was a cry of pain.

"No, I mean there's nobody to help."

"We'll do it without them."

"I'll go for the doctor. Should I go for the doctor?"

"No…" Another release of pain. "No, you'd never…no time."

Pigs were loose on the drainage deck now, squealing and skittering without footing.

"Do you remember what to do?" Jadwiga yelled. She didn't wait for an answer. "I'll tell you," she said. "Just get yourself braced." And then she repeated it, not because he hadn't heard it but because it was on her tongue when the pain came. "Just…get…yourself…braced."

The Dominiak children were in a state of confused alarm. Assaulted by the storm, they were now abandoned by their mainstay, Jadwiga, who was having troubles of her own. Franek was the only one not crying. "Is it going to be all right?" he wanted to know.

"Yes, Franek," Jadwiga yelled. "The ship is strong. Hold on."

The Frederika wrenched in a twist that felt as though bow would part company with stern. Paul had a conviction the ship would surely break apart.

Jadwiga cried again in pain. Paul was cold with wetness and hot with sweat at the same time.

Among the Poles outside the safety of the confined pigpen, Old Man Kradzinski was whiplashed by the ship pulling at ropes that tied him, sitting, to the foremast. His head struck the post with a cracking sound.

Inside the pigpen, Jadwiga cried out and Paul held new life in his hands.

Chapter 41

Jadwiga had known worse storms on the Baltic. Some were sudden off-shore storms that could pound anything on the Bay of Gdansk with the smash of a sledgehammer. Small fishing vessels were driven to shore far from home, damaged, sometimes with members of the crew missing.

In Gdynia the custom was not to speak of storms, at least not in certain ways. Those lost were mourned, boats repaired, and the injured treated. But it was believed that the fisherman who spoke aloud of his narrow escapes was calling himself to the attention of fate. Bad luck had to be faced and its consequences accepted. But good luck could only be chased away by speaking of it—except quietly, to God, in the thankfulness of prayer.

Her father taught that foul weather was something to be dealt with from the footing of solid ground, which was a refuge to keep in sight or clearly in mind at a specific point of the compass. But here on the ocean, one had to carry one's refuge along like a turtle.

She had a sense for discerning the deceptive lull in a storm from the real subsidence of nature's hostilities. It was a knowing—an essence of experience reduced to an interaction with each new insult of nature on its own terms. But this was no storm to strike and then quickly retreat. It was the kind that came with deliberation, grabbed at its targets and then held on, wearing strength and resistance away in a persistent test.

Had someone been relying on her to make a judgment, she would have guessed that the worst of the storm came and went with the coming of her baby. But at the time, she had been busy with matters other than sensing the subtleties of weather. Sometime in the last hour, praise God, the worst of it had come and gone.

She felt it would forever be part of this child: arrival to the crashing call of thunder, first breaths taken from charged air.

Gently, they held together now, man and wife with newborn, the holding more for each other than for the stability it gave against the thrashing of the weather. In the pigpen, there was the underside of the deck close above, fencing to the sides, little space in which to be thrown around, and there was always a secure grabbing place at hand. This made for an assured resting of the new mother, no less the new father, all the more their new child.

Silently, to herself, she let issue a small prayer, so that He would know she was not letting this mercy pass without thankful notice. And proper thankfulness, too, for a perfect child—one without deficiency or defect. She had taken note of all these things, despite the turmoil, and now she wondered if he had as well. She knew when he asked the question:

"Jadwiga, is it...is the baby a boy or is it a girl?"

She laughed aloud. She couldn't help herself.

Why would she laugh at his question?

He had, after all, been concerned about her and about coping with this momentous event without the assistance of the doctor, or even the women. And there was the heaving of the Frederika, the shouting and screaming of the others, and the Dominiak children close at hand, themselves in possible jeopardy if shaken loose from safe haven.

And his greatest concern was for the child's safe arrival in the midst of all this turmoil. And the light had been bad. And it had all happened so very quickly.

"Oh, Paul, I love you so much."

Perhaps she understood, then, why he had not noticed this most important detail of all. Or perhaps it was that she, too, was otherwise occupied and also had failed to note the gender of their firstborn.

"A girl, Paul. She is a girl. She is so beautiful."

This woman of his was crying through her happiness again, holding the new child to her breast but holding him, too, and answering as well. He felt such love at this moment that it didn't matter that she laughed.

"Isn't she beautiful?"

"Yes, Jadwiga. I love you."

"Why are you crying so?" she asked.

"Am I...I didn't know I was crying," he said. "Because I love you so much. I don't know."

It was the tension, of course, as well as the love. Finally secure in his sense of the movements of the Frederika, finally freed of the terrifying responsibility of the incredible moment of being the first to hold this new baby, finally at ease, he was at last free to let it out. He was emotionally exhausted, yet renewed by feelings of relief and gratitude.

As the storm gave up some of its thrust, the Dominiak children were able to release their tight holds on the fixtures of the pigpen and relax. Seeing that Paul and Jadwiga and the baby were snuggling, tired from all their holding on and fearing, they joined in, working close to enhance the feeling of greater security that came on with the waning of bad weather. Even little Konrad was brought into this community of warmth. Anyway, it was night, and time to sleep. As though making special provision, the storm abated, and the Frederika came more into harmony with the spaces she found between ocean waves.

When, in the middle of the night, Jadwiga awoke thirsty, Paul was able to move without disturbing the children. Outside the pigpen, the others had fallen asleep, too, except for the soft sobbing of Viktoria Murak. But he found the rainwater vat empty, sabotaged by the storm.

In the next compartment the Germans, like the Poles, were resigned to the disarray. They had made sleeping places as best they could amid the confused leavings of the storm.

There was a small drinking pail still hanging over the rainwater vat. He took it and climbed over the half-door. Taking little caution, he made his way to the cows.

Chapter 42

Morning brought a taking stock.

Stanisław Krulik moved about, solicitous of each family's welfare. Son Lancek carried the brightly burning lantern while son Władek helped tidy the debris of luggage tossed, spilled, and broken in the storm.

There was no certainty as to how Old Man Kradzinski had died. He was aged and frail enough that natural causes could be cited with some confidence, but they had little doubt that the storm made its contribution. He had been tied in, without the strength to do anything in his own defense. But the exact cause mattered the least to the old man, who was gone.

The grief was Viktoria's almost alone. Salomeya Steck relieved her frequently for the customary continuity of prayer. But the old man had been almost reclusive, certainly quiet, seldom a participant in conversation or discussion, so often withdrawn. Frail, too, even to the worrisome point of seeming to teeter constantly at the edge of death. Tadeusz did what he could to console his wife, but true consolation would be the work of time. Viktoria's compelling sorrow, expressed when any of the women sought to comfort her, was that her father did not live to set foot in America where, through the generous gift of his special military dispensation, he was sending his daughter and son-in-law and grandchildren.

To her four-year-old Jan and two-year-old Jakub, Viktoria said tearfully, "You must always remember Grandpapa. His gift to you is America."

For the rest of them there was more interest, and certainly more pleasure, in learning of the arrival of the new Adamik baby. Some had been aware at the fringes of their consciousness of the unusual goings-on in the pigpen occupied by Jadwiga and Paul and the Dominiak children, but in the intensity of the storm it had escaped the attention of most.

It was a miracle, Salomeya said, and they all agreed. A miracle that a tiny baby could choose such a time to arrive and then do so without the assistance or authorization of midwife or even the German doctor. A miracle that in taking from them the life of Bolesław Kradzinski, the Lord had given them a new life in his place.

A miracle, too, that such a wondrous tiny bundle could arrive unscathed under such difficult circumstances. It was an omen of God's blessing for all of them, Salomeya said, and there was none to dispute her.

One by one, quietly, the women came to the pigpen to make a gentle fuss over the baby girl and say the words, *cuda czynię*—miracle, and Jadwiga felt she knew now what it must have been like for Holy Mary on the First Christmas.

Paul stayed with them, silent and full of wonder, while mother and child slept and nursed and cuddled.

Among the others, storm injuries were mercifully light. Everyone had been frightened, and doubly so because they had suffered this storm without the reassurance of the sea-wise Jadwiga or Paul's interpretings from the words of German seamen. Fear had magnified small injuries into bigger ones which now proved less troublesome on calmer waters.

Little Bernadina Ran had banged her knee in the midst of the storm and it was showing the discoloration of blood released beneath the surface of the skin, but it seemed no worse than that. Her father Ignatz reported an ache in his head, which he attributed to its unplanned meeting with that of Paul Adamik when the crazy young one was hurrying to become a father. Other than these and a wrenched back of which Ludwig Karpczinski complained, there were no serious casualties in forward steerage—only those scrapes, bruises, and the odd splinter too minor for the men to mention.

Jadwiga was not even curious about damage to the Frederika. Now that her baby had arrived, she had little interest in the health of the ship as long as it could complete its trip, which it seemed to be capable of doing, for it continued on its way when the storm subsided, albeit with considerable seawater still sloshing about below the drainage deck.

As with the earlier storm, there was damage to more people in the midship section than in the forward section, though there, too, it was mercifully all minor in nature, the worst being a child's complaint about a painful elbow that suggested a broken arm.

Stanisław was about to try to pass the word to Herman that the doctor should be summoned because of the death of the old man, but it wasn't necessary, for by mid-morning he had arrived midship, visiting passenger sections to discover what work the storm had made for him. More important to the people of forward steerage, especially the Dominiak children, Delfinia had come with the doctor to help him.

She was received with joy appropriately tempered by the grief over the passing of Old Man Kradzinski. Even so, her return represented a welcome opportunity for a moment of subdued celebration. Even as her children surrounded her, Delfinia received several kisses of welcome from the other women.

Magda and Manya shouted "Mama!" in near unison. Hearing it and knowing what it meant, Konrad became agitated and reached to Franek to carry him. Franek handed the little one out of the pigpen to Pelagia. In conflict between wanting to run to his mother in glee and an impulse to act as adult as possible, he was the last to greet her, but when she lifted him and hugged him, he responded with a kiss and tight squeeze of his own, saying "Mama, mama!"

"I am so happy to see you, Franek," Delfinia said. "I think you have grown up a little just while I was upstairs with your father!"

"Papa?"

"Your papa is getting better, children, and he loves you all very much. He must stay upstairs, still, and I must go back when the doctor goes back, but we will all be together soon. Are you all being good children for Jadwiga and Polka?"

Each trying to be first with the news, Pelagia and Franek blurted it out about the new baby. "And we have our own place in the pigpen with Jadwiga, Mama," Franek added.

"Where? Show me." She let Pelagia and Franek lead the way even though she could have found Jadwiga's special haven with no help.

"Jadwiga, such a beautiful one you have!" Delfinia said, kissing the new mother on her cheek. "What have you named her?"

Paul, who realized by now that the doctor was present in the compartment, had been about to slip out of the pigpen to inform him of the birth, but Delfinia's question stopped him short.

Jadwiga glanced at him, then at the baby, then Delfinia. Looking at Paul, finally, she said, "Helena? For my mother? Paul?" Paul nodded his assent. He was grateful the child and Jadwiga were alive. He was not about to quibble over the name. He liked the name, anyway, he decided.

By now the doctor had asked for Paul by speaking his name several times. He was directed to the pigpen with gestures that suggested he would find a surprise there. Followed by the hunchback, he was almost on Delfinia's heels in poking his head into the pigpen.

"Bring the lantern to me," the doctor said to Herman, who turned to comply. Delfinia moved out of the way quickly when she heard his voice, and despite knowing he wouldn't understand her, she said "Jadwiga has a new baby."

Reasserting his authority over the lantern, Herman nearly dropped it in snatching it away from Lancek Krulik, who still held it for his father. But when he stuck the lantern inside the pigpen and his head closely followed it, the doctor spoke harshly to him: "Leave the lantern with the man who belongs here," he hissed, indicating Paul. "Go about your business." When the hunchback hesitated, perhaps thinking to reassert some authority over the pigpen, the doctor added, "You have no place here. Leave us."

Gently, not taking her from Jadwiga, the doctor examined the baby girl, paying special attention to her eyes and to her head. "It was a normal birth," he said to Jadwiga.

Paul, who could have answered, instead allowed Jadwiga to answer, and interpreted.

"Yes," she said. "Normal. Paul helped."

Doctor Hoffmeister turned to Paul. "You were the midwife." Paul shrugged. The doctor held out his hand. When Paul took it, he said *"Brunnen getan!"*

Paul realized he was being congratulated as much for being the midwife as for being a new father.

Chapter 43

There was joy, and there was sadness. From the assemblage of traveling trunks where the body of Old Man Kradzinski awaited burial, and from the pigpen where the new Adamik baby received the attentions of her mother and father, the two moods washed outward, contending dissonantly at mid-compartment.

Viktoria cried. Occasionally her voice rose to an indignant question: Why should her father be taken, so close to America but never to see it? Why an old man incapable of harming anyone? There was prayer, too—an unbroken murmuring from Salomeya, joined by Estella Poglicki, Kostanta Ran, or Polka Karpczinski in rotation.

From the pigpen came a polyphony of new life, whispered fascination, quiet excitement. Helena was serene, but already finding a tiny voice. Under lantern light, her fellow travelers remarked again and again at the blueness of her eyes.

Juliusz was at work with his carpentry tools, trying to mend the rainwater vat. The occasional pounding was an incongruity, but nobody stopped him; he was at last doing something other than grieving deeply. Anyway, the water was important.

This discordant patchwork of sound and mood separated celebrants from mourners until it was broken, unexpectedly, by the bereaved Viktoria herself. As the time neared for her father to be carried away by the men and then by the sea, she came to Jadwiga.

"Jadwiga, will you tie the rope for my father? Please, as you did for Maria?" Between the two, touching, there was a quiet intuition that neither could reach fully across the shattered spectrum of emotion separating them. For now, there would be only this one thing: the knots would be tied.

When Paul saw Jadwiga outside the pigpen without Helena, his head snapped around to see where his daughter might be. She was in the pigpen, asleep, secure in Franek's arms. Franek was humming a lullaby.

As son-in-law of the deceased, Tadeusz Murak selected the pallbearers: himself, Ignatz Ran, Paul, and—after asking Paul about conditions on deck—Kazimierz Steck. Prayerfully, the people of the Frederika's forward hold bade farewell to their eldest as he was carried through the hatchway, then past the German passengers, who paused respectfully in their clearing of storm damage.

A new team of seamen at the midship pump didn't stop work as the Poles passed through, nor did a galley worker who sorted foodstuffs taken in damaged condition from the locked storage area. Paul tried to see what the worker was doing, but had to attend to his part in carrying plank and body. But as the burial party climbed the ramp, another galley worker hurried past, bumping them. Paul turned to look back, and saw Fritz Adenauer watching intently.

His mind wasn't on the burial. He did his part passively. Clearly, the thefts had been discovered—one galley worker returning from topside, the other sorting, both agitated—this, where normally they would work together, arriving and leaving together as well.

He had promised Jadwiga he would return with warm water, so he went to the galley after the burial, hoping to overhear something while waiting for water to be heated. But there was only one worker and nothing to hear. Anyway, water was already boiling. The worker was puzzled that Paul wanted two containers—one of hot water, one of cold. "For a baby, for washing. I must have both," Paul said, pointing at the doctor's note. Finally, he simply took containers in hand, filled them, and walked out, annoyed at the German's lack of comprehension that boiling water alone was not useful—that two containers were necessary.

"Stupid Polack!" the young man said to nobody in particular as the door closed. Paul's impulse was to go back to shout in reprimand, but he was desperately eager to know what was happening below.

His fears were justified. When he opened the hatchway, a quiet midship spoke thunderously of trouble. The sounds of Germans cleaning up were gone, and only Herman's voice could be heard.

"Here's the other one, sir. The Polack Adamik. They did this while I was asleep, sir. These are the two who are up at night, always conspiring at the hatch." Fritz Adenauer, Herman, and the two galley workers all faced the First Mate.

The mate spoke to Paul, quietly, with authority. "I will question you and Herr Adenauer about these thefts. You are not under arrest, not yet, but I will require you to answer some questions."

Paul's heart was pounding, heavier by the beat. He responded in a hesitant German ravaged by his fear. "Sir, excuse me. I have this heated water...for my wife...for our new baby. I'll return in a moment."

Before there could be an objection, he strode down the gangway toward the half-door, where Stanisław held out his hands for the containers of water.

"Don't take them. Just open the door for me."

He thought the hunchback had seen him with Fritz only once—the night of the cow milking—but he could have been watching from his hammock at other times. Or perhaps he was grasping at anything to shift attention to others. Paul realized he mustn't delay, lest the First Mate think him hiding, unwilling to come out. He went straight to the pigpen.

"Jadwiga, here's the water. You'll have to mix them. One is cold, the other is boiling. I didn't think to mix them. Oh, damn, that's what the galley worker...Save some to drink. The rainwater vat is..." She looked at him in curiosity and surprise. She had never seen him in such a state. "Jadwiga, they've discovered the food is missing. Fritz and I are to be questioned. I have to go back to midship..."

"Paul, remember: You don't have to show how well you know their language. Don't show how smart you are. Be a stupid one." She leaned to kiss him, but he was already leaving. She caught his hand and squeezed it instead. "Stupid. Be stupid."

As he returned to the midship section, Herman was pressing the accusation. "It is a certainty. These are the two who conspire at all hours, sir. These are the thieves. They're the ones who sneak when the others sleep."

"What's this about?" Paul asked, trying to look and sound mystified.

"Something's missing," Fritz said. "Some food. And this twisted swine accuses us—you and me—of taking it."

Herman started to respond, but the officer cut him off. "This is not the place we will discuss this. Adenauer, come with me. Adamik, go back where you belong. I will be sending for you."

Fritz's wife had been listening, agitated, and now she came forward with a jacket for him. The mate walked aft toward the stores locker, followed by the galley helpers and Herman. Fritz's wife hissed quietly as she helped him with the jacket. "What will you do now? Are you going to take the punishment for the others?"

He shushed her. "Don't worry." He winked at Paul, showing a clenched fist.

Paul turned to go back to the forward hold. Amid water-soaked bales of hay, the rest of the Germans stood statue still, watching. Hans Koenig, maker of the illicit key, was also watching but his eyes darted from the group with the officer to the Adenauers to Paul. He seemed not so much agitated as evaluating, calculating.

Again, Stanisław opened the door for Paul. "What's going on? They discovered the thefts, didn't they?"

"Yes," Paul said. "I am to be questioned."

"Herman was accusing? What does he know? He doesn't know anything about it."

"I don't know."

"Did he see you dealing with Fritz?"

"Yes, but I don't think...Stanisław, I must think about this before they question me. I just have to think."

"I'll leave you. But call me if you want to discuss it."

Paul felt uneasy about Fritz, whose winks and signals made him all the more suspicious. Fritz could accuse him and the other thieves would condemn him, too. He remembered the officer's warning when the group first boarded: *If you abide by the rules*...It reminded him of how diminished he'd felt when the sailor slammed the hatchway double door on him, and he felt his mind go adrift in irrelevant thoughts.

He forced himself to concentrate. Jadwiga's idea—that he pretend to be dumb—would play on the Germans' traditional attitude toward Poles. He'd seen it repeatedly in the army. It was the one constant in their dealings with the Polacks. When he was promoted, he was seen as an exception—an oddity.

The idea of playing dumb grated on him. It wouldn't convince them he was innocent. And from the interview about Big Jozef's injury, the mate knew his German was at least passable. If he played dumb and then had to drop the pretense to defend himself...

He concluded it wouldn't work and discarded the idea. Immediately, he felt better that he wouldn't have to act as the Germans would expect.

Still, admitting even a little—even that he'd had food other than from the galley—would be a mistake. It would become a wedge to be driven hard by the officer. He wasn't a clever liar, not even in Polish. There would be inconsistencies in his story and he would be lost.

Would Fritz betray him? Fritz stood equally accused. If he admitted any knowledge in an attempt to shift blame to Paul, he would hurt himself. Fritz, he concluded, would keep silence out of self-interest.

Still lost in thought, Paul became aware of someone approaching him from the German side of the hatchway. It was Hans Koenig, followed by another German whose name he didn't know. Farther aft, several German passengers surrounded Herman, arguing with him and distracting him.

Koenig, a small man in his thirties with straw-colored hair and brush mustache, shot a question at Paul with no preliminaries.

"What is it with you and Fritz?"

Paul disliked him immediately. The other German, older, stocky and balding, said nothing. His attention was divided between the conversation and watching to be certain Herman was occupied.

"We didn't steal anything. At least I didn't. I don't know about Fritz." Paul felt bound by his promise he wouldn't reveal Fritz's side deals.

"What's all this about meetings late at night?"

"I don't always sleep so well. I spend time here at the door. He comes to talk sometimes. He helps me with your language. Gruenberg, too, sometimes, before he joined the crew."

"Was he selling food to you?"

"No."

"Did he ever give you anything to eat?"

"A piece of cheese once."

The other German reacted quickly. "No, he didn't! Fritz never gave you anything to eat. And you never saw any of us eating anything except what they passed out from the galley. Do you understand?"

"Yes, I understand."

"Listen to me," Koenig said. "They're going to work hard to get Fritz to talk. But they won't get anything out of him. We can depend on him. Can we depend on you?"

"I don't know anything to tell them."

"They're going to do the same with you, you know. It's not going to be Oktoberfest up there. You understand? It's going to be hard."

"I know."

"But if you say anything about any food Fritz gave you, you're implicated, you know. Just as guilty as he is."

"Just as guilty," said the other German.

"Can we rely on you?" Without waiting for a response, Koenig continued. "Remember this when you go upstairs, Adamik. If anything happens to Fritz, there will be a lot of angry Germans after a piece of your Polack hide."

"Let's get away from here before Herman sees us," said the German without a name. They walked away.

Paul was churning inside. Their manner made him want to turn in the whole bunch.

He shook his head sharply, trying to clear his mind. What would happen to Jadwiga and Helena if he were judged guilty? Would they all be sent back to Poland? Or to Germany where he would be imprisoned? Or could he be imprisoned in America? And if that happened, where would wife and child go? He held himself still, fighting a panic he felt overtaking him.

He decided to spend a few minutes with Helena and Jadwiga before the Germans came for him. As he passed the manure pile and rounded the rainwater vat, the situation had changed. Children were gathered to hear a story. Jadwiga, holding Helena, was perched on the ledge of the pigpen, ready to listen. He joined her and tried to answer the question in her eyes with a shrugging smile, feigning confidence he didn't feel.

Both Kazimierz and Salomeya were settling into position as story-tellers, so Paul knew that the children must have asked for the Kościuszko story again. They always told this one together. The children listened with intense concentration. Adults listened, too, for the Stecks were good storytellers, especially Salomeya. But on this particular story, Kazimierz always commanded rapt attention.

"One hundred years ago," Kazimierz told the children, "there was a great Polish general who fought many great battles and defeated many powerful foes. He was Kościuszko, the man of iron. He was a great fighter, strong and brave, who knew no fear. When he came upon the battlefield, his enemies would tremble and run away in fright, for they knew they could not beat him. After he fought many important battles and became known across all the world as a very great man, Kościuszko heard about a new country in a new place, where the people were having trouble with a very bad King who wouldn't let them be free and have a proper kind of country.

"Do you know the name of this country?" he asked, and all the children responded.

"America."

"This King did not live there, in America, you understand. He was King in another country, far away. It is like the Kings of the Germans, Russians, and the Austrians, are the Kings today in the various parts of our Poland. Do you know something? This King never even went to visit."

Now Salomeya took over.

"You can easily understand," she said, "this was not a very good situation. So the people of the new country wrote a long letter to this bad King, and they told him some things they thought he should know. And in America, this letter is a very important letter which, even to this day, children learn about when they go to school.

"Now you all know," she said, looking from child to child to be sure each was included, "because I have told you many times, that in America, in a place called Pittsburgh, Grandfather Kazimierz and I have two big grown-up sons. And in a letter to me, my sons Alois and Feliks told me that they have studied and learned about this letter the people wrote to the King. Would you like to hear what my sons wrote to us about this?"

All the children nodded their heads most solemnly, for it was the thing they were supposed to do at this point. Salomeya turned to her husband. With careful ceremony, Kazimierz reached under his jacket, unbuttoned a shirt and plucked a well-worn envelope from another shirt worn underneath. Slowly, because in these actions he had the rapt attention of the children, he removed the envelope and held up the letter taken from inside.

"This is the letter," Kazimierz said, "written to Grandmother Salomeya and me by our two grown sons who are in America. And in it, they tell about Kościuszko and the letter the people in America wrote to the bad King."

Now he unfolded the letter with great care, and with some ceremony, handed it to his wife. The light wasn't good enough, Paul knew, nor were her eyes. But the children didn't know, so she made a great show of finding the proper place in the letter and pointing to it.

"The people in America wrote the letter to the King as follows," Salomeya said. "God has told us certain things we think you should know about. Because of these things, we are not going to let you be our King any more. These are true things. All good men and all good Kings know they are true.

"When God makes children, he makes them all the same. God does not care about whether a child is born to good peasant parents or born in the finest palace. God's truth is that all children are alike when they are created.

"In the sight of God, every peasant is a King, and every King a peasant.

"So God, because he loves all his children, gives each of them the same opportunities to make their way in the world. And it is their duty to God and to each other, when they become grown-up people, to join together and make rules and laws and to promise, each one, that they will be faithful to these laws. These laws say that no man, not the merchant nor the farmer nor the King nor the soldier, can take things away from the other men. This is because they are equal, each with the other.

"Now this letter to the King goes on to tell him a thing or two," Salomeya said. She handed it to Kazimierz, who folded it carefully, but held it in his hands as she continued. "It tells the King that he has been very bad and he has treated the people in America very poorly. He sends the cossacks to beat them up if they don't give their *złotys* to the King. Sometimes he makes the people be the cossacks and hurt their friends. Can you imagine a King who would do such a thing?"

The children moved their heads, some for no, some for yes.

"Of course you can, because you know how it is in mother Poland, and you have heard the stories about the Germans and the Russians and the Austrians. But that is Poland. And as you know, this story is about another place."

"America," said Bernadina Ran, and several other children said the word.

"That's right," Salomeya said, "it is about America and the letter the people wrote to the King.

"And about Kościuszko," Kazimierz reminded, as he always did at this point in the story.

"Well, you can just imagine," Salomeya continued, "that when the King received this letter, it made him very angry. Especially that part about how they were not going to let him be their King anymore."

Children nodded their heads and their eyes widened in anticipation of the next part of the story.

"So the King gathered about him all his greatest generals, and all their great armies, and he told them to go to America where the people had these ideas about not letting him be their King anymore. He said, 'I don't care what God says about this. I am the King and the people are not equal to me.' He told the generals and the soldiers to go to America and beat people up and kill them and make them obey."

Now eyes flashed to Kazimierz, who always took over the story when it came to soldiers and fighting. "Well, you can see that this letter the people wrote to the King was stirring up great trouble." He held up his sons' letter. By now, for all the listeners, it had become the very letter to the King around which this story revolved. As he put it back within his inside shirt and buttoned his jacket, he continued. Throughout the Frederika's forward hold, all eyes were on him, all ears tuned to the subtlest intonation.

"This letter was so important, because as Grandmother Salomeya has told you, it was to the King...so important that it was called by a special word: *deklaracja.*"

Heads of the children nodded at the importance of this word.

"The letter was so important that people copied it down and sent copies all around the world. Soon, as I'm sure you can imagine, everybody was hearing about how the bad King was sending all his greatest generals and all his greatest armies to America to make the people obey him. And everybody knew that the King was very strong and powerful, and that he had many friends who were strong and powerful, too.

"Things did not look very good for the people in America. So do you know who decided to go and help them?"

The children said the name with reverence, for that was how it was to be when this story was told: "Kościuszko." Even the smallest ones said the last part: "Tchoozsh-ko."

"That's right," Kazimierz said. And he gathered up his fist, turning it and thrusting it upward in three movements as he said the three sounds of the name again: "Kościuszko." Then slowly, he said the great man's entire name.

"Tadeusz Andrzej Bonawentura Kościuszko. He was a very great Polish general, and he said, 'I will go to help the people of America.' He traveled across the ocean just as we are doing now, in a big boat with big masts and big sails, until he reached America, where the people were waiting for him, because by now they were in very great need of his help.

"'Come and follow me,' Kościuszko said to the people, 'and I will show you how to fight bad Kings and the armies they send.' And so the people did. They followed Kościuszko into battle, and do you know what happened?"

Franek had been waiting for this moment, and he responded eagerly, raising his arms. "They beat the bad King!"

Now Salomeya spoke.

"That's right, Franek. They beat the bad King. And so today, almost one hundred years later, America is a free country. There is no King anymore. And the people are all equal, as God told the people in America it should be."

"And all this is true," Kazimierz said to end the story, "because when he heard about the letter that the people in America wrote to the bad King, Kościuszko went to help them."

Chapter 44

"We require no confession, no admissions. We know the two of you did this, so we aren't asking you to confess. That isn't necessary. But we do wish to know exactly how you picked the lock, so that we can prevent such things from happening in the future. So that is all we require of you. Do you understand, Adamik?"

Paul stood at attention, eyes straight forward looking at a wall. The Frederika's First Mate sat at his desk. Paul was frightened; his knees even felt weak. He felt terribly unready. He fought consciously for control of himself, fearing his own potential for mistakes even more than he feared the power of the First Mate.

"Adamik, do you understand?"

The Mate had the upper hand. He was in control in this situation, appearing all the more so because the Second Mate stood to his left, pike straight even though not at attention. Paul thought the show of authority must be partly for this audience of one; the First Mate had not been so militaristic on the other occasion, talking about Jozef's leg.

"Adamik, answer me! Do you understand the question?"

Paul wanted to steal a glance at the junior officer, but couldn't while standing at attention. That led him to ask himself why he was standing at attention. Because these are officers, he thought, German officers acting like officers and expecting him to act like a soldier. But he was no longer a soldier in their army. And in any case, these were not German military officers. In authority, yes, with credentials of the sea, yes. But not *his* officers. He wanted to put his body at ease—perhaps then he could be less taut, less fearful...

"The question is, how did you pick the lock? That's all we need from you."

Picking the lock? Did Fritz tell them he picked the lock? Either that or...No, they had to be bluffing.

By now, they would be thinking him insolent, failing to respond for so long.

"Adamik!"

Insolent. So be it. Better insolent than frightened. He took his eyes from the wall and looked directly at the First Mate.

"Sir," he asked, "do you have a family name?"

"A family name?" The man was on guard, but disarmed.

"Yes, a family name."

"Of course I have a family name. Of what relevance..."

"I noticed that you were addressing me by my family name only. I wish only to follow the proper form."

"Do you understand..."

Paul didn't mean to interrupt the man but, in his nervousness, he did. Standing stiffly was ridiculous. "Did I hear you offer me a chair? Thank you."

He used this as his way of relaxing his body. He turned to a chair and sat. In his tense state, in the sudden release of his muscles, he felt the situation carrying him along, and he even crossed his legs. It was a momentum he didn't understand—adventurous, reckless. He thought of Jadwiga, pushing the half-door open after the hunchback slammed it.

"*Herr* Adamik, then." He said the honorific *Herr* with an overly enthusiastic rattling of the *rr* sound. It was a note of contempt. "Or perhaps you would prefer *Pan* Adamik."

He wasn't sure how far he could carry this, but he was well into it now. "If you prefer Polish, that's fine." Incongruously, he found himself wondering what Americans said instead of *Herr* or *Pan*.

The Second Mate, still stiff, was suddenly out of place. "Schmidt, sit down," said the First Mate, but he didn't take his eyes off Paul. "I am not attempting to address you with any particular respect, *Herr* Adamik. You are accused of thievery, and I am questioning you about it. About your picking of the stores lock. You could well be under arrest and in restraints before this day is done."

"I picked no lock," Paul said. "The hunchback lies."

The officer leaned far back in his chair, taking satisfaction that the conversation was now returning to his control. Paul, who now sensed he was letting the man regain his balance, decided almost instinctively that he should maintain his own footing.

"I have no idea what your cattletender is talking about. Perhaps he points at me to take…"—he searched for the word—"…revenge for the day he was scolded for slamming the door on my wife." He glanced at the Second Mate, who had given the reprimand. "But I appreciate that you are concerned—quite properly concerned—with shortages of food. You are concerned about shortages that seem to be due to theft." The German words were coming more easily now. He continued.

"I am concerned about shortages, as well. I'm concerned that there is not enough food on this vessel to properly feed its passengers, including the people in our section. This may be because the journey extends too long, which may be due to the misfortune of damage, or it may be that some member of your group of officers failed to purchase sufficient quantities, for which I'm confident you authorized expenditure." Paul realized suddenly that he was implying a theft of the ship's funds by the First Mate or the chief of galley.

"Adamik, you are angering me. Understand, you might as well simply admit your part in this. Your comrade's confession implicates you, and…"

"Comrade, sir?"

"Adenauer."

It had to be a bluff. "Then Adenauer—*Herr* Adenauer—lies. He lies if he says I had anything to do with any thefts. On the other hand, I have found him to be a reasonably honorable man…" Paul was tempted to throw in Jadwiga's phrase, *for a German*, but restrained himself; "…of whom I think it unlikely he would accuse me of anything, particularly since I've done nothing. Your cattletender, on the other hand, seems quite ready to accuse. But I don't think we—either of us—would speak of him as honorable."

"Your 'reasonably honorable man,' your Adenauer, is so guilty his tongue swells when he denies. He therefore has told the truth about his own and your involvement. You might as well do the same."

"I have no way of knowing what he may have told you," Paul said. "I can respond only to what you say, and what you say is not correct. The hunchback lied. If Adenauer is saying the things you say, Adenauer too has lied."

"Then tell us what you see as the truth."

"Of thefts of food, I know nothing."

"Nothing at all."

"No. Nothing at all."

"You may be interested to know that Adenauer will be spending the balance of this journey under restraint. He saw fit to take offense with our questioning." He gestured with his head toward the other officer. Paul saw a mark from a blow on the man's cheek. "For that alone, he is in trouble. You make the outcome worse for both of you if you continue in your insistence that you know nothing. You can make it better for yourself by telling what you know about these thefts, particularly Adenauer's role. Your role might be overlooked, perhaps, if you were forced by him or others."

Paul looked carefully at the man, measuring. He was being offered an opportunity to add his accusation to the cattletender's in exchange for a half-promise—a promise that might be made whole with negotiation—that he would not be charged. He decided it was, at best, a promise that could be broken, and at worst, an invitation to confess.

He stood. "Meine Herren," he said, addressing both officers and rattling the *rr* just a little too much, "I think I've made it clear that I know nothing of any use to you. If there have been thefts, I wish you success in discovering the guilty one. But I can make no contribution to the process, for I know nothing. It has been a pleasure visiting with you again, sir..." From the corner of his eye, Paul thought he saw the Second Mate's head move, almost imperceptibly, with the word *again*; "...but now, if you have nothing further, I must return to my wife and new baby." Neither man objected immediately, but Paul expected it. Because he didn't want to turn too abruptly to leave, he added something almost impetuously: "Sir, with regard to Jozef Dominiak's injury, I believe that with some additional time I can persuade my fellow passengers to accept the accounting you suggested."

The impulse seemed to be on target. The Second Mate's head turned to the First Mate, who glanced up at Paul. Trying to be very casual about it, he said, "That's of no importance. I will send for you if there are more questions, *Herr* Adamik."

Outside the cabin, Paul allowed himself the first full exhale he had taken the whole day. His heart was pounding at the walls of his chest, even harder than before the questioning. But now it was exhilaration rather than fear. He could hardly believe what he had done, and less that he had done it successfully.

He thought: *Thank you, Kościuszko.*

And then an afterthought: *Thank you, Jadwiga.*

Chapter 45

Leaving the Mate's office-cabin brought Paul out onto the starboard deck of the Frederika, rolling now with gentled after-storm swells of the Atlantic. Through the rigging, the sun splashed the deck, giving an immediate warmth to whatever it touched. This imparted a feeling of flexibility enhanced by sails pressed into a compliant, purposeful shape by unwavering winds. Even with the gap of sails missing where the mainmast had been ripped away by the December storm, he had a new feeling about this German ship—that she was finally doing what was expected of her on this journey to America.

Deep in thought, he was suddenly conscious of a new sound in the air. When he focused on it, he realized there was some excitement—yelling—on the port side. He mounted some steps and crossed over the ship's centerline. As he did, his eye fell on something distant in the water—another ship, sails fully rigged, passing diagonally and going in the opposite direction.

This was the first sign of life seen from the Frederika in over two months, and it brought crewmen and first class passengers out into the cold air.

At the rail, a well-dressed man turned to him and shouted in German: "We must be nearing port."

In his exhilaration, he hurried to Jadwiga, ignoring the Germans who tried to intercept him on the midship gangway. Because Helena was sleeping, he told his wife quietly, but enthusiastically, of the passing ship. But she wanted only to know about his appearance before the First Mate.

"It's all right for now," he said. "But they've confined Fritz."

"Did Fritz accuse you?"

"That's what was said. They were lying, I think."

"Will Fritz think you accused him?"

"He shouldn't. He knows I was interviewed afterward. They confined him for hitting the Second Mate, they say. They're sure to work on him, to try for an admission. Oh, the hell with it. I don't want to think about it. I have to go tell the Germans what happened."

"Not yet. Stay a minute. Hold your daughter, Paul."

He did, and held Jadwiga, too. He really wanted to be held by her, to escape, but his muscles jumped with the tension that was only now beginning to drain away. Wary of overconfidence, he fought a heady feeling of having bested the First Mate in their confrontation. He could hear his father's voice: *Embrace humility. Leave arrogance to others.* Thus torn, he found it hard to be still, even for a moment.

And the others found it hard to leave him alone. Stanisław wanted to know what had happened. Paul left the pigpen and told them all about the passing ship, but of the stolen food he said only that it wasn't over— that it was too soon to assume trouble was behind them. Then he went to the hatchway to lean on the door and wait for Hans Koenig.

Koenig was suspicious. He took Fritz's detainment as evidence that Paul had betrayed Fritz. "You know what I told you," the German said, and Paul had to resist an impulse to pull him up by his shirt.

"Wait until we disembark," he said. "You'll see. They don't know anything, and if they don't break him they'll have no cause to hold him. Just wait, you'll see." He felt his restraint going, and he couldn't help himself: "And forget about getting a piece of my Polack hide. If Fritz is in trouble, if you're in trouble, it's your own trouble and I have nothing to do with it. And this compartment is full of angry Polacks who'd like nothing better than to help me with you."

Now he turned, and it gave him satisfaction that he could walk away from Koenig just as the German had earlier walked away from him.

Paul returned to the hatchway later, when shouting was heard among the Germans. The cattletender was away, dumping manure, and the crewmen were finished with the pumps. Fritz's wife was yelling at Koenig and the other man in German so rapid and spritzy that Paul understood only phrases: "...if my Fritz goes...you will not escape...if he is taken...each one of you..." The others tried to calm her with reasoning, but it was only the hunchback's return that silenced her. Even then, she was hysterical, crying, and she shouted something more at Herman, denouncing him for accusing Fritz. Despite her aggressive threats toward the others, some of the women tried to calm her, but she was overwrought and rejected them.

In the middle of the uproar, Jan Poglicki asked Paul for the knife which had been taken from Piotr. Paul, wanting to be rid of him so he could listen, told him where he could find it. Jan wanted to take advantage of the distraction to slaughter a piglet, but Stanisław stopped him.

"I told him," Stanisław later explained to Paul, "that Herman and the others are on the lookout for thieving. We can't cook the damn pig before we arrive, anyway." So the piglets were left in the pens, and there was some laughter over the confusion the hunchback would experience when he found two more porkers than he had counted earlier.

When the evening meal was served, the word was passed from upper decks that passengers were to be ready for disembarkation the next day—all personal possessions packed, pasteboard tickets at the ready. From Salomeya there was a prayer in thanks, and then a raucous celebration fueled by two bottles of whisky miraculously produced from thin air by Jan. Only the Jakubiks were left out; even Viktoria had a drink when Kazimierz toasted the memory of her father.

Among the Germans, there was no celebration. Fritz's wife had dampened their spirits.

The news brought Jadwiga to her feet. She was truly up and about, even though Paul scolded and cautioned that it was too soon after the birth. He warned that Helena could be hurt, too. But Jadwiga knew better. She had her sea-legs, and eagerly helped with the packing, only slightly inhibited by the tiny child in her arms. Helena took it all in stride.

At bedtime, there was something new in Salomeya's praying: "We thank thee, Lord, for our deliverance."

Chapter 46

Paul had come to imagine that when he first saw the shores of America they would be sun-dappled and green. It was all the talk, of course—all the hope. But it was the middle of winter, and while the rising sun was shining, there was no green.

It came just after first light. His sleep had been uncertain, still troubled with speculation on the worst that might happen were the First Mate to bring charges. This was still on his mind as he walked the deck along the port rail, going to the galley in anticipation of Jadwiga's wish for warm water to give Helena a morning bath. Thus preoccupied, he failed at first to note that the Frederika's sails were luffing in a light breeze. In the normal course of things the sails would be drawn tight to their task of catching and using every puff of a light air, so the flapping sound did capture his attention at last. As he looked up toward the foresails his eye was caught by other sails in the distance—three small schooners like the Wdowiak fishing boat. In the mild breeze they were carrying full sheets and they were racing toward the Frederika.

Then, behind them, he saw the land. It was a thin strip of shoreline, grey and brown and snow, splashed with a cinnamon sun, bare trees like stubble on the face of a giant at rest. Even this narrow interruption of the usual continuity of sea to sky spoke of vastness, for it stretched to the north and to the south as far as the eye could see. Paul felt his sea legs leave him for just a moment as the Frederika rolled gently in a reminder that for all the attention he gave this land he saw, he was still aboard ship.

The land was not beautiful, he could see. There was the lack of green, for one thing. And as mild as the day was beginning, there was a hint of winter's punishments in the air. There were no houses, no structures. But it staggered him; he was so accustomed to looking overboard at only waves that the sight of land brought with it a sudden displacement of thinking: The Frederika, world that it was, was no longer the whole of the world. Though he had known this in his mind, his heart had begun to doubt. Now there was a combination of feelings: an exultant joy that relief from the grinding confinement of this ship was at hand; a somber ache in the gut that land, so close, was yet distant.

Then a spattering of fear: It meant so much in uncertainty. For the first time, he alone was responsible for resolving that uncertainty not just to meet his own needs, but those of his wife, too, and for the tiny child she held—and, lest he forget the prospect before him, all the Dominiaks.

But an intense excitement was the sum of the feelings. His heart raced. His impulse was to cry out—to alert someone—but then he realized that crewmen on deck were calmly aware of the land, which they had probably seen even before dawn. Their attention was on the schooners and the race. But he had to tell someone, so he burst in on Dr. Hoffmeister, who was just waking. Then he woke Jozef and Delfinia to tell them. In their half-sleep, they received the news with an enthusiasm more restrained than his own; he saw that for them, arrival represented even greater uncertainty: they faced all the same questions he faced, but with five young ones and with resources devastated by Jozef's loss of a leg.

It sobered him, but his excitement was still great and when the doctor had pulled on a light jacket, they hurried out on deck together.

Closer now, one of the three schooners was falling off, quitting the race. The other two were in a smart competition. It was evident the idea was to pull alongside the Frederika, and as they drew closer, position became more important than speed.

"Look," the doctor said to Paul, "he stole the wind." One schooner had turned in a tack that put his sails between the wind and the other boat, so that for just a moment, headway was lost. It was the decisive maneuver; the winning boat pulled even with the Frederika.

"Why are they coming?" Paul asked.

"They're harbor pilots," the doctor said. "They race for the work. The master of the ship can give it to any of them, but it is the custom to reward the winner."

At the edge of the Frederika's starboard deck, between the pin rails that terminated her spiderwork of rigging lines, a seaman stood ready to lower a rope ladder. He waited for a command from the First Mate, who now shouted down to the schooner: *"Sprechen sie Deutsch?"*

The voice came back, *"Ja, mein Kapitan."*

With a gesture, the mate ordered the rope ladder thrown overboard. Near Paul, a sailor handed money to another in settlement of a bet. As one man who had been at the helm of the schooner came up the ladder, the other drew sails tight, and the schooner turned away in a graceful arc. Within seconds, the pilot was over the rail, bowing very slightly but most formally, and shaking hands with the First Mate.

"He'll guide us to the quarantine station," the doctor said to Paul. "We are required to anchor and wait for the health inspector to come aboard before we continue into the port of New York."

"For how long, doctor?"

"Not long. We've been fortunate."

"How, fortunate?"

"No cholera, nothing else major. We have no epidemic. All the sicknesses are individual sicknesses. That's one reason the pilots race—German ships are clean. They know we're not likely to be held at quarantine. But they'd race even if we were an English ship. It's a matter of pride with them. We should be no more than an hour. Before the day is out, Paul, you and I will say farewell and you will be on American soil."

Paul noticed that the pilot made no reference or gesture toward the broken mainmast as he talked with the First Mate and they walked toward the helmsman's position.

"The order will soon be given for all steerage passengers to come to the deck," the doctor said. "You may as well tell your people. The sailors will wash down your section, the better to pass muster."

"And we won't go back there?"

"No. The officers would prefer the health inspector not see that your compartment was used for passengers. It won't be concealed from him, but the hope is that he won't notice. The Americans are always making new rules about ships that bring newcomers."

"Will Jadwiga have time to wash the baby?"

"Not below. When your people are called to the deck she should come to the sick bay to keep the baby warm. The two old ones, too, if you like."

"And the Dominiak children? They are worried they'll be left behind on the ship."

"That will be quite a crowd. But they haven't seen their father for...Yes, I suppose so."

From behind them, another voice intruded. "Doctor Hoffmeister, your records are ready?" It was the Second Mate.

"They are," the doctor answered. "Everything is ready."

When Paul arrived in forward steerage, a German seaman, frustrated despite his use of many gestures, was trying to tell Stanisław the orders with regard to people and luggage. Paul took over, and it was settled quickly.

"All of it," the seaman emphasized. "All of it, out. All the people, out on the deck. All out. Boxes, too. Raus. Alles."

"*Versteh*...I understand," Paul reassured the man, and then he explained to the others, even though most had caught the seaman's meaning. Separately, he told Jadwiga to take the Stecks and the Dominiak children to sick bay. Franek heard this, and excitedly told Pelagia, Konrad, and the twin girls that they were going to visit their father now.

"What's it like outside, Paul?" Estella Poglicki was unsure how to dress her two-year-old Stanisław and three-year-old Katrina.

"Cold, but not windy. Dress them warm," Paul said. "We'll be on deck for a while." Then loudly, so everyone could hear: "You can see America—the shore—out there."

The women immediately began repacking everything that was loose. Juliusz pondered his uncompleted repair of the rainwater vat, and packed his tools. The men started to move crates and boxes to the double-door hatchway.

Jadwiga organized the Stecks and the Dominiak children to leave, but when everybody else was ready, Pelagia was hesitant. Shyly, she was looking at Old Man Kradzinski's crutches among the things the Muraks were unable to cram into any luggage.

Viktoria saw this. There was a moment of hesitation, and then she handed the crutches to the little girl. "For your Papa," she said, and then she turned away quickly because tears were flooding her eyes.

In Jozef Dominiak's mind, the time aboard the Frederika would forever be divided into first part and second part. In the first part of this voyage, he had found it difficult spending so much continuous time with his children. The second part, after he lost his leg, was harder: he had never spent so much continuous time away from his children. Delfinia saw them when she went below. But for him, the loss of the loving hugs of his children had become almost as difficult as the loss of his leg.

Accepting her help, he moved to a chair facing the door. She placed a blanket in his lap so that it would fall to the floor in a drape—a shield. He had seen other men this way, disability hidden but not concealed. In this moment, he felt himself pass from status as patient—impairment forgiven and treated, to status as cripple—impairment forever his mark of differentiation.

And then his children burst in. Franek carried Konrad, but Delfinia took the littlest one immediately, and Franek ran to him, arms outstretched and reaching to be embraced. The twins were immediately behind. In pain, he wished he'd foreseen that they would climb onto his lap. But the hurt in his stubbed leg was overwhelmed by the happy tears, anyway, as he hugged all three of them. They were saying "Papa, Papa," and for a precious moment this made him feel like a whole man again.

And then past the trio of heads he saw Pelagia, standing back, ever shy. Cutting across the upright straightness of her frail body there were the crutches, taller than herself, her arms wrapped around them because her hands were too small to grasp them. He gave the two in his lap a special hug and then he turned his attention to her, tilting his head just so to tell her how very much he loved her. She took a small step, and then three big ones, dragging the wooden implements along the floor, and there was the awkward moment when she wanted to hand him these things she had brought for him, but wanted more to be hugged by her Papa.

He was able to hold Magda and Manya with one arm, and with the other he reached out and drew her to him, crutches and all.

It was only because the children might not understand—only for that was he able to keep the discipline of silence, and not cry aloud.

Now all the passengers were out on deck, excepting only the few in sick bay, and it made a mixed crowd of faces tired with sleep but more tired from the long confinement of travel. Each face gave its own evidence of inner feelings brought on by arrival. Children were held up to see the land. There was a chatter of shared excitement. A few women cried. Behind beards and collars turned upward, some men hid what they felt, but one older German man thrust his cane aloft in a gesture of celebration.

The Poles gathered in a cluster, luggage nearby, looking toward the land. Paul remembered them waiting in the railyard at Gdansk. It was a smaller group now, not just because some were in sick bay, but because there was no Old Man Kradzinski, because Juliusz was without his Maria, and because each was a smaller person—faces more drawn, eyes more stark, bodies less vital for lack of exercise. Everyone was weary. Other groups were much the same, though in some cases appearing considerably more prosperous, many women specially dressed for arrival in America.

After a while, people made themselves sitting places on luggage, some standing pieces on end so they could see overboard while sitting. To port, the land passed slowly as the Frederika leaned lightly on a course parallel to shore. Aloft, rigging hands furled topsails fore and aft. A passenger was occasionally shooed as ropes were hauled to adjust the angle of sails. The Frederika was gradually turning to port, more into the wind toward an opening in the otherwise continuous run of shoreline.

Suddenly there was a hand on Paul's shoulder, heavy and insistent, turning him.

"I want a word with you," Fritz Adenauer said, "a word while they're maneuvering."

"Fritz, they've let you out."

His eyes glared. "They told me you confessed."

"No. They told me the same about you."

"What did you tell them?"

"Nothing."

"Damn you, what did you tell them?"

"I told them nothing. What did you..."

"Have you been confined?"

"No."

"I've been confined until just a few minutes ago."

"They told me you hit the Second Mate."

"That's a lie. He was swinging at me and I...You understand, don't you, that if I'm sent back and you stay, you won't live to enjoy America. Do you understand that?"

"Fritz, be quiet."

"What?"

"Make no threats. I told them nothing and if you're smart, you told them nothing. They know nothing. We may still be questioned. Just keep quiet. Neither of us can gain by saying anything now. And don't threaten."

"Warned, then. Just consider yourself warned."

"All right, I am warned. *Genug.*" Fritz didn't believe him, he could tell. "Fritz, listen. They said I picked the lock. They kept at me with that. They don't know, and that proves it. But the minute one of us says a word against the other..."

He was interrupted by a cabin boy who addressed the entire group of Polish passengers. "Pardon, please. Which one is Herr Adamik?"

"I am," Paul responded.

"Please come with me. The First Mate wishes to speak with you."

Adenauer grabbed Paul's jacket. He whispered, hissing, "If you're telling me to keep quiet so I take the entire blame, remember what I told you."

Newly angered, Paul grasped the German's wrist and drove his thumb into the underpart to loosen the grip. He swung his right arm upward against Fritz's to break his hold, then turned and walked away. Fritz took a pursuing step but found himself stopped in mid-stride. From behind, Ludwig Karpczinski held him by the seat of his pants, and Stanisław Krulik was ready to assist.

"There is a minor difficulty," the First Mate said. "It is my hope you can help." At the ship's outside helm, steps above the deck, they were a short distance from the harbor pilot, who gave quiet guidance to the Second Mate, who directed the helmsman.

Surprised by the First Mate's solicitous attitude, Paul echoed it in his response: "How can I assist?" Pleased with this, the mate put a hand on Paul's arm as though they were old friends, and spoke in a confiding tone.

"I intend to lay over to have this ship fully repaired before returning. "The rule is that if anybody is rejected he is sent back with me. My line has no other ships currently in port here. Do you understand?" Paul nodded. "I want no passengers rejected. I want them out of my hair while the ship is repaired. It will take a few days, at least, once a yard for the repairs is arranged."

"Yes, I see."

"The one with the leg taken off will be rejected. I asked the pilot, this man over here, and the rule remains in force that a cripple must have a bond. It's money to promise he won't become a public charge. Do you understand what I'm saying— 'public charge?' Dependent?"

"Yes."

"Bond?"

"Yes."

"If no bond is paid, I'll be stuck with him. He wouldn't have been allowed aboard as he is, just because of this. I don't know what the bond will be. Perhaps the health inspector will know when he comes aboard."

"This is very bad."

"Does he have the money? Ask him, will you? Can you collect from the others?"

"Without knowing how much..."

"I'll find out. If absolutely necessary I will pay part of it. It's worth it to be rid of him, you see?"

"Yes, sir."

"Meanwhile, will you see what can be done? I appreciate your help."
Hesitantly, then impulsively, he reached out for Paul's hand and shook it.
Surprised, Paul drove his heels together in a dull click. He probably
would have saluted had his hand been free.

When he turned, his eyes met Fritz Adenauer's. From the deck below,
Fritz had been watching.

Chapter 47

If the First Mate wanted no stragglers to be taken back to Germany...

Although the bond was bad news, it seemed unlikely the Mate would ask his help and then cause trouble for him...

As he walked toward sick bay, Paul felt good enough to smile—small outward evidence of an inner elation. This made it all the worse with Fritz, who was about to accost him again but didn't because Ludwig and Stanisław were watching. Feeling good, even charitable, Paul resolved he would try again with Fritz, but later.

In sick bay, Delfinia stood beside Jadwiga, talking to her children.

"So who is this, now?" she asked, pointing at Jadwiga.

"Aunt Jadwiga," yelled Magda, Manya, Pelagia, and Franek.

"And who is this man who has just come in to see us?"

"Uncle Paul," they yelled. The twins even held out their arms for Paul to pick them up, and he did. Giggling, they kissed him, one on each cheek.

"I see you have it all worked out," Paul said. "I was just coming to make sure everybody understood about aunts and uncles and sisters and brothers."

"Jadwiga is my sister," said Big Josef. He was standing, trying the crutches. They were small for him, more canes than crutches, but better than nothing. His left pantleg was pinned up, out of the way. "And you, Paul, you are my brother-in-law. You are more a brother to me but today you are my sister's husband." The Stecks looked on approvingly. Paul decided that until he knew the amount, he wouldn't discuss the bond with Jozef. Enough mustering out pay remained to pay it, if it came to that.

When Delfinia took baby Helena, urging Jadwiga out on deck to look around, she agreed eagerly and took Paul's hand the way she had at the parade ground at Poznań, surprising him. She was fresh and gay again, newly excited with the idea of America within close reach.

It was beautiful, she could see. The land was beautiful. There was a crispness in the air, and a powerful dormancy in the shoreline winter-stripped of masking shrubbery. These shores were open to the sea, reaching down to narrow strips of sand as at Gdynia on the Baltic. From behind the ship, a morning sun rose to paint the land in all the colors of strong earth. Here was the land of freedom for which the promises were made, and it filled her heart with memories of her mother's words and dreams. She felt a pull from this land and it brought out her longing to set her feet upon it and breathe its air.

Overhead, deckhands furled the sails. From under the raised foredeck came the clanking of heavy chain as the anchor was winched out. This was the quarantine station. A sailing skiff was already making for the ship.

When Paul told Jadwiga about his conversation with the First Mate, she took it as good news, too; "Not yet a certainty," as she put it, but a good sign.

"There is only Fritz," he said. "He suspects I accused him. He saw me with the Mate, talking about Jozef, even shaking hands."

The health inspector, a fortyish man with thick mustache and bald head, walked with the Frederika's doctor among the passengers on deck. His eyes darted from face to face, looking for signs of disease or distress to be investigated more thoroughly. But it wasn't a meticulous effort, and it appeared he trusted Doctor Hoffmeister's report.

When it was certain they had passed inspection, the doctor introduced Paul to the official and there was a conversation, away from the others, about Big Jozef. The bond was likely to be about four marks, or around fifty of what the Americans called 'dollars.' But the exact amount would be determined ashore, the inspector told Paul, where each newcomer was considered individually. Jozef could be sent back, or he might be delayed at a special hospital for emigrants if he needed medical care.

Doctor Hoffmeister said he would try to forestall a hospital stay by writing a report stating Jozef was fully recovered. The inspector warned that this was no guarantee Jozef wouldn't be sent back or detained, but the doctor said he would do it anyway. "There is ample time," he said. "It is six miles yet to go up the bay."

In his office, he asked, "Paul, what are your plans? Are you taking the big fellow and his family with you?"

"Yes."

"Where are you going?"

"Where there is work. We will go where there is work."

"Do you intend to try to support Dominiaks and your family, too?"

"I don't know. I promised him his children wouldn't starve in America."

"And from what you said, you haven't yet picked out a place where you will go? You have no work promised."

"No." The questions were bringing back Paul's worst fears about this emigration to America.

"It will be difficult for you to earn enough, you know, if you intend to take care of Dominiak's family, too."

"I know." This worry was second only to the concern about being punished for the thefts.

"Will Delfinia take work?"

"Possibly. I don't know."

"I'm going to write a letter for her—about her work in sick bay. She really was much help, even beyond what her husband required. Explain to her that if she looks for work, it might be useful, will you?"

"Yes, sir."

"Now that I think about it, I'll write one for you, as well. For the translating you've done. You've been a good help, too."

"If it's no trouble…"

"No trouble. I understand there is a service inside the emigrant station, for writing letters back home. You should take my letters to the German table. Ask them to write the translation, in English, at the bottom of each letter. They might not be willing or have time, but ask."

"Yes, I will. Doctor, thank you."

When the letters were written, they shook hands, smiling, in a moment of goodbye.

"Good luck to you, Paul Adamik," the doctor said.

"*Danke, Herr Doktor,*" Paul said.

The First Mate gave Paul three marks toward Jozef's bond. "Just get him accepted," the mate said. "If he comes back to me, send him back with my three marks." Then, in an offhanded remark of goodbye that Paul took as final assurance there would be no further difficulty over the thefts, he added with a handshake: "Herr Adamik,"—the *rr* sound wasn't exaggerated— "I wish you good fortune in America. Don't pick any locks."

BOOK FOUR

Chapter 48

The striking thing about the first encounter ashore was the marking of Jozef. His jacket was marked with chalk. It was a casual act, without exchange of words, done by a young official who did it as though he had already marked dozens today and thousands in days past.

It wasn't that Jozef objected. On the barge that brought them from the Frederika to this point of land, while Juliusz added extensions to Jozef's new crutches, Paul had explained about the bond and the possibility of the special hospital. So Jozef expected to be treated differently. And it wasn't that it was done without exchange of words, for it wasn't expected that the official would speak Jozef's language.

No, it was conspicuous because Jozef was the only one marked, and everyone knew why.

When he had rejoined his contingent of travelers on the deck of the Frederika, working his body around the obstacles of luggage and children with his new crutches, they had greeted him with the warmth properly due a long-absent comrade. But there was the awkward combination of the looking and the not looking with which he was marked by their eyes. And now, the first American they encountered—at least the first official one on real American ground—this one marked Jozef, too.

Paul stepped forward, of course, and tried both Polish and German, but the man didn't understand. Paul showed the letter from the doctor, but it was in German and it didn't seem to be of interest. He pointed at Jozef's missing leg and at the paper, but the young man only said something in his own language which had no meaning for any of them.

When he finished with them—all the Poles and Germans from the bottom of the ship—he waved them through a doorway, and now it could be seen why his examination was so perfunctory. There was yet more to do.

They were in a huge hall that had been a theater for stage perform-
ances. There was a great domed ceiling over four tall central supports,
fluted and graceful. Great balconies of seating swept around the hall
except for the part where the stage once had been, where now instead
there were metal stairways leading to offices with windows where officials could look out on the hall. As yet, there was no large crowd this
day, but the wear and tear foretold that one would come, as they had
come and gone before. It was quiet enough that when a young man hurried down the metal stairs the click-clank of his shoes echoed from wall
to wall around the auditorium.

Despite past elegance, the place was tattered. But it had a haunting
beauty. Paul had seen construction like this only in a few great churches.
A faded magnificence drew the eye upward and away from the fencing
and signs and booths that littered the space where patrons once sat listening to concerts and lectures. Like this ragged group of people, this
place had known times of greater honor. Yet, neither place nor people
complained of present circumstances.

Now they all stood, the Poles and Germans of the hold, as one
blended group but like staying with like, except for the Jakubiks, who
were isolated and shunned. All awaited the next wish of someone, anyone, who would come with an instruction they could understand and
upon which they could take appropriate action. In lieu of an official to
point the way, several turned to Paul in the hope he would know something; at least he had been talking with the men who came from shore.

But Paul was at a loss, too. One sign, which pointed through a door
to another department altogether, was in German as well as the other
language, so Paul could read it and understand. It said *Arbeiter Bureau*,
but as inviting as this designation was, it was clear they weren't to go
there yet, because the fencing and ropes kept them penned in.

These few moments afforded Paul an opportunity for a reunion with
Hoyt Gruenberg, who looked healthier than the other men. He hoisted
Magda and Manya to his hips, hugging them even while remarking on
Helena's pretty eyes.

"It was the day you saved me that she was born, you know—the day
you pulled me up in the storm. It was just then she was born. I thought I
was gone, Hoyt. I would have gone overboard if you hadn't helped me."

"Your papa exaggerates," Hoyt said, speaking to Helena.

"No, I don't. I thank you, Hoyt. You really did save my life."

Hoyt had proved himself useful as a member of the crew, and had
spent much time in the rigging, he said. He was surprised, in the end,

that the first mate paid him the full amount promised; from the other crewmen he had heard stories of passengers pressed into crew duty without hope of payment.

Hoyt and family were going to a place named Baltimore. He had the name of a man there who would help him secure work related to the harbor and shipping. If that didn't work out, Hoyt said, he had another name in a place called Milwaukee. Paul copied the strange addresses, lightly, in pencil, on the back of his honorable discharge paper.

Among the Germans, Fritz Adenauer was being stern with his wife over something, but wanting to break away to talk to Paul again. He couldn't, because in addition to the controversy with her, Ludwig was still watching. But Paul wanted to reassure him, and started toward him.

What happened next startled Paul and led to some disruption. A young clerk wearing a leather eyeshade stood on a small box, pointed at two tall desks where officials waited, and shouted two names:

"Adamik. Adenauer."

Both names were perfectly pronounced. Heads in the German group swiveled toward Fritz and his wife, and there was an equal effect among the Poles for Paul and Jadwiga. Fritz's wife burst into tears. The young clerk waved his arm to show they were to step forward. In German, then in Polish, the young man added three words: "Wives, baggage, children."

Paul felt the bottom of his stomach drop away, and then caught himself with the reminder that he mustn't become panicky. Fritz glared at him and swore quietly. "I may kill you right here." Both their wives heard the hostility in his tone.

The young man said "Adamik" again and pointed to tell Paul to step up to an older clerk who sat on a stool behind the desk. The man was taking up a writing implement. By a similar gesture, he motioned Fritz to another clerk at another bench to the left. It was all very official.

Jadwiga rocked Helena gently to ward off any possibility of crying that might make her first impression in America a bad one. But Fritz's wife was still crying, able to control her sobs only a little.

In the surprise and confusion, there was a crossing of paths; behind Fritz there was Jadwiga with Helena, behind Paul there was Fritz's wife with no child but many tears.

The clerk spoke Polish to Paul: "You are Pan Adamik?"

"Yes."

"You can tell your wife there is nothing to cry about. This is only registration."

Glancing over his shoulder, Paul saw what he already knew—that it was not Jadwiga crying—but he saw the reason for the man's confusion. He also saw Fritz's wife in the final thrusts of a movement: She had taken a small package from within her dress and she stuffed it, quickly and forcefully, between Helena and Jadwiga. The movement surprised Jadwiga, who was about to let the package drop. Instead she obeyed Paul, who said, "Come here behind me so this man knows who belongs to me." In his anxiety, he was more snappish than he meant to be.

To the official, Paul said, "This is my wife, the one with the baby. The one with the tears belongs to the German."

"Oh, pardon me," the man said. "Sometimes the first ones called are afraid." To Jadwiga, he said, "Welcome to America, Pani Adamik," and Jadwiga brightened at this special greeting. "Full names, please."

Paul gave their names, Helena's last, and Jadwiga's smile was even brighter now that Helena's name was being written down for the first time. "But her name is not yet her own. We must go to church first for baptism," Jadwiga said to the clerk and Paul simultaneously. "Where is a church?"

Paul shushed her.

All the man wanted, as it turned out, were names, point of origin, and intended destination.

To this last, Paul said only, "Where there is work." He was distracted by the conversation to his left, in German, in which the clerk had asked the same question of Fritz, who answered with a name Paul had difficulty grasping: "Philadelphia."

With this distraction, Paul repeated himself: "Where there is work. I will go where there is work."

"I understand," the man said. "What you should do, then, is go first to the Labor Exchange—*Arbeiter Bureau?...*" He pointed and Paul nodded understanding. "Go there first and they will tell you about jobs. Go there first before buying a train ticket, which normally would be your next step, over there, you see?"

"Yes, sir."

"Go to the Labor Exchange, then, and when you know where you are going, buy your ticket and then come back here and tell me, so that your record will be complete."

"Yes, sir."

"When can we go to church? For the baby?" Jadwiga asked. Paul was growing annoyed with her, but the clerk was not.

"Catholic, of course."

"Yes," Paul said.

"It's only across the street, outside, that way. There's a statue of the Virgin. You'll see it right away when you step outside."

"When can we go?" Jadwiga insisted.

"You can go anytime. And then you can come back to finish your business here."

"What about my brother?" Jadwiga asked. "He is to be the godfather and his wife the godmother."

"Which is your brother, Pani Adamik?"

"This one over here," Jadwiga said gaily, and despite carrying Helena she flitted back to Jozef. As she did, she nearly dropped the package Fritz's wife had thrust upon her. She caught it and put it in a pocket.

"His name?"

"Dominiak. Jozef and Delfinia," Paul responded. This was all new to him, about Jozef as *ojciec chrzestny*—godfather—and Delfinia as *matka chrzestna*. He hadn't thought about it aboard ship with so many other worries on his mind, but he had no objection.

"Very well, I'll take them next, out of order." He waved at the Dominiaks to come forward. Paul suddenly realized why the "Adamik" and "Adenauer" had been called first, and felt foolish for having been startled. Jadwiga took Pelagia's hand. Together, they hurried forward.

"Ah, I see the man is marked," the clerk said. "He may be subject to a bond. He may not yet be able to leave here."

"We are all together," Jadwiga said. Paul looked at her sharply.

"We will be going together," he said. "We come as one family, all of us."

"And you are responsible for him?"

"Yes, sir."

"How much money have you brought with you?"

Paul thought for a moment, and quickly told the truth, because it didn't seem to him the man wanted to cheat him. "Do you want to see…"

"No, no need for that. It's just that if you have no money, there is the concern over how he and his family will eat at first, until there are wages." Paul nodded his understanding. "You have enough that no bond will be required. However, by the mark, there is the question of an examination to see if he needs medical care."

"I have this paper," Paul said, reaching into his pocket. It took him a moment to find the one about Jozef, mixed in with the ones about himself and Delfinia. When he found it, he saw that Jozef's name was spelled differently—Josef—but ignored the discrepancy. "This is from the doctor on the ship."

The clerk saw that the letter was in German, and turned to his colleague at the next desk. He said something in another language, and handed him the paper. The man looked at it for a moment in which Paul saw that Fritz was gone, and another German stood at the desk.

Further words were exchanged between the two clerks. Finally, the one who spoke Polish said, "Everything is fine. You can all do as you wish. At the door where you leave, tell the guard you'll return so he'll let you come back inside. Pan Adamik, come back to me when you know your destination. Welcome to America."

"Sir, I thank you," Paul said, standing straight, but not saluting.

Jadwiga now pestered Paul to go immediately to church to have Helena baptized, but he was equally insistent that he must first go to the Labor Exchange. He reasoned that before this huge place became crowded with people who would be standing in line for work, he wanted to put that matter behind him. Jadwiga relented.

It was a good decision. Already, people from another ship were beginning to form lines, but there was a wait of no more than a few minutes once Paul read the signs and put himself in the pen labeled "With References."

"What sort of work can you do?" asked the young man behind the counter, speaking a perfect Polish of the Austrian partition, judging from the rhythms of his speech. He looked at Paul's honorable discharge paper and the letter from the doctor.

"In the German army, I was a sergeant in a company of engineers. I grew up on a farm. And I speak German."

"You had construction experience in the army, then."

"Yes, sir."

"There is railroad construction work. It pays as well as anything you will get until you speak English."

"Building a railroad?"

"The New York Central Railroad company is adding a parallel track across the state. There is a need for men in Dunkirk now, in the western part. The train fare to go there is about ten dollars, but if you sign up for it here, they will give part of it back to you when you report for work. Are you interested in this?"

"Yes, sir."

"Good. Here is information you need. It's in Polish and in English, too, in case you have to ask for help. You should read this…" he watched Paul's face for the sign of hesitancy that would suggest he couldn't read; "...and then fill out the one form and bring it back to me. Do you have any questions?"

"No, sir, not...Where is this work?"

"Dunkirk. Dunkirk, New York. Dunkirk is the name of the village, and New York is the name of the province. If you have questions, you can come back. Or if you want to consider other things...but this is the best we have now, for wages."

"Thank you, sir. Thank you very much."

Paul was beaming when he turned, and it caught on Jadwiga's face, too.

"Pan Adamik, don't forget your papers."

In his elation over having work so easily and quickly in prospect, Paul was leaving behind his honorable discharge papers and the doctor's letter.

"Thank you, sir. Thank you!"

Chapter 49

"Forgive me, Father, for I have sinned.

"Aboard the ship, I bought stolen food from thieves, even while knowing that this would encourage their thefts.

"I lied to the officers of the ship so that I would not be punished for my part in this.

"I lied to the American authorities by telling them that my friend Jozef is my wife's brother, so that he would get into America."

His parents, Paul thought, would understand about the food for Jadwiga. And about the lies to avoid punishment. And they would even understand about the lies to get Jozef into America without paying a bond for him. But all these things, they would tell him, would require his confession to a priest. The lying, especially.

"Forgive me, Father, for I have sinned.

"My husband was present with me when my daughter was born."

In the Wdowiak family, lying to authorities was not something one confessed to a priest. Lying to authorities was something one did to disrupt their hold on one's life—to gain a little freedom and flexibility.

The priest gave holy communion to all of them after confession. Jozef, who insisted on kneeling despite having to do it on only one knee, was moved by this first visit to a real church in so long a time. The emotion he felt was founded in his gratitude that these Adamiks not only were standing up for him to enter America, but then, as the priest baptized Helena, there was even this special honor of his selection as Godfather to their newborn child.

When the ceremony ended and they all were feeling happy and full of love, the priest took the adults aside. Franek was left to mind his sisters, though Jadwiga held Helena, who had slept through all the day's events.

The priest was from Poland—Torun—which explained his perfect speech. His assignment to America had not been sought, he said, nor had he welcomed it. But he had come in service of God. He told them that they would all find America a good country, perhaps better than they had dared hope. He said there would be difficulties with some—those who had come before—over their Polishness and perhaps even over their being Catholic. But wherever they would go, he admonished them, the Church would be their bastion, their refuge.

"On the ship," Jadwiga said to him, "there was talk that when we arrived in America we would walk until we would find a church, and go inside until the priest would find us, and when he asked what we wanted, we would say that we were looking for work, and the priest would tell us where to go." Mother Church, she said, was never far from their thoughts.

"I am better at baptism than I am at finding work," the priest said. "But there is much work here. At Castle Garden—the theater where your names were taken—they have people who know where to find work."

"It's not a problem," Paul said. "I have already spoken with them, and I have papers for work."

"Good. What will you do?"

"Railroad construction." Paul looked at the paper and tried to read the name, 'New York Central,' then was grateful when the priest held out his hand and took the paper and the tickets.

"Some of these words are hard," the priest said. And then he pointed in surprise at the handwritten place name on the paper. "Oh, my. *Dunkirk*. You're going to Dunkirk."

"Yes, sir," Paul said.

"If you advise it, Father," Jadwiga said.

"Oh, yes. My brother in Christ Jan Polowy is there. He writes that it is a lovely place. He even sent me some sketches. Wait, I'll show them to you."

Paul was again annoyed with Jadwiga, this time for taking it upon herself to contradict him with the priest, but with Jozef and Delfinia present, he said nothing. Fortunately, the priest was not disapproving of this choice he had made.

When he returned, he had a letter and some drawings.

"Polowy is really quite an artist. He loves to spend his free hours near the lake. He is a painter, really, but these are just sketches. Look, here you can see he's drawn this point of land into Lake Erie. He says in his letter—let me find it—here: 'This point makes a natural harbor protected from the worst of weather from the beginning of spring to the end of fall.' One of these sketches, if I have it here, shows the harbor..." He found it, and slipped it out from among the pages he held.

Jadwiga, so quickly as to be impolite, reached for it when she saw it. "And schooners," she said.

"Yes, sailing boats. I think these are..."

"For fishing."

"Yes."

"What does your friend the priest say about this lake?" Jadwiga asked.

"Well, I remember most of it. It's one of the very large lakes, perhaps one hundred fifty or two hundred miles long, twenty or thirty miles wide. Are you interested in lakes, Pani Adamik?" Studying the drawing, Jadwiga seemed not to be hearing the question. The priest continued, "There are many villages built up on the shore. One side is Canada, the other the United States—America."

Paul answered. "Jadwiga comes from fishing people."

"When you arrive there, you must find Father Polowy, and tell him you have spoken with me—that you have seen his sketches. He'll be delighted. Here, you must see the one of the church where he serves. You must tell him you have seen this one or I will never be forgiven. Wait— I'll write him a short letter."

It was a modest church, but with a tall steeple. Paul felt a reassurance knowing that in this strange village they would know someone, a priest yet, even before arriving.

Jadwiga insisted that she would carry the priest's letter. She would deliver it herself, she said.

"One night, I need," said Jan Poglicki. "I need one night with a good bath, and good food, and a good bed." There was almost complete agreement on this. When the Adamiks and the Dominiaks returned to Castle Garden from the church, they were several steps behind the others in their processing. The Stecks had purchased their railroad tickets to Pittsburgh, in Pennsylvania, but the last of the day's trains would leave before they could be transported to the terminal, so they, too, were planning to stay in New York for one night. Without exception, everyone felt the need for a bath, having been deprived by the Frederika's broken rainwater vat of recent opportunity to wash. Paul, hoping Jadwiga would not be so eager to go to this Dunkirk to see the schooners in the harbor, proposed that they stay one night, as well.

"For the food if for no other reason," said Jadwiga.

"And for the chance to sleep on something softer than German hay and a German deck," said Ignatz Ran.

Juliusz Sczepaniak joined the group at that moment, having just returned from the Labor Exchange. "I have carpentry work," he said. "I have carpentry work!"

"Where is this work, Juliusz?" asked Salomeya Steck, and when Juliusz responded his pronunciation was so amiss that none of the Dominiaks or Adamiks heard that what he was saying was *Dunkirk*.

Ignatz Ran and his powerful Kostanta and their brood of five had already purchased their tickets to a place called *Saint Louis*, where they were to seek out their friends who had secured work for them on a farm. Ludwig and Polka Karpczinski and daughter Franciska, who still wanted to call herself Teresa, were planning to go to a place called *New Jersey*. It was nearby, they said, but no one cared—it was the least of their concerns.

Tadeusz Murak and wife Viktoria and children Jan and Jakub, four and two years old, intended first to go to see friends in an altogether different place called *Harrisburgh*, and Paul theorized that these 'burgh's might be the same as cities in Germany, like Hamburg.

"He will pretty soon have us all speaking German," Juliusz said, and the others laughed, happy to hear a bit of the funmaker coming out again.

Stanisław Krulik, good with machines, had papers which directed him to yet another village with an unprounouncable name, *Buffalo*, where he would find work with a foundry. There might even be work there for twelve-year-old Władek and fourteen-year-old Lancek.

When Jan Poglicki rejoined Estella and the others in the main rotunda of Castle Garden, he informed them that he planned to stay, for a time at least, in New York City. "I didn't think to bring references," he said. "It wasn't very smart. But I will find some work here in New York."

"Does anyone know," Big Jozef Dominiak asked quietly, "where the Russians are going?"

"Going?" asked Stanisław. "Where are they going? They are going back, that's where they're going. They've been taken away already."

"Why?" Paul asked.

"Nobody knows. I think the man said Piotr tried to get in once before. I didn't hear much of it. I was too concerned with my own..."

"Damn him to hell," said Big Jozef. "I had plans for him."

"Just think of it, Jozef," said Delfinia. "He and his ugly wife and his two big fat sons have to turn around and go all the way back now. Just think of that."

"I would like to send him back but keep his legs here," Jozef said.

All of them spent several more hours in the Emigrant Station. There was money to be exchanged. Some had yet to buy railroad tickets, and many wanted to use the services of the letter-writing department to send word that they had arrived safely. The trip had taken so long, said Kazimierz, that by the time letters arrived, people would be giving them up for lost. Even his sons must be worrying in Pittsburgh.

While others conducted these various pieces of business, Paul was given the task of negotiating with one of the boarding-house representatives. The first he found was delighted to have eight families and the one single male, for these would fill his boarding house and he would no longer have to wait at Castle Garden for others to take additional rooms. He even made a special price, dinner and breakfast included.

He didn't bargain for their hunger. Dinner became a long goodbye, and even after the children fell asleep and were carried to their beds, the parents talked and ate.

Now they were human beings again—civilized people who sat at a table on real chairs to eat with plates and proper cups and knives and forks and spoons. Even napkins. And they could talk, and laugh, and look each other in the eye because there was enough light.

For a time, there was a recounting of memories of the Frederika, but these common experiences were not something of which they had to speak to share them, for each knew them, the good and bad, too well to require spoken recollection. Anyway, their memories would be of each other, they agreed, rather than of the incidents that marked their crossing of the ocean.

The man of the boarding house, who had heard the stories of many such trips, told them they were fortunate to have had only three deaths. "There is still a ship anchored at quarantine which has been there many weeks. Cholera. On some ships they lose one in three."

To spare Juliusz, Salomeya changed the subject.

On small pieces of paper Paul laboriously copied the unfamiliar words of the address of the Stecks' sons, for among all of them, it was the one certain place to which letters could be sent. Around the table, there were promises that they would keep in touch, perhaps even visit.

The man of the boarding house tried to fill their heads with advice about America and about learning the new language and about buying in the shops and about innumerable other subjects, but it was all too much for them to absorb. As much as they knew they must look ahead, more than that they wanted to give themselves this one night together of looking back. It was almost comfortable to do this, now that the Frederika and its travail was placed, in this one day of transition, firmly behind them.

Finally, Salomeya said a long, thankful prayer, and then softly sang the song of the watchmen of Lubownia:

Zapierajcie swiatlo, ogien
A idzcie spac z Panem Bogiem

Dim the fires, put out the light,
And may God keep you safe this night.

BOOK FIVE

Chapter 50

Together, Delfinia and Jadwiga worked small miracles that proved inadequate. They shopped carefully, bought sparingly. No morsel went to waste. Every last potential for nourishment was taken from every bone or scrap.

Clothing was mended and mended again. The pantleg Jozef didn't need became the patch for the seat of Franek's pants. One shoe could be patched from the inside with the leather from the outside of another.

But it wasn't enough. There were ten of them, and only one of Paul to earn. It was testament to the truth of the stories about America that it was a wage on which Paul and Jadwiga could have lived well. But it wasn't enough for all of them.

Outside, there was the snow. This was the lee of the Great Lake Erie where easting air, heavy with wetness, let go its burden in the transition from lake to land. It was beautiful in its softness, but oppressive in its relentless reappearance day after day. Franek cleared the walkway to their little rented house on Beagle Street, just down from the post office near the lake, and when an overnight accumulation was too great, Delfinia and Jadwiga shoveled, too, so there would be nothing left for Paul to insist he must do.

Jozef tried once to manipulate the shovel, but it was not to be. He drove himself off balance trying to push snow and stay upright on only one foot.

He was constantly depressed. When one of the makeshift extensions Juliusz Sczepaniak had added to the crutches on the transfer barge to Castle Garden split and broke away, it was days before he troubled to fix it. Even then it was only because Pelagia was more sick with her cough and Delfinia decreed that she must be kept warm in bed, be fed there, and have warm milk hourly—duties Jozef assumed when the women were away from the house.

Paul came home cold at the end of each day. He longed for a day merely too cold to set tie and lay track—or one so cold that his Irish foreman would be frozen in place and left behind forever. There was a rivalry between railroads, it seemed, and there were bonuses for the bosses; they intended to double-track the New York Central first despite snow and ice and tomb-cold rail that tore at hands and frigid air that froze sweat in a man's stubble.

But there was work, as the promises had said there would be. In this, there was a satisfaction.

Paul brought home news one day that surprised them all: After work, in a tavern where he stopped for beer with fellow workers, he had encountered Juliusz Sczepaniak. Juliusz was here in Dunkirk, too, also working for the New York Central. He was doing carpentry, yes, building forms for concrete, though longing for work more suited to his cabinetmaking skills. Addresses were exchanged, and Juliusz would come to dinner one Sunday.

"Spring is coming," Jadwiga said, but she thought of Maria. "We'll have a picnic when the snow goes away. We'll have a picnic and Juliusz will come." Maria's death seemed so long ago, as though in another life.

Jadwiga counted blessings. And she looked forward to Spring. *Spring is coming*, she said often. Spring, with sunshine and new growth and fish in the harbor. She would fish, she told Delfinia, and bring home a fresh catch for each day's table, free, from the great *jezioro* Erie. Delfinia would start a garden and through the summer at least, there would be vegetables to eat and perhaps even some to sell. And Paul would soon be complaining about the heat rather than the cold.

Franek came home daily with new words of the American tongue learned in the church school, where the nuns spoke his own Polish language but helped with this English that everybody spoke. His sisters and Konrad were not yet old enough for the American school, but he sat them in chairs, anyway, and pretended they were his students. Pelagia pretended so well that soon she was making strange sounds in the new tongue, and showing them off to her Papa and her Uncle Paul. The adults listened, too, and tried to learn, but the words were of little use and it was hard. Even so, this learning was a blessing Jadwiga counted.

She counted blessings and gave thanks to God. She prayed for Pelagia's health while thanking the Lord for baby Helena's strength and growth—quietly so as not to scare it away. She thanked God for the lake, despite the ice that made it lifeless and chilling to the eye. She walked that way every day, not only because she longed to see the water in motion but also because when she walked the other way she passed the post office and it reminded her.

It reminded her she had not written to Salomeya.

But she counted blessings, and she thanked God for her special secret, which she took to the priest on a Monday late in March.

"I should have brought the letter more than a month ago, Father, so it wouldn't be delayed. But I wished to speak with you of another matter and I first had to think about it."

"You must come to me at any time you wish, and for any reason, Pani Adamik. But I am pleased to have his letter. He showed you my drawings."

"Yes."

Father Jan Polowy, still a young man though older than Jadwiga, relaxed and waited. In the warm sitting room of the orphan asylum across Buffalo street from the church named for the Virgin, Helena lay on the floor, on a blanket, kicking her legs and reaching up to grip her toes.

"On the ship," Jadwiga began, "I was hungry. I was carrying Helena, and I was hungry. We all were hungry, and because my husband could speak the German tongue he was able to buy food for me and for the others from a German passenger.

"It was stolen food, Father, taken by some of the German passengers from locked storage. They sold it to us, to the Polish passengers, for very high prices—for too much, really, but we were all very hungry, especially the children. But I started it, with my hunger and my baby's hunger. The German—the one my husband was dealing with—accumulated a great deal of our money.

"These thefts were discovered. The German and my husband were accused. When we arrived the German's wife thought there was to be punishment for the stealing, and when their name was called...She had the money, and she pushed it upon me—in a package—she pushed it upon me. I didn't know what it was, then, but later I looked. It was the money.

"I have told no one of this, until now."

Father Polowy began to lean forward, ready to speak, but stopped when Jadwiga continued.

"I could get the addresses of the people from the ship, Father, if I would write to the *babka* who traveled with us. The people have her address, and it was promised that we would write. I haven't written yet. It's because I don't want the addresses, not yet. They don't know I have the money, but I think it should be returned to them. That's what I think should happen to the money." Jadwiga looked up at Father Polowy, but his expression conveyed no opinion—no confirmation, no hint of any alternative that might be crossing his mind. She looked away and spoke again.

"But I haven't written yet. I have been spending some of the money, Father. On the ship, a friend was hurt, and a leg was taken from him. My husband promised to stand by him in America, and the man is with us now, and his wife, too, and they have five children. I've been spending some of the money because there isn't enough of my husband's pay, after the rent, for food for all of us. Some weeks it's almost enough, but usually not. I've been spending from the money because I don't want my Paul to know he isn't earning enough for all of us. He was reluctant to come to America in the beginning, and..."

Here, Jadwiga stopped speaking and made no effort to finish. For a moment, she cast her eyes down. Then she looked up. Despite the guilt she felt, her eyes challenged the priest's.

"Do you feel you have done wrong?" the priest asked.

"I want to do what is right. I think what is right is to send the money to the people who had to give it to feed their children and themselves. It shouldn't go to the shipping company. It was the ship's food, but they were already not giving us the food we paid for. The money shouldn't go back to the thief. I think it should go back to the people who gave it for the food. But..."

"But you want to use it..."

"To use it but only for a while, Father."

"...to use it for your friends."

"Yes, but I...Yes, Father."

"You are troubled over this."

"Yes."

"Have you prayed for guidance?"

"Yes."

"And God tells you...He tells you as you have told me—that you should return the money to those who had it before."

"I don't know. That's only what I think."

"What your conscience tells you."

"Yes."

"It could be God is speaking to you through your conscience."

"But if I send it to them, there is the question of our friends and how to help them."

"Surely the money will run out."

"Yes, but not for some while."

"But then you will have to tell the truth to your husband and your friends."

"Yes, Father, but Spring is coming and I'll catch fish and there will be a garden, and the money my husband brings home will last longer then. Perhaps he will earn more by then."

"What is his work?"

"The railroad. The tracks. He puts tracks down."

"A laborer."

"Until he learns English, at least."

"Or until the track is finished and the work runs out."

Jadwiga just looked at the priest. This possibility was not one she had considered.

"Pani Adamik, it's not something to worry about soon. Not before Spring, certainly. I didn't mean to raise this additional trouble, but you should know that the work could end when the track is completed."

"But all the railroads are building."

"They were, and yes, some are. I don't know about this area— Dunkirk, I mean. In any case, you shouldn't be troubled now. But you may have to tell your husband, eventually, what you have been doing."

"I know."

On the floor, Helena's face contorted and grew red, and Jadwiga saw it would soon be time to leave the priest.

"Have you been coming to mass?"

"Yes."

"On Sunday, will you bring your husband to the eight o'clock Polish mass? And bring him to meet me? At the door, after church."

"Yes..." Jadwiga's face showed worry. "But..."

"Oh, no, no...I won't tell him. No, don't be concerned about that. But I'd like to meet him."

"Yes, Father."

"About the money..."

"Yes?"

"It troubles you because you are a good person, I think. If you pray for the Lord's guidance, you will have a clear understanding of what you should do. But it could be that it isn't yet time for the Lord to tell you. It could be that what you're doing now is acceptable to God. That could be, you know."

Jadwiga cast her head down, then brightened and looked up.

"And there is help, Pani Adamik, from the church, if you find...if your friends need it."

"We—our families—have always given to the church, Father, not taken. I think our friends would feel shame to take..."

"I understand. It needn't be a worry now. As you say. Spring is coming."

Chapter 51

After supper, in his favorite chair, holding Helena to lull her to sleep, softly humming a lullaby, Paul heard the news that he was to meet the priest.

"I took him the letter," Jadwiga whispered, and when a question appeared on Paul's face, she said, "You know, from the priest in New York—where she was baptized."

"Oh, yes. I almost forgot."

"Well, I took him the letter and we talked and I promised that on Sunday I would take you to meet him after the mass."

"I'll have to get something to wear, Jadwiga. I can't just...Saturday, I'll have to get something to wear."

"Saturday, after work, go to confession instead. I'll get you something to wear. I have almost the whole week. You have so little time."

"Sure, you get me something." He spoke more loudly than he intended, and Helena stirred. Jadwiga reached for her, but Paul kissed her head and patted her back. "You only now took the letter to the priest?" Delfinia came in from the kitchen, trailed by Magda and Manya and the sound of Jozef setting the draft of the cookstove so the fire would burn out slowly during the night.

"And Delfinia and Jozef and the children must meet him, too, Jadwiga said. "He's nice—the priest."

The cracking and breaking of the sharded ice of the southeastern shore of Lake Erie comes each Spring as though its day is appointed in the Book of Time. There is first the sun, and when it has held on for a few days so that the ice below knows it is serious, the ice gives up its death grip on the shoreline.

The sounds of yielding ice—now and again mistaken for distant thunder by the visitor or newcomer—are beautiful, for they mean that winter has at last gone its overdue way into the recesses of a plodding calendar.

It can happen in a day and a half—from ice to open water.

So it was in the spring of 1870.

So it was that Delfinia took from Jadwiga the sewing and reworking of Paul's army uniform to be worn to meet the priest. "I'll do it," she said. "You go down to see the *jezioro*."

Jadwiga was grateful. It wasn't just that she wanted to see the lake. Delfinia was far better than she with scissors and threaded needle, and Jadwiga wanted Paul to look his best on Sunday.

She spent all that day wandering the shoreline, Helena kept warm in her arms or in the seabag made into a pack on her back. From the battery cliffs to the northeast where, it was said, the Americans once fired on English warships on the lake, past the docks reaching into the harbor, to the southwest where outcroppings of slate jutted into the lake to form a natural point of land and give calm harbor to the calling vessels of lake commerce—all these things Jadwiga explored. Except for the salt missing from the air, it was like the Baltic—like Gdynia. There was a fish house. There were pines, and even the willows.

Coming back toward home near a dusk brought early by clouds reluctant to clear, she walked the dock that extended Dunkirk's Center Street into the lake and gathered up a tattered treasure she had noticed earlier. A fish net, discarded because it was torn beyond reasonable prospect of repair, went into the pack with Helena.

Delfinia had preparation of supper well under way when Jadwiga appeared. Paul would be home soon, hungry and sore after a day with heavy rail. Pelagia, out of bed, feeling better than usual, met her at the door asking to hold Helena.

"She must sleep now, little one. But I have something for you—a good surprise, in the bag with her."

Pelagia's shyness was wearing away, at least among those in the house. She brightened with the promise of a surprise and hurried to tell her father while Jadwiga took Helena to the Adamik bedroom.

"Here, you see this? It's a fishing net I found for you, down by the lake. Somebody threw it away, but I think you and I can make it good again."

Jozef, who had been looking through a borrowed catalog, treasured and passed around because it was one of the few with Polish words instead of English ones, now watched Jadwiga and Pelagia. Jadwiga showed her how to tease open the knots along the most frayed edge of the net to save the string for mending the middle.

"You can borrow your mama's sewing needle and poke it inside there, into each knot, and it will be easier, you see?"

"When it is fixed will we get fish with it?"

"Yes, and with a line and hook with bait, too, but look. First you must knot the string to the other part to make the squares all good again so your fish won't get out, you see? Watch."

Pelagia was interested and attentive, but following the movement of hands, string, and net was hard for her. Jozef, who quickly saw what Jadwiga was trying to teach, raised himself off his chair with his giant arms and lowered himself to the floor to help just as Pelagia was becoming frustrated with the difficulty of the manipulation. His involvement renewed her interest and she held her own piece of net, trying to do as her father did while Jadwiga directed both of them.

Franek, carrying his brother Konrad, came from the kitchen to watch.

"Where did you go, Jadwiga? After school, where were you?"

"Down by the shore, Franek, seeing the *jezioro*. Through here, little one, that's it. Like your papa."

"The Americans say '*lake*.' The water is called '*lake*.'"

"*Lake*." Jadwiga tried the strange word. "*Lake*. What do they call it when it isn't frozen?"

Franek laughed, thinking Jadwiga was making a joke.

"'*Lake*' is good for when there are no waves. But there must be another word for when there is movement." She made a flowing movement with her hand. "You know: *jezioro*."

Franek laughed again. "I don't know."

Pelagia looked up at Franek. "Mama and I have a special secret," she said.

"What?" Franek asked.

"It's a secret."

"Tell me."

"Promise you won't tell."

"I won't tell. Tell me."

"Promise."

"I promise, Pelagia. Tell me."

"We took Uncle Paul's army uniform all apart and we're sewing it back together for him."

Jadwiga made a shushing sound. "Oh, you must keep that secret very well, both of you. That's a special surprise for your Uncle Paul. You won't tell, will you?"

Both Franek and Pelagia pulled their heads down, turtle-like, shaking them. Pelagia put her finger to her mouth.

"Here," Jozef said. "See this, Pelagia." He had finished his second knot and was testing it.

At supper, Paul was at first quiet, then talkative when Jadwiga pressed him for what was on his mind. Again, it was his foreman.

"He thinks he will be understood better if he yells," Paul said. "He yells and then when somebody doesn't understand he yells even louder. We're putting in a damned switch and it's all new…"

"Don't the other Irish ones tell him he doesn't have to yell?" Jozef asked.

"No. For them, better he should yell at us. One day he will say these American words 'Stupid Polack' one time too many. It means…"

"I know," Jadwiga said. "It's like the Germans. When you know English someday you can say back to him, 'Stupid' Irishman."

"He may not live long enough," Paul said, looking at his fist. "First he may be dead."

Jozef smiled faintly, raising a fist.

"We have a secret," Pelagia said, smiling at Paul.

"You do?"

"I can't tell."

"Tell me."

"It's a surprise. I can't tell you until…"

"Until Saturday," Jadwiga interrupted. "On Saturday, you can tell your Uncle Paul."

"When is Saturday?"

"Saturday," Franek said, "is the day I don't go to school. It's the day before church day. Saturday is the day after tomorrow."

Chapter 52

His *uniform*. Changed.

Saturday had come. Work and confession were behind him, and this was the surprise they had for him. Pelagia was allowed to tell it, but it was Jadwiga's surprise, and Delfinia's, and the women were proudly displaying what Delfinia had brought forth from the garment, expecting pleasure and gratitude and praise.

It brought a wash of feeling over him.

He was impressed with the handiwork, to be sure. Delfinia—Jadwiga attributed all the accomplishment to her—had somehow closed buttonholes that were once there, taken the adornment from sleeves, even slackened the fall of the jacket past his waist. The handiwork was very much to be admired.

But—his *uniform*.

His uniform was the one thing he had accomplished—the one thing for which an established, official organization had accorded him recognition. He had gone through a mired hell for the Germans, never fighting except against his own crushing feelings of inferiority. He had withstood their mistreatments and crude jokes and had given them proof he was made of their same disciplined steel, and when the time came, they had recognized his strengths and put him in the blue uniform and even gave the rifle to carry. It was an accomplishment, recognized and rewarded.

Now the uniform was gone. And he was expected to be delighted.

He still had the discharge papers, but it wasn't the same.

Oddly, he didn't feel anger that they had done this without asking him. He wished they had asked, but understood that they wouldn't. They were women, after all, unconcerned with military things and the achievement of discipline and strength. To Jadwiga the uniform was nothing more than the costume in which the Germans had delivered him to her.

But even these were not the things that raced across his mind, and it wasn't until later, sitting quietly after dinner, that he knew it for the feeling it was.

Jadwiga, looking up from the net she was mending with Jozef and Pelagia, saw it cross his face.

"Paul?"

He looked at her, his thoughts keeping him from smiling as he usually would.

"What is it, Paul?"

"Come for a walk, Jadwiga. Come with me for a walk, down by the lake."

"I'll come, too," Franek said.

"No, Franek, not tonight," Delfinia said. "We must get the twins to bed, you and I."

But even by the lake, Paul said nothing. And Jadwiga knew by now that what he said inside, to himself, was more important than the words he spoke aloud. They were almost to the battery cliffs, outlined in faint moonlight, before he said it.

"We're not going back," he said. "We will stay here."

She held his arm tighter, but she didn't speak. There was nothing more to say.

Church was home.

More than the others who spoke Polish, because they were in various stages of their own adaptation to America, and more than the occasional letters that came from Poland, more than anything else, church was home. There, all things were familiar: the prayers, the hymns, the statues, the cross. And the feeling.

When mass was over, Jadwiga left Helena with Delfinia to make her special visit to the statue of the Virgin as she always did. Then she took Paul's arm and looked him over. She straightened a lapel that didn't really need to be straightened, and smiled at him from deep inside. It was the look and the smile that said, without the words being spoken, *You are the one.*

The Dominiaks were on the street already, having gone ahead because it was easier when Jozef could take the crutches at his own pace. There, splashed by a patchwork of warm spring sun that shone past new growth in the maples, the priest talked with the people. It was the tradition, here and everywhere, that these talks after services were of pleasant matters, except perhaps for the occasional appointment that was made for a later conversation, in private. So there was smiling and conviviality and a warmth of feeling.

The Dominiaks stood back, waiting in a group, Franek holding Konrad, Pelagia standing between Magda and Manya holding a hand of each, Delfinia still holding Helena so Jadwiga could be free to take her Paul to her new friend the priest.

"Pani Adamik, it's good to see you."

"Thank you, Father. This is my Paul, Father."

"Father," Paul said, a little embarrassed. Jadwiga was being so proud of him.

The priest extended his hand. "Pan Adamik. It's good to meet you. Welcome."

"We have a beautiful Sunday, Father," Paul said, taking care that in his nervousness he wouldn't grip the priest's hand too tightly. He couldn't imagine what else to say. He had in mind to say something about the mass, but he was holding this in reserve for when he would need it, for he couldn't think of what it might be that he could talk about with the priest.

"Yes, Spring is wonderful. Your baby, Pani Adamik?"

"Over here, Father, with our friends."

Jadwiga started toward the Dominiaks, pulling Paul, but Father Polowy held back, keeping Paul's hand, and Jadwiga waited. The priest turned now, just a bit, saying "Teodor" as he did, and this caught the ear of a good-looking man, smiling, standing nearby and talking with other worshippers. From these he excused himself with a goodbye and a smile, and he came to stand next to Father Polowy. "Teodor," the priest continued, "I want to introduce to you Mr. and Mrs. Adamik..."

It was the first time anybody used this word *mister* with Paul, and it sounded odd amid all the Polish words. The priest went on. "Pan Adamik, Pani Adamik, I introduce Teodor Weiss."

Now Paul shook hands again, and it was easier, because this man wasn't a priest and there was hope of something to say other than about religious matters. Jadwiga said something by way of greeting, and the man smiled broadly.

"You are here how long?" Teodor Weiss asked Paul, who felt Jadwiga leave his arm, stepping toward Jozef and Delfinia with the priest.

"Since February," Paul said.

"It is a pretty community, isn't it? I've been here three years now."

"Yes. Yes, now that the snow is going, yes, it's pretty." Paul glanced and saw that the priest was occupied with Pelagia and the twins.

"Are you walking…?" Teodor Weiss said, waving a finger to ask what direction Paul meant to go.

"Toward…" Paul said, gesturing in the direction of the lake, and Teodor Weiss turned with him. They walked slowly, for Paul didn't want to leave Jadwiga and the others behind.

"All this time you've been here, and only now the priest introduces us. The Father is slowing down in the warmth of spring coming."

"He only just now met me," Paul said. "Jadwiga…My wife had a letter for him, from the priest in New York, but it was only just this week that she took it to him."

"Pan Adamik, we are planning to petition the Bishop, for a church of our own—a Polish church. More are coming from the homeland, like you and your friends, and soon we will need our own church. It will take some time, bringing the Bishop along, raising money, building, and we must start now, if we are to bring all Poles together instead of having them part in the German church, part in the Irish one."

"Yes."

"Will you help?"

"How would it be that I could help?"

"There will be a good deal to do, eventually. Not so much now, but as time goes on, more and more."

"If I can help, I will help." Paul felt he couldn't refuse so vague a request, but he didn't see what he could do to help. He felt honored, too, being asked. "I work long hours," he said, thinking he should warn Teodor Weiss that he might not always have time.

"No matter. Each of us will do a little part, and when we do, it will all get done. But what is the work you do?"

Behind them now, Jadwiga and Jozef and the others were walking, slowly catching up, as they approached Third Street and the tracks that streamed down its center.

"With the railroad," Paul answered, gesturing southward with his chin. "I lay track." He stood straight as they walked, and after a moment of hesitation, said, "I am a laborer. I work under a foreman. It is the work they gave me in New York, when we came. Cold, and hard. But not so bad now that it's warming up."

"Have you made application for other work? Since you've been here, I mean."

"No, I…I'm grateful for any work. Before we left, I didn't know what I would do—what my work would be in this country."

"Ah, but there are many other things to do—many good jobs—but of course they don't tell you."

"For example, what other work?" Paul asked.

"Well, they are building locomotives here now, you know—locomotives for the railroads."

"I have heard about the plant."

"Now, that is a place to work. It's going to grow. They're putting railroads all over this country—all the way out to the Pacific ocean now, there is a track. Many locomotives will be needed."

"And they are hiring new workers?"

"I believe so. Brooks Locomotive, it's called."

"That is where you work?"

"No, no, I have other things. But it's something to consider, Pan Adamik, something to consider. When the railroad has the track all put down, who knows what happens? They may want you to move away, to another place, to put down more track."

They stopped at Third Street now, and Paul pointed to the west, where the track disappeared in the distance. Jadwiga and Helena and the Dominiaks stood close by, having caught up. "There will be the maintenence and repair of the track here," Paul said.

"Yes, that's true. Well, I go that way," Teodor Weiss said as he looked the way Paul pointed, then he turned and extended his hand once more. "I will call on you, then, to help to get our own Polish church?"

"Yes," Paul said.

"Nice to meet you, Pan Adamik," he said, and turning toward Jadwiga, he touched the brim of his hat, saying "Pani Adamik," before strolling away.

Chapter 53

It was as Jadwiga had said it would be. Spring made things better.

Paul was grateful for the chance to lay tie and track without constantly fighting the accumulating snow and frozen earth. Konrad discovered that there was a world, after all, beyond the wall of the little house near the lake, and he was turning his determined walk into a tentative run.

Delfinia did start a garden, but it soon became Jozef's special project. He was already half-way down on his haunches, he said, already naturally adapted for cultivation. Saying nothing, Delfinia had spaced the rows just the imperceptible amount farther apart so he could be comfortable between them.

Spring brought out the schooners in the harbor, and the fishermen who knew well how to sail them. The sails were something to see, brisking off over the horizon, or returning, slower, the boats heavy with fish. The fish market grew active, and Jadwiga soon understood two new American words: *wholesale* and *retail*.

Jadwiga fished. With Helena in the sling on her back, she consulted with an old Polish man who fished the edges of the lake. She learned the preferred baits for whitefish and pike. On good days, with fish left over, she was able to sell a few to a young German who packed them with ice into a barrel, which he then took on his wagon to the railroad.

Spring meant that the budget balanced without resort to Jadwiga's special account at the savings bank.

Spring brought storms on the lake. They were frightening, sudden upheavals of water and lightning and wind that could come without fair warning, often at the ebb of day as boats were making for home. Sometimes their thunder would last through the night, rattling windows, the winds tearing at roof and doors.

In the morning, the face of the shoreline would be changed. Jadwiga would walk the beach in search of the treasures the lake yielded. One early afternoon, she even rolled home a perfectly good barrel to put under the corner of the roof to catch rainwater.

It was after one such storm that she found her prize.

It was on that day that Paul, seeing that the track his labor gang was laying was now passing Dunkirk and stretching farther to the West with each day of work, had his serious talk with himself.

On the Frederika, he remembered, he had told himself that one day the circumstances of his life would thereafter be his own creation. Hefting ties, fighting stubborn sod to make them level and satisfy the foreman who could never be satisfied, he thought that soon the rails would be too far from home, and he resolved that it was time.

When she saw the schooner where it had come aground, its stern wallowing at the edge of an outcropping of slate, it took Jadwiga's breath away, but then her heart dropped. A living thing, it was near death.

Cautiously, holding Helena, she started down the slate cliff, dividing her attention between her footing and the boat. The smaller foremast was mostly gone, the mainmast probably sprung. The foresail was missing, the jib torn, the mainsail loose and partly wrapped around the stern. With each wave coming ashore, the hull rocked across a boulder where a hole was being worn ever larger.

A man watched too, his horse feeding on grass growing in the soil above the slate cliff, and it was evident man and boat belonged to each other, for his heart too was torn by this sight. He, too, made his way down the slate that broke away under his boots, going quickly, hand under hand on a rope tied to the horse's saddle. She could see he had just come upon this disaster, and he was hurrying to save his boat. She watched him only long enough to see that he disappeared into the hull and came out with a coil of rope, intending to do what he could for the boat. Hurrying, but with a care for Helena in the pack on her back, Jadwiga continued downward as the slate broke away under her feet.

She was sure he would speak no Polish, so she said nothing. But as he tied one end of the rope to the lower part of the mainmast, she could see that he intended first to pull the boat over so the hull would no longer grind upon the rock. She took the other end, just as he saw her, and ignoring the strange words he spoke, took up the slack end and cinched it around a scraggly tree persistently growing from the slate. It wasn't sturdy, but it took the pressure off and the boat rocked less. The grinding sound stopped.

The man yelled something to her, but Jadwiga could only wave her hand. "No English," she shouted, using up all her American words except the few from the fishmarket. But he saw that she meant to help and knew what to do.

As Jadwiga tied off the rope on the small tree, she looked for something more appropriately sturdy for keeping tension on a rope with a schooner at its other end. There was nothing. As she approached the boat, she saw the man now, for the first time, more closely. He was near her father's age, clean-shaven, and though he seemed to be experienced with boats, he hadn't the ruddy look of a man who spent day after day on the lake.

He went around the hull and looked at the boulder that had been doing all the damage. For a moment Jadwiga thought he was going to try to move it, but he couldn't do it without more help than Jadwiga could give. He looked to his horse, but the rope tied to the saddle wasn't long enough. He ran back to the rope, tugged on it so his horse would know the pull was coming, then climbed back up the cliff.

He pulled in the rope and then mounted. He meant to bring the horse to the boat, but he'd have a quarter-mile ride to a place the horse could descend, and he started out the wrong way. She yelled to get his attention and pointed the other way, and he turned the horse.

The problem was to relieve the strain on the rope, which would soon pull the small tree out of the slate with the constant rocking of the boat. Jadwiga slipped the pack off her back and put baby Helena down in the pebbly sand well up from the water, and climbed onto the boat. There, she found a gaffer's pole twisted in some fishnet which itself was twisted around the stub of the foremast. She untangled it and threw it down to the waterline, then slid down the hull from the high side of the deck. Bracing the pole on a stone, she propped it under the gunwale, wedging it farther along each time the boat rocked, restricting the movement.

The man arrived, his horse picking its way through the shallows and rocks. Seeing what Jadwiga had done with the pole, he helped by extending a leg and kicking it when the boat rocked and more strain could be taken. Now the immediate danger was past and he dismounted.

He said something, but the sounds were without meaning for her and she shrugged. "No English," she said again, to which he responded by saying something in acknowledgment.

He led his horse into the catchment formed by the outcroppings of slate and left it to stand waiting. Jadwiga watched to be sure the horse wasn't near Helena.

The man spent only a moment looking at the edges of the hole in the boat's hull, then sat on a ledge of slate to contemplate the damage.

With gestures now, Jadwiga talked to him. She pointed at him, at the boat, and then made a possessive gesture. *Do you own this boat? Is it yours?* was her question, and he nodded to say it was.

Then she examined the craft. It had come ashore stern first, already on its side, keel dug into the sand. Lettering in the fashion of American fishing boats gave her the name *Florence H* and a harbor, *Barcelona*. Barcelona, Jadwiga knew, was miles to the southwest—an inconvenient distance to haul a damaged fishing vessel foundering on a shore where access would be difficult.

The hole in the hull might, with God's blessing, be repaired. The masts would be a challenge, but they might be replaced or fixed with effort and, perhaps, a compromise or two. The rudder was damaged, but such was to be expected from the way she had come across the shallows near shore. It could be repaired, as could any rudder.

The boat, Jadwiga concluded, could be saved to serve again on open water. She looked at the stern again, and in her mind the American words there changed, and they were now *Maria S* and *Dunkirk*.

She walked to the man whose boat she now understood this to be. She had his attention, for he was curious about her performance; perhaps he had judged that she knew boats, or was just surprised that she would put a baby down among the stones. She pointed at him, then at the boat, then at herself. Again, she made the possession movement, arms brought to her chest.

He didn't understand her immediately, but when she repeated the gestures, then pulled some money from a pocket, he did understand, and he smiled at her, at first amused that a young woman, a mother, would presume to buy his broken boat. She repeated the gesture again, and with a piece of driftwood, scratched a dollar sign and numbers—$100—into the wet sand near his feet.

Now he merely looked at her. She could tell he was uncertain of whether to take her seriously, so she underlined the number. He was still doubtful. She underlined it again.

He looked at his boat, then at Jadwiga, then at the numbers in the sand. He stood, picked up a stick of his own, and crossed out her numbers. He wrote his own—*300*.

It would have been a fair price, but Jadwiga pretended shock. She pointed at the hole in the hull and stamped out his number with her foot. She pointed at the sand to tell him she wanted him to write other numbers. He shrugged, looked at her and at the boat, and now wrote *250*.

Jadwiga threw up her arms, looking away. She walked to the boat, pointed at the ruined foremast, and threw her hands at the boat as though to push it away. Then she strode up the catchment to Helena, squatted down to put her arms through the sling, stood, and started to leave.

But she turned and approached the man again. She took up a stick and wrote once more: *125*. She underlined it three times and, to show it was her final offer, broke her stick over her knee and threw down the pieces. She looked at him, ready to walk away.

Now he shrugged, rolled his head back and raised his hands in a gesture of helplessness. Then he held out one hand, palm up, and with the other hand, pointed into it.

Jadwiga pointed where he'd been sitting. He sat. She turned away, took several bills from within her dress, turned back, put the bills on the sand, then drove her fish-cleaning knife through them. She gestured again, palms out, that he should wait. He shrugged and nodded; he would wait.

It was unusual for Paul to arrive home before Jadwiga and Helena, and this night he found it annoying because he burst in with decisions on his tongue, ready to tell her, and instead found only Delfinia and the Dominiak children. Knowing that Jadwiga spent time on the beach after storms, he was immediately concerned that this time, her love affair with the water might have claimed both her and his baby daughter.

"She came home in the middle of the day, Paul, asked Jozef to go with her, and they left. She was excited about something."

"Where did they go?"

"I don't know. Maybe back to the beach."

This meant nothing to Paul—there was too much beach to go looking, even if he could guess the direction. He could only shake his head in frustration. He decided to change his clothes and, as Delfinia and the children were doing, wait.

But it wasn't long before the two of them appeared at the door, Jozef in a sweat from having gone much distance on his crutches, Jadwiga all brightness about the eyes. She put Helena in Paul's arms and kissed him hello. "Did you tear an arm off that foreman of yours today?"

"No. But I'm not going back tomorrow."

Everything stopped. Everyone looked at Paul, waiting, wanting him to continue.

"The day after tomorrow, maybe, but not tomorrow," he said, but this only served to confuse everyone further. No longer annoyed, he was now enjoying the full attention he so seldom commanded from everybody at once.

"What happens tomorrow?" Now it was Jadwiga who was annoyed.

"Tomorrow, I will go to apply for different work, at the locomotive factory."

"Brooks," Jozef interjected.

"Yes," Paul said. "I will apply at Brooks Locomotive and when they have a place for me I'll stop putting down track for the railroad, and I will go to work there."

There was something of the reckless in this—risking a good job, a paying job, by not going to work, in order to apply for another. There was no comment.

"I have thought it over," Paul said, "and I have decided."

Still silence, until Jozef spoke: "Then it is decided."

Delfinia was first to break the tableau of everyone simply staring at Paul. She bustled to the stove, moved a boiling pot off to the sink, and gestured to the table. "Sit, eat," she said. "If you're going to get a new job, you'll have to look strong."

"Where were you today, Jadwiga? By the lake?"

"Yes, Franek, by the lake. And all over. Your papa will tell you after we eat."

They let Paul talk further about his decision, and he told the story of how, on the day Helena was born, he had made himself the promise. There was doubt and uneasiness around the table, but he was the provider, and the doubts were not expressed.

Jadwiga and Jozef kept back their news until after supper, when they gathered in the front room, as they called the sitting room that faced the street.

"We bought Jozef a boat today," Jadwiga said, watching Paul and Delfinia for reaction. Franek was immediately excited, but with a gesture Big Jozef showed he should listen and wait. Quickly, Jadwiga added, "A damaged boat, from the storm."

"Really, Jadwiga bought a boat for herself, not for me," Jozef said. "It's only that there was a requirement for a man to sign a paper, so Jadwiga fetched me and the priest."

"The priest?" Paul asked. He didn't know what question to ask first.

"To speak for us," Jadwiga said. "He spoke American words for us, as you spoke the German words on the Frederika. He talked for me to the man whose boat it was. Then at the bank, he talked, too."

"At the bank?"

"I took out some money I had saved up," Jadwiga explained, "and then the man of the bank signed papers for us, for Jozef really, to show he is now the one who owns this boat."

"It's Jadwiga's boat, but I signed the paper as a man so there would be no questions."

"And so that we could complete the papers. The man had to ride his horse back to Barcelona."

"Where is this boat?" Delfinia asked.

"Out by the cliffs," Jadwiga said. "It got away last night. It was blown up the lake. It came ashore out by the cliffs. Damaged. We'll fix her up."

"How much damage?" Paul asked.

"A great deal. She'll never be the same as she once was, but with new, good sails, she will pull nets again."

"You plan to go fishing with this boat?"

"Yes, Paul, with nets instead of hook and line. We'll go after the yellow pike and the whitefish."

"You and Jozef...?"

"I'll be a fisherman, Paul. What do you think of that?" Jozef said.

"And we'll get a helper, too, after a while," Jadwiga added.

For a moment, Paul was doubtful. He recalled Jadwiga, pregnant, going over the side and down the ladder of the moving flatcar to take pails of water from him, and he imagined Helena clinging to a mother hauling nets. But he said nothing, for protestations would make no difference. Anyway, he was beginning to trust Jadwiga's care for Helena even in unusual situations.

But they were waiting for his reaction.

"How is the boat damaged?" he asked.

"The hull—there's a hole near the stern from when she hit rocks on the beach. And a mast must be replaced, and some of the sails, as well."

"Where is it? Where did you say?"

"Around by the cliffs. We tied it in and the priest made a notice to put on the boat that there is a new owner."

"How will you fix it? How can it be sailed?"

"We'll patch the hole somehow, just temporarily, so we can float it over here to the beach at the end of the street. We'll work on it there."

Paul was quiet again. Franek and Pelagia both had questions, but they held them, quiet, waiting until it would be all right to speak.

Finally, Paul looked around at all of them. "Sunday, after church, let's have a picnic."

"A picnic on Sunday?" Jadwiga asked.

"Yes, out by the cliffs. We'll ask Juliusz to come. I'll ask him to bring his tools."

Afternote

Theodore Weiss headed a lay committee which successfully petitioned the Bishop of the Archdiocese of Buffalo for a Polish Catholic Church. The cornerstone of St. Hyacinth's was laid in June, 1875. Paul Adamik was a member of the committee and was active in fundraising.

Jadwiga Wdowiak Adamik's correspondence with the people of the Frederika's forward hold, which forms the basis for much of this chronicle, suggests all were eventually paid their due, and more, of the money recovered from Fritz Adenauer. Her fishing enterprise grew in production and profits over a period of years, though barely surviving the panic of 1873, which struck the same year the original Maria S was damaged beyond repair, at anchor, in a storm.

There are some obscure indications that Jadwiga started a system of raising small flags on her boat to notify workers ashore how many wagons would be needed for the load of fish she was carrying, a system later replaced by whistle blasts. She is also said to have been the first to give the leavings of fish cleaning to farmers to be plowed under as fertilizer.

Paul Adamik, whose position as a moulder at Brooks Locomotive Works (later American Locomotive, Brooks Works) was eliminated during the nation-wide economic difficulties of 1873, became active in the fishing company that year. Its records suggest that both his contribution of labor and his management were instrumental in the company's survival.

County records show Paul Adamik purchased a house in the late 1870's; because no change of address was recorded, it is likely the property was the rental property the families first occupied upon arrival in Dunkirk.

No records of Juliusz Sczepaniak exist after 1870. It is probable he changed his name or moved. He may have returned to Poland.

Jadwiga appears to have been active in the formation of Dunkirk's women's Political Equality Club in November of 1887, though there are no records of her participation thereafter. She was one of 65 women who formed the Women's Educational and Industrial Union, a social welfare organization, in the spring of 1888.

Pelagia Dominiak died in 1872. At the wake, members of the family tied a stone at her feet with white ribbon. The custom of burying a stone with members of Dunkirk's Polish immigrant community survived for many years, though its origin had apparently been forgotten by 1930.

Jozef Dominiak (who became Josef upon admission to the United States; and later, according to local records, Joseph) was nominally the owner of the fishing company and active in it for many years. He introduced the triangular-grid pound net, which he insisted (without lasting effect) be called the Pelagia net. In these, fish were impounded in a kind of round-up technique. His nets may have been the initial key ingredient in the development of successful shallow-water pound-netting on southern Lake Erie. Joseph was later co-founder of a commercial fishing equipment company that operated under various names beginning in the late 1880's.

Skipper Edmund Wdowiak arrived in Dunkirk in 1875. His sons and their families either accompanied him or immigrated shortly thereafter. He became active in the Adamik Fish Company, as it was then known. In his later years he was often seen at Dunkirk's Central Avenue dock, fishing with a pole, accompanied by his extraordinarily ugly mongrel dog he had named Bismarck.

Records of Konstanty Wdowiak's family are lost, but it is believed he became active in the local brewing industry, then returned to Poland in the mid-1880's. His brother Konrad remained active in the Lake Erie fishing industry and may have been among those lost in a severe lake storm in 1893.

Paul and Jadwiga had two additional children, a son Edmund and a daughter Pelagia (who was better known locally as Anna).

Franek Dominiak was appointed to the U.S. Military Academy at West Point. In 1891, he and Helena Adamik were married at Saint Hyacinth's Church. After service in the army, he became a principal in his father's equipment company, then known as Erie Marine Supply. Franek ultimately originated the "circulating net" system in which boat operators rented nets rather than owning them, leaving their winter repair to the supplier.

Descendants of the Adamik, Wdowiak, and Dominiak children still live in Dunkirk and other communities of Western New York.

About the Authors

Aloysius A. Lutz grew up in a Polish home, in a Polish neighborhood of Dunkirk, New York, near the shores of Lake Erie. One of eight children, he was born in the early years of the 20th Century and grew up hearing stories of his grandparents' immigration to America. During the Great Depression, he promoted amateur boxing in Dunkirk, and later worked in Dunkirk industries, including the Allegheny-Ludlum Steel Corporation. He began work on *Jadwiga's Crossing* in the 1950's, but died in 1966 before completing it.

Richard J. Lutz, a lifelong broadcast journalist and media specialist, is the son of Aloysius and Lena Hartlieb Lutz. He worked in commercial and public radio and television in Michigan, Illinois, Pennsylvania, and Wisconsin before moving to New York City as a consultant on the nexus of digital technology and mass communications. He holds degrees from The University of Michigan, where he was also a journalist in residence in 1978–79. In retirement, he edits and publishes *The Main Street WIRE*, the fortnightly community newspaper serving Roosevelt Island, New York City.

978-0-595-38127-2
0-595-38127-8

Made in the USA
Middletown, DE
21 August 2017